BONEYARDS

Books by Robert Campbell

Jimmy Flannery series:

The Junkyard Dog
600-Pound Gorilla
Hip-Deep in Alligators
Thinning the Turkey Herd
Cat's Meow
*Nibbled to Death by Ducks**
*The Gift Horse's Mouth**
*In a Pig's Eye**

Jake Hatch series:

*Plugged Nickel**
*Red Cent**

Whistler series:

In La-La Land We Trust
*Alice in La-La Land**
*Sweet La-La Land**

other titles:

*Juice**
*Boneyards**

*Published by *POCKET BOOKS*

BONEYARDS

Robert Campbell

POCKET BOOKS
New York London Toronto Sydney Tokyo Singapore

This book is a work of fiction. Names, characters, places, and incidents are either products of the author's imagination or are used fictitiously. Any resemblance to actual events or locales or persons, living or dead, is entirely coincidental.

POCKET BOOKS, a division of Simon & Schuster Inc.
1230 Avenue of the Americas, New York, NY 10020

ISBN: 0-671-70319-6

POCKET and colophon are registered trademarks of Simon & Schuster Inc.

Printed in the U.S.A.

Dedicated to

Elizabeth and Jim Trupin
Wise Representatives
Protective Colleagues
Affectionate Friends

BONEYARDS

Prologue

THE WINTER SUN SLIPPED IN AND OUT OF THE CLOUDS, GLANCING off the dome and towers, piercing the stained glass windows of Nativity of Our Lord on Thirty-seventh and Union in the Bridgeport section of Chicago. A section composed of Irish, Polish, Germans, Lithuanians, and some Italians, still living in separate little neighborhoods as self-contained as rural villages, who had successfully fought off the invasion of the blacks but had allowed the infiltration of a considerable number of Hispanics. They were civil, sometimes even cordial to one another.

The body of the old woman in the white coffin, signifying virginity, lay upon a draped gurney before the altar, and the priest was winding up the Catholic service for the dead.

There were many attending, the generations of the family, acquaintances and neighbors, all scattered among the pews. The members of the older generation—the dead woman's generation—in their late sixties and seventies, sat in ones, twos, and threes, like the last leaves of autumn in their rusty brown, forest green, and black winter coats and ladies' hats.

The women sat heavily above canted hips, resting their feet. The men with thick Irish faces sat severely upright, their heads and necks crushed down into their shoulders, dignified, dutiful, respectful, uncomfortable in their shirts and ties.

The next generation, the forties and fifties, were fewer in

number, having had less association with the dead woman. They were mostly relatives: nieces and nephews, a few second cousins.

These women still resisted the idea of wearing all black or even other somber colors, paying less attention to the rituals and frauds of grief.

The men especially were uncomfortable in the church, strange to them in the middle of the week. It felt like going to a movie when they should be at work. Practically none of the men wore black bands of wide grosgrain ribbon on their sleeves. That was old-fashioned.

Those in their twenties and thirties, some with children, some without, were of mixed mind about the whole business of corpse display and funerals at which some priest, who probably hadn't even known the dear departed, recited kind words written down the night before.

A good many among all the generations cast their thoughts forward to the funeral feast.

Where would it be held? At her brother's, Municipal Judge Jerry Sharkey's, house? They'd probably ask for invitations at the door, for Christ's sake, the way those Sharkeys put on airs.

Would old man Sharkey be in the Judge's living room, sitting in the corner, in some ancient mohair club chair smelling of his sweating backside? Would he be crouching there, chewing on his gums? How old? Ninety, for God's sake. A bunch of goddamn elephants, the Sharkeys lived forever.

What kind of spread would they put out over to the Judge's? Some little finger bits and pieces, celery sticks stuffed with cream cheese, potato chips and green dip that worked its way up under the fingernails? Nibbles of no consequence. Not like the old days. Casseroles, stews, baked funeral meats and fricasseed chickens, fresh breads and cakes, brought in by the neighbors.

Pray at least there'd be something to drink besides sweetened punch or jugs of wine.

Christ, would the priest never make an end of it, droning on and on, the smell of incense enough to make you puke?

In the back of the church, in front of the banks of votive candles, a latecomer picked up a small piece of paper, roughly scissored out of a larger piece, and read:

BONEYARDS

Never Fail Novena

May the precious sacred heart of Jesus be praised forever. Sacred heart of Jesus please hear our prayers. Hail Mary Mother of Jesus pray for us. St. Jude pray for us. (Make your request and say a Hail Mary.)

This prayer is to be said in a church for nine days in succession and each day two copies of this prayer left in the church. On the eighth and ninth day your request will be granted. This novena has never been known to fail.

He was a fair-skinned Irishman with hair gone white, a man in his early seventies who carried himself with the slope-shouldered assurance of a prizefighter and had the eyes of a cop.

One or two of the mourners, glancing back at the door as though checking the way out when the last prayer was spoken and the last bell rung, spotted the latecomer and recognized him as the dead woman's brother, a cop gone bad who'd been released from prison just lately . . .

"Is that the brother? How long since he was released? Two weeks ago? Was it two weeks ago?"

. . . and had, they said, gone to ground in some furnished room, not even visiting the old father, the dying sister, the one-legged brother who drank.

"What the hell is he doing here at all? You'd think he'd be ashamed to show his face. He'd been sleeping with a nigger, wasn't it? Shot her dead, didn't he? Something like that. Should be ashamed to walk into the house of God, for Christ's sake."

"Well, it's his sister dead. Give the man a little mercy. Show the man a little forgiveness."

"He don't deserve any mercy. He don't deserve any forgiveness just because he's attending his sister's funeral."

"Well, he's here, doing the right thing, don't you know. Suffering the humiliation. Him a cop sent up for murdering a nigger whore he was sleeping with so . . ."

The whispers going around, savoring the scandal, lingering over the details of his transgressions, heads turning and craning to catch a glimpse as though a celebrity had come among them.

". . . let's do the Christian thing and welcome him home, now he's here satisfying the family obligation."

"Well, I'll give him that. They always said he did his duty

by his family. But I'm not going to be a hypocrite. I'm not going to shake his hand or kiss him on the cheek and say I'm glad to see him."

"He loved his sister, Della."

"God rest her soul. But he'll get no embrace from me."

A woman, in her late fifties, still very trim, very stylish, red lipstick, penciled brows, green eye shadow, wearing a red hat wound round and nearly covered with black ribbon, stepped up beside the latecomer. "Long time no see, Ray."

He embraced her and kissed her on the mouth. "Hello, Wilda. Why didn't somebody tell me about this novena, never been known to fail?" he said, holding out the slip of paper. "I could've saved myself fourteen years of trouble and pain."

She glanced at it as though seeing it for the first time but she'd clearly read it before because she said, "You take a copy and you leave two copies of your own every day for nine days. Eighteen copies."

"Also you leave a couple of bucks each time."

"They don't say that."

"It's one of them things goes without saying. You're standing here, so you'll light a candle and drop some money in the slot. So that's all right, the church needs the revenue."

"Oh, Ray," Wilda said, smiling at her older brother.

"I thought the Catholic Church only invented bingo," he said. "Here's the proof they also invented the chain letter."

She captured his arm and drew him out into the foyer, across the vestibule, almost to the door where she might get the daylight on his face. The sun broke through the overcast and drew a halo around them.

She lay her hand along his cheek. "Ah, Ray, you don't look well. Your color's not too good."

"I'm two weeks out of prison, Wilda. In prison the niggers get glossy and the spics get browner—all that exercise out in the yard, in the sun, no living to make, no women to rape, no goods to steal, plenty of dope to deal—but white men turn yellow or they turn gray."

She flinched as though he'd struck her, knowing that he meant to hurt her, meant to taunt her, not able to control himself, all the bitterness welling up and filling his mouth.

A bell rang. It had the appealing sound of a calling dove.

She glanced back over her shoulder, through the doors, into

the nave. "He's prayed her gone. They're walking past the coffin for a last look. Do you want to go in, see Della?"

She could tell he didn't want to walk back into the arms of friends and family, what there was left of them, the generations separating like patches of oil upon the water, coming together only now and then, on occasions such as this, right then and there. Probably afraid to suffer the memory of their abandonment of him all over again, though he was the one who said very early on in his imprisonment that he wanted no visitors, not even now and then.

"How does she look?" he said.

"You know what they say."

" 'Looks like she's sleeping. Looks better than she did when she was alive,' " he mimicked, in a thin, high, feminine voice, recalling accurately a thousand such remarks.

"They gave her a new hairdo. Washed out the dye." Wilda touched her own dyed red hair. "White as snow. Beautiful."

"She wouldn't like it."

"No."

He looked away, into the church, down the aisle toward the altar and the woman in the coffin as though wondering if she'd heard.

The mourners filed out, having had their last look at a woman they'd scarcely known, so quiet in the corner she'd been all her life, everyone anxious to get out of the echoing church into the open air. Most of them cast a furtive glance his way and one or two even pasted wan smiles on their faces as they nodded past, but only a few came over to actually press his hand, to offer him condolences or give him welcome.

A few of the women pressed their cheeks to Wilda's, for she, the wayward daughter, was as much an outcast as the rogue cop.

When the departing people thinned out, Ray and Wilda started down the aisle, passing the few still leaving, the old ones, the slow ones.

One man, struggling up the raked aisle by means of a cane, paused for breath and looked up into Ray's face with a rueful smile, commenting on his own failing strength. But his eyes were bright and knowing.

"Ray Sharkey, ain't it?"

Sharkey didn't say. They looked almost the same age standing there, though at least twenty years separated them.

"You don't remember me? Frank Cromarty. Your father's

friend? We used to hang around Schaller's Pump together." He laughed, remembering. "Sorting out the city. Keeping the politicians on their toes."

"The Pump still there?" Sharkey asked.

"Sure, it's still there, right on South Halstead across the street from the Eleventh Ward Democratic Headquarters. Some things never change, thank God."

"It's nice seeing you again, Mr. Cromarty."

Cromarty reached out and laid a withered hand on the sleeve of Sharkey's ill-fitting camel hair topcoat with the old-fashioned black mourning band on the sleeve.

"You don't mind my asking, I never could figure it out."

"What's that, Mr. Cromarty?"

"I never could figure out how come they convicted you for shooting that colored whore," he said, very softly, so as not to give offense.

"Well, they did."

"Also I could never figure why they gave you the sentence they gave you. That was a lot of time for shooting a whore."

"She was dead, Mr. Cromarty."

"So, all right, but it seems to me you served a very long time. How long?"

"Fourteen years."

"That's too long for shooting a nigger whore," Mr. Cromarty said. "It was political, wasn't it? Somebody had it in for you."

"Well, they give me life and I only had to serve fourteen," Sharkey said.

"It was political," Cromarty said.

"You okay now?" Sharkey asked.

"What?"

"You can make it out of the church okay by yourself?"

"Hell, yes," Cromarty said, shaking himself like an old dog, proving he still had the stuff, three-stepping it up the aisle and into the vestibule.

Sharkey and Wilda walked down the center aisle to the coffin before the altar, an aging woman, an old man, clinging to each other, going to look at their dead sister.

At the coffin Wilda rearranged the prayer beads in her sister's hands more to her liking. Sharkey leaned over and kissed the corpse on the brow.

"The first time I kissed a corpse I was only seven. You

weren't even born. Dad lifted me up and I kissed Great-grandma Gowan. I never forgot. All those years ago."

Ray put his face close and stared into Della's closed eyes, as though looking for some mystery she could no longer conceal now that she had no kitchen corners to hide in, no dark bedroom behind closed doors.

"What is it, Ray?" Wilda asked.

He shook his head and twisted his mouth as though commenting on his own foolishness. "She kept her secrets, didn't she?"

"It's a Sharkey trait, wouldn't you say?" she said, letting him know by the impress of her voice that if anyone could be said to have kept secrets it was he.

"It might even be an Irish habit," he said. "I saw Jerry but I didn't see Gabe or Michael," he said, dropping the subject of the family's and his own Irish love of secrecy, the conspiracies of silence, moving his head stiffly from side to side, like a boxer working out the kinks before a bout.

"Gabe didn't come. He sent a spiritual bouquet and said he'd pray for Della's soul," Wilda said. "He's not been feeling well."

"She'd have liked it if her own brother had been the priest to do the service for her," he said, as though blaming his brother for being ill. "How about Michael?"

"He was here. Sitting right down in front, over to the side, nearest the side door. That was the way he went out, without anyone seeing, I wouldn't be surprised."

"Will he be over to Jerry's? That's where they're having the reception?"

She nodded. "He'll be there, sitting in the kitchen, making drinks for anybody who wants one mixed, always helpful and polite, making himself useful like he always does," she said.

"How would you know?" Sharkey said, sounding not unkind, merely curious.

She looked at him, as startled as a cat pinned in a dark alley by the beam of a flashlight, wary, frightened, ready to fight or run. She put her hand up to her face as though afraid that he might make some comment about her makeup, equating disguise with stupidity. It was Ray's way, pinning a person down to explanations, letting no remark go by unchallenged, forcing you to examine what you meant, revealing what you didn't know and how carelessly you spoke. A cop's way of holding conversation.

"I've been coming home more often, these last ten years or so, and staying longer," she said.

"You living here now?" he asked, as though pleasantly surprised.

"Yes. I've got a room over on Mospratt."

"Back in the old neighborhood, are you?" he said, seeming to be praising her.

She smiled, and suddenly looked startlingly young and sweet.

The undertaker's assistant, standing off to one side, cleared his throat.

"Everyone'll be waiting in the cars for Della to leave for Resurrection," Wilda said.

"Is that where we're burying now?" he asked.

"Well, I think there was no more room in the plot over to St. Mary's."

"I don't think I want to go to the graveside," he said.

"Whatever you say."

Sharkey turned away from the coffin and Wilda took his arm. They walked along the ambulatory and up the aisle to the front door.

"We've always been a scattered family, ain't we, Wilda?" he said. "Even in death we can't seem to come together, buried here and there all over the city."

"Does it matter? The time to be together is before you die."

He looked at her and grinned. It was his playful, sarcastic, editorial grin. Here's the runaway, the vagabond, the tramp preaching sermons about togetherness, it said.

"It's all right, Wilda, maybe you was just born to be a leaf in the wind," he said.

She felt her heart squeeze in her chest. For a moment she mourned, on his behalf as well as her own, the passing of their childhood.

"Did you come with somebody?" he asked suddenly, as though an urgent thought had just struck him and her answer was of some importance.

"No, I came by myself."

"Taxi?" he asked.

"I rented a car."

He stopped her at the curb. "Maybe we should go out to Resurrection," he said.

"Maybe we should," Wilda said. "The trumpets are blowing for this generation. Our generation. We might as well get used to the music."

1

WE'RE ALL LIKE THE MAN IN THE ROWBOAT. WE SPEND OUR LIVES rowing in one direction while looking backward in the other. If you want to let it happen you can let your mind bounce back through the years like a stone skipping across water, laying down a pattern of ripples, diminishing into the past until the stone sinks and no longer disturbs the river of time.

You can wish for things to have been otherwise. You can imagine that you've managed to retain your youth, your enthusiasm, your passions, and your innocence.

But fourteen years before ex-Sergeant Ray Sharkey stood outside the Nativity of Our Lord, he was Sergeant Ray Sharkey with twenty-six years on the Chicago Police Force, going all the way back to the time when cops walked a beat, and his innocence was already lost and gone forever.

He'd done it all. Lofts and Warehouses. Burglary. Juvenile. Bunko. Vice. Homicide.

He'd been partnered with Charlie Minifee for the first five years, but after Minifee had been murdered in a back alley around Cabrini-Green in 1956, Sharkey had become a loner.

In sixteen years, before he made detective, he'd walked a beat with four or five partners and, after a new superintendent of police put everybody into cars back in '61, ridden in a car with maybe half a dozen others. Subtracting the five years with

Minifee and then averaging it out, he'd been married to a different cop for maybe a year and a half at a time, with lots of space in between marriages. So the truth was, he never made a hell of a lot of close friends.

A couple of his partners had been Italian. One Polish. One Bohemian. A Mexican. A colored—which was what Sharkey called Negroes in civilian company, being unable or unwilling to keep up with the change to "black" and "Afro-American" or whatever over the years. The rest had been Irish.

In the locker rooms of the Eighteenth District Station and around the cop bars, he called Italians guidos or wops, Poles polacks, Bohemians hunkies, Mexicans spicks or greasers, and African-Americans niggers or darkies. He would have been surprised if anybody had told him that they took offense. He viewed such casual insults as signs of good fellowship, the easy, rude, irreverent ways of family, fellow soldiers, brothers-in-combat, laughing when they called him a harp or a cat-lick.

He was known as a bachelor, a cop who didn't work well harnessed to another cop, keeping everything to himself, going off and investigating angles on his own and sharing what he learned only when he got damned good and ready.

Some said he'd never gotten over mourning his friend Minifee and didn't want to risk getting too close to a partner anymore, going through that kind of grief again.

Some said he'd somehow been to blame for Minifee's death and wasn't to be relied upon, the word passing down from cop to cop through the years, all of them trying to avoid being his partner until it got to be a habit—avoiding him—even after the original reason for it was forgotten, misremembered, or never even known by many.

Some said he was just a plain and simple bastard—for all his smiles and Irish honey cake—not to be believed, not to be trusted, a rogue cop who liked working alone because it gave him plenty of spread, plenty of opportunity for shady deals and shady ladies.

Everybody said he had a quick trigger finger. He'd been in the Big Two and had come out a war hero, having been among those who'd fought their way up the boot of Italy and past the slaughterhouse known as Monte Cassino.

So he got to the force a little late, thirty years of age, and maybe it had been hard for him to slow himself down, but anyway he'd been involved, more than once, more than twice, in shootings and deaths that might have been avoided. In those days, they said, in uniform and out, he'd gone looking for trouble. Now, the whispers said, for all his connections down at City Hall, trouble was looking for him.

He'd accumulated his share of nicknames. They called him the Lone Stranger. They called him the Merry Prankster, because of the elborate practical jokes, with sharp edges of cruelty, he pulled on other cops. They called him the City Hall Pimp for certain services he performed for the politicians and visiting firemen.

His supporters, and there were a few, said you had to understand Ray Sharkey and forgive him for a lot because underneath it all, you looked close enough, there was a sadness in him belied by his ready smile and easy manner, traces of pain and bewilderment behind the eyes. He was tight-mouthed about his troubles and his deepest feelings.

He had a retarded kid, over twenty-five years old now, here in '77, tucked away in some institution, and a wife who'd been dying of cancer for the last four or five years. The man had his troubles. He had his sorrows.

2

HE'D BEEN WORKING ALONE THE LAST EIGHTEEN MONTHS AND then they'd handed him Wally Dubrowski—that disgusting hippopotamus—for a wife.

He and Dubrowski had walked a beat together for about three months, fourteen, fifteen years ago. They didn't like each other then and they probably wouldn't like each other now, so why team them up?

The reason Captain Kronen gave was that Dubrowski's partner was out with a heart attack and Dubrowski wasn't the kind of detective who worked well on his own.

But Sharkey worried that there could be something more—he didn't know what—but twenty-six years of walking the mine field of city-hall politics and police favoritism had given him a barometer, a seismograph, whatever you wanted to call it, and something was giving him the tingles.

But being handed a fat partner wasn't a big worry, that was a small worry.

The big worry was over Mayor Richard J. Daley dying the way he did, keeling over in his doctor's office a few minutes after being told he was fit as a fiddle, just a couple of weeks ago, a few days before Christmas. So there was this special election coming up in February '77, about a month from now. Any kind of election seasons were always pockmarked with mantraps. Loyal soldiers were given up for no apparent gain, everybody playing Byzantine games in the Stygian dark. So you had to be very careful.

They'd locked the black alderman, Wilson Frost, out of the mayor's office, even though he claimed that as mayor pro tempore he was the legal successor to the position. There was no way white aldermen were going to allow a black man to serve as acting mayor. They'd put Michael Bilandic, the chairman of the finance committee, in the chair on the fifth floor and to hell with protocol.

There were a lot of bizarre, upsetting things going on as the pecking order changed and dozens of wannabes dreamed of glory and assessed the new opportunities opening up.

Funny things happened even in ordinary election years, so you could just imagine what was going on now that Daley's reign was at an end. It was going to be a cat and dog fight. The blacks were pissed off about what was done to Wilson Frost for one thing and were putting Harold Washington up as their candidate.

Also it wasn't altogether certain that Bilandic, acting mayor or no acting mayor, was going to be the choice of the Democratic Central Committee aka the Regular Organization aka the Machine. Chances were that he would be, but there was always the possibility for change.

There was talk that a young, prematurely retired scion of a famous father was thinking about tossing his hat into the ring. Nobody was naming him by name yet, but there was mention of The Candidate.

But even that wasn't the most of Sharkey's worries, the battle for the mayor's job.

He worried because the acting mayor looked at him a little funny every time they met, as though Sharkey was a doubtful piece of garbage and he, Bilandic, was a new broom looking for something to sweep. Sharkey was involved in a couple of enterprises that he didn't consider illegitimate but other people might think were illegitimate. Especially anyone who, because of political circumstances, had been infected with reformer's zeal.

He worried because he had many acquaintances and associates, some people might say were friends, partners, and even lovers, who would not be acceptable in what they'd consider polite society.

He couldn't stop worrying. He had a feeling.

It was like the feeling you got smelling danger behind some closed door, down in some dark cellar, on a rooftop late at night. Somebody waiting to kill you or do you a terrible injury. Somebody, something, waiting to bring you down, tear out your throat. You didn't know who or what but you knew something was out there waiting.

He felt like he was being stalked. He felt like he was being targeted.

It was in the way the other cops looked at him a little sideways lately, as though if he laid a hand on them, he'd infect them with the plague. None of them knowing any more than he what the hell could happen in case anybody got a wild hair up their ass and started some internal investigations, but, like wild animals, sensing that one or more of those among them might be marked for destruction by some animal more powerful than any one of them. By some politician looking for a head to hang on the wall. Seeing in Sharkey a likely candidate.

It was in the way he no longer had such easy access to the office of Deputy Superintendent Finny Cavan, who'd been his Chinaman, his mentor and protector, from practically the beginning of his service, and who was now closing the door on him. Not altogether. No smart man cut off all his options until every last card was on the table face up. Sharkey still got a good-morning when they met and a slap on the back in passing, but he felt the greeting and the touch weren't to be trusted.

He had no reason to feel secure.

Not with all the potential candidates poking around looking for an issue, maybe a rogue cop, a little police corruption to spice up the campaign and tempt the voters' palate. Was he about to be selected by somebody as the designated sacrificial goat?

Maybe he should lie low, pull in his horns, proceed with caution, do the prudent thing.

But he couldn't afford to shut down his little stores, his little enterprises, that *some* people might call illegitimate.

Not with Florence, his wife of thirty-four years, dying on him. Still dying on him after four years of suffering. But clinging to him, reminding him of his devotion to family, his infatuation with duty and obligation, forcing him to repeat promises made a thousand times a year never to abandon their child, Helen, hidden away in an institution since she'd been ten years old. The money pouring out of him like blood. Exciting his appetite for martyrdom.

Not while he was playing house with a black hooker stashed away in the Eighteenth Ward down in the black South Side almost on the city line.

Not when Shelley Orchid, his partner in a gambling operation over on the Near North Side in the Forty-second Ward, was mouthing it around that Sharkey was a greedy sonofabitch who was about to get his ass kicked out into the gutter.

They were coming at him from all sides.

He'd be lucky to be retired with a pension. He'd be lucky to be allowed to resign with no pension. He'd be lucky to stay the hell out of prison. He'd be lucky to get out of it alive.

And here he was, cruising the streets in an unmarked car, with Wally Dubrowski, the cop they called Moby Dick because he was as big as a whale and could probably drop dead of a heart attack any minute, for God's sake.

The fat man was behind the wheel, just barely making it even with the seat pushed all the way back to accommodate his gut, his feet hardly reaching the pedals.

Sharkey was slouched in the runner's seat, his hat tipped over his eyes, nearly concealing them, staring out the window, cracked to catch a little fresh air even though the air was cold enough to cut skin.

In the twilight, three kids were playing marbles on the dirt meridians that separated street curb and sidewalk.

"Look at that," Sharkey said.

"Look at what?"

"Them kids playing marbles."

"They should go home for supper?"

"No, I mean it's winter. You don't play marbles in winter. Marbles're for summer. What's the matter with kids nowadays? They got no sense."

"Oh," Dubrowski said, figuring kids playing marbles in winter was no cause for alarm, definitely not a major issue.

"You play marbles when you was a kid?" Sharkey asked.

"I didn't play marbles much," Dubrowski finally said. "I didn't have the hands for it." He lifted hands like a couple of baseball mitts off the wheel for a second.

"I used to love playing marbles. I'd go all over looking for a game," Sharkey said.

"Why'd you have to travel to find a game?"

"I was good. I was so damn good I used to win all the marbles in the neighborhood. Had this big stoneware pot I'd keep them in. Thousands of them. I don't know how many. The kids in the neighborhood wouldn't play with me after a while. I had to go looking."

"Like a pool shark," Dubrowski said. "A marble hustler, you was."

Sharkey sat up straight, excited and agitated by his memories.

"I had to go six, eight blocks to get a game. You understand marbles?"

"I told you I didn't play that much."

"So you don't have to play to understand the game. I don't play football, but I understand the game."

"So tell me about marbles," Dubrowski said, knowing that was what Sharkey wanted to do.

"Well, there was a lot of different games. Shoot to a line. Play inside a big circle. The one we played, you dug a pot, then you stepped back say twenty, thirty feet and drew a line. Each player put his toe on the line and tossed his marble, trying to get in the pot. If nobody got in the pot on the first throw, the closest to the pot took the next shot to get in. Like that. When a player got in the pot he had a chance to shoot at any other player's marble. Hit it and you won. Whatever. One marble. Two marbles. Whatever you bet. You never bet your shooter.

You never put that on the line. Jesus Christ, I bet I could go out there right now, get one knee down in the dirt, and beat those little suckers."

"I'll bet you could. Then their folks would call the cops. Old white-haired man taking the marbles from their kids. Probably a pervert waiting for the chance to pat them on the ass."

"I'll bet I could clean the little buggers out," Sharkey said, not listening, savoring his imaginary triumph.

They rode in silence for a few blocks.

"You learn things playing marbles," Sharkey suddenly said, as though breaking in on a conversation they were actually having, coming to a conclusion that logically derived from long discussion.

"How's that?"

"One summer I'm looking for a game outside my neighborhood. I'm maybe twelve blocks from home, practically a foreign country, you understand? I get into a game in this neighborhood. We throw from the line. I make the pot first. I'm about to shoot at the nearest marble, which belongs to this kid maybe seven feet tall—"

"Hey!"

"Well, he *looked* about seven feet. So, he was maybe five feet tall. You got to understand I was very small. I didn't start growing until I got into high school."

"So, this giant kid . . . ?" Dubrowski said, nudging Sharkey along.

"This kid says to me 'Backsies.' I says, 'What?' He says, 'Backsies.' I says, 'You don't mind my asking, what the hell is this here backsies?' He says, 'I yelled backsies, which means you got to shoot from the back of the pot.' I never heard of such a thing. I tell him, 'Screw you and your backsies.' He says, 'You ain't from this neighborhood, are you?' I tell him, 'No.' He says, 'In this neighborhood that's the way we play. You bring an army with you to tell me different?'

"So I hunker down and shoot from the back of the pot and take his marble anyhow.

"The next go-round he lands in the pot first. Before I can say anything he yells, 'Fen backsies.' I says, 'Now what the hell is this fen backsies?' and he explains that if you yell fen backsies before the other guy yells backsies then the shooter don't have to go to the back of the pot."

"What the fuck. So then what?" Dubrowski said.

"So then the next time he gets in the pot and yells fen backsies, I yell, 'Knuckles in.' "

"Knuckles what?"

"Knuckles in. I explain to this big asshole that when a player yells knuckles in, the shooter's got to stick his knuckles in the bottom of the pot and shoot *up* and *out.*"

"Sheee*it!*"

"Exactly. For the rest of the game we're yelling this, yelling that, making up these crazy rules. We ain't playing marbles anymore, we're playing Make Up New Rules and Shout the Other Sonofabitch Down. Finally I'm getting fed up. The next game, I yell "Fen everies," and when the big kid asks me what *that* means, I punch him in the nose and run like hell."

Dubrowski started to laugh, it came out of his belly and rolled up out of his mouth, and for a minute there Sharkey actually liked the man.

Dubrowski laughing made him laugh and that made him feel good for a minute, forget his troubles for a minute.

"You know what's the moral of that story?" Sharkey asked.

Dubrowski couldn't speak for the laughter, but just shook his head from side to side.

"The moral of that story is," Sharkey said, "some bastard makes up new rules on you, you make up new rules right back."

After a minute, Dubrowski said, "Also punch the sonofabitch in the mouth and run."

"Also that," Sharkey said, pleased with himself.

They drove along for a couple of miles in a comfortable silence. Maybe it was the air of good fellowship in the car, maybe it was the remembering, that made Dubrowski say, "Sorry to hear about your wife."

"Who told you about my wife?"

"I don't know. One of the old-timers."

"Why would anyone tell you about Flo?"

"I don't know. I must've asked about her. After all I used to know her—I mean you introduced me to her once or twice—years ago. So it's natural I should ask were the two of you still together and whoever it was I asked told me she wasn't well."

"She ain't been well for more than four years, almost five."

"I'm sorry."

"She's dying."

"So, it must be tough being on your own."

Sharkey looked at Dubrowski out of the corner of his eye. Was the polack making a crack? Had he been told some rumor about the black hooker some people might be saying he was keeping for company and comfort? Dubrowski was looking straight ahead, the expression of an innocent cherub on his kisser, so probably he wasn't trying to be a smart aleck. But it'd be nice if people minded their own business, Sharkey thought.

"So, I just wanted to say I was sorry about your wife," Dubrowski said.

"Okay."

"How about your sister? Wilma, was it?"

"Wilda. What about her?"

"She doing okay?"

"Never mind about my family."

"I was just making conversation," Dubrowski said, thinking that Sharkey, the Irish sonofabitch, hadn't changed much. He was still a close-mouthed bastard in spite of the stories he liked to tell.

3

THE STREET LAMPS WERE COMING ON, GROWING LIKE FLOWERS IN glass bottles. The storekeepers were turning on their lights. Kitchen windows popped out like squares in a crossword puzzle and, here and there, the surgical blue light of televisions watched by early-evening addicts glowed in otherwise unlit parlors.

"Another day, another dollar," Dubrowski said.

Oh, for Christ's sake, Sharkey thought, here it comes again, more old-time sayings from the gab-bag of Granny Dubrowski. Every day, just about this time, he said the same thing as though he'd just invented it. Then you got another little walk down memory lane. He never should have brought up that story about the marbles last week. That gave Dubrowski the idea that he had the right to dig back into the past. Sharkey wanted the goddamn past left alone. It only hurt to think about how things could've turned out, should've turned out, starting back when. All the wrong moves he'd made. So, you had to live with your mistakes, but why dig it all up, one memory inviting another?

"So here we are," Dubrowski said, trying to prime the pump of conversation again when Sharkey didn't respond to his first overture.

"Where's that?" Sharkey replied.

"Back working the streets. Just like old times. Remember how we used to hang around that tavern over on Superior?"

"What tavern on Superior?"

"You remember. That tavern where we used to have a nooner with that hunky twist."

Sharkey was staring straight ahead through the windshield, pretending that he didn't know that Dubrowski was tossing glances at him as he drove the car.

Sure he remembered the tavern and the woman. Why not? Did that mean he had to listen to one of Dubrowski's goddamn fuck stories?

The man was impossible, had always been impossible, when it came to sex and women. Always had his nose up some bint's ass. If he could he would've worn tits for earmuffs. Goddamn gash hound is what he was, always telling war stories. You tell a story about a marble game, remembering the innocent past, and you had to get back a war story. So, all right, he didn't have to listen or he could listen with half an ear. The man was impossible.

"The Gateway, that's what it was called," Dubrowski said. "And the twist's name was . . . I got it on the tip of my tongue."

"Alice Wegrzyn."

"What?"

"Alice Wegrzyn. That was the woman's name."

"I can't believe it. A harp like you remembering a hunky tongue twister like that. I couldn't even remember it."

"There's a lot of things you don't remember, Dubrowski."

"Oh?" Dubrowski said, his back going up at Sharkey's tone of voice. "How's that?"

"You don't remember we only went in there together just the once," Sharkey said, suddenly unbearably irritated that Dubrowski should be making up things that never happened, dragging him into his memories, the shitty games he used to play. "You don't remember I never shared any nooners with you. You had the good times with Alice Wegrzyn and every other amateur fuck in the neighborhood. I never did. I never even had any friendly conversations with those bimbos. You understand what I'm saying?"

"So, all right, I hear you," Dubrowski said.

All of sudden Sharkey yelled, "Stop!"

Dubrowski stood on the brakes.

"What?" Dubrowski exclaimed.

"In the alley," Sharkey said. "Back up. Back up."

Dubrowski backed up thirty feet and parked at an angle. "What in the alley?" he asked.

"Somebody parked in the alley."

"There's no law against parking in the alley."

"Looks like somebody's sitting in the car slumped over the wheel."

"So what?"

"So we should have ourselves a look," Sharkey said, already getting out of the car, anything to keep Dubrowski from telling another one of his goddamn war stories.

Dubrowski heaved himself out from behind the wheel.

They approached the mouth of the alley. There was a car parked halfway along where the fading light of day hardly reached.

"I can't see nobody slumped over the wheel," Dubrowski said.

"Then you must be going blind," Sharkey replied.

"All right, suppose there's really somebody in that car. Suppose there's somebody in that car slumped over the wheel. Maybe it's somebody dead. Now we're up the rest of the night waiting for the medics, waiting for the crime lab, doing paperwork."

"Dubrowski, you know what your trouble is?" Sharkey said. "Your trouble is you're not ready to put out the extra ounce, walk the extra mile. You got no ambition."

"We're past the age of ambition," Dubrowski said.

"Maybe you. Not me. Maybe you got all you want. Not me."

Sharkey checked his gun in the belt holster. He could see something—somebody—slouched behind the wheel. It could be somebody with his head dropped forward on his chest.

He could feel his pulse racing, the old familiar tension across his chest, the coppery taste in his mouth from the surge of adrenaline. Every time, knock on a door, walk down an alley, poke into any dark, unfamiliar place and the fear—like the rising excitement preceding sex—pounded through him.

Old man Kiley back at the academy used to say all cops were junkies, high on their own juices, addicted to their own adrenaline, pinning themselves in the arm every day of the year with shots of fear. Hungering for violence.

The drill was supposed to be that one man stayed behind the open door of the vehicle, near the radio in case help was needed, ready to make the call, hand on gun butt, ready to join in.

But these were two old dogs who didn't go crying for help at the least sign of danger. They walked down the alley together, one on each side, Dubrowski slightly behind Sharkey, letting him have first call because Sharkey'd spotted the possibility, watching Sharkey on the stalk, hand on the butt of his gun under the skirt of his camel hair topcoat. Glory hound. Making every reconnaissance a major battle. Irish bullshit artist, actor, game player. Fucking adrenaline junky snaking down the alley on the soles of his shoes, doing the Indian shuffle, making no more than a whisper on the broken cobbles. Wyatt Earp and Doc Holliday walking the dusty street toward the O.K. Corral.

There *was* somebody in the driver's seat. No doubt about that now. Whoever it was had his head down like he was looking at the steering wheel or the floor.

Sharkey was about five steps away when the man lifted his head. He could see the man's face reflected in the rearview mirror, eyes drawn tight into slits, lips drawn back. He could see a head bobbing up and down in the driver's lap.

He knew that Dubrowski was seeing everything he was seeing. Sharkey put his hand up, cautioning Dubrowski, then went up alongside the car on the driver's side and tapped on the window with one hand, showing his shield in the other.

The man was caught in the moment, release pulsing up through his loins at the same time surprise, maybe terror, registered in his eyes. They were opened wide. His head snapped around, the rictus of climax still pulling his lips back from his teeth. He started to yell, trying to turn toward the threat, ejaculating at the same time.

The woman's head came up fast, face twisted in a fright just as severe as the man's, her makeup garish in the wash from Dubrowski's flashlight.

"Would you mind opening the window, sir?" Sharkey mouthed the words, pretending he was speaking aloud, letting the man believe he'd gone momentarily deaf.

The driver was a white man about sixty, gray-haired and sallow-skinned except for bright spots of sexual excitement high up on his cheeks.

The woman was black. She was wearing an auburn wig and her eyes were made up with green shadow and silver glitter.

The driver scrambled to conceal himself and retrieve his wallet from the inside pocket of his jacket in the same motion.

He handed it over. His hand was trembling.

"Will you please take out your identification and hand it to me, sir?" Sharkey said.

The man did as he was told.

The whore sat up and looked straight ahead, quickly rolling down the window with her right hand. She turned her head aside, ready to spit.

"You'd better watch where you're spitting, sis," Dubrowski said.

The whore looked wild-eyed for a moment, then took a red bandana from a little beaded purse and cleared her mouth. "What seems to be the trouble, detective?"

"Would you like to step out of the car, please?"

"Oh, dear," the whore murmured in a husky voice.

Sharkey finished examining the license. He stepped back two paces. "Would you mind stepping out of your vehicle, Mr. Gole?"

"I was just driving my maid home when she said she felt faint."

"Felt ill did she? Would you just step around to the back of the car, Mr. Gole?"

"Yes, she said she was afraid she was going to faint."

The initial shock had worn off quick, Sharkey thought. Now the bastard starts shoveling the shit.

But Gole moved where he was wanted without argument or hesitation.

Getting out of the car, the whore's wig brushed the top of the door opening and got knocked askew. She gave a little yelp which made Sharkey look.

"Oh, fachrissake, is it you, Pennyworth?" Sharkey said.

"Didn' recognize me did you?" Pennyworth said, obviously delighted that his disguise had succeeded so well. "I knew auburn was my hair color."

"I would've recognized you, Pennyworth. It's dark in this goddamn alley and you wasn't exactly sitting with your head up high. You was busy at your trade. But I would've recognized you. Sooner or later."

Gole was looking at the male prostitute, wig cocked over one eye, as though the fake hair had turned into a mess of writhing snakes and Pennyworth—the lissome lady—into a monster beyond description.

"Have we got a case of mistaken identity here, Mr. Gole? Is it possible this ain't your maid but some impostor who managed to sneak into your house and take your maid's place?" Sharkey asked. "Would you mind stepping around to the other side of the car?"

Gole did as he was asked, shaking himself like a dog shedding water from its fur. He stuck out his chest like Harry Truman used to do and seemed to take on some authority.

Sharkey felt a little shock of recognition at the way the man was handling himself. The quick recovery. The way he turned his head and stared into his eyes, sizing him up. Ready to turn the situation around. He was ready to bet a fifty that the man was a lawyer or a politician or both.

Dubrowski reached for Pennyworth's purse and Pennyworth protested.

"Mind your business, Pennyworth," Sharkey said. "Hand over your purse and let Detective Dubrowski take a look inside."

"What's a big man like you doing tossing whores?"

"Keeping the peace."

"You got a warrant?"

"We caught you in the act, fachrissake, what are you talking about a warrant? You trying to get smart with us?" Dubrowski said.

"I just don' see why you got to go messin' with my property."

"We're not going to mess. We're going to have a look in case you got any dope, any hash, any speed, any il-legal substances, Penn-y-worth," Sharkey said, using black cadence, splitting the syllables, laying down the rap. "Get your hat on straight fachrissake, Penn-y-worth, you look like a drunken sailor."

"I ain' no drunken sailor, detective. I *do* sailors, drunk or otherwise." Pennyworth giggled.

"Don't giggle, Pennyworth, you black charmer. Please don't giggle. Makes me want to throw up," Sharkey said, enjoying himself. "You look like a pile of burnt toast with a gob of strawberry jelly on top."

Which made Pennyworth giggle all the more.

Dubrowski frowned, wondering what the hell was going on here, Sharkey insisting on pursuing nothing but a vague impression, some shadows in an alley, and now making a joke out of it, doing the dozens with a black transvestite hooker.

Dubrowski turned to face Gole and stepped in closer. "You seem to be in a little difficulty here."

The shake Gole had given himself seemed to have restored his confidence. He looked at Dubrowski as though measuring him for a suit.

"It looks that way, doesn't it? Caught out in a minor indiscretion, one might say," Gole said insinuatingly.

"Indiscretion," Dubrowski said, repeating Gole's word while making a face of disgust.

Gole's face tightened up. When he spoke again it was in a very low, quick, hard voice.

"We can play games or we can do business. Officer . . . ?"

"Detective. Detective Dubrowski."

"Detective Dubrowski, I'm not going to stand here like a mouse and let you play the cat. I'm not going to let you scold me or reduce me to begging on my knees. I'm not going to discuss the sociological ramifications of this situation, about what my appetites and desires have brought down on my head. And I'm not going to let you threaten me by innuendo."

He looked at Sharkey. Didn't just glance, but looked hard as though to say, Haven't you made me yet? Don't you remember the face, let alone the name? Don't you remember the circumstances under which we met? Don't you know who the fuck I am?

The voice. The manner. The penny dropped. Sharkey knew who Gole was and Gole knew he knew. Gole had been a member of the state legislature and used to come down from Springfield for this function or that affair. They'd partied together more than once, more than twice. Sharkey remembered the man had a taste for dark meat. It had seemed a disgusting perversion to Sharkey at the time. What was it? Five, six years ago? Before Roma Chounard had come into his life, that was for sure. Even if Gole was out of action he'd still have his connections. He could still have considerable clout.

"Hey, Detective Dubrowski," Sharkey said softly, laying his hand lightly on Dubrowski's sleeve, "I don't think we have to keep this up. I don't think . . ."

Dubrowski shook him off.

"You finished, Mr. Gole?" Dubrowski asked. "I hope you're finished. What I heard sounded to me just like the threat you say you ain't going to take from me. I hope the next thing you're going to say ain't going to be that you're a man of influence and that you got friends in high places."

Sharkey closed his eyes, wondering how he was going to smooth this thing over.

Dubrowski kept rattling on. "What you was doing here tonight is a dirty act. It ain't bad enough you're in a back alley letting a whore suck on your lollipop but it turns out it's a black whore. On top of which it's a male homosexual transvestite black whore."

"I didn't know that when I contracted for the service," Gole said, as though he were discussing a lube job for his car.

Dubrowski put up his hand.

"I won't argue that. I don't care you knew, you didn't know. I'm telling you something. I'm not scolding you. I'm not trying to humiliate you. I'm not threatening to tell your wife and kids. You got any kids?"

He put up his hand again before Gole could respond, if he meant to respond, and said, "I don't want to know. I don't want to know if you got a nice wife who loves you . . ." Gole's mouth twisted slightly as though he was disdainful of the hypocritical sermon Dubrowski was laying on him but helpless to do anything about it. ". . . and maybe a couple of nice daughters who think a lot of their old man. Maybe daughters with kids of their own. I don't want to know do you have some pretty little granddaughters who'd get sick to their stomachs if they knew the filthy things their grandpop was doing with a nigger."

"Listen . . ." Gole started, but couldn't get past the one word, couldn't get past the shame and rage and frustration he was suffering dealing with this cop. This cop who said ain't and was spraying him with his spit.

"Wally, let's settle down, look at what we got here," Sharkey said. "What we got here is what the man says we got, a little indiscretion. It's the holidays—"

"What the fuck you talking about?" Dubrowski snapped. "The New Year was a couple of weeks ago. We're in January, fachrissake."

"Well, I'm just saying we're close enough, we should maybe show a little charity in this situation."

"I understand that. I understand charity," Dubrowski said. "I hope you ain't going to laugh, Mr. Gole, when I tell you that I'm going to pray for you. That might not mean anything to you, but I'm a Polish Catholic and my partner here is an Irish Catholic and we both believe in prayer. I'm going to pray that you find the strength to do better with your life."

"I don't have to stand here and listen to this crap," Gole managed to choke out.

Dubrowski took a step toward Gole, so sudden it made the man start.

Dubrowski's eyes had gone flat. What had started out as a game was no longer a game.

"What we caught you doing was more than just an indiscretion," he said. "It was a danger. This Pennyworth is one type. He gives value for your dollar and he don't pull a knife. He ain't dangerous unless he bites down and gives you an infection. But we got others would cut off your nuts and cock, stuff 'em in your mouth, and steal your wealth if they got it into their heads to do so. You people come down here around Robert Taylor, around Cabrini-Green, looking for cheap sex in your eight-hundred-dollar sports jackets, forty-thousand-dollar cars. You incite these people to commit dangerous acts. You offer yourself up for killing and if they kill you it's me and Detective Sharkey what got to clean up the mess."

Gole looked away from the raging Dubrowski and stared at Sharkey.

"You understand what I'm saying to you?" Dubrowski asked, grinding the words out, spraying spit onto the side of Gole's face.

"I understand, detective," Gole said, his voice struggling up through the thickness in his throat, his eyes still on Sharkey, outraged by the treatment he was getting but reassured by the look of sympathy in Sharkey's eyes. "How much?"

Dubrowski blew out his breath, expressing his dismay at the stupidity Gole was displaying.

"Let the man talk," Sharkey said, seeing bribery as the only quick way out of the bind they were in.

Gole was crying silently now, enraged beyond any other expression, crying while he skinned bills off a roll he'd plucked from his pocket. "Fifty? A hundred? Two hundred?"

Sharkey took a couple of steps back into the shadows, distancing himself a little, letting the man deal with Dubrowski, buying his way out the easy way, hoping that Dubrowski's rage wouldn't overcome his greed.

"Pennyworth?" Dubrowski said. "What's your going rate for cleaning a client's pipes?"

"Fifty when I can get it," Pennyworth said, laughter lurking in his voice.

"So, what do you think is fair, Mr. Gole? I mean comparing service and value here?"

Gole handed over two hundred dollars.

"I'll be happy to make this contribution to the Policemen's Benevolent Society for you," Dubrowski said, taking the money. "Now, go on home and stay away from hookers, fags, and niggers."

"What about me?" Pennyworth asked, as Gole got into the car and drove away.

"What about you?" Dubrowski said.

"That sonofabitch didn't pay me."

"'Call a cop."

"You at least going to give me a lift back uptown?"

"Take a cab," Dubrowski said.

"You interrupted me at my business. You scared my customer away. He gave you my pay."

"Fachrissake."

"You stole my livelihood."

"Take a fucking stroll before I bust your ankles," Dubrowski said. He was laughing but only a fool would have failed to see he meant it.

"Come on, Pennyworth," Sharkey said, "get in the goddamn vehicle. We'll drive you back to the stroll."

"Well, I should hope-fucking-so," Pennyworth said, flouncing back and getting into the backseat as Sharkey held the door. Pennyworth smiled at him as though thanking him for being such a gentleman to a lady in distress, then gave the still-laughing Dubrowski a hard look of disdain.

When they let him off on the avenue where Pennyworth strutted his wares, Pennyworth got out, showing a lot of leg, tossed Dubrowski another disdainful glance, batted his eyes at Sharkey, fluffed the back of his wig with his carmine-tipped fingers, and walked away doing hip-rolls, accepting the hooted congratulations of the other strollers and night-birds.

"Fuck you, ossifer," he crooned back over his shoulder. "Not you Sergeant Sharkey, the other motherfucker. Here's a kiss for you," Pennyworth cried out on a note of triumph, cutting a fart before disappearing into the dark.

"Maybe I ought to catch that insulting bugger and break his nigger ass," Dubrowski said.

"Don't get yourself excited thinking about such things," Sharkey said, making a joke out of it.

Dubrowski laughed again. "I got to admit that jig's got a pretty nice pair of stilts on him."

"He has that."

"If he was a she I don't think I'd mind. How about you?"

"How about me what?''"

"You like dark meat?" Dubrowski asked, glancing at Sharkey in a way that made Sharkey wonder all over again if there was word about Roma going around.

He slumped down in the seat, threw his head back, tilted his hat over his eyes, and made an impatient motion with his hand, telling Dubrowski to shut up and drive.

If they kept on talking, the first thing you know he'd have another enemy, if Dubrowski wasn't already an enemy or in the enemy's employ, Sharkey thought.

4

SHELLEY ORCHID'S REAL NAME WAS SALVATORE OSMONSKI, HAVING received the last name from his Polish father and the first name from his mother, who was Calabrese.

Just before his engagement to the daughter of Pete Governale he was calling himself Stanley Osmond and was known in the neighborhood as a petty thief and grifter, smart but without much face.

Governale, on the other hand, had face. He was a man who put in fourteen-, sixteen-hour days in his construction yard from which he rented out earth-moving machines with operators at ninety to a hundred forty dollars an hour. He had connections. He had friends. You're in the construction business in Chicago, it's hard not to have friends and connections.

Governale had not been all that elated about his daughter, Gia, marrying the asshole who called himself Stanley Osmond, but she said she loved him and wouldn't have any other, so what was a loving father to do? He had to give his blessing or risk losing his daughter. Children never obeyed their parents nowadays. It was all the fault of television.

On the other hand the idiot was half-Italian and that was better than nothing.

With his father-in-law's help, Salvatore Osmonski aka Stanley Osmond rose in the world and bought an old mansion in the Forty-second for himself, and his wife and daughter, nicely located—not too near, not too far—around Lincoln Avenue, which was a very popular entertainment area.

He started running a crap game out of the parlor on weekends.

It was his dream to be asked to sit down with the Families. They didn't know he was alive.

Later on, after Ray Sharkey worked a deal on him, a couple

of tables for poker, a roulette wheel, and a restaurant and a couple of bedrooms for the comfort of high-rolling patrons were added, and the money started rolling in. Now the Families knew he was alive and even looked with interest on his operation, but with such a well-connected cop for a partner they weren't about to do anything about it. The *capo* did, however, nod when he happened to bump into Osmond, which was not very often.

By this time he'd bought another house seven blocks away, not wanting the business to affect his daughter's upbringing or his wife's standing among the other wives in the neighborhood or the Women's Sodality at St. Joseph's.

He started calling himself Shelley Orchid and took to wearing a diamond pinkie ring. He also started playing around with glossy women, whom he wined and dined over at the Canton Restaurant on Wentworth, reputed to make the best moo shu pork in Chinatown.

Every Monday and Friday night, rain or shine, he could be found with a glossy hooker on each arm and a bunch of regulars like Billy Chicklet, the bookie, Frank Leddy, the hoodlum, Connie Too-Too, the loan shark, Jasper Tourette, the whoremaster who supplied the hookers for Orchid's enterprise, and a handful of others who came and went with time and tide, scarfing up the moo goo gai pan, the chow mein, and the fried rice, telling the story of Sharkey's abuse between swallows. His companions thought he was an asshole and a dumbbell but he picked up every check in sight and he did business with each and every one of them.

So, the way he told the story was that back in '74, after four, five years of running a quiet game, some person or persons unknown had brought him and his enterprise to the attention of the Special Crime Squad, that bunch of freelancers commonly known as the Cowboys, who'd kicked down the door to his living room, with his wife and daughter sleeping upstairs (no hookers on the premises at that time), and dragged him off to jail at East Chicago Station, where he was visited one evening by this red-faced, white-haired, grinning Irish cop, Ray Sharkey, the City Hall Pimp.

Every one of Orchid's acquaintances knew the City Hall Pimp. They would've known him even if they didn't know him because they'd heard about Ray Sharkey every Friday night for several months.

"I'm sitting there in a cell being very annoyed, you understand," Orchid said each and every time he told it. "I mean they busted my establishment three times in less than three weeks. And now they done it again. Kicked in my goddamn front door. Those goddamn Cowboys everybody knew was friendly with Sharkey. Three times I paid a fine and spread a little butter on this piece of bread, that piece of bread, and somebody still wasn't satisfied."

"This goddamn Sharkey," one of the hookers, a redhead named Belle, piped up.

"You got it right, honey," Orchid agreed. "He was out to get me for reasons which I didn't know about—"

"But which you was about to find out about," Chicklet said, trying to rush along the story he'd suffered through twenty times before.

"You going to tell this story or am I going to tell this story?" Orchid demanded.

There was a look in Chicklet's eye that said he'd like to tell Orchid to shove his story up there where the sun don't shine but since Orchid always picked up the check he kept his mouth shut.

"So this time it's even worse," Orchid went on. "This time my wife and daughter's been arrested, too. They was residing in the women's facility with me momentarily unable to do anything to help them. All I wanted to know was who I'd offended and in what way, and who I had to pay off, once and for all, and how much. So when Sharkey comes strolling up, that's the first thing I asks him, how much."

Jesus Christ, you can sure pile it high, Frank Leddy thought. He had the story a different way from Manny Pockets, who'd been busted for drunk and disorderly and had been enjoying the hospitality of East Chicago Station's holding tank with Orchid that night.

The way he told it, Orchid had been beside himself, weeping and cursing and carrying on for an hour before the starch leaked out of him and he'd just sat there on his bunk staring at the floor between his shoes as though hoping that a map would appear there marking an escape route. He'd even gone down on his knees (which Pockets figured was a first) and said a prayer just before Sharkey arrived.

But why bring that up? Why not let Orchid have his story the way we wanted it.

" 'Hey,' Sharkey, the fucking pimp . . . you should excuse the reference, Jasper . . . says, throwing up his hands like he's afraid I'm gonna hit him. 'Why you coming at me? I'm here to help. I'm here to clear up these misunderstandings,' he says. '*Several* fucking misunderstands,' I says."

The way Pockets told it, Leddy remembered, Orchid stood there grasping the bars, with this sick cat's smile pasted on his kisser, like he was ready to get right down on his knees and kiss the cop's ass then and there. It was a terrible temptation to stick a pin in the asshole and let the farts out all at once. Except he had a favor to ask, so he decided once more that it would be better to let Orchid tell it the way he wanted to tell it.

" 'You don't look too good, Mr. Orchid,' Sharkey says to me, like he's really concerned," Orchid went on.

" 'I've got a little indigestion. You can understand. I ain't been able to finish my dinner lately. I keep on getting interrupted,' I says."

"That was a good one, Shelley," Leddy said.

" 'I'm sorry about that,' Sharkey says, and I says, 'You're sorry?' " Orchid went on.

Jesus Christ he hits a long ball, thought Tourette, the whoremonger. If he was a baseball player he'd be a regular Joe DiMaggio.

" 'I really am,' Sharkey says. Then he takes a key out of his pocket and opens the door. I pick up my tie and jacket, ready to get the hell out of there, but he taps me on the arm and ask me to sit down, he wants we should have a little chat. I says I don't want a little chat, I want to get out and see about getting my wife and daughter, which are innocent of any wrongdoing, out of Women's Detention."

"It must've been awful for them," Belle piped up.

Her girlfriend stopped shoveling the noodles in long enough to look up and say, "Detention ain't so bad."

"Well, I mean for girls who ain't used to it," Belle explained.

Orchid looked at them like they were a couple of cats who'd learned to talk and they shut up and went back to eating, going uh-huh and catching their breaths every now and then just to let him know they were listening.

" 'In a couple of minutes you can go upstairs and see the night magistrate,' Sharkey says. 'He's a friend of mine. Judge Abramowitz. It's not his regular court, you understand? It's just that the regular magistrate is out with the flu and Abramowitz likes to cooperate and make everything nice for everybody. He's a very sensitive and compassionate man.' He's feeding me this Irish bullshit like I'm supposed to believe it's chocolate pudding. I'm getting sick and tired. I'm fed up. 'How fucking much?' I says."

Orchid pulled himself up as though demonstrating exactly the pose of authority and defiance he'd struck.

" 'Twenty-five thousand,' this thief says to me. I nearly fainted. This gonnif's got illusions of grandeur. 'You're out of your mind,' I says. 'I've been taking heavy losses here and there lately. On top of which you cops've scared away all the customers from my establishment,' I says. 'Look, I'm going to be perfectly honest with you,' he says, like we're asshole buddies. 'This I know. Ever since your game got busted the first time, I've had some people looking into your finances. You understand what I'm saying? You've taken a lot of bad knocks. The track. The wheel. This and that. You've been on the edge for a while and you're just about ready to fall through the ice. So, when I say the price is twenty-five large, I don't mean *you* pay *me* twenty-five large, I'm saying *I* pay *you* twenty-five large.' I'm dumbfounded. What's he talking about?"

"That's what I'd like to know," Connie Too-Too said, who knew the rest of the story like he knew his own toes.

" 'Is this twenty-five large a present?' I asks him. 'Well, I ain't the Pope,' he says. 'I can't go around spreading that kind of charity. I got to have something for my money,' he says, and then he goes on to tell me he wants a piece of my enterprise. I don't mean only the game, I mean the house and the furniture and everything attached."

"I can't believe such a person," Belle said, which was an allright thing to say, because Orchid smiled at her and patted her hand.

" 'You're out of your mind. I got a big investment there,' I says. 'You got a big mortgage and credit payments there,' he says. So what can I say? I can't deny it. I had a streak of bad luck. He's been poking around and he knows. So he's got me over a barrel and he knows it. I'm sitting in jail and he's got the key. My business is going down the toilet. Then he tells me how besides the twenty-five he'll put in something for improvements."

"Which he done, you got to admit," Chicklet said.

"He gets me a permit for a couple of parking lots in a residential zone. He gets me a license to run an eating establishment. He works it so we can put up a little neon advertisement. I'm not denying it. What I'm saying is he's been paid back. Triple. Quadruple. Enough is enough."

"The man's greedy," Too-Too said, poking Leddy's shoe with his foot.

"You should put a stop to it," Leddy said, working the gag on Orchid the way they did every now and then, working him up.

"I mean you put up with something like that, the first thing you know this sonofabitch gets the idea he can walk all over you," Chicklet said, cranking it up.

"I mean you got a wife, you got a daughter," Leddy said.

"What the hell you mean by that?" Orchid demanded, sensing that he was being worked but not understanding in just what way.

"I didn't mean nothing by it. I'm just considering that you've got a very attractive wife there."

"How old's your daughter?" Chicklet said.

"What are you trying to say here?" Orchid said.

"Well, that old Irish cop's a powerful man with the ladies," Tourette said, going along.

"He ever lays a finger. He ever lays a fucking pinkie," Orchid said.

"No doubt," Leddy said. "We got no doubts."

"But how you going to manage it?" Too-Too asked.

"Manage what?"

"Taking the sucker out. Bringing that sucker down. Doing for that sonofabitch," Leddy said.

"I speak to my friend. I speak to the don. He gives me the nod every time he sees me. I'm not unknown to the right people."

"Hey, what you're saying there? You got to watch yourself. You ask the favor from them people and the next thing you know you got some partners you ain't counted on," Tourette said.

"I understand what you're saying," Orchid said, "and don't think it wouldn't be a consideration. But sometimes I think I'd rather have them for partners than have some crooked harp sucking my life's blood."

"There's other ways," Leddy said, in the quiet, dangerous way of talking he had.

"What's that?"

Leddy smiled a secret smile. "Well, you got other friends."

Orchid reached over and squeezed Leddy's hand.

"Thank you, Frankie," he said.

"That's all right."

"You want some more sweet-and-sour?" Orchid said.

"There's no more left," Too-Too said. "You want I should order another dish?"

"Also some long-life noodles," Orchid said, looking fondly at his companions, his friends, deeply touched by the declarations of affection and loyalty he read in their eyes, unable to read the laughter there.

"Can you do a favor, Shelley?" Leddy asked.

"You just name it."

"I'm coming up on a hijacking charge and I could use an introduction to your friend Sharkey."

"My friend?" Orchid said, snorting through his nose disdainfully.

"Well, maybe it could help."

"Why the hell not?" Orchid said, thinking it over and smiling. "We might as well use the sonofabitch while he's still around. But I don't want to ask the favor. I don't want to be beholden to the sonofabitch. You can understand that? But Jasper, here, can set it up for you."

"I'll do that," Tourette said, wondering what was going on here, Leddy looking for Sharkey, acting like he wanted to bribe the cop over a piece of dogshit, buying a howitzer when a fucking .22 pistol would do the job.

5

"THIS IS THE PLACE," DUBROWSKI SAID THURSDAY MORNING as he and Sharkey drove up to a run-down residential hotel on Kinzie Street in the Twenty-seventh Ward, in a neighborhood called the Patch. Not far away was Lake Street, under the Lake–Dan Ryan elevated tracks, said by some to be one of the toughest areas of the city.

There were three blue and whites in front of it, blocking the north side of the boulevard.

Dubrowski wheeled in and parked along the flank of the first squad car. When the uniform started toward them, Dubrowski pulled his badge holder and showed the cop the gold. Sharkey kept walking.

In the last remodel of the Westley Hotel—maybe twenty, thirty years before—somebody'd decided on distempering the walls up to the chair rail to look like parchment. They looked like they'd been pissed on.

Where it wasn't worn away, the carpet had once been maroon. Now it was a reddish-brown mess with five broad rivers worn into it almost down to the cord. One went to an abandoned newspaper and tobacco kiosk, one to the check-in desk, one to the elevator cage, one to the stairs going down to the public toilets, and one heading toward the staircase going up.

It wasn't yet a welfare hotel but it was getting there.

A small black man with round spectacles half-concealing his eyes with their reflection, wearing a shirt and tie, the sleeves shortened with old-fashioned arm bands, was sitting on a caved-in pouf in the middle of the lobby with two uniforms talking to him.

One of the cops was seated next to him and the other was standing looking down at him. There was something both intimate and intimidating in their manner toward him. The seated cop looked over at the approaching detectives and got to his feet.

Dubrowski raised a hand in greeting and Sharkey said, "You the man on the scene, Dolan?"

"Kramer and me caught the squeal."

"Why ain't you with the victim?"

"I assigned the next team to stand over it. The steam heat in here. It's very ripe in that room and my ulcer's been giving me hell lately."

"This the hotel manager?"

"Clerk," the man said. "I'm just the day clerk."

"This officer says the body's in a state of putrefaction," Dubrowski said. "What would you say, Dolan? Three days? A week?"

Dolan shrugged, unwilling to make that assessment. "Coroner can tell you that when he arrives."

"I know that, Dolan. I know that. I was asking for an estimate for the purposes of this conversation I'm having with Mr. . . . uh?"

"Kendicott," the clerk said. "Orville Kendicott."

"Mr. Kend-i-cott, here."

Dolan grinned.

"Anyway, Officer Dolan says it stinks to high heaven up there," Dubrowski said. "So let's figure it's been laying there rotting a couple of days at least. How come you waited so long to report it, Mr. Kend-i-cott?"

"I don't go around sniffing under doors," Kendicott said, offended by Dubrowski's manner.

Sharkey was amused. There was Dubrowski, the stupid, clumsy sonofabitch, trying to use black cadence on this Orville Kendicott in the same way that he himself had used it on Pennyworth, a goddamn male hooker.

"Okay, so it's going to be that way, is it?" Dubrowski said. "We ask you reasonable questions and you give us smart answers."

Kendicott's mouth twisted and he turned his head away. Sharkey could guess that Kendicott was a man who'd worked his ass off to get an education, his mother maybe scrubbing floors in public buildings all hours of the night, seven nights a week, to help him get it. Him getting up in the dark to deliver newspapers or paper sacks full of hot rolls to people's houses, working in some grocery store after school, swabbing out saloons on Sunday mornings. And when he had the diplomas in hand all he found out was that it wasn't time for educated colored yet. He was a couple of decades too soon. All the work he could get was work he could've got without the diplomas. Found out that a lot of whites actually resented a nigger having an education better than theirs. So here he was, an aging man, working as a clerk in a third-rate hotel slipping into decay. Him and the hotel growing old and ragged together, listening to the fading music of the parade that had passed them by.

"All we want to know," Sharkey murmured, "is how come you didn't smell something like a body rotting away for two, three days—who knows how long—up in that room."

"I just said that I had no reason to be in the hallways. I stay at the desk," Kendicott said.

"So, that's all right, then," Sharkey said, getting up close as though closing out the others. "You wasn't being a wise guy, I understand that. My partner understands that, but he's easily irritated. You know what I mean? So, how come the maid didn't notice something like that? How come one of your regular tenants didn't notice?"

"All the maid'd smell is an open bottle and my regulars wouldn't report anything even if they found a stiff under their own bed. They'd just check out."

"Unless the stiff was a good-looking piece of ass," Dubrowski said.

"Let's keep this clean and dignified," Sharkey said.

They were falling into it naturally, the asshole cop who might flip out, you said the wrong thing, and the quiet, reasonable cop, giving you smiles and chances to make brownie points with him.

"How come the maid makes the bed and don't see the body?" Sharkey said.

"The room's clean when the guest checks in. Weekly tenants get maid service only once a week. It cuts a couple bucks off the rate. This guest had the weekly rate and he checked in on a Sunday night, so he wouldn't get service until Monday week."

"Why don't we step over to the desk, have a look at the registration," Sharkey said.

They all got up and trooped over to the desk.

Kendicott went behind the counter and took a small wooden box out from underneath it. He took out a couple of dozen registration cards and handed them to Sharkey.

"What am I looking for?" Sharkey asked.

"Sunday afternoon."

Sharkey fingered the registrations as though he were counting the cards in a hand of gin rummy and plucked out three. Then he discarded one. "Woman," he said. Then he asked Kendicott if he'd watched the guest sign in.

"I don't recall."

"Try."

"I see five hundred people a month sign registration cards," Kendicott protested.

"Close your eyes and imagine him standing there."

Kendicott did it.

"Long name or short name?" Sharkey asked

"Short, I think. I wouldn't swear."

"So it ain't Stanley Wyszynski. Pick or Pike?" Sharkey asked, giving Dubrowski a look at the registration.

"Pike," Dubrowski said. "C. Pike."

"You want to try remembering the time he signed in?" Sharkey asked.

Kendicott closed his eyes and made an effort. "Late afternoon. I'd say three or four o'clock, Sunday afternoon."

"He have any luggage with him?"

"A Val-Pac. You know, one of those fold-overs with pockets."

"What color?"

"Dark green. With labels and tags all over it."

"What kind of labels and tags?"

"You know, the usual. Claim tags and destination labels."

"How come you remember these details all of a sudden?" Dubrowski asked suspiciously.

"I suppose when you start remembering you can't stop remembering," Kendicott said. "That bag had been places I could never hope to go," he added, with a certain sadness in his voice. When he opened his eyes he blinked as though the light hurt his eyes.

"Who found the body?" Dubrowski asked.

"I did."

"How come you was up there in the hallway if you always stay at the desk?"

"A check-in called the desk and complained about a backed-up toilet. He smelled it going by room 224. I went upstairs to have a look. The minute I got a whiff, I knew it wasn't a backed-up toilet."

"How's that?" Dubrowski asked.

"I've smelled backed-up toilets and I've smelled that other smell."

"Two?" Sharkey said.

"Korea."

"You call the owner?" Sharkey asked.

"I don't know who the owner is," Kendicott said. "I called the management company."

"They sending somebody down?"

"They didn't say so."

"Well, they better send somebody down because we're going to freeze everybody we can in place—no checkouts—until we can ask everybody some questions. So there could be some bitching and moaning around here. Also you're out of business. No check-ins either, at least not until after the coroner's through and we've had our look around."

"I suppose we better go up," Dubrowski said.

"You think you can hold your breath for fifteen minutes?" Sharkey asked. He reached into his pocket and came up with a sample-size jar of Vicks VapoRub.

"You got to watch it with that stuff, you could become a junkie," Dubrowski said.

"Upstairs, second floor," Dolan said. "You'll have to walk it."

"How come?"

"Bloodstains in the elevator cage. I got it taped off."

"Hey, you ain't as dumb as you look," Sharkey said.

"Probably just some drunk had a nosebleed," Dubrowski said, stealing the praise away.

Sharkey crossed the lobby and trudged up the stairs with Dubrowski and Dolan right behind him.

When they reached the second-floor landing, Dolan said, "Just follow your nose."

They walked along the corridor to the room where another uniform, looking white around the gills, stood guard.

"Go downstairs, get some fresh air," Sharkey said. "But come back when the coroner arrives."

The young cop threw him a salute and a grateful glance and hurried away.

"I don't think I'm going to enjoy this," Sharkey said, dipping his finger into the VapoRub and dabbing some on his upper lip just under his nostrils. "You want a couple dabs, Wally?"

"You remember Kiley back at the academy?" Dubrowski said.

"Sure. I remember Kiley. Loved chili and beans."

"He'd lay a fart, you'd think an elephant died."

"That's right."

"So, this is nothing compared to Kiley."

Sharkey laughed and said, "Suit yourself."

They went into the room. It was torn up pretty good, clothes and newspapers scattered everywhere, but there was no blood except some drip marks on the carpet.

Sharkey went over to the door of the bathroom.

The corpse was that of a naked man, fifty, fifty-five, tipped sideways, half-squatting over a cut-down cardboard toilet paper carton filled with a layer of Kitty Litter three inches deep. The man had crapped himself from fear or from punches in the gut. His feces were smeared all over the litter and his legs as though somebody had been poking at it.

His hands had been tied behind his back with a length of clothesline which had then been looped around an overhead pipe and hauled up. The weight of his body dragging on his arm sockets would have given him hell when he was alive. His face was swollen, his eyes completely shut, lips split, teeth broken, and one cheekbone caved in. A sock was stuffed into his mouth.

"Stripped him bare-ass naked," Dubrowski said.

Sharkey pointed his chin at the tub and the shower curtain, which had been torn half off the rod. There was a cake of soap sitting on the bottom of the tub. "Caught him taking a shower."

There was a suit, a shirt, and a pair of shorts crumpled up on the floor as though they had been knocked off the hook on the back of the door.

Sharkey put on a pair of surgical gloves, squatted down, and went through the trouser pockets, removing a money clip holding some bills, a soiled handkerchief, a comb, some change, and a practically new wallet. He tossed the money clip and the wallet to Dubrowski, who snatched them out of the air one after the other and gave them a quick once-over.

"Airport baggage checks and a gate pass from Tel-Aviv to Chicago on Pan Am. Temporary driver's license from the state of Illinois made out to Calvin Pike, seven seven seven Seventy-seventh Street, Cicero."

"Wise guy," Sharkey said.

"You think there's really a seven seven seven—"

"What do you think, for God's sake?"

"I mean if there really was a seven seventy-seven Seventy-seventh Street and this victim really lived there maybe it'd be a bet for the numbers or maybe the seventh horse in the seventh race over to the track."

"The nags ain't running in the winter."

"I just mean it could be a bet on whatever."

"Take a look. I don't think you could exactly call this gazooney a lucky man," Sharkey said.

"You got a point."

"Anything else?"

"Two hundred and thirty-eight dollars and a scapular."

"Roman Catholic," Sharkey said.

"I know what a scapular is," Dubrowski said.

Sharkey straightened up and stood there staring down at the battered corpse. "This traveler blew into town to transact a little business and didn't even have a chance to jump into his own skin."

"You think he's a local?"

Sharkey shrugged, declaring the obvious. At this stage of the game who was to tell?

"How you doing?" Sharkey asked, taking out the jar of Vicks again and giving his nose a couple of dabs.

"You really need me in here?" Dubrowski asked.

"It's only going to be another minute."

"So, maybe I'll have some of that."

He smeared some of the salve on his upper lip and stuck his pinkie finger into each nostril.

Sharkey looked the body all over, leaning against the far wall behind the toilet so he could catch every angle. His back was to Dubrowski. Dubrowski capped the jar and slipped it into Sharkey's coat pocket from behind.

"They busted his legs. What we got to look for, is we got to look for a baseball player toting around a Louisville Slugger," Sharkey said, making the kind of black joke cops make to keep themselves from going nuts.

"You think he owed somebody something and couldn't pay?" Dubrowski asked.

"Couldn't or wouldn't."

"I think somebody starts doing that to a person, that person would decide pretty quick that he would if he could."

There were voices out in the bedroom. Dubrowski turned around and walked out of the bathroom and Sharkey followed him after a minute.

Dubrowski was at the foot of the bed talking to the man from the coroner's office, a youngster by the name of Charlie Press. He was already wearing a molded paper mask over his nose and mouth and was snapping on a pair of gloves.

"That piece of paper ain't going to do you no good," Dubrowski was saying. "What you got to do is stuff some Vicks VapoRub up your nose." He patted his pockets as though he carried a jar of it around all the time.

"I already got some cotton plugs soaked in cloves up my nose," Press said, sounding like a man stuffed up with a bad head cold.

"So, that's okay then," Dubrowski said, going over to the chest of drawers and starting to open them one by one.

"Some juiceman had him beat to death over a bad debt or a drug deal went sour, that's our bet," Sharkey said.

"So, I can save myself the trouble of an autopsy?" Press said.

"If it wasn't for the fact that you're the man who's got to tell us is he dead, ain't he dead, we could've saved you the trip."

"The boys from scene of the crime here yet?"

Sharkey shook his head no.

"Well, bread and butter," Press said, going into the bathroom. "Got to earn my bread and butter."

Sharkey stood where he was and watched Dubrowski toss the room. He searched the closet, even getting up on a chair to check the back of the top shelf, the wooden chair creaking and groaning under his weight. He stepped down and tested the floorboards with a penknife. He lifted the corners of the worn carpet.

You had to admire the economy and efficiency with which the fucking mastodon did the job, Sharkey thought, walking over to the bathroom and standing in the doorway.

"Time of death?" he said.

"You're pulling my leg," Press said, laughing through his mask. It sounded like he was softly strangling.

"I read about it all the time," Sharkey said, kidding Press along, having a little fun. "Rigor mortis. Postmortem lividity."

"Useless for timing death," Press said, as though really believing that Sharkey didn't know.

"Maggots?"

"You see any maggots? If there were any maggots, I could give you an idea, an approximation, but it's the dead of winter. Not that many flies. The couple of flies in here now weren't in here when the subject got it. They didn't lay any eggs in the wounds. You want to hang around a couple of days, I'll show you some maggots."

"Give me a window," Sharkey said.

"More than thirty-six hours. Less than ninety-six."

"Between a day and a half and four days?"

"You can count."

"Ah, you're such a funny man, Charlie."

"It's the jokes that keep us sane," Press said. "Anything else or are you going to hang around for any pearls of wisdom I might utter?"

"We trust you. When SOC gets here just tell them to bag everything in sight, okay?" Sharkey said.

"You want the body cellotaped for particles and hairs?"

"Not unless the poor sonofabitch was raped."

Dubrowski was finished looking. "No Val-Pac. Not even an overnighter."

"That's really traveling light," Sharkey said.

Sharkey and Dubrowski pushed their way past Dolan and the guard at the door and walked on down the hall to the staircase. On the way they passed the trapdoor to a garbage chute set in the wall. There was a sign that said INCINERATOR on the wall so scarred and stained it was scarcely readable. Somebody had welded a hasp onto the bottom of the door and a heavy staple was screwed to the wall. There was a padlock securing it.

They walked on to the top of the stairs.

"We can close this one out right now," Dubrowski said. "All we can do is see if we can connect this dead guido to some shy. Even then, what've we got? A sucker goes to one shark, he goes to more than one. How do we point the finger? We're never going to find the bone-breaker what done it unless somebody gives him up for reasons of their own."

"Early times, Dubrowski. It's early times," Sharkey said. "We got to ask ourselves how come somebody beats the life out of this poor fucker because he can't pay his bill and then leaves two hundred and thirty-eight bucks in his wallet."

"Maybe they figured it was nothing but small change."

"Nothing's small change to these goniffs looking for an easy profit. They'll steal a fifteen-cent newspaper when they got a hundred dollars in their pocket. It ain't always the size of the score that counts."

Two men from SOC, the portable lab, both known to Sharkey and Dubrowski by name, Joe Ostriach and Harry Friar, came trudging up the stairs with their wooden boxes of paraphernalia.

"Oh, Christ," Friar said. "Look who it is. Them two. They tramped all over the place, put their prints on everything, used the victim's comb, took a dump in the toilet, left dandruff on the pillow cases—"

"Chartreuse cunt hairs," Sharkey said. "That's what we want you to look for, chartreuse cunt hairs."

They jostled one another in passing and then Sharkey and Dubrowski were walking across the lobby.

Sharkey detoured back to Kendicott, who was still standing behind the desk. Dubrowski wandered after him.

"You happen to see how Mr. Pike arrived?" Sharkey asked.

"I don't recall. I really don't recall," Kendicott said.

Sharkey turned his back, leaning an elbow on the counter to bring himself down to Kendicott's perspective and looked across the lobby toward the entrance.

"If a taxi pulled up you could see it right through the glass in the doors," he said.

"Well, you could if there was room for a taxi to pull up in front. Drivers ignore the passenger loading zone there more than half the time."

"Thank you, Mr. Kendicott," he said and started leaving the hotel again, Dubrowski falling into step beside him.

"What's next?" Dubrowski asked.

"What you've got to do is check the register, see how many permanent, how many long stay, how many transit," Sharkey said. "Question the transients first. There could be people got to get somewhere. You know what to look for. I don't have to tell you."

"What's this 'you' bullshit? You planning on taking a nap?"

"There's no reason for two of us to do what one can do just as well. I'll go check that address."

"Fachrissake, all you got to do is check a street map."

"Not if somebody's really living there," Sharkey said, picking up the pace and breezing out the door.

"Hey!" Dubrowski shouted. "How you going to get there?"

"I'll take a cab," Sharkey replied.

"It must be nice to be on the expense account," Dubrowski shouted.

"Maybe you ought to call in, get the captain to send down a couple of teams to help you with the interrogation," Sharkey shouted back. "You understand what I'm saying? We can't be expected to do it all."

"Fuck you," Dubrowski said.

Sharkey laughed and waved without turning around. Fuck you too, he thought, you work your side of the street and I'll work mine.

6

THE KILARNEY TAVERN ON SACRAMENTO AND TWENTY-FIFTH, just up from the Criminal Court and the Department of Corrections, had been there for sixty, seventy years. It had a lovely smell of beer-soaked wood, frying sausages, sauerkraut and pickles, corned beef and cabbage, and just a trace of vintage urine. Time was when ladies were not allowed in the taprooms but only in the dining room saloon.

Since the war that'd all been changed. They sat where they

pleased to sit. Still, there were some who refused to believe that more than thirty years had passed since the end of Big Two and that there'd been two more wars involving America since.

It was a huge place, as big as a warehouse, broken up into maybe eight different rooms on three different levels. You could get lost in there trying to find the toilets without a map.

There were isolated tables standing out in the middle of the floor here and there, the idea being that nobody could get close enough to overhear any confidential conversations between jurists, attorneys, defendants, or co-conspirators without being seen.

There were booths tucked into dark corners and even a few small private rooms, not much bigger than large closets, where really private affairs could be conducted up to and including afternoon "affairs of the hearts and belly buttons" as Patrick Cooney, the regular afternoon bartender, liked to call romantic interludes or daytime quickies.

Sharkey was sitting in a booth—a table in the middle of a moat of empty floor not being available—with Frank Leddy aka Frankie Blue Shoes, a versatile criminal who'd come to Sharkey with a recommendation from an acquaintance and associate of Sharkey's by the name of Jasper Tourette.

Leddy had not been unknown to him before Tourette's introduction, but they'd never had reason to break bread before.

Pretending to a certain carelessness in his posture, leaning in close, head cocked a little to one side, one hand sometimes slipping up behind his ear, Sharkey reminded the thief and ball-buster of a priest listening to confession.

His red face shone where the bone was closest to the surface as though it had been waxed and the white hair had a handful of red in it like rust stains on bride's satin. Big teeth as white as pieces of a broken china cup. Blue eyes those of a young man.

Sharkey's gray fedora sat on the seat at his side, carefully placed there with one hand while the other had twice checked the surface of the scarred wooden tabletop for wet spots or the sticky remains of the last customer's beer, protecting his camel hair topcoat from stains. He'd planted his elbows so that his hands were held aloft and free to move. Hands more eloquent even than his mouth, weaving images with his fingers in the air. Concentrating Leddy's attention. Dragging him under his spell.

"My acquaintance, Jasper Tourette, indicated to me that you desired a meeting here in Kilarney's," Sharkey said. "You wanted to buy me a ginger ale and have a chat in a venue that guaranteed a modicum of privacy. Is that right?"

"That's right."

"But over there, sitting in that booth, you got your runner with a pair of felony sneakers on his feet, you got your bone-breaker wearing gloves in a tavern—for God's sake, what's the matter, his hands are cold or he thinks somebody's going to call him out for a gunfight?—and you got your lawyer, J. J. Finnegan, with a briefcase full of motions and continuances. I thought you were a hard man."

"I carry what help I might need with me."

"But what help you need you need from me. Is that right? Did I get the right impression? Do you want some service—some favor—from me? Did I misunderstand my acquaintance, Jasper Tourette?"

"No, you got it right."

"I thought I did. How do you happen to know my acquaintance, Jasper Tourette?"

Leddy smirked. "I sometimes got occasion to use his services. I'm putting on a party and I need some girlfriends for visiting businessmen. I get an urge in the middle of the afternoon. You know. Just like you."

Sharkey's eyelids fluttered a little, but Leddy apparently didn't notice or, if he did, had no idea what it meant.

"Just like me what?"

"Well, I mean," Leddy said, still grinning his suggestive grin, "I understand you also got occasion. I mean to say I hear tell you ain't altogether unacquainted with Tourette's merchandise. Wholesale *and* retail."

Sharkey's eyelids fluttered again. What did this asshole think he was doing? Swapping war stories with a buddy, matching peckers with an old friend, indulging in a little male bonding before getting down to business?

"You heard that?" Sharkey said. "What else did you hear?"

Leddy backed off a foot, getting a little distance from Sharkey's face thrust forward at him in what was about to become a threat display, the grin turning to dust on his mouth, licking it off his lips with his tongue.

"I heard you snapped up Tourette's main woman the second time you laid eyes on her," Leddy said.

"What else you hear?"

"That's all, that's all," Leddy said quickly.

"So, you discuss this with people?"

"What?"

"You bandy my name about? You and your shyster and your runner and your bone-breaker swap a few stories about me before coming here? Have a few laughs at my expense?"

"Fachrissakes, nothing like that. We was just remarking," Leddy protested, clearly confused about Sharkey's anger. After all, in his world, to his way of thinking, for a man to steal a top pimp's main woman was no mean accomplishment.

"Because what I'd like to do," Sharkey said, as though Leddy hadn't apologized, "is point out to you that you shouldn't let what you hear come flying right out of your mouth without you give the parties involved some consideration. You understand what I'm saying to you?"

Leddy nodded.

"Show a little discretion. Be smart. You come around asking a man for favors, you don't wave a snotty handkerchief in his face."

"I wasn't being snotty. I was just—"

"I hope it's not now your intention to entertain me with a few ironical remarks."

"—upset."

"I didn't think you were a man easily upset. You've got a reputation."

"So have you got a reputation."

"Oh?" Sharkey spoke the word like a gunshot, like a warning.

Everything about the Irish cop was a threat, right up front, Leddy thought. Right from git-go. Showing his teeth while he shook your hand. Letting you know who was going to be the boss in the relationship.

He could understand that. Everybody had his own means of intimidation. His was a quiet manner and the screen of mirrored glasses and the people he always had around him. Sharkey's was Irish bluster, Irish honey cake.

"So, tell me what you're doing for your living lately, Mr. Leddy," Sharkey said.

Leddy hesitated.

"A little numbers wheel?" Sharkey said. "A little dope? A little freelance procuring? Child porn? A little burglary? A little smuggling? A little loan sharking?"

"Nothing like that. No, I don't do that."

Isn't that odd, Sharkey thought; of all the nasty things I name the one thing he rises to deny is loan sharking. He filed it away in the back of his head.

"So, what have we here?"

"What?"

"I mean what've we got on your plate here."

"The charge against me is a piece of dogshit," Leddy said.

"Well, you know, that's what people in my end of the business hear all the time from people in your end of the business. What's the charge?"

"Hijacking."

Sharkey raised his eyebrows. "Where?"

"Midway Airport."

"They catch you with the stuff?"

"There wasn't any stuff. I'm telling you it's all a misunderstanding."

"Somebody turn you in?"

"Some crooked watchman rolled over on me, looking to save his own ass."

"You had no business with this man?"

"Well, I knew him. I had conversations with him."

"About baseball, football, like that?"

"Yeah, like that."

"About a load of sporting gear?"

Leddy's brows shot up in surprise. It was a right move because Sharkey lost his grin and eased back a little, pleased that Leddy was impressed how thoroughly he got on top of things.

"Which you definitely did not hijack?" Sharkey went on.

"I won't lie and say I wasn't giving the proposition some consideration."

"But you didn't?"

"I didn't lay a finger."

"So, no crime, no time."

"Well, the thing is, somebody unknown to me must've had

the same idea. They can't find whoever done it so they lifted me. They got the watchman's testimony."

"So, stand up in court. Your word against the watchman's."

"I can't take the chance. If I'm convicted on this one it makes me a persistent felon."

"Oh, oh," Sharkey said, smiling as though Leddy had just made a funny remark.

Leddy tried to smile too, but it wouldn't stay on his face.

"You're looking at five, minimum," Sharkey said. "What's your intention?"

"It's my intention to find out if there's some way this misunderstanding could be settled."

Sharkey flicked a speck of dust from his sleeve and rubbed the bridge of his nose with his thumb and finger as though pinching weariness from his brain.

"Who's hearing your case?" he asked.

"Judge Jeremiah Sharkey."

"Convenient. Ain't that convenient?" Sharkey said with the air of a mouse sniffing the cheese in the trap.

Leddy knew that cops didn't trust anybody or anything. Not the mirrors and not the walls.

They avoided the truth. They told lies when the truth was just as easy and would serve just as well, maybe even better. So they figured everybody in the world was a liar. They ran around setting mantraps, deadfalls, and snares, so they were always walking very carefully because they believed that somebody was laying such devices to catch them.

All of a sudden Leddy wasn't too happy with this little frame Finnegan had talked him into with vague promises of good times to come when and if a certain candidate was elected to office with a little help from him.

"So what did you have in mind?" Sharkey asked, after a minute.

"I had in mind . . . well, let me hear what you got in mind."

Sharkey slid out of the booth in a hurry, took seven strides to the booth where Leddy's people sat, and snatched up the lawyer's briefcase.

Finnegan said, "Hey!" but didn't make a move to snatch it back.

Sharkey carried it back to his table, laid it down, and snapped the latches. "You know they got microphones nowadays can catch a fly's fart fifty feet away and put it on tape?" He opened the case and searched it quickly and thoroughly. It contained some documents and a sausage in a bun wrapped in waxed paper. It also contained a miniature recorder and a directional shotgun mike concealed in a false bottom.

There was a little circle of dull copper mesh, almost the same color as the leather, the port for the microphone head, set into the expensive custom-made case.

He popped the recorder cover and stripped the tape from the cassette before dropping it in the ashtray. He put the recorder back, closed the case, and held it out at arm's length.

Finnegan scrambled over to retrieve it.

"Let me make a suggestion, Finnegan," Sharkey said. "Why don't you and your friends go someplace else, have yourself a drink, eat your kielbasa? There's a nice coffeeshop down the block. Tell the waitress I sent you. Or go outside, sit in your car. Take the other assholes with you. You understand what I'm saying?"

Finnegan looked at Leddy as though accusing him of giving the game away.

"Don't look at him to see if it's all right, Finnegan. All you got to do is listen to me," Sharkey said.

Finnegan gathered up the runner and the bone-breaker and left the Kilarney.

"I ought to get up and walk out of here," Sharkey said. "Let you stand up in my brother's court and hear him sentence you to five. Let those buggers at Cook County tear you a new asshole."

"Listen, I want to explain—"

"What the hell did you think you were doing? You think you were fucking around with an amateur?"

"Finnegan told me to let him record the meeting. A little insurance policy in case you took my money and then decided not to deliver. Something to have on record."

"Anybody who listens to lawyers like J. J. Finnegan should have their brains examined. Why're you sweating?"

"Well, now you won't do me the favor—talk to your brother."

"Stand up," Sharkey said, looking around to see how much privacy they enjoyed, now that Leddy's people were gone.

"What?"

"Stand up, if you still want a negotiation."

Leddy stood up. Sharkey slipped out of the booth. "Unbutton your jacket."

When Leddy had done as he'd been told, Sharkey searched him for a wire. It was over in a minute but he hadn't left anyplace untapped or unprodded.

"Unless you swallowed the mike and you're carrying the battery pack up your ass, I think we can talk some more," Sharkey said.

He sat down and indicated that Leddy should do the same. "So, we make a Chicago contract. Nothing on tape. Nothing on paper. No outside witnesses. We don't even have to spit on our palms and shake." He chuckled, remembering—reminding Leddy of—the way agreements were sealed in the playgrounds and on the streets in the neighborhoods when they were kids. "A Chicago contract. A couple of nods. An understanding."

Sharkey's hands opened up in front of his face, showing ten fingers spread out like fans. He manipulated his fingers like a deaf man signing, showing this many, that many. "We got this many I got to spread around among the uniforms what arrested you, they shouldn't feel they wasted all that energy for nothing. This much for the court clerk, make sure you stay in the right court. This much for the prosecutor, he shouldn't decide to make an example out of you. This for the judge, whose name you forget one minute after you stand before him for the dismissal of charges." He was counting out hundreds. "You understand what I'm saying?"

Leddy nodded, thinking there were conversational habits Sharkey ought to watch.

"So a little and a little," Sharkey went on, his fingers flourishing in the air between them, "and there you got the number." His fingers became still again, no fingers showing, two fists held up in the air between them. "And then there's me. So altogether . . ." He displayed one five-fingered fan.

"You're asking too much. Five bones is too much," Leddy complained.

"If it's too much, it's too much. I'll see you in court, like they say," Sharkey said, picking up his hat and sliding out of the booth. He took his time putting on his hat, arranging it just so, at a conservative angle. Nothing flashy. Nothing unruly.

"Wait a second," Leddy said quickly. "What can I say? You got me by the shorts."

"So don't make me feel bad by acting like I'm forcing you to take the favor."

"You want the money now?"

Sharkey's eyes went flat. He hesitated for a New York minute, staring at a spot between Leddy's eyes.

"Sure, why not? You got it, I'll take it."

"Well, I don't carry money. I make it a policy. My bodyguard does it—"

"Your bodyguard?" Sharkey said contemptuously.

"Well, Albert."

"The asshole with the gloves?"

"He carries my money. I can go get him."

"No, no. That's all right. I can wait. I'll do the favor and I'll wait."

"When do I pay you?" Leddy asked.

"I'll send you word in the next day or two. Never mind the checkbook. Cash. Small bills. You know the drill."

Sharkey walked out, settling his topcoat on his sloping shoulders—boxer's shoulders—throwing up a hand, waving bye-bye to the bartender, Patrick Cooney. Ray Sharkey, the businessman cop. There was a greasy stain on the right-hand pocket of his expensive topcoat.

So, fuck you, Dandy Dan, Leddy thought.

J. J. Finnegan, the runner, and Albert the bone-breaker, sitting in a car across the street, watched Sharkey flag down a cab.

"Pretty good, a police sergeant can fart around in taxis," Finnegan said. "You don't get that kind of pocket change from sucking on the public tit."

They went back in. Albert and the runner went to sit in the booth they were sitting in before, like dogs taking up their guard positions. Finnegan sat down with Leddy.

Leddy already had a fresh double whiskey with a ginger back on the table. His hands were shaking so badly that he could hardly get the shot glass to his mouth.

"What's the matter with you, you got a chill?" Finnegan asked.

"That Irish sonofabitch scares the shit out of me," he said.

"I don't mind saying. He comes right at you. He don't even leave you time to think."

"That's Irish bullshit."

"I don't know. I think you make the wrong move, say the wrong word, he'd put a pea in your eye before you could blink."

"You trying to up the ante on this little favor you're doing for me?"

"No, no. I wouldn't do that. I mean it."

"So, all right, you make an agreement?" Finnegan asked.

"Five large."

"You didn't pay him?"

"With what? Albert carries the money, I don't carry the money."

"So, all right," Finnegan said. "That gives us another chance to nail the sonofabitch with the evidence. Where and when are you supposed to pay him?"

"He'll tell me where and he'll tell me when."

Finnegan's expression changed, hope replaced with disappointment.

The Candidate isn't going to like this, he thought.

7

"WHAT MAKES YOU THINK MY ROBE'S FOR HIRE, RAY?" JUDGE Jeremiah Sharkey asked, staring at Ray over his steepled fingers.

"Hey, Jerry, you telling me I don't know my own brother? You telling me I don't know you do this one that one a little favor for a favor?"

"No, you don't know that. You may have heard that, but you don't know that because we never talked about it. But let's give you the benefit. Let's say I've done a favor now and then. That's politics. That's not hiring out."

"It's the mention of cash makes the difference, is that it? You never took a dollar to look the other way, squash a motion, declare an arrest tainted that wasn't tainted? You never done that?"

"Why is it you still talk like a truckdriver, Ray?"

"Hey, Jerry, some of my best friends're truckdrivers. I didn't go to college. You're the one the family sent to college."

"Gabe went to college."

"Gabe went to seminary, then he went to college. Mother Church picked up his tuition and his board once they knew he was going for the collar. No expense to the family."

"I was just mentioning."

"I understand. Keeping the record absolutely straight. Gabe went to college and you went to college. I wasn't reminding you I chipped in so you could go to college."

"You just reminded me."

"I mentioned it in passing, is all. You don't want to do this little thing for cash, then do it for your brother. I mean since you never took money under the bench."

"Okay, let me get this straight, Ray," Jerry said. "You never came to me before with anything like this. Now you're asking me to run a cut-rate court. You're asking me to kick this Leddy—this goniff, this hustler, this persistent felon—loose for three hundred dollars. You think my court's a discount house?"

"I don't think your court's a discount house, Jerry. What I think is you could use the three hundred dollars. Myra's fur coats don't come cheap and if we get another brute of a winter like last winter she'll love you for it. So think about it."

"I think about it or you get the case assigned to a different court, is that what you're saying?"

"I could go to the clerk and ask the favor, Jerry. You know I could always do that."

"There'd be a charge."

"Well, there's a charge already. With Harry Mungo there's always a charge. Mungo's got eyes in his ass. He's got ears on the end of his prick. He gets wind of my desire to have Leddy appear before Judge Sharkey, even if Leddy's already on your docket, and all of a sudden Leddy's floating. This court, that court, all around the town. If I want to make sure Leddy's case don't float, I got to give Mungo a little taste. There ain't no other way to do business around Criminal Court."

"What are you going to have to give the clerk?" Jerry asked.

"A hundred and fifty."

"So a judge is only worth twice as much as a clerk?"

"If I don't buy the clerk, I don't get the right judge."

"What judge would you want to buy if it wasn't me?"

"I was thinking Abramowitz."

"That pussy won't kick Leddy loose for three hundred dollars and you know it."

"That's why I come to you on this one. Abramowitz is getting greedy. I'm looking for a price."

"Abramowitz is the judge you've gone to in the past?"

"Don't ask me such questions. Besides . . ."

"Besides what?"

"Besides I don't want to deal with strangers anymore."

Jerry laughed through his nose at that, but his eyes were serious.

"You've known Abe for fifteen years."

"He's still a stranger, Jerry. He ain't family."

"So, all these years you ignore me and now, all of a sudden, I'm family and you don't want to deal with anyone but family."

"I didn't want to give them anything to wonder about before. One brother a judge, the other brother a cop."

"What changed your mind this time?"

"I got nobody else I can trust," Ray said.

"I understand."

"Oh?" Ray said.

"Rumors are going around that The Candidate—actually the people advising him—are looking for a rotten cop to hang on a tree. It's a crowded field and everybody's looking for a cause."

"Is that what you think I am, Jerry, a rotten cop?"

"For Christ's sake, no. Don't go putting words in my mouth. I'm just saying somebody could have an eye on you. This Leddy could even be part of a sting. You ever think of that?"

"Yes, I thought of that. It's another reason why I come to you. If you heard the rumors, Abramowitz heard the rumors. I see Abe in the corridor today, he might not even say hello. I don't want to beg the man, maybe end up insulting him."

"But you're willing to endanger me?"

"I wouldn't put one of your pinkies at risk. You shouldn't even have to ask me if I would. You know and I know this persistent felon bullshit is honored in the breech and not in the application. The case they got is no case. It's a witness testifying to conversations because they made him a deal. I doubt anybody's taking it seriously. In fact I think the prosecutor goes along with it just to do the favor for The Candidate in case he winds up sitting in Daley's chair. You understand what I'm saying? They gave the fucking scheme away."

"How's that?"

"Leddy's got that asshole, J. J. Finnegan, supposed to be representing him, sitting at the next table with a microphone pointed up my ass."

"How do you know that?"

"Because I took the goddamn toy away from him, what do you think? I'm too old a cat to be fucked by a bunch of kittens."

"The Candidate's no kitten. He's had plenty of experience in state government."

"Then maybe he's getting old before his time, underestimating me the way he's doing. Or maybe he learned a lesson from Nixon's mistakes. He wants something done but he only wants to look at it with one eye. He don't want to own it, in case anybody should ask."

"Why don't you play it safe? Why don't you just give them the back of your hand?"

"Because I need the money. Helen and Flo together are draining me dry. I can't keep five dollars in my pocket." He paused, watching Jerry's expression, waiting to see if there'd be any comment about Roma Chounard forthcoming. Waiting to see if *that* rumor had reached Jerry's ears. Nothing. "Because they insulted me, pointing a mike at me that way. Because if I know what they're up to, I know how to play them. I'm going to teach those fucks a lesson. I'm going to pick their pockets and they ain't going to be able to do a thing about it. I guarantee you."

"You want a drink?" Jerry asked.

"Is that a yes? You'll give Leddy the air?"

"You said it. If the prosecution presents the kind of case you say they have, there's not a judge on the bench who'd invoke the persistent-felon law."

"Well hardly any." Ray grinned. "I'll have a bourbon and branch. Use your phone?"

"Go ahead," Jerry said as he walked over to the mahogany sideboard to pour a couple of drinks.

Sharkey dialed up the city registry over in Cicero, identifed himself by badge number, and asked about the address with all the magical numbers.

"Streets stop at Sixty-first? Thaaank you."

"What was that?" Jerry asked, coming back with the drinks in two square-cut crystal tumblers.

"Phony address on a temporary driver's license we found on a corpse over at the Westley Hotel."

"Wouldn't they know that down at Motor Vehicles?"

"You'd be surprised what people who are supposed to know don't know."

8

EVERY TIME RAY STOPPED BY HIS FATHER'S FLAT IN BRIDGE-port—the flat just downstairs from the one in which he'd been born and raised—he was filled with a sweet melancholy, an inarticulate regret that things had changed. There were memories collected like dust in every corner of every step up the two flights to the second floor.

He remembered how his mother, Cora, had always talked about moving to the flat on the first floor when they'd lived on the third. Three dollars a month more on the rent, which they'd never been able to afford back then.

His mother and father would sit for hours discussing the advantages and disadvantages of such a move.

Living on the top floor you got more sun and fresh air and you didn't have anybody tramping around over your head, Dan argued.

He walked around barefoot in the middle of the night sometimes and the old lady on the second floor complained bitterly about the thumping.

Living on the first floor saved a person three flights of stairs, Cora said. Running up and down those stairs six times a day, sometimes with your arms full of groceries, wasn't a pleasure.

On the other hand, it was only one flight up to the roof to hang out the clothes where they could get the best sun and air. Hanging clothes out in the backyard, on lines strung between two poles, the way people on the first floor had to do, meant the possibility of leaves and grass blowing onto the sheets and pillowcases.

He smiled at the memory of his mother drying her underwear inside a pillowcase, concealing her bras and panties from the lecherous glances of the men of the neighborhood.

He remembered helping her on washdays when he was sixteen, seventeen, carrying the creaking wicker basket filled with wet laundry up to the roof surrounded by wooden railings, where wooden catwalks kept your feet off the tar.

He remembered one day when the wind had come kicking in off the lake. It smelled like fish and clover. He was unfolding a sheet when he happened to glance over his shoulder. Cora was standing on the lower rail of the wooden barrier that circled the roof, trying to tighten a clothesline on its hook. She was reaching up, poised on one foot, the other leg held straight back for balance, like a bathing beauty on the calendars.

The line slipped from her hand. She grabbed for it and started to swing out over the railing, as if she were holding on to the pole of a merry-go-round, reaching for the brass ring. She seemed to be falling. He could already see her tumbling off the roof.

He dropped the sheet and ran to her, yelling to her. Calling her back. She turned her head to look at him, glancing over her shoulder as though she were flirting with him, a smile on her face, affectionate but distant, a look in her eyes amazed and innocent.

Ray clutched at her skirt. Caught it. Pulled her back. She came tumbling into his arms, knocking him to the roof, breaking her fall with a hand and arm beside his shoulder, crushing him with the weight of her breasts, smiling into his face as though they were lovers.

"What are you trying to do?" she asked. "You trying to knock your mother off the roof? You trying to kill me, for God's sake?"

He could smell the beer on her breath, the sharp sting of whiskey spicing it.

She had her quart of beer every day as she worked around

the house. She joked about how Dan let her have her quart of beer because she could work like a nigger with a quart of beer. Not enough to make her drunk, just enough to give her the energy she needed to get through the day. But Ray had never known about the whiskey before. Except at parties. On Saturday nights. Not during the day.

What you don't want to know, living in a family, won't hurt you.

Cora had rolled off Ray and gotten to her feet as though she were made of fluff and feathers, one hand going to her hair, which had come undone from the bun at the back and hung loosely around her face and neck.

It was only a couple of years later that she took her life with a highball with some rodent killer mixed in it.

So now Dan and Della, the eldest daughter, the mother surrogate, lived on the second floor, one flight down being a big step up. And now the old man complained about the people walking around over their heads in the middle of the night, while the people downstairs complained about him getting up to take a pee six, seven times a night, the flushing toilet running through the pipes in the walls like a cataract, waking people out of a sound sleep with a start. The worst of all possible worlds.

Ray stood in front of the pane of pebbled glass in the front door and realized, all of a sudden, that he'd only started coming to the front door since his mother's death. Until then, he'd always come up the back way, looking through the curtained window beside the back door in winter and through the screen door in summer, seeing his mother at the stove or bending over the washing machine in the corner or sitting at the table having a cup of tea or a glass of beer in the daytime, seeing mother, father, and sister having supper, reading the newspapers in the evening.

He rapped on the glass pane with his ring and in a minute he heard his sister call out, "Coming," just the way his mother had done long ago. He watched her shadow come closer until she was at the door.

"Who is it?" she asked.

"It's me."

"Who's me?"

"Jack the Ripper."

She opened the door, stepping back to let him in, then closing it and standing there smiling at him, smoothing her skirt with her hands, touching her hair, looking so much like Cora.

"You think you're funny," she said. "It's not funny. Things are different nowadays. I can remember the time you never had to lock a door. No more. You never know what danger's outside the door."

He kissed her on the cheek. Her hair was a little damp as though she'd just left the bath.

"Things don't change in Bridgeport," he said.

"That's what you say."

"Where's Pa?"

"In the kitchen combing his hair. Getting ready to go out again."

"Why the hell shouldn't I go out?" Dan yelled from the kitchen as they walked down the hallway, Ray going first with Della behind him.

"He's deaf, half the time, but he hears what he wants to hear," Della said.

Ray stopped in the doorway to the kitchen and stood there watching his father comb his hair just so in the mirror above the sink, as he'd watched him do ten thousand times before.

Dan moved in and out, trying to get his reflection into focus without his glasses on. He slipped the comb into the back pocket of his trousers, then ran his hand over his jaws, one side and then the other. Ran it up and down his neck. Checked the corners of his mouth, where the lines were deep, with his thumb and forefinger, searching out stray hairs and stubble. He seemed satisfied that it wasn't a bad shave.

Who'd believe he was seventy-six? he'd often ask, and you'd have to admit he looked sixty. Okay, sixty-five. Nice ruddy complexion, clear eyes, not too much sag under the neck.

He was attending to his bow tie.

Della asked Ray if he wanted a cup of tea.

"I just stopped by to see if you and Pa wanted to drive up to Fond du Lac with me on Sunday."

Della didn't answer. Neither did Dan. Ray let them think about it. Every decision was very large and came very hard in this house.

"I've got some beer in the icebox," Della said.

Ray wondered why she called the refrigerator an icebox after all these years. The mind-sets people got into.

"No. I don't want a beer."

"I can give you a shot of whiskey," Dan said.

"Never mind. I don't want anything. All right, maybe a cup of tea."

It always pleased Della to be given something to do, even something as simple and commonplace as making a cup of tea. She fidgeted otherwise.

"You know," Dan said, glancing at his son in the mirror, "if I saved up two thousand, twenty-five hundred, maybe I could have a little face-lift."

Della made a sound of amusement and derision.

"You read about it all the time, men having face-lifts."

"Actors," she said.

"And athletes and business executives and others. A youthful appearance's got dollar value in the marketplace. Why not? I could go back to work with the sheriffs."

He winked at Ray in the mirror, letting him know that he was just carrying on to get Della's goat.

He started to sing, softly at first.

> "Whataya gonna do for McCoughlin?
> Whataya gonna do for you?
> Are ya gonna carry your precinct?
> Are you gonna be true blue?
> Whenever you wanted a favor,
> McCoughlin was ready to do.
> Whataya gonna do for McCoughlin,
> After what he done for you?"

He sang into the mirror, doing little eye winks and stressing the trills on the *R*s.

"There he goes again with that song," Della complained. "He knows how I hate it."

"Sit down, sit down, sit down," Dan said, turning away from the mirror.

Ray picked his father's topcoat off the back of the kitchen chair closest to him and sat down, folding the coat in half, ready to hold it on his lap.

"Here, I'll take that," Dan said, reaching out for the coat.

Ray started to hand it over, then noticed the weight of it. He reached into the pocket and took out a gun wrapped in a rag wrapped in a scarf.

"What the hell you doing carrying a piece around?" Ray asked.

"He takes it down to Schaller's Pump and shows it off to all those beer-guzzling old bums he calls his friends," Della said, setting out the cups and saucers, the sugar bowl and the hot pad, the pot of brewing tea and a plate of cookies.

Dan frowned and shook his head angrily at Ray, then raised his eyes to heaven, expressing the extent of his suffering.

"Trying to impress his new girlfriend, that Maggie Hennessy," Della went on, getting a small pitcher of milk out of the refrigerator.

"New girlfriend?" Ray said.

"I ain't dead yet," Dan said. "Della'd like me to roll over and die."

"Jesus, Mary, and Joseph, what a thing to say," Della said, collapsing into a chair as though she'd just climbed a mountain. "What a thing to say." She reached into her pocket and got out a handkerchief as though she wanted it ready in case he said some other cruel thing and made her cry.

Dan sat down and picked up a cup and saucer, glaring at Della as though accusing her of neglect.

She poured the tea into his cup.

"Never mind the girlfriends," Ray said. "Where'd you get this old revolver?"

"It's my service gun from when I was a sheriff's deputy."

"I hardly ever saw you wear it."

"What did he need a gun for, watching Hinky Doyle run the freight elevator down at City Hall?" Della said.

"I was protecting a principal access to the building," Dan said.

"Hoo, hoo, hoo," Della said, chiding him.

"What I want to know is," Ray said, "I want to know how come you didn't turn in the gun when you retired."

"Nobody asked me for it."

"Are you kidding me? They didn't check out this piece against the registry and reassign it?"

"I'm telling you nobody asked me to turn it in. They didn't ask me to turn in my badge either."

"A badge is different, for God's sake. You got to keep records on guns."

"Who gives a rat's ass?" Dan said, annoyed with the whole conversation. "What the hell good are records? They all end up under a blanket of dust down in the basement anyways."

"They keep them on computer."

"Not when I left the department," Dan said triumphantly.

Ray wrapped the gun in the oily rag and the scarf again and dropped it into the pocket of his own topcoat.

"What do you think you're doing?" Dan asked.

"I'll keep it for you."

"I don't need you to keep it for me, for Christ's sake."

"Ooof," Della said, as though he'd just said an awful thing.

"I don't carry it around just to show off, the way Della says," Dan said. "You need to carry something for protection nowadays."

"Stay out of mean neighborhoods," Ray said.

"Draw me a map."

"Let it go, Pa," Ray said.

"I like to have it in the house in case of prowlers."

"You start waving a gun around in the middle of the night, it's likely you'll shoot Della by mistake."

Dan looked at his daughter and grinned.

They were like an old married couple, Ray thought, sniping at each other, winking and grinning and arguing, their days filled with the comfort of eloquent silences when they weren't bickering, living on Dan's pension and the contributions Ray, more than any of the other children, made to their household.

He wondered what his father's life would be like if Della hadn't remained unmarried. If she'd not lost the baby conceived out of wedlock. If she hadn't finally decided against becoming a nun. Where would his father be living now? Probably with him. Probably they'd be living together in Ray's flat several blocks away. The last flat he'd shared with Flo, for nearly twenty years, married almost thirty-seven.

"I was over to your flat the other day," Della said, as though she'd read his mind. "Don't you ever go home?"

"What do you mean? Of course I go home."

"Well you haven't been home lately. Not for days. I can tell."

"How can you tell?"

"She's a witch, don't you know?" Dan said. "She reads chicken gizzards and tea leaves."

"You shut up," she said.

Dan laughed and winked at Ray.

"I can tell because when I let myself in the air was stale, at least three days old."

"For God's sake she can taste the air and tell its vintage," Dan said.

"I should take the key to my house away from you," Ray said.

"Welcome," Della said, instantly offended.

"I mean the next thing I know you'll be poking around looking for ladies underwear."

"You want to tell your girlfriends not to leave their underwear around, then," Della said, slapping out at his hand. "You're as bad as Pa."

Ray reached over and placed his hand over hers. She turned it over and squeezed his fingers against her palm.

He stood up and settled his coat on his shoulders, the weight of the gun making him feel all lopsided.

"You don't have to take the gun," Dan said. "I'll put it back up in the closet."

Ray didn't answer, he just shook his head and raised his hand in a gesture that said that the subject was closed.

"So, have you made up your mind about Sunday?" he asked.

Dan turned sideways on the chair. He was pouting.

"That's an awful long drive for Pa," Della said. "His hip's giving him trouble again. It's all that running around."

Dan ignored her.

"All right, I just thought I'd ask," Ray said.

"Don't go," Della said. "Have you had your supper?"

"I stopped in a tavern for some kielbasa and cabbage an hour ago."

"That's not good for you, all that fat."

"What's not good for him?" Dan said. "These crazy notions people get from the television, the magazines. What's not good? I been eating corned beef and cabbage, kielbasa and cabbage all my life and look at me. Seventy-two years old—"

"Seventy-six," Della said.

"—and I got the figure of a young man."

"It's all that cabbage you eat along with the fat," Ray said.

"Makes you fart," Dan said. "Della should eat more cabbage. Get rid of all that gas what makes her so mean."

"I've got a chicken," Della said, ignoring her father's rude remarks. "Stay and keep me company."

"I got a hundred things to do."

"You do too much, Ray. You should get more rest."

"We'll all be a long time resting," Dan said.

Ray went over to his father and hugged him from behind. "Hey, Pa, you don't want to show Maggie Hennessy this gun, you want to show her your pistol."

"Jesus, Mary, and Joseph," Della said, but she couldn't help smiling.

Dan laughed outright and patted Ray's hand.

"Oh, my God," Della said.

"What's the matter?" Dan said, practically jumping out of his chair.

"Look at the pocket of your coat, Ray. The grease on that gun went right through your pocket."

"See?" Dan said, as though Ray had only gotten what he deserved, taking a man's possessions from him.

Ray was looking at the ugly stain as he stuck his hand in his pocket and came up first with the gun wrapped in the scarf and then with the jar of Vicks VapoRub. The smell filled the kitchen. Then he plucked out the lid.

"Sonofabitch, that Dubrowski," he raved. "That polack jack-off handed me back the jar and never tightened the cap."

"I don't know if I can get that out," Della said.

"It's like pure grease," Ray said. "Goddammit. It's okay. It's okay, Della. Don't try anything. It'll probably set it."

"You get that coat to the cleaners as soon as you can."

"One more thing to remember," he said.

Della walked Ray to the door.

"Give Floie a kiss for me," she said. "Tell her I'd come, only . . ."

"It's okay. Maybe next time."

"Yes, next time. And say hello to Helen when you see her."

Pretending that his daughter, that poor, dull-witted, fit-racked woman, would know or care.

Ray's hand was in his trousers pocket removing a bottom bill from his money clip. He knew it would be a fifty. If he took the clip out and peeled off a bill, Della would turn away, ashamed, before he could stuff it into the pocket of her apron. He had to do it smoothly, like a magician's sleight of hand, so as not to offend. He had to do it like a pat or a caress.

"No," she said, as he slipped the bill into her pocket. "We don't need it."

"Buy yourself a Cadillac."

"You don't have to, Ray."

"I know I don't have to. It's for keeping my place straightened up."

"You ought to spend more time there."

"It's easier out on the streets, Dell."

"Oh, I know, I know," she said, her eyes filling with tears, a rueful smile on her tender mouth.

She kissed him on the corner of his lips.

"You're a good man, Ray," she said.

He turned away and started down the stairs. He was halfway down the first flight before he heard the door to the flat close behind him. She'd been looking at him just the way Flo used to do when he went to work, just like his mother had done when he'd gone off to school.

9

HALF THE BUSINESS OF THE CITY AND ALMOST ALL OF THE POLITICAL business was conducted in saloons and taverns.

The Candidate's Committee to Elect held their meetings in the permanently leased back room of a Bridgeport neighborhood saloon called 'Hara's. It had once been O'Hara's but the *O* on the sign had been torn off in a windstorm ten years before and had never been replaced.

When service was wanted there was a bell on the table which summoned a waiter from the bar but as a rule there were pitchers of beer already drawn on the table and whiskey and water for those who wanted something stronger nearby, along with some nibbles for those not afraid of ruining the evening meal.

The committee—sometimes with The Candidate, sometimes without—met every afternoon between four and six, at which time everybody was supposed to go home for supper, except usually the meeting went on so long they had a late supper right there.

The committee, aka the Kitchen Cabinet, boasted first of all J. J. Finnegan, the attorney, who was consulted in practically all things and gave advice in practically all matters.

Jack Quinn, hair like thistledown blowing softly in every passing breeze caused by something even so small as a child walking by, round cheeks, bulbous nose, a Santa Claus who drank, was said to have been The Candidate's secret mentor and backstage adviser throughout a good part of The Candidate's political career. He had the wide-open Irish face and manner, the quick quip, the dry kiss on the cheek of child or woman, the pink and white friendliness of a bartender concealing the shrewd brain of a professional assassin.

It was said he'd taught The Candidate the value of a soft voice, of patience and equivocation as much or more than The Candidate's father ever had. It was said of him, by friend and enemy alike, that had he not chosen Chicago politics as the arena in which to exercise his talents, he would have made a marvelous prince of the church.

Brian "Bud" Kenna, a young man, but already bald on top, six feet two, forty pounds overweight, round face as smooth as a baby's bottom, himself a gigantic baby of short attention span and careless habits who walked around leaving a trail of crumpled cellophane packets and bits of soda cracker, discarded notes, and pencils with broken points, was the political consultant, a new breed of animal raised on statistics and polls instead of favors and cigar smoke.

The Candidate didn't quite understand Kenna, with all his charts and graphs, straw polls and people-on-the-street interviews. Still and all he seemed amused by Kenna, tolerant of his excesses, and could be seen smiling upon the brilliant eccentric every now and then.

Kitty Brennan, the only female in the group, dyed her hair such a vivid red that it looked as phony as a hooker's Dynel wig. She tried to make her small blue eyes larger with eye shadow and liner but succeeded only in making them look smudged and weepy. The rest of her makeup matched the treatment of her eyes, messy and much too colorful.

She was in her late forties and was shy, impatient, overbearing, quarrelsome, and self-protective, concealing with great effort the vastly needy child inside her hard, nervous body and petulantly frowning face. She seemed to thrust herself in front of people as though seeking their affection and, though living a celibate life since her husband's death, she looked at every attractive man with a breathlessness that made them half-expect an invitation into her bed even at first meeting. Yet when anyone reached out to touch her she shied away like a skittish mare.

She was not a token female among them, but the kind of down-and-dirty politician, full of foxy tricks and guile, most admired and understood by The Candidate. In fact it had been his father's hand that had personally picked her out for a spot in a previous administration.

It was Kitty Brennan who'd put forward the old strategy, tried and true, of singling out police corruption as the principal issue concerning the public. It was she who'd suggested they target Ray Sharkey, the City Hall Pimp, making of him, if they could, the sacrificial goat. And it was she who had devised the sting involving Leddy, a stand-alone scam guaranteed not to scoop up any friends or potential friends that Sharkey might be involved with in other enterprises of the moment.

It had once been rumored around town that Kitty Brennan had sought comfort from Ray Sharkey shortly after her husband's demise and had offered it to him when his wife was gone to Fond du Lac with her illness. He'd turned her down both times, they said, perhaps none too gently, and she'd had it in for him ever since.

Chicago is a city of rumor and gossip.

Sam Speaks, a retired newspaperman, a skinny old man who looked like a rag rug and had the rat-like nature of the professional snoop, never spoke of Sharkey without calling him a sonofabitch as though that were Sharkey's Christian name.

At one of the earliest meetings, The Candidate, a man who liked to know why one man hated another man, asked Speaks when, where, and why he'd given birth to this vendetta against Sharkey.

And Speaks told them how years before, when he'd been a young reporter, he'd become friendly with Sharkey's old man,

Dan Sharkey, a sheriff's deputy whose job it was to supervise the running of the freight elevator down at the old City Hall.

"Not run it himself, mind you. Just sit there to make sure that the man operating the cage—pushing the lever to go up and then pushing it to come down—didn't take a nap in the basement or otherwise jeopardize the workings of the machine.

"He had six kids. There was Ray, the oldest, and the next, a boy by the name of Michael. There was Della, the oldest girl, a sad, plain girl about fourteen, and then two more boys, Gabe, who became a priest, and one you know."

"Jerry Sharkey, the Judge," The Candidate said.

"Then another girl, Wilda, who ran away before she came of age. Got the hell out of there. I don't blame her. You can imagine why."

"Well, no, I can't," The Candidate said. "You're not suggesting that the father or the brothers were messing with the girl?"

"I wouldn't go so far as to say that."

"Well, I should hope not. You're talking about a good Irish Catholic family here."

"The mother was a suicide."

"God rest her soul," The Candidate said. "We don't know that for sure. It was just gossip."

"I do," Kitty Brennan said. "I lived just down the block and Cora Sharkey—"

"And I lived just around the corner," The Candidate said in that voice that told everybody the subject of Cora Sharkey's death was closed. He nodded at Speaks, telling him to go on.

"I thought Michael could make a boxer. I myself had an interest in taking up the game at one time, though I was never strong enough to make much of it. But Michael had no interest. It was Ray who came down to the gym and went into training. He was very promising. An opportunity came along for a bout with an up-and-coming young black fighter by the name of Leroy Scarlet."

"I remember the fight," The Candidate said. "I was only a kid, but I remember that fight. Scarlet was very good, with a lot more experience than Sharkey had."

"But fighting out of his weight," Speaks said. "Sharkey outweighed him by twenty pounds."

"Even so, Sharkey was very green," The Candidate said.

"Well, you're right about that," Speaks said. "Sharkey was a lot greener than I thought and afraid of Scarlet to boot. It was supposed to go six."

"Supposed to go?" Quinn said, speaking up for the first time.

"I mean it was scheduled for six. By the third Sharkey was taking such a terrible beating"—Kitty Brennan winced and paled, freckles blooming across her nose and cheeks—"that I wanted to throw in the towel but Sharkey wouldn't have it."

"Is that the way it was?" The Candidate murmured, and the way his lids half-concealed his eyes anybody with an eye in their head should've been able to tell he believed something otherwise, but neither Speaks nor Kitty Brennan seemed to notice.

"He was getting himself slaughtered," Speaks went on, two spots of color burning on his cheeks, excited by the memory of the beating Sharkey had taken that night. "So he did what his sort always does."

"And what's that?" The Candidate murmured even more softly than before.

"The sonofabitch turned and ran."

"And then turned around again and knocked Scarlet out with a single punch," The Candidate said. "Crushed his cheekbone and broke his jaw as I recall. Ended that black boy's ring career."

"That was an illegal punch," Speaks said, his voice gone high and thin in his rage.

"I don't remember that being mentioned," The Candidate said. "I don't remember my father—God rest his soul—saying anything like that."

Finally Speaks got it. The Candidate and his old man had been there on that night nearly forty years before—The Candidate would've been maybe ten or twelve—and his father had been one of those who'd exulted in the black man's defeat. Common sense informed him that it was best not to tamper with another man's prejudices, new or old, but the temptation to knock Sharkey one more time couldn't be resisted.

"Who'd mention it?" Speaks said. "Who'd declare a nigger had been beaten by an illegal blow? Who'd dare say *that* in a hall filled with practically nothing but whites?"

"I'm merely making the observation," The Candidate said. "What I don't understand . . . are you telling me that you're still angry with Ray Sharkey because when he was a young fighter he defended himself after being tossed into the ring against a better, stronger man for the crowd's amusement and Leroy Scarlet's exercise?"

Having said that, The Candidate turned his glance away as though he'd lost interest in whatever else Speaks had to say.

"No, not because of that," Speaks said.

"Because of what then?" Quinn asked.

"He beat me up afterwards."

"Sharkey beat you up for being a bad matchmaker?" Quinn asked.

Speaks looked around for some safe place for his eyes to light. They looked like a couple of bugs trapped in little glass jelly jars.

"He claimed I had something to do with his sister."

"The littlest one or the plain one?" Quinn asked.

"For God's sake. With the oldest one. With Della."

"The fourteen-year-old?"

"I took her to the movies once or twice. She was maybe fifteen, sixteen by then. I just took her to the movies and maybe kissed her once or twice. Because I felt sorry for her. I don't remember why. But that was all."

"This Sharkey beat you up for kissing his homely sister?" Quinn said.

"He claimed I'd made her pregnant."

"Did the girl say so?"

"I don't know. I never had the chance to ask her."

"And had you?"

"No."

"What?"

"I said, no."

"Well, now we know your reasons for wanting to bring Sharkey down," Quinn said, "but you've got to cool your passion. If we can make a case against Ray Sharkey and if we decide it'll be useful in the campaign, we don't want news of your old grudge against him muddying the water. You understand the reasoning here?"

Speaks said he did.

"And what about you, Kitty?" The Candidate asked, speaking up again, turning the corner on the subject, looking at it from another angle. "What's your reason for suggesting we go after Sharkey?"

"Because he's vulnerable," she said.

Finnegan arrived, rushing into the back room like a Pony Express rider who had just barely escaped the clutches of the raging Sioux.

Finnegan poured himself a glass of beer, examined the head, deplored it with a blink of his eyes, took a swallow, declared it stale, and brought it back to the table.

"How did it go?" Kitty asked.

Finnegan shook his head in disgust.

"That Sharkey's an evil force. I had the scene set, with Frankie Blue Shoes—"

"Who?" The Candidate says.

"—and Sharkey," Finnegan finished, and then asked, "What who?"

"Who's this Frankie Blue Shoes?"

"Frank Leddy, the goat we staked out for Sharkey."

"Okay, go on," The Candidate says.

"Frankie Blue Shoes—Leddy—is sitting at one table and I'm sitting at another."

"Sharkey knows you, does he?" Kenna said, hinting that Finnegan has committed his first tactical error right there, practically anticipating the story that the lawyer was about to tell.

"Perfectly natural for an accused person to have his lawyer close at hand," Finnegan said. "Besides, who else was available to be a credible witness? I didn't see you raising your hand to volunteer."

"Well, I never thought much of the plan," Kenna said.

Kitty tossed him a glance but made no complaint or protest.

The Candidate smiled and waved a hand, the royal permission to go on.

"They're talking away, sparring around," Finnegan said, "when all of a sudden Sharkey jumps out of the booth, runs over, and snatches my briefcase out of my hand. I told him what he was doing was illegal but that didn't stop him."

"No respect for the law, that Sharkey," Kitty said.

"Searched my personal and private property right there. Manhandled my sausage sandwich."

"Found the microphone and recorder," Kenna said, pinning Finnegan with the truth of the matter, that he had, himself, been engaged in an illegal act.

"Jesus, Mary, and Joseph," Kitty said, expressing her disappointment in the strongest possible terms. "So that's the end to that."

"Not exactly," Finnegan said. "Sharkey went on with the negotiation. They made a contract. We'll have another chance to witness when Frankie Blue Shoes—Leddy—hands over the fix money."

The Candidate pursed his lips. He obviously didn't like it that Sharkey was going ahead with it after finding the wire in Finnegan's briefcase. "Could the cop be that dumb?"

"He could be that greedy," Finnegan said. "The prospect of money blindfolds some people."

"There's that," the Candidate said, sharing a quick wink with Quinn. "Is there a way we can put an eye and an ear on Sharkey?"

"He's usually on his own, but the last couple of weeks he's been teamed up with an old shuffle by the name of Wally Dubrowski," Quinn said.

"So, maybe somebody should talk to this Dubrowski," Kenna said. "A man like Sharkey can't inspire much loyalty. A little sugar for this Dubrowski might buy us an ear in Sharkey's pocket."

Everybody looked at Quinn who nodded his head. "We'll have a beer, this Dubrowski and me."

"One question more, J.J.," The Candidate said.

"What's that?"

"Why in the hell is this criminal type, Leddy, known as Frankie Blue Shoes? Was he wearing blue shoes?"

"No, he was wearing black boots."

"I don't understand these people," The Candidate said.

10

SHARKEY AND DUBROWSKI HAD TO SHARE A DESK. ACTUALLY IT was Sharkey's desk and he allowed the partner of the moment to have a piece of it.

A gray herringbone topcoat—his other topcoat—was draped over a chair. He was waiting for Dubrowski to make some comment about where the camel hair was and then he'd tell him the camel hair was in his closet waiting to go to the cleaners because Dubrowski had failed to tighten the cap on the jar of Vicks VapoRub.

But Dubrowski was reared back in his chair, with his feet up on the desk, reading some pages of the lab report and chewing on a meatball sandwich—for breakfast, for God's sake—which threatened to spill out of the Italian roll all over his vest and tie.

Every second or so Sharkey's eyes flickered up from the pages he was reading, waiting for it to happen. It was the kind of thing that made him nervous about having a partner. Everybody had a habit could get on your nerves. He might even have a couple of habits could get on somebody else's nerves. But the point was, you couldn't go through life with a partner who got on your nerves or did things that courted small disasters, like eating meatball sandwiches loaded with olive oil and tomato sauce.

The report in his hand was the rap sheet he'd plucked from the files on one Alberto Carbonne aka Albert Bug-Eye aka Al Chooch, Frankie Blue Shoes aka Frank Leddy's deposit box. The man who carried his cash. The asshole sitting there with gloves on in a heated restaurant showing everybody what a hard type he was. Sharkey wanted to know more about this Albert because he had the feeling that one of these fine days he might want to drop a hammer on the sonofabitch.

It wasn't a pretty picture. The man was stupid and violent, his crimes mostly petty but harmful to the well-being of a lot of people. Under "notes"—a grab bag of observations—it was mentioned that he had a fondness for cats. Which made Sharkey think of the box of Kitty Litter. You could make a connection there if you were eager, Sharkey thought, but he'd long since learned that life was a boiling stew of casual connections and if you acted upon every coincidence you stumbled upon you'd be arresting half the people in the city for murder and mayhem.

"The blood in the elevator?" Dubrowski said.

"Yeah?"

"It wasn't a drunk with a nosebleed. It's a match with the victim's blood."

"That's good," Sharkey said.

"Why's that good?" Dubrowski asked, looking up while he took another bite and the meatballs shifted in their soup.

"Because now we know the whole thing didn't happen behind closed doors. We know that at least one blow was struck outside the room. In the elevator, maybe in the lobby. Which means there's a good possibility somebody saw the violence."

"Nobody I interrogated saw or heard a fucking thing," Dubrowski said in a voice that sounded as though somebody had him by the throat.

"Maybe outside the hotel," Sharkey said. "We check the taverns, the candy stores, the diners in the neighborhood."

"You going to give me a little help on this?" Dubrowski asked.

Sharkey glanced up. Dubrowski was glaring at him.

"Huh," Sharkey said, finally recording the message. "Oh, yeah, I'm sorry I didn't get back to give you a hand. The captain send you any help?"

"He sent me Baker and Dunleavy."

"So?"

"So, you should've come back and done your share," Dubrowski said.

A rivulet of sauce flowed along the edge of the roll and trembled there. Sharkey couldn't take his eyes off it.

"Also—" Dubrowski said.

"I wish you wouldn't do that," Sharkey said.

"Do what?"

Sharkey was about to say that he wished Dubrowski would stop eating dangerous foods which demanded Sharkey's attention when he should be concentrating on other things, but instead he said, "I wish you wouldn't always say *also*. You got something to tell me, I wish you'd just tell me and not say *also* first, which I then got to say also what. So also what?"

"The victim didn't die of the beating."

"What'd he die of?"

"He drowned on his own blood and vomit. Charlie Press says here that the man got sick behind the sock stuffed in his mouth and couldn't get it out so he breathed his own blood and vomit and choked on it."

"So, that sounds to me like he died of the beating."

"Well, yes, he died of the beating, but not directly. Charlie

Press says here it probably happened after they were finished working him over."

Sharkey went back to the examination of the report as Dubrowski licked the sauce from the sandwich's rim.

"Round up the usual suspects," Sharkey said.

"What?"

"I said round up the usual suspects."

"What the hell does that mean?"

Sharkey looked up and smiled his sweetest smile. "Don't you remember that line?"

"From what?"

"From that picture *Casablanca* with Humphrey Bogart and Ingrid Bergman."

"She say that?"

"No, Claude Rains said that."

"Who the hell's Claude Rains?" Dubrowski asked.

"Never mind. What we got to do is get on the eary, find out if there's any rumor about a shy having to make an example out of some deadbeat. You got any snitches down that part of town?"

"I got to look in my little black book."

"Well, I got maybe one or two. So you ask and I'll ask and we'll see. That don't work, we got a lot of taverns, smoke shops, and candy stores to visit."

Dubrowski groaned at the thought of all the donkey work they might have to do. In the beginning of a homicide, when the corpse was still a little warm and everybody very eager for a quick fix, you could get some help. But it didn't take long for the killing of a man hiding behind an alias like this Pike to cool down. Then it was up to the first detectives on the scene to put it in their caseload and do all the foot-soldiering.

"You think it could be a mob killing?" Dubrowski asked. "You know these guidos are doing it to one another all the time."

"They do it, they leave the victim with a fish in his mouth, or his eyelids sliced off, or something like that. They do him with a couple peas behind the ear. Besides, how do you know the man's Italian?"

"What I could see, he looked Italian. You check on that address over to Cicero?"

"There's no such address."

"You run over there?"

"I called the city directory."

"Jesus Christ, you don't want to strain yourself."

"Give it up, will you, fachrissake?" Sharkey said.

"The papers are running the story—"

"I saw."

"—with the name C. Pike in it," Dubrowski said.

"That ain't going to get a rise out of anybody."

"Maybe they should run a picture," Dubrowski said.

Sharkey stared at him. "Maybe they should run a picture of a pound of hamburger."

"Oh, yeah," Dubrowski said, and laughed.

He started to raise the sandwich for another bite. The sauce shifted on the roll. It started over the edge. Suddenly he straightened up in the chair, his feet hitting the floor, his hand with the sandwich in it pushing straight out, away from his body. He stood up and bent over slightly. The drip left the roll and landed between his feet.

"Sonofabitch," Sharkey said.

"Almost got me that time," Dubrowski said. "Carla raises hell when I come home with tomato sauce on my shirts."

Some guys courted disaster and won every time, Sharkey thought. Other guys courted disaster and ended up dead meat tied to the plumbing.

"On the subject," Sharkey said. "You notice I'm wearing a different topcoat?"

"Now that you mention it," Dubrowski said, "what happened to your fancy camel hair?"

"I'm going to tell you over lunch."

"You better tell me now. I got a date for lunch."

Sharkey folded up Albert's rap sheet and put it into his breast pocket. "Well, okay," he said, suddenly hot with irritation, "this shouldn't take more than a fucking minute."

11

YOU WOULDN'T THINK IT TO LOOK AT HIM, BUT DUBROWSKI WAS very careful about his person. He showered twice, sometimes three times a day, and always used deodorant spray under his arms and sprinkled baby powder in his crotch. It was just that twenty minutes after he was freshly showered and shaved, hair combed, teeth brushed and flossed, shoes polished, tie carefully knotted, he started to fall apart. He stumbled here and there, scuffed the toes of his brogans, the collar of his shirt wilted, the knot loosened up and the tie fell askew, his hair became rumpled, and he looked like he'd picked his outfit out of a rag bag.

Quinn on the other hand could've bathed once a week, worn the same suit and tie for two, and he still would've looked like he'd just stepped out of a barbershop. Except for the flossy hair, blowing all around, the one casual, unruly note in his otherwise impeccable appearance.

These two men were sitting at a table in the Little Naples Restaurant, red-checked napkins as big as tablecloths tucked underneath their chins, going at platters of antipasto, bowls of lasagna and linguini with mussels, side dishes of angel hair spaghetti dressed with cream enriched with seven cloves of smashed garlic. Two decanters of red and two of white sat alongside the food.

They ate in silence, men who enjoyed the good things of life, especially the pleasures of the table, now that other appetites were beginning to grow a little dull around the edges.

Of the two, Dubrowski seemed the least interested in conversation, though he was the one who was waiting for the other shoe to fall after Quinn had greeted him with the information that Dubrowski could perhaps do Quinn, The Candidate, and himself a favor.

It was over the spumoni that Quinn finally got to the point and then only after Dubrowski took the bull by the horns and said, "That was very nice. What do I owe you?"

Quinn believed that whoever opened negotiations was put at a subtle disadvantage, though, to be accurate about it, this was by way of being an exploratory interview, not a negotiation.

Dubrowski had no theories. When he wanted to know something he asked.

"You owe me nothing," Quinn said. "I invited you."

"That's right. You invited me but you didn't invite my partner."

"Did you tell Sharkey who you were having lunch with?"

"You asked me not to mention it, so I didn't mention it. Also he didn't ask."

"Oh? Don't you take your meals together during the working day?"

"Sometimes we do, sometimes we don't. Today he went one way and I went the other."

"You know where he might be at the moment?"

Dubrowski made an elaborate show of looking around. "Well, he ain't in my pocket."

Quinn held up a hand. "I wasn't prying."

"I didn't say you was. We got this case. A man had the shit beat out of him. I mean literally. He could be working on that. He doesn't always tell me everything until he's got something to tell me," Dubrowski said, working himself up.

"So, he don't tell you everything and you don't tell him everything?" Quinn said.

"Except what the other person has to know."

"Absolutely."

"We ain't joined at the hip," Dubrowski raved on.

"I understand."

Dubrowski suddenly saw himself spinning out of control over nothing. He took a deep breath. "So, what's the reason for the invitation?"

"I'm afraid to ask."

Dubrowski waved his hand. "You can ask anything you want. I don't guarantee I'll answer."

"How come you're working with Ray Sharkey?" Quinn asked.

"Nothing mysterious. My partner had a heart attack and me and Sharkey was married since he had no wife at the moment."

"I thought he liked to work alone."

"Right now, it ain't what he likes what counts."

"How's that?"

"The special election's coming up. Everybody's looking for something to hang their hat on. Cops on the take are nice. Cops in business for themselves are nice. The acting mayor don't want any of that kind of crap hitting close to City Hall. Sharkey's close to City Hall."

"Are you saying the mayor's got reason to believe that Sharkey's engaged in activities that might bring discredit on the force?"

"I never said that. I'm just saying that would be the sensible thing to do. The incumbent don't even have to make mention. The superintendent tells the chiefs, the chiefs tell the captains. It comes filtering down. Like that. I don't have to draw you a picture, Mr. Quinn, you know these things better'n I do. You understand what I'm saying?"

He smiled inside. For Christ's sake, he thought, I'm starting to talk like that fucking Irishman.

"So, are you saying that you were married to Sharkey to keep an eye on him?" Quinn asked.

"Maybe it's the other way around. Maybe we was married so Sharkey could keep an eye on me."

"But *you* know that *you're* not engaged in any illegal, or even questionable, activities."

"Yes, I know that. Unless you heard something to the contrary?"

Quinn shook his head. His hair blew around as though caught in the vortex of a fan.

"And how about Sharkey?" Quinn asked.

"We been working together less than two weeks. You think if he had anything going, he'd be sharing it with me in less than two weeks?"

"You got eyes and ears."

"I also got a mouth and I know how to keep it shut."

"We'd depend upon that."

"Oh? What are we talking about here?"

"We'd like to know if Sharkey's involved in anything indictable."

"Like he's dumb enough to tell me."

"You can find out a lot of things, working as close as cops work. They get like soldiers in combat, I've been told. They get like brothers."

"Practically taking dumps together, getting your ashes hauled together?" Dubrowski said, being deliberately gross, making the old Irish fart pay a price.

Quinn blinked, but that was all. "He does that a lot?"

"Takes a dump? I guess once or twice a day. How about you?"

"Gets his ashes hauled."

"I don't follow the man into the bedroom."

"How about stags and smokers? You ever been in his company at stags and smokers?"

"Hey, I thought that was neutral territory. I mean unless a man goes out there, fucks a politician's wife in the window of Carson Pirie Scott or goes running through the streets bare-assed with some two dollar whore, I thought a man's private business was a man's private business."

"Oh, it is. We don't want to invade anyone's privacy when it comes to matters sexual."

"Otherwise half the aldermen, and maybe a couple of the alderwomen, wouldn't look so good. I mean running around with their pants down and all."

"Like you say. I just wanted to point out that men open up in situations like that. They say things they otherwise wouldn't say. Male bonding. That sort of thing."

"You mean you want me to listen in on what Sharkey might have to say while he's doing the old in and out?"

"One never knows."

"Well, if he ever shouts out any names and numbers while he's on the rise, I'll let you know. But you got to understand we never break that kind of bread together."

"I understand. I'm just talking about a notion here. Men together a lot usually end up telling war stories."

"Correct me if I'm wrong but ain't you been a guest at some of these smokers and stags you're talking about?" Dubrowski said.

"But I never partook."

"I was never even invited."

"Well, there might be opportunities in the future," Quinn said.

"You're taking a chance here."

Quinn popped his eyebrows. "How's that?"

"I could tell Sharkey you got him in your sights."

Quinn shrugged. "There's always plan C."

"You telling me I'm plan B and you already got plan A going against him."

"What I'm saying is a smart man's always got plan A, B, C, D, E, and however many letters of the alphabet he needs to get wherever he wants to go."

12

"YOU TOLD US THIS C. PIKE SIGNED IN ON YOUR SHIFT?" SHARkey asked.

"That's right. We been through this."

"Well, pardon us," Dubrowski said.

"If you don't mind, just go along, Mr. Kendicott," Sharkey said. "We're not trying to trap you here. Would you say this Mr. Pike was hiding out or on the run? Would you say that?"

"I wouldn't know something like that. Though I can tell you a lot of people come to a place like this to get lost, one way or another."

"You see him anytime after he checked in?"

"Sunday afternoon and Sunday evening, but not Sunday night or anytime after."

"He come and go?"

"Yes, he came and went, but don't ask me how many times. He went out once and came back with a bottle in a bag. I remember that."

"How come you remember something like that?"

"I keep an eye on the bags. They're not supposed to cook in

their rooms. Bottled goods are okay but they're not supposed to cook."

"You search the bags?"

"No, I just take a look. I can tell when somebody's got just a bottle in a bag."

"Where would he get a bottle around here?"

"If he went down to the corner and walked south along Western there's a package shop halfway down the block. If he went east there's a drugstore which also sells bottled goods."

"You get a lot of drunks coming through the door, don't you, Mr. Kendicott," Sharkey said.

Kendicott snorted through his nose, his mouth twisting up in what was supposed to be a derisive grin. They wanted to know about wine and roses, the expression said, he could tell them about wine and roses.

"So, it's understandable that somebody could come through the door with a couple of buddies holding him up, he shouldn't fall on his face getting into the elevator. Did that happen anytime that night? Or maybe anytime Monday, Tuesday—"

"—maybe even Wednesday morning?" Dubrowski finished, sticking his oar in.

There was a sheen of sweat on Kendicott's forehead and a line of small beads along his upper lip, sprung there in an instant.

"I didn't see anything Monday or Tuesday and I don't work nights. If I'd seen anything like what you're asking about on Wednesday morning, it'd depend what time. I don't come on until eight. Don't you think if I saw anything I would've told you?"

"Not necessarily, Mr. Kendicott," Dubrowski said. "Sometimes people don't want to get involved."

"You understand what we're saying here?" Sharkey said. Before Kendicott could answer, he went on. "What we're saying here is that people decide not to tell us what they see or hear. Maybe they got reason not to cooperate with the police. Some old beef. Maybe somebody pays them a nickel, pays them a dime, to forget what they see or hear. Maybe somebody threatens them with bodily harm if they tell the police what they see and hear."

"We just want to be certain that this ain't one of those cases," Dubrowski added.

"We just want to give you assurances that if you tell us that you just remembered something you forgot, we'll understand."

"Nothing. I didn't see or hear anything," Kendicott said.

"When did you first notice the blood in the elevator?" Sharkey asked.

"I never said I noticed any blood in the elevator."

"You didn't?" Sharkey looked at Dubrowski, seeking confirmation. "Have I got it wrong? Don't you remember Mr. Kendicott, here, telling us that he noticed blood in the elevator?"

"I didn't notice any blood in the elevator," Kendicott said.

"You telling me you never noticed any blood in that elevator?" Sharkey insisted. There was a sharp edge of belligerence in his repetition of the phrase, even though he was smiling and pretending to be a puzzled but reasonable man. "You telling me there was never one time that you saw blood in that elevator?"

Kendicott looked like he was about to cry. "I never said that. I never said I *never* saw blood in that elevator. I'm saying I never noticed any blood in the elevator at that time."

"What time?"

"Anytime lately. Monday, Tuesday, Wednesday, like you said."

"Or Sunday night," Dubrowski said.

"Night or day," Sharkey said. "We were called in yesterday, a Thursday. The body was decomposing there at least a couple of days, maybe more. So Monday, Tuesday, maybe Wednesday morning—"

"And maybe Sunday night," Dubrowski said, poking in again.

"I don't work nights," Kendicott said, repeating himself, growing more agitated by the minute.

"But you live here," Dubrowski said. "You goddamn live here, don't you?"

"I got a room," Kendicott said, his face coloring with the rage and humiliation blooming under his dark skin.

"So, you didn't notice any blood?" Sharkey said. "For maybe four and a half days there could've been blood in the elevator and you say you didn't see any blood in the elevator?"

"That's hard to believe," Dubrowski said.

"I'm telling you I never saw any blood in the cage until the police officers mentioned it and taped off the cage. I've seen it other nights, other times, but not this last week, couple of weeks."

"You telling me you never used the elevator since maybe last Saturday?" Dubrowski said.

"That's right, I never did," Kendicott said, shaking his head.

"That's hard to believe," Sharkey said again.

"So, maybe it's something you just get used to around here," Dubrowski said, looking at Sharkey. "Blood in the elevator."

"Okay then," Sharkey said, as though that clarified a major point that had been bothering him. "How well did you know Mr. Pike?"

"I didn't know him at all," Kendicott insisted.

"He never checked into this hotel before?"

"Never that I know of."

"He never used this hotel to do a little business every time he came into town maybe?"

"I don't know. That was the first time I ever saw the man."

"Okay. You say you didn't see him with anybody. Could he've had any visitors?" Dubrowski asked.

"Of course he could. He *had* visitors, didn't he, for God's sake. It's obvious that the poor bastard had visitors." Kendicott said, his voice thinning out like a wire, his eyelids fluttering in his agitation. "I never saw anything or anybody while I was on the desk. You could ask the night clerk. You ever stop to think that if this Pike walked in here with a couple of buddies and a bloody nose it'd probably have been at night? I mean you should be asking the night clerk all these questions. If anything like that happened it probably would've been at night."

"That was going to be my next question. You got the name and address of the night man?"

"The night man's a woman by the name of Mamoo Johnson."

"Mamoo?" Dubrowski said.

"You know. Big Mamoo? They call her Big Mamoo."

"So where does this Big Mamoo live?"

"Room 209. In the back. But she ain't in."

"Oh? How's that?"

"She went to visit her sister over to Cicero for a few days."

"A few days?" Dubrowski said, exchanging what he would've called a significant glance with Sharkey, meaning for Kendicott to read the look, giving him a little something extra to worry about.

"Two shifts."

"You going to work her shifts till when?"

"Sunday night."

"This is only Friday and you're going to work double shifts for three days?"

"Two nights. I do the favor for Big Mamoo and she does the favor for me."

"She go visit her sister last Friday, Saturday, Sunday?" Sharkey asked.

"No."

"You swap shifts on Sunday afternoon, Monday morning? Maybe she was on Monday morning? Was she here on Monday morning?" Dubrowski asked.

"No."

"That was quick," Sharkey said.

"What do you mean, that was quick?" Kendicott said.

"Just what I said. You didn't even take time to think about it."

"I didn't have to take any time to remember a thing like that."

"What'd you have for lunch last Wednesday?"

"What are you talking about, for God's sake?"

"I'm asking you a simple question here, Mr. Kendicott. I'm asking what you had for lunch last Wednesday."

"How do you expect a man to remember a thing like that?"

"Just my point," Sharkey said. "You were quick enough to remember that this night clerk, this Big Mamoo, didn't ask you to take a shift for her last weekend. So how come you can't remember if you took her shift Monday night, Tuesday night?

"I *can* remember. I *didn't*. I *told* you."

"What I'm saying is that you *might've* been on the desk say Sunday night."

Kendicott didn't say anything. He just stared at Sharkey as though he were some sort of demon come to bedevil him.

Sharkey pressed the bridge of his nose with his thumb and finger as though he were very weary, disconnecting, giving it up.

Kendicott took off his glasses and wiped them, blinking as though he was very tired, too.

Sharkey grinned at him and Kendicott grinned right back as though they, the men who had carried the fight, were the men in the know and Dubrowski was nothing but an outsider.

"So, when's Big Mamoo coming home?" Sharkey asked, smiling lazily.

"Sunday night. Monday morning the latest."

"So I guess all we can do is wait."

"Unless you want to go over to her sister's house."

"It's the weekend. Even cops got to have some personal time."

"Mr. Pike, he won't be going anywhere anyway."

They smiled at each other, understanding the game while Dubrowski looked on in something like bewilderment.

"Well, so, it's goodbye for now," Sharkey said. "You remember anything about the blood, about anything, you give us a call. Will you do that?"

Kendicott took the card that Sharkey offered him and said he would.

Sharkey held out his hand and after a slight hesitation, Kendicott shook his hand.

Out in the car, Sharkey grunted as he settled himself in the runner's seat.

"Motherfucker's lying through his teeth," Dubrowski said.

"I don't think so," Sharkey said, feeling greatly disgusted with the interrogation, with police work, with himself. "I think it was just we scared the poor sonofabitch half to death and he was too proud to show it."

13

SHARKEY DIDN'T KNOW WHICH HE HATED MORE, GOING UP TO Fond Du Lac to see Flo or driving down to Tinley Park three, four times a week to see his daughter.

Not hated. That was the wrong way to describe the feeling. Feared. Dreaded. Sometimes he felt a kind of horror, sometimes a terror so real that it shrunk his scrotum. He could feel his genitals cringing away, trying to bury themselves in the cave of his gut, as though knowing that they'd been the cause of it all.

That fuck in Flo's father's Ford when she'd driven him back from the club fight—which he'd almost lost to that colored boy, Leroy Scarlet, but had retrieved with an illegal punch—had changed his life forever.

That one fuck, after her holding him off for so long, him bleeding through his pores, the shirt sticking to his back, her struggling to get her panties off over her tennis shoes. For God's sake, it'd been a fucking comedy, them struggling to get it in, knowing practically nothing—either one of them—about how things really worked for all his bragging to other young men about having this one or that one.

And the consequences. The quick marriage six months later with Flo already showing when she walked down the aisle.

The baby coming out all wrong, suffering a dozen serious ailments, one right after the other. Scarlet fever, mumps, rubella, and other sicknesses. Epileptic seizures ravaging the child. Beating her up.

Beating up Ray and Flo. Taking all their love away in arguments over what was to be done about Helen, for Helen. Until the seizures got worse and worse, unmanageable, the anxiety about having another seizure bringing the next one on.

Sometimes she shook with them, her back arched against the power of it, strong as a bull inside the fit, Ray on his knees straddling her little body, trying to keep her from throwing him off, forcing a folded handkerchief between her teeth so she couldn't bite or swallow her tongue, three or four times inside a half an hour.

Sleeping for hours after. Exhausted. Hiding from the beast in sleep.

More than once, more than twice, she'd said to him how she'd like to go to sleep and never wake up. He'd hold her hand and take her in his arms, the child of ten or eleven, the woman of thirty, and tell her that he couldn't bear the loss of her. If she could just hold on, they were discovering new medicines, new treatments, every day. Feeling inside, afraid to put the words to it, that, yes, it would be better if she passed away in her sleep. How much could she take? How much, for Christ's sake, could *he* take?

He could take what he had to take and do what he had to do. Week after week through the years, going to see Helen in this institution, that institution, finding private hospitals for her when the public hospitals for the developmentally impaired shut down, the mental incompetents thrown out into the streets to make their way the best they knew how.

Even after he found a way to get her back into one of the few public facilities still in business, trying to get a little relief from the expenses that were eating him alive, Flo wouldn't let him move Helen. The private hospital was so much better, the grounds so much prettier, the room nicer, the attendants kinder. . . .

That's when he'd stopped paying for his own beers and shots when they were offered. That's when he'd started on the take.

So, driving down to the private sanitarium in Tinley Park, slow one minute because he felt a rising panic that came on his worst days, fast the next because he wanted to get there, get it over with, he thought about something Kiley, his old academy instructor, had said way back when.

"Bad cops don't start out running a string of whores, robbing stores, dealing drugs, or taking out contracts on somebody's life," Kiley'd said. "They all start out with a nickel heist."

"Amen," Sharkey heard himself say aloud.

He thought about the murder at the Westley. He thought about the way he'd humiliated and frightened Mr. Kendicott because they meant to humiliate and frighten him, believing, as all cops believed, that the citizens hated them and would conceal anything and everything from them.

He found himself approaching the long drive that led up to the red brick administration building where you had to go to sign in before each visit.

Maybe, he thought to himself, she'll be feeling good enough we can go over to the shopping center to that ice cream parlor and have a sundae.

They had a good hour over in the ice cream parlor.

Helen looked good. Somebody had brushed her hair until it shone, and the thickening of her features, caused by some manifestation of her suffering, appeared softened under the pinkish lights of the shop.

They had a corner table, away from the rest of the people in there for a treat, never mind it was winter. Ice cream wasn't only for summer.

Driving back she had a fit, not a major one, not a bone-cracker, but bad enough. Still driving with his left, he grabbed her hand in his and she squeezed down, crushing his fingers—as strong as his hands were—until he thought his bones would splinter.

When she came out of it she murmured, "Jesus Christ."

Which he thought he'd tell Flo on Sunday because she'd take it as a sign of hope.

After Helen left the car and walked away up the path, promising to tell the attendant she'd had an incident, Sharkey noticed she'd left a spot of urine on the front seat of the car.

"Ah, Jesus Christ, indeed," he said, touching the spot with his fingertip.

14

THE FUND-RAISER THROWN BY THE COOK COUNTY CENTRAL Committee of the Regular Democratic Organization in the banquet rooms of the Bismarck Hotel was unusual. First of all because it was not a regular election year, second because the Republicans were running a token candidate of no consequence, and third because the proceeds of the hundred dollars a plate were actually earmarked for the general election two years down the line, when, of course, there'd be another fund-raiser. So, whoever put up a hundred dollars for this chicken dinner was buying sight unseen. They might even turn out supporting somebody they couldn't stand.

Fifty years ago it would have been practically an all-Irish affair. Now you had your Bohemians, your Germans, your Italians, your Jews, your Hispanics, and you even had your colored.

If you checked around the room, the different tables, the speaker's table, you could see how the power was sorted out.

On the dais you had the acting mayor and his wife, smiling upon one and all, because it seemed certain that he would win the endorsement of the Party. You had John Keir, the president of the Cook County Board of Commissioners; Con Quirty, chairman of the Democratic Central Committee of Cook County; Finny Cavan, the deputy police superintendent; Alderman Patrick McMullen from the First, nominal host of the affair; and so forth and so on.

Three or four tables to the right of the main table as you faced it were reserved for ranking cops and firemen.

The ones in the center were for other commissioners and city government and party notables who would be honored by some mention during the course of the evening.

Former Congressman Roman (Pooch) Pucinski was seated at one of them, state Representative Harold Washington at another, and Edward Hanrahan, former Cook County state's attorney, sat with his supporters at still another, all three declared challengers to the acting mayor's nomination as the Democratic Party's candidate.

The Candidate, undeclared but considered by many to be a certain runner and odds-on winner, sat with Kitty Brennan, Bud Kenna, and Jack Quinn at a table well off to the side, in a discreet corner practically in the slipstream of the swinging kitchen doors, the purpose being that he wished to be present but inconspicuous (as if anybody as notable as he could go unnoticed), remaining well above the battle that had already begun.

Pucinski had only yesterday charged that acting mayor Michael Bilandic's supporters had thrown bricks through the house windows of *his* supporters and Bilandic had countered by accusing Pooch of engineering the vandalism in order to gain sympathy.

Hanrahan accused both Bilandic and Pucinski of being hypocrites, pretending an affection for the late, great Hizzoner, Richard J. Daley, but secretly being definitely anti-Irish.

Washington, on the other hand, accused one and all of harboring severe racial bias, proven by the fact that many of the very delegates who would endorse the Democratic nominee were the very same people who locked out Wilson Frost.

The tables on the left were for important building contractors, clergy, the judiciary, and others who had earned or bought their way into that first crescent of tables.

And the wives and girlfriends.

The dozens of tables crowded into the huge banquet room

accommodated the rest of the Democratic faithful including Dan Sharkey, who had escorted Maggie Hennessy to the do, much to Della's disapproval.

Ray Sharkey, who would have been there in any case, had accepted his brother Jerry's invitation and sat with Jerry and Myra among other judges.

The crowd had been called to their seats for the third time, only Bilandic, Pucinski, Hanrahan, and a dozen of their supporters still out there circulating, working the crowd, the fruit cups already on the tables, some of the guests already dipping in. Maybe another dozen latecomers hurrying to find their tables, embarrassed to be walking around like stray dogs, waving to this one and that one.

"I don't think you've got anything to worry about," Jerry said to Ray under his breath. "With such a crowded field, I doubt The Candidate will even declare at this late date."

"That's not what the smart money says," Ray replied. "The smart money says that's his way, send out his scouts, Kenna, Quinn, and that Kitty Brennan, count the dead and wounded in the preprimary fight between contenders, do what he can to shoot the wounded, then come in at the last minute, like the pope, ready to heal the faithful that are left and put things back together."

"There's a notion that if you don't say you want something, you're not going to get it," Jerry said. "Ever since Johnson said he wouldn't run if nominated and wouldn't serve if elected, the voters aren't going to shove it in your pocket. Bilandic's got the Bohemians, he's got the chair on the fifth floor, and he's got the ear of the Committee to Nominate. Pucinski's got the polacks which, though not overwhelmingly large in number, are very noisy. Washington's got the blacks."

"And The Candidate's got tradition and affection."

"He could still be leaving it too late."

"Well, I hope you're right."

15

THEY WERE JUST FINISHING UP THE CHICKEN, FIFTY WAITERS AND waitresses having hustled a barnyard full of the birds from the kitchen to the tables in about five minutes flat. One thing you could say about Democratic fund-raisers, you didn't have a situation where the last to be served were just starting the main course while the first to be served were already finished because there weren't enough waiters or because the service was too slow.

Jerry sat there thinking about chicken dinners, how every chicken dinner he'd had at every banquet he'd ever attended had always tasted the same. Too oily, too salty, sometimes running a little red close to the leg bone. Dangerous that. Salmonella. He'd been sick on salmonella more than once, more than twice. You took your life in your hands eating dinner at Democratic Party functions.

Now, the Republicans served steak as a rule. Nice little fillets. On occasion he'd even been asked how he'd like it prepared, well done, medium, or rare, and the steak had come back to him with a little wooden paddle stuck into it which had told the cook which was which. Lovely that. A nice steak with a baked potato, sour cream and chives, perhaps a nice green vegetable.

A dessert appeared in front of him, a ball of vanilla ice cream rolled in coconut and splashed with chocolate sauce. Every year the same thing. So, that was all right. Tim Neely, the toastmaster, was about to speak and he could sit there watching the ice cream melt, hypnotizing himself until the speeches were over and done.

After the usual greeting Neely delivered his opening joke. "Well, here we are at the Bismarck Hotel once again, ready to launch another season of political fun and games with a chicken dinner. A couple of months ago I was at a similar affair and I failed to finish all my bird. Damned if I didn't find it back on my plate this year. I could tell because it was wearing a button urging me to elect Mayor Bilandic, a button which I'd pinned to it when last we'd met."

Jerry leaned in closer to Ray and said, "What did I tell you. There's the giveaway. They're going to endorse the incumbent. The Candidate left it too late, just like I told you." Then he went back to his contemplation of the ice cream.

Neely waited out the obligatory laughter and launched into the body of his speech.

"There are those among us who'll remember that before gathering here at the Bismarck, this loyal band of brothers . . . and sisters . . . would gather at the Sherman House. And before that at the Morrison Hotel. Both of those beloved and venerable hostelries long since condemned and torn down. Long before that, back at the turn of the century, when the bones of what would become the Democratic Party Regular Organization were first being formed, Bathhouse John Coughlin and Hinky-Dink Kenna, the aldermen of the First Ward—they had two aldermen for every ward in those days, one to watch the other being the theory—would hold an annual holiday campaign fund-raising ball at the Coliseum. A celebration attended enthusiastically by politicians and ranking cops, madams, pimps and working girls from the brothels, blue-blood socialites, and criminals of every stripe. Fifty cents a ticket. Tickets selling in the thousands. Most of the fifty grand or more collected finding its way into the pockets of Hinky-Dink and Bathhouse. Never so little crime on the streets or so few cops checking on the city the night of the ball."

Neely accepted a surflike swell of laughter and went on.

"Police corruption and political favoritism were commonplace in those days but these times, thank God, there's precious little of it."

A good number of people in the audience were nearly overwhelmed with admiration at the way he was able to say that with a straight face.

"Oh, I'm not saying a person can't get the occasional favor from an alderman or a city employee. After all that's the way the city that works, works. Honest concern for one's friends and neighbors is not a bad thing."

Applause.

"And I'm not saying that every once in a while, every now and then, we don't come up with a crooked cop. For God's sake we're not perfect, we're only human. Remember, one bad cop does not a rotten police force make."

Ray's eyes, cop's eyes, were roaming the room. One of the things about a cop, their eyes were never still.

His glance paused here and there, acknowledging a returned glance, recognizing this one, that one, and then they stopped cold. Kitty Brennan was looking straight at him as though trying to direct the attention of one and all toward him at mention of the crooked cop. He could read dislike, even hatred, in her pale blue eyes, even from across the room. For a second he wondered what it was all about, this aversion she had for him. They'd been neighbors when they were young. He seemed to remember a homely kid with orange hair, a playmate of his sister Wilda's. Just a neighborhood kid he scarcely ever noticed. So, what was it all about?

Why was that Irish bastard staring at her the way he was, Kitty Brennan wondered. Was he remembering? Was he remembering the time she was coming home alone from the movies when she was sixteen and had passed him where he was standing beside an empty lot under a leafy tree on a summer night, staring down the street as though about to run and never stop.

He'd scarcely noticed her, but she was used to that. She was just his little sister's friend and he was Ray Sharkey, the boy who'd shattered some colored fighter's jaw some years ago, the man who, going away to war, came back to his family, his wife and child—his neighborhood—a hero and seemed to be waiting, her parents said, for the world to hand him a living.

He swayed slightly as she passed and bumped her softly, turning, taking a step back. "Very sorry," he said, starting to reach up to tip a hat he wasn't wearing.

"That's all right, Ray," she said.

"Who is it, then?" he asked, putting an old-country lilt to the words, smiling this smile he had that made her buzz in the strangest way between her breasts and down there where her legs met.

"Kitty. Kitty Brennan," she said.

"Sure it is. My sister's little playmate." He thrust his face closer, peering down at her. "Not so little. Grown up."

"Are you all right, Ray?"

"There's some would say that I'm a sorry mess. I've had what to drink. I can always manage to drink myself half a load down at the tavern, the old boys buying me drinks just to hear the stories of how men got shot, blown up, shattered, dead. But that's just the half of it. I've got a wife and a sickly child and no way to keep them."

Kitty had heard about his daughter's illnesses. Not from Wilda, she was already gone, run away at thirteen, three years gone, who knew where? Heard about it from gossip here and there. Helen Sharkey, Ray and Flo Sharkey's only child, suffered fits. She'd even witnessed one outside the grocery store, the child lying on the cement, arching her back, shuddering, her eyes rolled back in her head, fists clenched, a bloody froth on her lips.

He rocked on his feet, back and forth, back and forth, and seemed about to fall. She moved in close and he threw his arms around her, making them both stagger back through the bushes and weeds growing on the lot, like a couple of cockeyed dancers under the summer moon. Her heel caught on a root or stone and they went down. It seemed almost in slow motion the way he struggled to keep them upright, holding them up with one leg, then giving way from her weight, with her clinging about his neck.

He was on top of her. She could feel him through her summer dress, his summer slacks. The film she'd seen had been a love story. Maybe that had had something to do with what happened that night, she caught up in the memory of the love scenes, becoming the actress surrendering to passion, there in the dirt and weeds of the empty lot with Ray Sharkey breathing beer and whiskey into her face, saying, "Ah, Jesus, what's a man to do, what's a man to do?" over and over again.

When it was over, he rolled off her and lay there with his arms flung wide, his fly undone, exposing himself, his eyes closed, moaning softly.

She couldn't rouse him. Repeated attempts had only caused him to thrash out in drunken, sleeping rage, so she'd left him there and hurried home.

When they happened to meet along the street about three or

four days later, she'd colored and said, "Hello, Ray," knowing that her voice was giving her feelings away, and he'd looked at her with his vague friendly grin and distant blue eyes and said, "Oh, hi . . . uh?"

"Kitty," she'd said. "Kitty Brennan."

"Sure. You ever hear from Wilda? We never do."

She felt a nudge at her elbow and roused herself from her memories and her intense regard of Ray Sharkey long enough to tilt her head and flash one of her brief, automatic, robotlike smiles.

"Time to go, darlin'," Kenna murmured. "Neely just introduced the acting mayor. He's about to deliver himself of a peroration on the virtues of loyalty and humility. So now's the time for you to take your departure, in the middle of his opening remarks."

"That would be rude," she said, automatically responding to her genteel upbringing.

"That's the idea," he said, and gently took her elbow as she rose to her feet.

Bilandic was up there ready to begin as the applause died down and now stood staring as The Candidate and his entire entourage made their departure, unnecessarily threading a path through the center of the room when they could more easily have gone around the perimeter.

They were heading right for the table where Ray Sharkey sat, Kitty saw. Her legs were still weak with the old memories. Every time she took a step, she had to lock her knees; her legs had lost all feeling and she feared that if she didn't feel the click and bump of the knee joints, she'd fall down in her tracks.

She threaded her way through the tables, holding her skirts aside and offering little murmured apologies as she navigated the narrow passages, feeling the occasionally comforting pressure of Kenna's hand on her back or shoulder. Letting her know that he was just behind her.

To catch her if she fell, she thought wildly. A giggle threatened to explode from her mouth and then she stopped, ready to make the public declaration they'd agreed upon.

She was looking down at Ray Sharkey, who was looking up at her with a quizzical expression on his still handsome face.

"Having a good time?" Sharkey asked tentatively.

"I beg your pardon?" Kitty said.

"What's going on, Kitty? It's me, Ray Sharkey," he said, standing up.

There were a couple of people with cameras approaching on either side.

Somebody's going to be shot, Ray thought wildly.

"That's right," Kitty said. "I didn't recognize you for a minute. You're Ray Sharkey, the City Hall Pimp, aren't you?"

The flashes of the cameras went off in his face, him standing there looking like an angry traffic cop, his mouth open, momentarily lost for a comeback.

Before he could respond, even absorb the insult she'd just flung into his face, say something to the brazen bitch, she'd clicked her smile on and off a couple of times and was on her way, with Kenna right behind her, his hand on her back, steering her like she was a little ship.

Ray sat down.

"I've got a feeling," Jerry said, "that The Candidate just declared himself in the race and also named his issue."

16

ON THE WAY HOME, JUST MINUTES AFTER ELEVEN, RAY WAS THINKING about the way Kitty Brennan had insulted him right to his face, in front of his brother and sister-in-law, in front of the judges and cops, in front of everybody. If a man had said what Brennan had said, he'd have knocked him on his ass, right then and there. As it was he had to chew on the goddamn piece of gristle she'd shoved into his mouth. She'd left him no choice.

Either he chewed on it and stayed up all night staring at the ceiling or he swallowed it and got a sour stomach which would keep him up all night staring at the ceiling.

Women could box you in that way. You couldn't hit them so all you could do was stay awake all night until your brain got so tired worrying about it that you finally had to let go in order to preserve your life.

The average man took a look at the grief in his life and ten to one it was a woman who gave it to him. His mother, his sisters, his wives. Look at Flo—God bless her, dying up there in Fond du Lac—clamping her legs shut on him all those years because she thought God was punishing them for the fucking they'd done before marriage with a defective child. For Christ's sake, where was the wise, all-knowing merciful God they kept on yapping about? They ought to get their act straightened out.

And how about Wilda, running off when she'd been only a kid. Wartime. Living God knew where, God knew how. Wrote when she goddamn pleased. Called up once or twice a year, on Christmas, on his birthday. Didn't hear from her for months and months on end. Giving him such heartache.

Look at Kitty Brennan—back to that—who the hell did the little fart think she was, coming on to him that way? Walking right up to him at a political affair, walking out right when the mayor was about to speak. Goddamn rude. No manners, the Irish bitch acting like she was one of Chicago's aristocracy. A shanty Irishman just like him. Used to play with his sister. Homely little scrawny kid with the ugliest orange hair anybody'd ever seen. So she married some fucking aristocrat from Sauganash. So what? That gave her no right to insult him the way she did. Taking pictures. A photo opportunity for The Candidate. He wanted to toss his hat in the ring, let him toss his hat in the ring. He didn't have to use Ray Sharkey for the sacrificial goat. Where the hell did they come off playing games like that?

On the other hand, you had to give her credit. It took a lot of guts to walk up to him and call him what she called him to his face, with everybody watching and the goddamn flashes going off.

"Oh, what the fuck," he said aloud. "What's it all going to mean a hundred years from today?"

He parked his Chevy in front of the apartment house on Artesian, locked it up, and stood there at the curb feeling the quiet. All the working-class people, black and white, inside their homes. Some watching the late news. Most of them asleep, the men done with work, the kids in off the streets, the dishes washed up, the women resting their feet, waiting for another day.

The way it'd been in the flat in Bridgeport for those three or four good years early in the marriage before little Helen started getting sick with one thing after the other and then the seizures. Before everything started falling apart.

And the woman waiting for him in the flat upstairs. A puzzle. The erotic, exotic Roma Chounard, his black woman, his New Orleans whore, with her exhausting appetite and sexual inventions that sometimes made him feel depraved.

Not the legendary whore with a heart of gold but a woman who'd sold herself, and was selling herself to him, everything very businesslike, yet, every once in a while, showing another side of her, deeply soft and womanly.

He fitted the key in the lock and opened the door to the top-floor flat, knowing the instant his foot stepped over the threshold that the place was empty.

There was a rich smell of some sort of jambalaya she'd made a couple of nights before. Their meals were catch as catch can—his hours irregular, her interest in household matters minimal—but every now and then she'd rouse herself into a frenzy of domesticity, cleaning the four rooms and bath, asking him when he came home was the master of the house pleased by the labors of his nigger maid, cooking up great pots of overspiced jambalayas and gumbos which gave him heartburn and the runs, grinning at him as though it was her joy to do for him the way a woman was supposed to do for her man.

He knew the flat was empty not because the television or the radio weren't playing, sometimes both at the same time, all hours of the day and night, her need for voices, music, company, action, a hunger as deep as his need for an hour's peace and quiet now and then.

Not even because his cop senses, alert to empty places and places that only seemed empty, told him that there was no one there.

But more specifically, something in him that had become attuned to her lately in a way he'd never been aware of another human being before—to just one person—told him that she wasn't in the flat. Not even in their bed, asleep. Not even in the building or on the roof looking at the city lights, or anywhere along the block from the grocery store to the apartment house. Not anywhere near. Gone away? Gone away as he always feared she'd be one day when he came in off the streets.

Then he remembered that there was a party going on at Jasper Tourette's club, the Pussy Cat, over there on Orleans just down the road from Cabrini-Green, where once she'd lived. He'd been late and she hadn't waited for him.

Was she telling him that if she wasn't welcome at his party he wasn't welcome at hers?

This woman he lived with who was not his woman.

17

THERE WAS NO SALOON, TAVERN, COCKTAIL LOUNGE, RESTAURANT, bar, night club, blind pig, private club, or beer joint in the Eighteenth Police District unknown to Ray Sharkey, though there were, of course, some less well known than others. Also it was a fact—which sometimes bothered him a little because it was getting harder to keep up—that the ownership and management of one or another of the several hundred establishments changed hands practically every week or so. After a while it was very hard to sort them out even when this was the nation you lived and worked in.

For instance, you take clubs with the word *cat* on the electric sign, the painted sign, the neon sign. You had your Pussy Cat, your Kit Kat, and your Kitten Paws. There was Kittens on the Gold Coast and Tiger Cat by the zoo. There were three City Cat Club lounges in three different parts of the city, and Sharkey remembered a club called the Cat's Pajamas somewhere around Cabrini-Green, maybe even on Orleans, right about where Tourette's Pussy Cat now did business. That was about thirty years ago when he and Minifee had walked a beat in this neighborhood. Before Minifee had died—one night when Sharkey had called in sick because he was chasing pussy and Minifee walked the beat alone—a broken Coke bottle shoved up his rectum, not far from the Pussy Cat.

He didn't have to think about where he was going. When he drove through the city he put that part of his brain on automatic. It noted the landmarks, a building in ruins, an empty lot, a billboard, an electric sign, and sent the signals to turn right, turn left, straight ahead to the supermarket, north to the underpass, west to wherever.

Making his way through the boneyards of the city, third garbage can from the corner where a corpse was found dismembered one February night, second roof from the brownstone with the purple door upon which a disemboweled hooker had expired on a Christmas Eve, the alley where he'd once plucked the body of a dead child from a cardboard box half-filled with kitchen trash. Everything recognized but little that was truly known. Too much data. Too much information. Too many layers laid one on top of the other, printed on transparent sheets of time, so that the shapes and numbers became confused, formed a pattern that could not be thought about but merely sensed, followed as a dog follows his nose, sorting out the smells.

He understood that for all his long-practiced cop's skills something was lost because of it, some acuteness of perception, memories conflicting with one another, information of value slipping through the cracks.

There was a big hand-lettered sign, red on white, that read CLOSED—PRIVATE PARTY. Two young black couples were standing there on the sidewalk, staring at it as though they expected it to change its meaning if they looked long enough.

When Sharkey parked his car in front of the hydrant on the corner, they all turned and looked at the white man taking a chance, leaving his car out there at the curb begging for a ticket or a tow-away. He put the official card in the front window and they stopped looking at him, moving off a few paces like a clutch of sidling crabs, giving him clear passage, turning their attention back to the offending sign.

One of them said, "Motherfucker," the catchall word of joy, misery, expectation, and disappointment in the black ghettos.

"Who, me?" Sharkey said, grinning to let them know he was kidding them along.

"This," the young black said, jerking a thumb at the door. "Club's closed. They having a private party."

"I can see that," Sharkey said.

"It's Saturday night."

"That's what I been told."

"So, I mean it's the best jazz night they got. Charlie Lincoln and Billy Smith be playing."

One of the girls said, "You here on official business?" as though making fun of Sharkey and a hundred television shows and maybe herself.

Her boyfriend frowned at her as though she'd given something away.

"I'm here to join the party," Sharkey said.

"Hoo-hoo," the girl crooned, flashing him a smile that could have busted a bronze horseman's heart. It made Sharkey happy to see her giving him such a friendly smile, little dimples plucking at her cheeks.

"You don't believe me?"

"Who's not goin' to believe a white policeman in nigger town on a Saturday night?"

"So you don't believe me, you come with me."

He held out his hand as though to take her hand and her boyfriend grabbed her by the arm to haul her back.

"I mean all of you. All of you come with me as my guests."

"The guest of a guest?" the girl said doubtfully, ducking her head flirtatiously, still giving him her million-dollar smile. Everything right out there, the fun of it all, the joy of life on a Saturday night.

The boyfriend let her take Sharkey's hand but he still held on to her. When Sharkey stopped and tried the door she bumped into his hip, laughing about that too, her body moving as though she were already dancing, hips canted, ass held high, accentuating the deep curve of her back. "Hoo-hoo," she crooned.

He held on to her with one hand and knocked on the door with the other. The judas hole popped open and a piece of black face filled it.

The door opened up. "Come along on in, Mr. Sharkey," Waylon Carteret, Tourette's majordomo, said.

"These are friends of mine, Waylon. Are they welcome, too?"

"They with you, it's okay. I don't even got to ask."

He pulled the door wide and let them through.

The club was in its nighttime dress, colored lights spraying the perimeter of the small dance floor jam-packed with bodies like one great multicolored, many-headed snake that writhed and undulated to the edges of the uncarpeted wood, like a creature captured by the white-clothed tables and wooden chairs.

A five-piece band gave up its music softly. Softly manufacturing dreamscapes on the smoky air, a curtain of piano runs, a heartbeat of drums, a clarinet crying like a baby coming from the open window of a ghetto flat on a summer night, the throaty lament of the saxophone like the rising chorus of a choir. Suddenly rising above it the silvery notes of a cornet, a child's horn almost lost in the great black hands of the musician. Sweet Saturday night.

Black men wearing furry hats and splashy vests, pointed shoes and trousers so sharply pressed that the creases folded like cardboard, were sitting around looking sly and fly.

Black women and white women dressed in cocktail gowns frothing down and away from their breasts, made bold by stays and padding, short skirts showing long lengths of thigh, some in skin-tight trousers, ending just below the knee, in shades of iridescent pink and yellow, feather boas, long silk scarves. Signage of the working girls, attention getters that could be flaunted and waved, drawing eyes to tits and ass and crotch.

Designer cunts, Sharkey said to himself, arming himself in that way against their considerable appeal, nearly overpowering allure.

Tourette was sitting at a table next to the tiny dance floor and the even tinier bandstand, sitting there like a king, his court close to hand at other tables, big black men wearing black leather, black denim, black silks and satins, black sunglasses like holes in their black faces, pretending to have balls of brass and nerves of hammered gold.

A man to be admired no matter how you looked at him, Sharkey thought as he walked across the floor, wending his way through the tables, still holding on to the black girl's hand.

Tourette was looking elsewhere, his hand on Roma Chounard's neck, his fingers tapping on the slender column of her neck as though playing a duet with the trumpeter.

Just as he'd been doing when Sharkey had first laid eyes on her.

She'd sat there beside Jasper Tourette as he'd fingered her neck as though she were a trumpet.

Sharkey's scrutiny had started at her feet and risen along her body, long-legged in sheeny stockings (or was it only her skin?), coffee taffy pulled taut until it shone. Sheeny, shiny emerald skirt rising along her thighs accentuating the brown flesh. Green and golden brown. Electric-green sheen passing over flanks and belly, clothing belly and breasts, revealing hips and belly and breasts, commercial come-on, priced too high for ordinary men.

Sharkey had felt a tightening in his scrotum, an excitement, electric lace spanning the bottom of his belly, across the white skin, the pubic hairs coming alive as though they had senses of their own, aware of the friction of his underwear, the pouch of his Jockey shorts cupping him, suddenly grown heavy as his eyes saw the swell of her breasts above the emerald sheen. The bones arching from throat to shoulder like delicate cantilevers of copper. The cup of her throat filled with honey.

"This be Roma Chounard," Tourette said, extending a hand toward her, pink palm facing up as though offering her for Sharkey's consideration, a secret smile lurking in the lines fanning out from his eyes behind the glasses while his mouth smiled an ordinary smile, his everyday smile. "She be from New Orleans, come up here only three days ago."

"To escape the humidity," Roma said, and then coughed delicately, clearing the honey in her throat.

"She be French on her mother's side," Tourette said.

"The cream in the coffee," Roma said, reaching over to lightly slap Tourette's wrist, cutting her oriental eyes, green-gold cat's eyes, at Sharkey, laughing as though she was laughing at him, reading every cell of his body reaching out to her, longing for her, showing the white man that she belonged to the black man because that was her choice.

"Something to eat? Something to drink?" Tourette said, as though offering a meal to a beggar, making Sharkey seem small.

Sharkey could hear the women, the whores, twittering away softly back there in the banquettes along the shuttered windows behind him; bird talk. He could feel Tourette's hookers laughing at him behind his back.

"Rib sandwich?" Tourette asked. "Fat back and collard greens?"

"You got any fruit? You got any bananas, any grapes?" Sharkey asked.

Tourette lifted his hand and one of his bodyguards was across the room, at Sharkey's back, quiet as a cat.

"You go out to the kitchen, Waylon," Tourette said. "You go out there and see does the cook have any fruits in the refrigerator."

"Fruits," Waylon repeated, not quite a question.

"You know. Bananas, grapes." Tourette looked at Sharkey. "Apples, oranges, kumquats?"

"Kumquaaaaaaats," Waylon said.

"Mmmmmmmmmangoes," Roma hummed.

"Oh, yes, mmmmangoes," Tourette said, pulling Sharkey's leg, jerking his chain, having fun with the white cop come to see the king.

Waylon did the pimp roll past the table out to the kitchen in the back.

They sat there in silence, Tourette, Roma, and Sharkey, smiling soft smiles meant for themselves more than they were meant for one another, waiting for Waylon's return.

Waylon came back in three minutes, four minutes, with a bowl of various fruits and placed them in the center of the table. Tourette nodded and he sat down.

Sharkey chose a banana, peeled it, looked at Roma, offered it to her. "Bite?"

She laughed again, a throaty little gurgle that didn't pass her lips.

"Fruit is a very healthy thing to eat," Sharkey said, chewing on a bite that had taken half the fruit. "Ribs is greasy, they'll make you fat, they'll give you indigestion."

"I'll remember that," Roma said.

"You going to remember that too, Jasper?" Sharkey said.

Tourette, puzzled, stared at Sharkey through his mirrored shades and said, "I'll remember that."

"Because you know what else? I shove this fruit up your ass, you'll be shitting fruit salad for a week. You understand what I'm saying?"

Tourette and Waylon stiffened, and Roma shifted uneasily in her chair, caught off guard by the sudden brutality.

"What's the matter, Ray?" Tourette asked.

Sharkey tossed the half-eaten banana on the table.

"You got this new woman here. This pretty woman here," Sharkey said. "You want to impress her. Show her how you can make the white cop look like a fool. Oh, yes, that's exactly what you're trying to do, Jasper. I understand that. In front of a pretty woman like this a man can't help whipping it out, matching peckers, showing the new bitch just who the daddy dog is around here."

The blood came up under the skin on Tourette's cheeks, brushing it with copper. "You don't have to carry on like this. We was only having a little fun. Just doing the dozens."

"Oh, yes I do. I've got to make it plain I didn't come for free samples like some cops might do. I didn't come to ask you for money. I came to offer you the chance to make some money. I came to talk business."

"We can do that. You want to do it private?"

"It don't have to be private. The woman and your bone-breaker can stay if they promise to be quiet."

Roma turned her face away as though he'd slapped her.

"Is this going to be a negotiation or an offer?" Tourette asked.

"A proposition. I'm going into partnership on a new enterprise. You know a gambling joint run over to the Forty-second in an old mansion on a hill."

"Orchid's place?"

"That's the one. I bought in. We're going to improve and expand. We're going to want a couple of shifts of hostesses."

"Girls and women?"

"Just women. Nothing that looks too young. That ain't the desires we intend to cater to. Dignified companionship. Celebrations for the winners. Comfort for the losers."

"If they can still afford comfort," Tourette said, laughing, showing the treasure of gold and a diamond chip in his mouth.

"If they made a contribution large enough, the club picks up the tab. The woman gives us a rate in that case."

Careful business between businessmen.

Roma, used to being merchandise, sitting there with her head turned away as though it meant nothing to her.

"What cut does the house take?"

"Very small. Enough to cover favors and any insurance policies we may have to buy."

"I understand," Tourette said, and raised his eyebrows, waiting for more, waiting for Sharkey to say what was in it for Sharkey.

"For this concession all I ask you to do for me, is keep an eye out for me, now and then. Count the house."

"I ain't no accountant."

"I don't need an accountant. Orchid's an accountant. I need somebody with eyes and ears. Lots of eyes and ears. Your girls and women pay attention, tell you the gossip, count the action, and you tell me. That's my cut for giving you the concession. You understand what I'm saying?"

"You want a drink to sign the deal?" Tourette asked.

Sharkey had looked at Roma, who looked back at him.

"I'll have the drink and then I'll have a little of that privacy you offered a minute ago. I'd like to know more about New Orleans."

"Okay, okay," Tourette had said, smiling softly, certain in his knowledge of what made men run.

"To seal the bargain," he'd said, looking at Roma, handing her over to the aging white cop as though she were nothing but a little sweetening in the deal.

Now, as then, Sharkey's scrotum cringed as he spotted Roma sitting there. He stumbled on some unevenness of the floor, took a misstep, rolled to the side, and felt himself coloring, red layered on red, his eyes blazing out of his brilliant face like the pure blue of argon.

Tourette looked at him and quickly took his hand away from Roma's neck.

She'd been watching Sharkey's approach all the time, out of the corner of her eye, and smiled now.

She was wearing something black, made of a million tiny sequins, that rode her body on two straps over her shoulders as thin as wire, so the top of the dress seemed about to fall.

"You have a good time with the men what run the city?" she said, something contemptuous, something mocking in the way she said it.

The girl holding on to Sharkey's hand bumped his hip with her ass and said, "I dance with you, you want. My price of admission."

The girl was jerking and jumping with small subtle motions, slipping and sliding inside her dress like a snake in its skin. She dragged at Sharkey's coat, snatched his hat from his head, said, "Hoo-hoo," at the sight of his white hair. Took the pile of hat and coats and placed them on an empty chair at a table, asking permission with a smile. Bumped Sharkey out into the crush of dancers with her hips and thighs, took him in her arms as though he were an old lover and drew pictures on his belly with her belly.

She had her head thrust back so it seemed her neck would break, her face glowing up at him in the shine of colored lights, her lipstick gone purple, her cheekbones gold, her eyes as brown and sweet as caramels.

When the music stopped, Sharkey felt as though he'd just been softly raped. "Hoo-hoo," the girl crooned softly, her expression for all occasions, and slipped away from him to join her friends, turning away from the white man, white cop, middle-aged white cop, turning her back on him.

Sharkey stood there for a minute as though he'd found himself lost in some alien nation, brought there by some unknown machine, and then he heard his name called. Respectfully. Insinuatingly. He turned his head and saw Jasper Tourette with his hand up over his head, a signpost showing Sharkey the way.

Sharkey slipped into the booth beside Roma. She wove her hands through the crook of his arm.

"You have a good time?" she asked, smiling into his face, as though she'd given him the gift of the girl. "You fucked that girl standing up. You want to fuck that girl laying down?"

She threw her head back and laughed.

"You want a slab of ribs?" Tourette asked. "You want a drink?"

"Yeah, bring me some ribs and some coleslaw and some sweet potatoes. And bring me a rye and ginger back," Sharkey said.

He ate and drank. From time to time he stood up and went out and joined the many-headed creature writhing on the floor, reading the thighs and bellies of a dozen women, licorice, coffee, chocolate, and cream.

Feeling the soft weight of Roma against him from chest to groin one time, the last time, when the crowd had finally thinned a little and was thinning out some more, trickling out the door like wine from a bottle.

For a time, there, he found himself alone with Tourette, sitting knees to knees, talking head to head, old friends, members of the same brotherhood, Sharkey feeling more black than black, feeling affectionate, Tourette telling him about overtures made to him by Shelley Orchid.

"Asks me what I'm doing being a white cop's prat boy. Asks me what do I need with you for a sponsor. Offering me a piece of your piece if I help him squeeze you out, bust your nuts. Asks me how come I let an old fuck like you steal my main woman. I tell him I give her to you, as a gift, but he just laughs at me, trying to make me feel small. I tell him to fuck off. He gets mad as hell. Turns colors like a fucking lizard he's so mad. Says he'll get your ass, one way or another, even if he has to call on his connections and invite them in. Give the guidos a piece of the club even, just to take you down."

"Put out a contract on me? He said that?"

"Well, he didn't exactly say that. It's what he in-ti-mated."

"He ain't got the stones for that. It's just his polack-guinea pride talking. He's just showing off for that Chinese dinner crowd of his."

"I join them now and then—listening like you say—but I ain't part of his Chinese dinner crowd and he was making these offers to me."

"We'll have a talk. Shelley and me'll have a talk," Sharkey said.

He ate and drank some more, forgetting about all the people out to get him.

Sometime in the small hours his head turned to glass. He grinned foolishly at Jasper Tourette and called him his nicest friend, knew that the blacks were laughing at him but didn't care because behind their derision he thought he felt a grudging liking, of a sort a man might feel for a dog he didn't ask to have as a companion but which was too friendly to ignore or abuse.

Why, hell, he thought, didn't he speak their language? Hadn't he learned it walking the beat with Chick Minifee years ago? Didn't he know the nuances of the meaning in the music of their speech? Like the note of a cornet when slurred meaning one thing, when struck another, and when muted meaning something else altogether.

He wanted to tell his friend Jasper Tourette, and his other friend Waylon Carteret, and his beautiful black mistress from New Orleans, just how much he liked them and their people. He leaned forward to tell them but they weren't there.

18

HE WAS NAKED, LYING ON HIS BACK. HIS CHEEKS WERE WET WITH tears, the salt of them burned his lips.

He'd been dreaming of his wife when she'd been a girl. He'd been dreaming of the night he'd struck Leroy Scarlet that vicious blow, crushing the fighter's cheekbone, breaking his jaw, ruining his career. Dreaming of how Flo had given herself to him in her father's Ford afterwards. Dreaming of his daughter struggling on the pavement. Of Kitty Brennan lying under him somewhere in an empty space underneath a sky with a moon in it. What the hell?

It was dark in the room. His eyes wouldn't focus as he tried to pick out some familiar object that might tell him where he was. He made long, sweeping gestures with his arms on both sides of the bed. It was empty. He was alone. Had she left him? Had Floie run away? For a second a terrible charge of panic raced through him, shocking him into false sobriety. Had *Roma* left him? Had she abandoned him? Had Tourette ordered her back into his stable?

He scrambled out of bed, reaching for his genitals, feeling vulnerable to some unknown attack. He had a partial erection.

There was a crack of dull light marking the bedroom door which widened as he stared at it.

Roma stood there in a robe opened in front.

He read contempt in her eyes as she glanced at the short white pole sticking out from beneath his belly. He turned his hips and covered himself with an edge of the blanket.

"My God. I'm going to have a head in the morning and I got to drive up to Fond du Lac to see Floie."

"So what do you want me to do about that?" she asked. "Kiss your ass or cry?"

19

THERE IT WAS. THIRD DAY BACK IN CHICAGO AND THERE WAS her brother's name in the paper. "Sergeant Ray Sharkey Called Pimp by Candidate's Aide," and the story that followed. It was almost funny. She could just imagine her old playmate, Kitty Brennan, standing toe to toe with Ray, looking up at him, spitting the insult in his face. Though why she'd want to do it was beyond her, except where there was politics and political advantage to be had, people did some very funny things.

It felt very strange being back in the city without anyone from the family knowing she was there. She had so few friends or even acquaintances in Chicago that they were of no consequence. It was like being a thief in a familiar, darkened house, all the rooms filled with softly breathing, sleeping men and women, fragile souls hovering on the edge, vulnerable to her will. She could shatter sleep and contentment, peace and confidence, with a knuckle rapped on a breastbone, a finger poked into a belly, a hand closed over a mouth. Stir things up with a couple of telephone calls.

She wasn't without fear of being startled from her own sleep, her own reverie and concealment. If she was suddenly awakened how old would she be?

She sat there in the cheapest room in the cheapest hotel she'd been able to find, thinking about the upset she could cause. The delinquent daughter, the bad penny, back home again to draw upon the family's charity, draining their emotions, making demands on them in a hundred ways.

"What's the matter with you, Wilda?" her father, Dan, would say. "Can't keep a job. Can't find a husband."

"What kind of work do you find for yourself out there in strange cities? What do you *do* with yourself so far way from the family?" her older sister, Della, would ask a dozen times that first night of celebration for the wayward child returned, pouring her endless cups of tea, envying her cheap red shoes and black stockings, things Della would never dare to wear.

Her brother Jerry, the Judge, would tell her, "Wise up. Stay here. We'll see to it you get a job in civil service. A clerk at City Hall. Maybe I can even swing you something in the courts. You can move in with Pa and Della, get back on your feet."

On the phone from his parish in another city, Father Gabe would ask her was she well, did she take communion, concerned for her immortal soul but apparently caring little for the comfort and safety of her body.

Michael would clump across the room on his wooden leg, picking her right up off her feet in his strong arms, kissing her with his oddly tender mouth, soft bewildered eyes studying her face as though making sure she was really his baby sister and not some changeling come to hide among them and steal their breath in the night.

Ray, the oldest, all but another father to her, taking her to his chest, embracing her with something that felt like hunger and letting her go more quickly than she thought he meant to do, than she wanted him to do. Not scolding her, not saying much, but looking holes through her right into her brain and heart.

Squeezing in on them, milking them for suggestions, forcing them to make plans for her, forcing them to pay attention as they waited for her to grow restless and be on her way again, full of tears and rage after a fight everyone knew would come sooner or later.

Then they could sit around and be dismayed and despairing, wondering what was wrong with a woman on the hard side of forty who insisted on dressing and acting like a woman half her age who just could not, or would not, stay put and behave herself.

Well, not this time, she thought. Not this time the excited hugs and kisses with the irritation behind the smiles and outcries. Not this time the conversation into the wee small hours before she could finally slip into a bed that smelled of memories, bringing a tightness to her breast.

This time she'd go on about her business without them, putting her life in order, getting a job for herself, as a salesgirl in

Carson Pirie Scott, a file clerk in a law office, this or that, even a waitress if that's the way it had to be. The hard way of hard work, and no depending upon men now and then for favors. For the rent. For the gas and electric. No little loans to tide her over just until the next job, the next pay check, and all the little favors that went along with little loans.

She'd rent a nice furnished room, maybe a little flat in Bridgeport or Pilsen among the artists or on a modest street in Lincoln Park. A nice neighborhood, wherever it might be.

And one fine day when she was settled in, living an orderly, modest, becoming life, she might be standing in front of the monkey house at Lincoln Park Zoo and she'd feel a nudge, hear a voice, and she'd turn around and see her sister Della with the old man, or her brother Jerry with one of his grandchildren, or Father Gabe, in town on a visit, or maybe even her older brother Ray, standing there saying, "When did you come home?" Saying, "I can't believe my eyes." Grinning and saying, "Where the hell have you been? Gimmie a hug."

Her big cop brother, Ray Sharkey, pulling her close, burying her face in his chest, his shirt smelling of starch and his cheeks smelling of lime aftershave. Letting her go too soon.

Or one of them might be shopping at Marshall Field's or Carson Pirie Scott, looking for some shoes, buying some underwear, trying on a dress, one of her sisters-in-law or aunts or cousins, and she'd step up to them, nice as you please, and say, "May I be of some help?"

In a church. Even in church, at her awkward prayers, she might find one of her own family waiting, having sat there through a thousand days and nights, telling their beads, making their Never-Fail Novenas, waiting patiently for her to appear.

Fate could lay a trap for her nearly anywhere, she thought, delighted and excited by the fantasy. In a movie house, a drugstore, a nightclub.

It were as though a mirror broke and the pieces fragmented the reflected light, distorting the shadows on the walls. It were as though the sound of traffic shattered the window and careened around the walls like the sound of a hundred falling cymbals.

She imagined herself sitting in a club with some companions, listening to the music, the rare old jazz that made her buzz, her breasts filling with it, the root of her belly vibrating with it, and Ray walking in (cop on the prowl), looking over the clientele, his contempt for the white women sitting with black men plain on his Irish cop's face, searching for someone to humiliate. Who better than she, his own sister, who sometimes consorted with blacks?

Her breath grew quick and shallow. It was all so foolish and dramatic it made her want to cry.

Maybe tomorrow, or the day after, she'd get on the telephone and call someone. Ray or Michael or Jerry. Call her father, visit with him and Della in the flat where they lived almost like man and wife, the daughter taking care of the father in his old age.

20

THE CANCER HOSPITAL WAS CUPPED IN A CRESCENT OF PINES AND firs on the summit of a long slope that swept down to Lake Winnebago. It had once been a resort hotel but had been sold to a consortium of doctors who specialized in most of the rare and intractable forms of cancer. Physicians and surgeons came from all over the world to study and learn.

They took chances and persevered, seeking cures and arrests when other institutions would have long since given up trying.

The hotel pool had been outfitted to provide water therapies for patients severely mutilated by radical surgery.

The hospital boasted that its restaurant provided foods of such variety and excellence that its cuisine could match the finest restaurants in Chicago.

Experimental drugs and medicines were available in its pharmacy that were unavailable in practically any other facility in the country.

All this cost a bundle.

Sharkey was no fool. He'd been advised by physician acquaintances at Cook County General, Passavant, and other hospitals throughout the city that what they did up at Fond du Lac was largely palliative. Lavishing such care on their patients undoubtedly made them more comfortable and might give them hope but when it came to arresting or curing the disease the cancer wards of city hospitals usually did just as well.

It broke his heart every time he came to Fond du Lac to see his wife bundled up in a wheelchair, one arm sticking out of the blanket like a twig, holding a cigarette between stained fingers.

The doctors allowed her to smoke, they said, because the cancer was ravaging the bones, not the lungs, and they doubted if taking away Flo's only pleasure would have much affect upon the treatments given her.

They told Sharkey in confidence that they counted it a rare victory to have kept her alive the last two years, her bones as brittle as sticks of chalk, ribs breaking from a cough, limbs fracturing from a careless bump. They counted it a victory, but all Sharkey could see was the pain in his wife's sunken eyes.

He kissed her on the cheek. Her skin was as dry as newspaper and for a moment he feared that her cheek would stick to his lips, the skin peeling away when he drew back.

"How you doing?" he asked.

"Do you care?" She was in one of those moods. "How long has it been? Three weeks, four weeks, more than a month since you been up to see me?"

"It's only been a week. Ten days. Remember? I came up the middle of the week about ten, eleven days ago."

"So," she said, not giving him an inch.

"I've been up to here," he said, making a cutting motion at the level of his eyes. "I call you on the telephone four, five times a week, don't I?"

"I'm usually asleep when you call."

"Well, I grab the chance when I can. It's not that I don't check up on how you're doing all the time."

"There'd be nothing to say to me anyway, would there?" she said.

"What do you mean?"

"I mean nothing happens to me up here. Just the same thing over and over again. The shots, the death rays, the shits, and the vomiting."

"You shouldn't talk that way, for God's sake, Floie. I mean it's not like you to use that kind of language."

"What? Did I use a dirty word? Did I shock you?"

He laughed, trying to make things a little lighter.

"Well, no, you didn't shock me. It'd take a lot more than that to shock me."

"I guess," she said, and cut her eyes at him as though she knew the things he did, the dirty, depraved things he did, with her so far from home. With her dying.

"Dotty Merton passed away day before yesterday?" she said, lifting the end of the sentence as though asking a question.

"I'm sorry to hear—"

"You remember Dotty Merton?"

"Tell you the truth, Floie, I can't put a face to the name. Or the other way around."

"That's what I say."

"What?"

"Nothing that happens up here matters to you. Why should it?"

"You matter to me."

"You're so tired of me you'd give up ten years of your own life just to see me go."

"You shouldn't say things like that."

"Well, I'm going to goddamn well say things like that. I'm dying, can't you see that? I'm falling away to skin and bones. Pretty soon that's all that'll be left of me, just skin and bones, and they can toss me on the pile."

"Why are you mad at me? I didn't give you the cancer, Flo."

"It's God's punishment."

"For what? For Christ's sake, for fucking what?" he asked, whispering harshly, trying so hard not to get angry.

"That's what for. For all that fucking we did before we got married."

He turned his head away. "I can't believe this."

"What did you say?"

"I said here we go again. Why do you have to start on that every time I come up here for a visit?"

"You're not even repentant. Your daughter's in an institution because she has fits and your wife's dying young and you won't even get down on your knees and pray for forgiveness."

He put his face close to hers and with a soft fierceness that was supposed to convey love as well as rage said, "There's a lot of things I could ask forgiveness for, Floie, but two kids fucking in the front seat of your father's old Ford ain't one of them."

He kissed her on the mouth then.

"You ask God or Jesus Christ or the Virgin Mary, the next time you have a little talk with them, if love ain't supposed to count for something," he said.

"Is that what it was?" she said, practically in a whisper, her eyes softening and her lips starting to tremble.

"We thought so. Didn't we think so?" he replied.

21

SHARKEY ASSUMED THAT PRACTICALLY EVERY MARRIED MAN thought about what it would be like to have a woman on the side, one time or another. It was only human nature, wanting something different, wanting that feeling of early times, the excitement of it again. The way it had been between Flo and himself when they were just starting out.

He'd had plenty of opportunities, walking the beat when he'd been a young cop. All kinds of women. Waitresses, hair dressers, shop girls, secretaries, housewives and hookers, barflies like Alice Wegrzyn, Dubrowski's piece of ass, plenty of what they called streetwalkers back then. So you took a taste of the professionals and repaid the favor, giving them a pass when you should've pulled them in for soliciting. And you had your occasions with the respectable women, watching out for the married ones because a man who shot a cop having it off with his wife was likely to have the edge in court. You couldn't go talking about law and order standing there bare-assed in some gazoony's bedroom. It wouldn't have been right.

But the truth was, anybody wanted to know, he'd partaken

less rather than more. He certainly hadn't been as eager for it as Wally Dubrowski, just to name one.

Even after Flo started getting the idea in her head that Helen's sickness was God's punishment, he'd strayed very rarely. Even after he'd started booking the entertainment for the smokers and stags down at City Hall.

Elvira Leeds, the madam he did business with, said it was because the Catholic Church had him by the balls and maybe she was right.

Or maybe it was just because he wanted something more than a professional treatment or the sneaky sex you could have with a married woman, and building up some decent girl with a lot of honey cake about how your wife'd turned the faucet off on you—true as it might have been—was a lousy thing to do. You'd get some poor woman out there hanging on a hook, both of you maybe believing that what you said about settling it with the wife was true when you said it, both of you knowing the Catholic training was part of the whole setup, something not easily cast aside, especially when you had a daughter who was mental. That had to be considered.

What you wanted was somebody you could have a relationship with. True, it started with wanting the body but after a while even the most exciting body in the world got a little stale. It was conversation you wanted sometimes and not the other.

So what had he been thinking of when he took up with Roma Chounard, who was a colored hooker, no matter how you tried to slice it? At first all it was supposed to be was satisfaction. Then it was jealousy. The thought of her doing things to another man—other men—drove him nuts.

So he'd gone to cut one deal with Tourette, saw Roma, and right then and there added a little something. Asked Tourette to keep an eye on his interests over to Orchid's enterprise, not because he needed anybody to measure the take but because you ask somebody to watch your wallet it makes him think you're friends. Just so he could see Roma when he wanted and, later on, so he could move her around a little, take her out of the business bit by bit.

She'd never been on the streets in Chicago but she'd been on the Rolodex and available for parties and appointments.

He'd stopped that. He'd pushed it and paid for it one way and another until he had her in the flat on Artesian. She'd accepted it because she'd been told by Tourette to accept it. Sharkey thought she might even enjoy it a little. It was a nice, lazy way to make a living, waiting for just one man to stop by.

She acted like she had no trouble with that. She wasn't locked up. She had her girlfriends to go shopping with. She went to Tourette's parties, so she wasn't his prisoner.

He was the one that was having trouble with the arrangement. She was there, ready to do what he asked her to do, once a week, twice a week, every night, during the day. Talk to him, watch television with him, take drives with him, drain him dry with her educated mouth and pussy, sleep next to him if he wanted to stay over—which was what he wanted more and more.

She'd told him more than once, more than twice, that he'd picked a nigger mistress because she wouldn't, couldn't, make severe demands on him. Wouldn't demand to be taken to a restaurant in the Loop, or to a political dinner. Didn't insist that he introduce her to his family and friends.

So he'd gotten his hands on exactly what he'd thought he wanted and now he didn't know what he wanted anymore.

Because he also wanted a wife, or at least a woman to take the place of the wife who was dying, and a black whore wouldn't do for that.

If he wanted out, she said, that was all right with her. She never thought that what they were doing was more than temporary. She was surprised that it had lasted as long as it had, in fact. So anytime he wanted to make a new arrangement, that would be hunky-dory with her, she said, and then went about ensnaring him in a hundred subtle ways. Playing whore's games on him, making him needy for her when he didn't want to be needy.

At least that was the suspicion he had. She'd found a butter tub to stick her ass in and didn't want to give it up. He could understand that.

Once, maybe twice, he even thought that maybe she'd come to care about him a little bit. Sometimes when she was sweet and kind above and beyond the call of duty. Never mind love. Who the hell knew what love was? But maybe she'd come to care just a little and that was more than he was getting from any other woman, except maybe his sister Della.

Sunday was gone, but it was still light by the time Sharkey got back to Chicago.

He stood outside the door to the flat he provided for Roma—the kind of accommodation they used to call a love nest in the tabloids—waiting and listening, wondering as he always wondered practically every night if Roma would still be there when he put his key into the lock and opened the door and stepped inside. And if she was inside, who would she be? What part would she be playing? The black, cat-eyed New Orleans whore who liked to play whore's games? Sometimes a nurse, sometimes a schoolgirl, sometimes a foreigner who didn't understand English, sometimes a cock-teaser. Putting him on, showing her amused contempt for the white Irish cop who'd gotten himself hooked on a hooker.

Once inside the flat he was struck by the quiet. The heavy drapes of bright colored cloth she'd hung at the windows closed out the street sounds, except for the insistent driving beat of a boom box down in the street and the occasional screech of brakes.

It had the remoteness of an empty chapel, the impersonal chill of a surgery, the odd, lingering echoes of a morgue, all the color muted in the shadows, all turned to purple and mauve.

His heels were as sharp as gunshots on the hardwood floor of the entry hall. He hung his hat and coat in the closet. One of the colorful shawls she sometimes wore draped about her body instead of a robe hung from the hook. He took a handful of it and covered his nose and mouth, closing his eyes, smelling her smell, allowing himself a moment of passion, the passion he tried never to show her. He walked from the wood to the carpets layered on the floor of the living room and pulled up short, startled by her appearance at the window, the drape held aside with one hand held high, staring down into the street, his instinct for empty places failing him that time.

She didn't move, though she clearly knew that he was there. It was in the way she held herself, her elegant back straight above her hips as though she were reaching for the ceiling with her whole body, forming a little arc of tension just there, where the buttocks began to swell, breasts tautly thrusting against the thin, clinging material of a dress the color of cigar ash. A dress he vaguely remembered buying for her. An expensive dress, worn a few times, then tired of. Thrust to the back of the closet until she might stumble upon it one day and pretend to herself that it was something new.

"Going out?" he asked.

"Thinking about it."

He had a half-erection curving out in front of him, pushing against his underwear. He walked up behind her and settled it in the separation of her ass.

She shifted, relaxing her knees slightly, then jerking them straight, locking him out.

"Seeing your wife got you horny, Ray?" she said.

"What?"

"I got friends work in the hospitals. They're horny all the time. They say it's from being around the sick and dying."

Trying to shame him, ridicule him.

"You don't have to say things like that," he said.

She laughed, a low chuckle deep in her throat, like the purring of a cat.

He pressed harder against her. She refused to relax but had to give way so that her thighs leaned hard against the window sill because she could retreat no farther. He put his chin on her shoulder and looked down at the place where the dress folded over itself, saw the clasp on the hip and put his hand there to open it.

"No," she said. "No."

His fingers were clumsy at the fitting. She made no move to stop him physically, to push his hand away, but kept her arms as they were, one pushing the drape aside and the other lying across her belly, the elbow leaning on her hip.

"Sonofabitch, Roma. Always the fucking games."

He fought the closure, ripped it loose, pulled the end of the loosened panel. Pulled it hard, spinning her around in spite of her struggles, the cloth tearing, her saying, "No," over and over again in a flat, uninflected voice, her eyes veiled as though her mind were fleeing elsewhere, one hand slapping at his face, the other flailing around behind her looking for an exit. She found the pull and the drape opened, caught, held by their bodies until she thrust against him, forcing him back a step, and then opened with a rush. The drapes rushing open to reveal them to anyone in any of the flats in the building across the street.

When she wouldn't cooperate, he ripped the dress along the seams, tore off her bra, and lifted her onto the sill, so that her toes were bent, just touching the floor, her shoes kicked off somehow, her legs stockingless, her buttocks spreading, her back against the cold window glass.

He unzipped his fly and released himself, awkwardly pulling his testicles through the opening in his underwear, giving himself room, fingering the sheer ribbon of nylon between her thighs, covering her treasure, planting his feet on the carpet, giving himself purchase, entering her, her moans and protests hammering at him, driving him to greater effort.

He felt manipulated, which was exactly how she meant him to feel, the whore making him pay the price for trading Tourette a place at the table for her. Making herself a fucking cross to bear. An Irishman's punishment.

He came too soon, letting go of her, letting her slide off the sill, her heels touching the floor, thighs trembling against him, eyes brightly seeing now, staring at him with cool contempt.

"Well, didn't we give the neighborhood a show?" she said. "How about I make some supper or you want to go out for some soul food?"

She turned away from him, waiting until he stepped back so that not even her hip should brush against him. She closed the drapes, then sidled past him in the narrow space between his body and the window.

"I've been thinking. It doesn't have to be this way," Sharkey said.

"What way is that?"

"You acting like you're nothing but a kept woman. Like all I'm doing is paying for your time."

She gave him a long look, slanting and unreadable.

"I'll go make some supper."

22

THE PHANTOM LIMB OFTEN AWAKENED HIM IN THE EMPTY DARK hours of early morning.

Michael Francis Sharkey was the second brother, younger by a year than Ray, but just a trifle taller and broader, a little thicker all around. Heavier shoulders and heavier thighs.

The same red hair gone white. The same smile, if a little more wistful and etched with pain. The same blue eyes, if a little less alert, more thoughtful, dreamier.

He was sometimes mistaken for Ray. When together, people often took them for twins at first glance.

Sometimes the stump was hot to the touch, fever raging along a leg no longer there, concentrating in the shortened thigh, bringing back the old fear of infection.

He grasped it in his two hands, willing it to go away, then looked at his hands in the dim light of the bedside lamp, staring at the scars and shortened tendons produced by so many years gripping the fletching knife. Remembering the day that had cost him his job and his leg and nearly cost him his life. Trying to turn his thoughts away. But no matter how much he tried to divert the mind it insisted on probing the most painful wounds, worrying the bones of things that couldn't be changed, endlessly at war with the dead past.

A past that couldn't be retrieved.

No way to bring back and change the day when he'd intervened in the fight between Owney Farrel, the fastest pig decapitator in the plant, and the quiet black man from Georgia, Buddy Doll, flashing knives there on the blood-and-grease–slick floor of the hog-butchering shed, tempers exploding for no reason except the work left them irritable and weary and pain-racked. Stepping in the way he did and taking the accidental knife slash high on his leg, near the groin, the razor-sharp blade slicing through leather apron and denim jeans, cutting off one of his balls as slick as a surgeon's scalpel and dropping it into his rubber wading boot, giving him the infection that took his leg.

That kind of looking back burned and tortured.

There was another kind, sweetly melancholy, manufactured memories of places unvisited, pleasures unfelt, women never experienced, bushel baskets of lost opportunities. Out of those, at least, you could weave comforting fantasies which might become fact if dreamed often enough and hard enough.

It occurred to him, that minute, that second, with his hands holding in the pain and fever of the phantom limb, that it was well after dawn, well into the next day and it was now his birthday.

There would be cards and greetings in his mailbox, sitting there from the end of the week before.

There'd be a card from Gabe and a note enclosed quoting from the Bible, a strangely cold sort of greeting, seeming more an attempt to lure him back to the church than to wish him a happy birthday.

The one from Jerry and his family would be funny, some insulting remark about growing long in the tooth and short in the pecker, something like that, bawdy jokes which went to prove that the Judge was neither stern nor humorless when off the bench.

Ray's would be outrageously sentimental, the inscription florid, smacking of Irish honey cake, not to be taken seriously, a sort of generic expression of love Ray poured over everything having to do with family, keeping his secret heart secret. Not once, not even when young boys and men, spending nearly all their time together, fighting and fucking (what little there was of that), together, had they ever had one long, revealing, truly intimate conversation.

Most of the greetings and remembrances would be from the women of the family. All the aunts and nieces and cousins. One from Della, as oddly formal as a message from a stranger. Della no stranger to the vow of secrecy as well, never letting anyone lift a corner of her dreaming life.

A card with a note from Wilda, maybe, mailed from some city far away, pouring out her heart in as many lines as would fit on it, even lines filling up the margins for lack of room. She was the only one who wanted to come close, to get inside your head, inside your heart, and asking you do so the same with her. Never finding what she wanted . . . needed.

First thing in the morning he'd have to check his mailbox.

Ah, for Christ's sake, where had it all gone? How had it happened that he'd never married, never lived with anyone? How had he ended up in a room that smelled of medicine and old books?

"Well, every man his cross to bear," he said aloud.

He pulled out the drawer of the bedside table and got out his daybook (black and white marbled cardboard covers, blue-lined pages, used to cost a nickel years ago, fifty-nine cents now, for God's sake), in which he kept a record of his weekly expenditures for food, medication, rent, electricity, and other necessities. Sometimes he tried to compose a verse, thinking of the attempt with a certain amount of shame, as though contemptuous of something with which teenage girls and love-sick youths wasted their time. He found a pencil and the page upon which he'd been slowly and with great difficulty composing a poem.

Its title was "Birthday."

There were eight lines, some of them crossed out with heavy, angry, frustrated scratches, some words no more than illegible scrawls. He went to a dog-eared paperback dictionary frequently as he labored on it, plucking out words that suited which he would never have spoken in everyday conversation, but reaching for something all the same, hearing a certain rightness in the rhythms when he spoke the lines aloud.

Finally he seemed satisfied. At least for that day.

Today I harvested last year's crop of melancholy,
Packed it away beside diaries sugared with dust,
Rustling with shadows,
Pictures of footprints left on the meadow.
Baled them and boxed them, memories of nights all gone to seed.
Lonely and loveless, fit only for journals.
Pages and pages tied with old string.
Birds frozen in Winter, buried in Spring.

"Fucking lonely, womanless, bastard Irish poet," he said aloud, not entirely unpleased with himself.

He often talked to himself in his furnished room, which, though it was filled with clutter, had the air of a monk's cell, austere and stark, no pictures on the walls, no curtains at the windows, no cloth on the table, smelling sharply medicinal. The green shades drawn during most of the day, living in perpetual gloom (the bottom of a pond), reading his books, formulating the thoughts he rarely bothered to convey to another human being except on those rare occasions when Wilda came home to visit for a while. Understanding the language in them but unable to put them on his tongue.

He hopped to the window and let up the shade. The sun was sending long shadows along the street, the gutters clogged with the rotting leaves of the autumn gone and past.

A woman in a cloth coat with a fur collar, wearing a cloche hat like one that might be worn by a ghost from the thirties, her gloved hands clutching the cloth at her throat, stamping her feet against the cold, was looking at his window. She turned away and Michael saw a glint of red hair, and then she turned back, knowing she'd been seen, smiled, waved, and started to run toward his building.

Wilda was home again.

He motioned her to come in and, grabbing his crutches, went first to open the door to his flat and then the inner door to the vestibule.

Wilda flew into his arms, nearly knocking him down, him standing there in the underwear in which he'd slept, feeling the cold air cooling the feverish stump of his lost leg.

Inside the flat, Wilda looked around, her face glowing with the cold and her excitement, filling the place with the uncommon energy, the air of expectation, even of danger and high adventure, that was the public posture she shared in common with Ray, as Michael struggled into a robe.

"What were you doing standing out there in the cold?" he asked. "You want a toddy?"

"Well, I couldn't sleep. I was riding the buses and got off at your stop. Then I realized what time it was and I wasn't sure you'd be awake. Isn't it a little early in the morning for a drink?"

"So, if I wasn't awake, you'd wake me. All I'm offering is a little something to warm you up. Your nose is white. It'll fall off. When did you get back in town?"

"I didn't want to wake you up so early. Okay, a short one."

He humped his way into the tiny kitchenette and put the kettle on to boil.

"Anytime you can't sleep and you're feeling blue, all you got to do is come on over," he said. "How long you been home?"

"Well, I mean, I was going to give you a jingle. I was going to let you know I was back in town."

"It don't matter. It don't matter at all. Don't you know how goddamn glad I am to see my sister, day or night? I want you to call me anytime you start feeling blue. So, how long do you think you'll be staying this time?"

"I don't know. Maybe for good."

He turned away, getting the whiskey bottle and the glasses and the sugar bowl, and looked at her over his shoulder.

"You mean that, Wilda?"

"Would it make you happy?"

"What do you think?"

He put a shot of whiskey in each glass and added another to his own. He muddled a teaspoonful of sugar into the whiskey and then added the water, which was steaming but not yet boiling. He went to the little refrigerator and found a lemon, cut off a slice of the part that had dried up and squeezed a little juice into each glass. Then he stirred both drinks and wrapped a folded paper towel around Wilda's glass before handing it to her.

"Don't want to burn your hand," he said.

She could've cried at the sweetness of the man. He was forever doing thoughtful little things like that. For a second she thought about how nice it might be setting up housekeeping for him, taking care of him, going out to work and coming home to cook him dinner. They could sit in front of the television and make rude remarks about the actors and actresses, about their sex lives, like Pop and Della did practically every night. Della and the old man. Wilda and the crippled brother. Irish couples.

"Take the easy chair," Michael said, dragging a wooden kitchen chair across the rug for himself, juggling crutches, glasses, and chair expertly, through long practice. He sat down, took a swallow of the toddy, made a sound of appreciation, then settled back, looking around the shabby flat as though he'd never seen it before.

"It's not so bad," she said, as though reading his mind, as though he'd apologized for the place aloud.

"I'm not the neatest person in the world."

"Well, you've got good reason," she said, and then wanted to bite her tongue, realizing how he might take it, her saying that he was handicapped after all.

But he didn't remark on it, just smiled softly and took another sip.

All of a sudden she jumped out of the easy chair and hugged him and kissed him. Still holding her glass, she snuggled onto the kitchen chair alongside him.

"How have you been keeping?" she asked, her arm around his neck, smiling into his face.

"Well, you know, I don't go out too often."

"You should."

"Yes. How about you?"

"Oh, I *do* go out too often. I go out all the time. I can't stay home no matter where I'm living. I try to stay home, watch the television, read a book, when I get home from work, but I can't stand it. I can't stand having nobody to talk to."

"Did you go out a lot when you were married?"

"Well, you know Carrigan. He was never home himself."

"Too bad I never had a chance to meet him."

"You wouldn't have liked him," she said, getting up off the kitchen chair and taking the easy chair again. "It wasn't working out."

For a second Michael didn't know if she was talking about Wilda's marriage, which had failed, or her trying to share the chair with him.

"It wasn't much of a marriage, even from the beginning," she said. "Ray met him once."

"He told me."

"When he came back from that cop's convention in New York?"

"That's right."

"They didn't like each other much."

"I got an idea Ray wouldn't like any man you decided to marry."

"He doesn't like any man I even say hello to. He's the most jealous brother I ever heard about. You'd think we were lovers or something."

That remark struck a strange, hollow note. It seemed to flutter up into the corner of the room and hide itself in the cobwebs there.

"You're not interested in getting married again?" Michael asked.

"Oh, I'm interested," she said, "but I've had so many bad experiences when I try to have a long-term relationship that I'm afraid. Hey, I'm not saying that I'm a one-night stand. I'm not easy. Oh no. When I go out, I'm not looking to meet a man, except for maybe a little conversation. I just go out someplace where there's some music. A little life. You know?"

Michael nodded and smiled and she jumped up and leaned over to hug him again as though afraid he'd disappear if she didn't touch him every so often.

"Ray doesn't understand that," she said.

"Sure, he does."

"No, he doesn't understand I like good music. I've got a lot of friends who are musicians. All over the country. Musicians who play jazz, you know? I love jazz. I don't like all this new stuff, hard metal, acid rock, rock-a-billy, country-western. I mean it's just a lot of noise, isn't it? I like the old blues, the old jazz. Ray doesn't understand that."

"Sure, he does," Michael said again.

"No, he doesn't, goddammit," she said, sitting down on the footstool beside Michael's chair. "He doesn't understand that a lot of the jazz musicians are black. He hates it that I've got all these black friends."

So that's what the argument Ray'd had with Wilda back in New York had been all about, Michael thought. It hadn't been about her husband, Carrigan. At least not entirely. Ray was one of those closet bigots who made remarks like, "Some of my best friends are colored," and, "I've walked a beat with niggra men and let me tell you, I'd as soon have one of them beside me walking into a fight than some greaser or guido." He'd drink with them, even sit down and eat with them, talking in the soft syncopated rhythms in which they spoke when in friendly celebrations, and, Michael supposed, he'd even gone to bed with a black woman more than once, more than twice, but just the thought of any black hand on the white skin of any woman in the family—on Wilda's milk-white skin—would surely be enough to throw him into a rage.

"Well, Carrigan wasn't black, was he?" Michael said, trying to make a joke.

"Black Irish is what that sonofabitch was," she said.

She jumped up off the footstool, leaning over to hug and kiss him again.

"You know what I was thinking, Michael?"

"What was you thinking?"

"I was thinking, if I decide to stay put right here in Chicago this time, you and me, maybe we could get ourselves a bigger flat. You know, three or four rooms with a real kitchen and maybe even two bathrooms. Though we could get along with one. We got along with one bathroom, the whole family, eight of us when we were small."

"When are you going to tell Pop and Della and Ray that you're back home?"

"Listen to me. Listen to me. Listen to this idea I've got."

He listened to her dream the dream she dreamed aloud each and every time she came back to Chicago. After a while, even though he'd heard it many times before, this time he began to believe it. He made a comment now and then and, pretty soon, they both were sure it could really happen this time. She'd stay put. To the benefit of all.

23

YOU DIDN'T HAVE TO BE A BRAIN TO FIGURE OUT WHY THEY called the night clerk Big Mamoo. She made Dubrowski look like a midget. She was nearly four hundred pounds, a mound of flesh who half-filled the tiny hotel room, sitting in a huge chair, reinforced with steel bars, shoved up against the window that framed her head.

She had bleached her kinky hair until it shone like phosphorus, a pile of dead leaves and pale yellow straw piled on top of her head. It contrasted harshly with her mottled brown skin, rouged cheeks, carmined lips, penciled eyebrows, and violet eye shadow sprinkled with glitter.

"Hello there, Officer Sharkey," she said in a husky voice. "Hello, there, you old motherfucker."

Sharkey frowned, started to laugh in shocked surprise, caught it in time and choked it back, felt the anger rising up in his chest, the color flooding his face. He felt Dubrowski's hand on his arm, restraining him, keeping him from smashing the grotesque creature in the face.

Except there was something in the way Big Mamoo had greeted him. Except the inflection of the word had been the way old friends used it against one another. Except it came to him with a second shock of recognition that the monstrous she wasn't a she and he knew it was somebody from the past.

"Virgil," she said. "Don' you remember Virgil from way back, from on the streets down by Cabrini-Green when you was a little man in blue?"

"Ah, ah, ah," Sharkey said, probing the past, tickling his memory, spinning the Rolodex like a prayer wheel.

"Vir-gil Hath-a-way, the man with the 'M' for mothafucka on his baseball cap," Big Mamoo said.

"Ah, Jesus Christ," Sharkey said, "I can't believe my eyes. What have we got here? It's ten months until Halloween."

"Oh, it's me, all right. This is me. This is who I am," Big Mamoo said softly.

He'd once been just a big, grinning teenager and Ray had been an easygoing cop, with a way of making people like him, even when he was busting them, putting the cuffs on them, kicking their feet apart as they leaned against a wall.

He joked and kidded around, as though what he was doing—but didn't want to be doing—was just part of a job which embarrassed him. He made out as if he and the person or persons he was arresting were buddies, pals, *compadres*, dancing the dance—the old two-step—to keep the boss man contented, keep him looking the other way.

"What we got here is a little difference of opinion, Virgil," he said, as he put the cuffs on a colored boy, sixteen years old, as big as the side of a house. "Wouldn't you say that's what we got here?"

"Shitfuck," Virgil said, disgusted with the whole affair. "What I want to steal his fuckin' woman for? I got womans of my own. I got more womans than I can manage."

"Wait a minute here, Virgil, you telling me you're a pimp? I don't want you to go telling me you're a pimp. I don't want you to go telling me you make your livelihood from the bodies of girls and women."

"I ain' no pimp, I's a *lover,*" Virgil said, showing his teeth, laughing like hell, his hands cuffed behind his back, doing the two-step, bouncing his head, knocking the baseball cap with a big initial *M* off his head.

Ray picked up the hat, brushed it off, made Virgil stop dancing, and put the cap back on his head just so.

"What's the *M* stand for, Virgil? It don't stand for Montreal, does it? It don't stand for Minnesota, does it?"

Virgil laughed.

"So tell me what it stands for."

Somebody from the crowd watching Virgil getting rousted said, "Stands for mafia, stands for murder."

"Stands for *may-hem,*" Virgil said.

"Where you learn a word like mayhem, Virgil? You go back to school?"

"Fuck school," said Virgil.

"Maybe *M* stands for motherfucker," Chick Minifee, Ray's partner, said, grinning from ear to ear, wanting to have the same soft, easy camaraderie with these people that he saw Ray enjoyed. Not understanding a bit of what was going on, the dance that was taking place between Ray and Virgil, while the other big black kid—the offended party—and the woman who had been the cause of the dispute looked on.

The crowd, having fun, watched like hawks, touchy as a collection of open wounds, waiting for the white cops to put their feet wrong but enjoying the dozens all the same.

"So does it stand for motherfucker?" Minifee asked again.

Ray winced and moved in close on Virgil, who was giving Minifee a cold, hard look. He pushed into him as though they were brothers and Ray wanted to soothe his anger with his touch.

"Don't listen to the fool," he murmured.

"Who the fuck he think he be?" Virgil murmured back. "Don't even know when to call a man a motherfucker, when not to call a man a motherfucker."

"He's not calling *you* a motherfucker. He thinks he's making a joke about the *M* on your cap."

"So fuck him, then," Virgil said.

"I'd say so, except I got to walk a beat with him eight hours a day, five days, sometimes six days, a week."

"Poor you."

"Oh, well, we got to do what we got to do. That right, Virgil?"

Virgil nodded, considerably calmed by the soft, slurred sound of the young Irish cop's voice.

"Now, I'm going over and have a word with the complainant," Ray said.

"Who what?"

"Your friend who blew the whistle on you. Going to see

what we can figure out here. Save ourselves a trip. Now, you promise me you're not going to escape on me?"

"Shitfuck," Virgil said, twisting his body around so the cop who put the cuffs on him could see what he'd done to an innocent boy. "How I gonna 'scape wid dese?"

"I know you, Virgil. I know you're a sly man. I know you can turn yourself into a shadow. I know you slip and slide through the cracks in the sidewalk. I know you are a clever motherfucker."

Virgil laughed again, one brother to another.

But, as time went on, Virgil hadn't been so clever. More than once, more than twice, he'd failed to slip and slide through the cracks in the sidewalk and he'd ended up in the slam.

Sharkey stood there, looking down at the weird mountain of flesh, and wondered if the Virgil who'd had so many "womans" of his own when not much more than a boy had been turned easy or hard up there among the animals.

"I'll be a sonofabitch," Sharkey said, amazed at what had become of Virgil but not too much dismayed at meeting him again after so many years. It was the kind of thing that happened often in the city. It was the kind of thing that happened practically every day in the confines of the half-world in which cops and crooks lived and worked. Half-world, small world.

"Hardly room to sit," Big Mamoo said, apologizing for the cramped condition of the room.

"That's all right, you old motherfucker," Sharkey said, "we do the best we can."

He sat down on the bed. Dubrowski remained standing on the other side of the bed, practically in the doorway.

Sharkey and Big Mamoo were sitting so close that their knees were touching.

"We ain't going to fuck around here, are we, Virgil?"

"What, what?" Big Mamoo said, his eyes getting big, drawing his head back as though afraid Sharkey was going to strike him. "You come to talk about that man was beat to death in room 204, ain't you? What've I got to hide about that?"

"Everybody's got something to hide, Virgil. We all know that. I mean, there's the smell of dogshit in a room and somebody asks has anybody got some on their shoe, everybody takes a look and says, no, it ain't me. Why give up the truth when it might cause you some embarrassment, some trouble?"

"You got that right."

"So, I'm asking for your cooperation up front and we start right in chewing on the bone. Okay?" Sharkey said.

Big Mamoo's expression turned sly. "You going to pull that shit about old times' sake?"

"That's what I'm going to pull. Mr. Kendicott tells us that you just came back from visiting your sister over in Cicero."

"That's the truth," Big Mamoo said.

"You visit her often?"

"One night every weekend if I can. It's my one journey out of this place. She comes gets me in her van."

"You visit her last Sunday night?"

"Uh, no. No. Last Sunday night she couldn't make it."

"So, you were on the desk Sunday night?" Dubrowski asked.

"That's right."

"You see the man who got hisself killed?"

"I never saw him check in, so I can't really say who I saw."

"I got a picture. The man's dead but it should give you an idea." Sharkey showed Big Mamoo the morgue photo.

Big Mamoo looked and didn't flinch but when he spoke his voice sounded clogged. "Who could recognize the man from that? That don't look like nothing human."

"You see two men—maybe three men—come in anytime Monday, Tuesday night? One might've looked sick or drunk?"

Big Mamoo hesitated.

"How about Sunday night? How many people caught your special attention getting into the elevator Sunday night?"

"Two. One of them was bent over holding his gut. The other man was helping him. I took them for drunks, one of them ready to be sick."

"What time?"

"Close to midnight."

"You see any blood?"

"Now that you mention, the man doubled over had a handkerchief to his mouth."

"Now that we mention," Dubrowski said, sarcastically.

Big Mamoo gave Dubrowski a look. For a minute he was the tough street kid, all the lady-looks and little flutters blown away. You didn't have to be a brain to read what his eyes were saying. If Dubrowski and another cop had come to ask the questions, they'd have gone away empty. It was only for Sharkey and old times' sake that Big Mamoo was cooperating.

"You didn't ask if anything was wrong? If you could help?" Dubrowski asked, pushing it, responding to the look.

"Not a chance. A woman sticks her nose in somebody's business she better be ready to fuck, fight, or run. I can't fight and I can't run and I only fuck my friend."

"Can you describe the man who wasn't acting sick?" Sharkey asked.

"He was a bulky white fella. Average height. Average coloring. A bone-breaker."

"How'd you know that?" Dubrowski asked, suggesting that Big Mamoo was giving a little so he could hold back a lot.

"What the fuck is it with this man?" Big Mamoo said, looking at Sharkey.

"Okay, Wally, butt out, you don't mind. Let me and my friend here sort this thing out."

"Ah, fachrissake," Dubrowski said, but went to lean against the doorjamb, half in, half out of the room.

"So, how'd you know?" Sharkey asked.

"He was wearing thin leather gloves. The kind that cut."

"But you didn't know him from around?"

"It's a big city and I don't get around like I used to."

Sharkey stood up. "So, is that your best?"

"One other thing," Big Mamoo said. "The bone-breaker was carrying a cardboard box with a sack of something—"

"Kitty Litter."

"—and a hank of clothesline in it. What the hell was he carrying Kitty Litter around for?"

"He was a tidy bone-breaker," Sharkey said.

Big Mamoo sighed heavily at the marvel of it all. "There's something else."

Sharkey waited.

"While I was paying attention to the two of them, I got the impression that somebody might've come through the side door—the one by the tobacco stand—and flitted up the side stairs."

"You got a look?"

"I got an impression. I turned my head and I caught a foot out of the corner of my eye."

"What kind of foot?"

"Well, I don't know—"

"Describe to me this foot you think you saw," Sharkey said.

Big Mamoo laughed. "You want me to describe a foot?"

Sharkey laughed right along with him. "Was it naked? Was it in a sneaker? Was it—"

"It was in a running shoe, I think."

Both of them laughing like a couple of kids sharing a secret joke.

"One of those flashy colored ones. Red and yellow. Something like that."

"You didn't think that was funny, somebody running up the stairs?" Sharkey asked.

"Nothing seems funny to me around here," Big Mamoo said, laughing, his whole body shaking. "People use the stairs all the time."

Sharkey controlled his laughter, wiped his eyes, stuck out his hand. "Thanks, Virgil."

"Big Mamoo."

"Whatever makes you happy."

"I just put myself in harm's way," Big Mamoo said, all the laughter gone like a blown-out match. "You understand that?"

"If you're alive you're in harm's way," Sharkey said.

"That's bullshit. You sound like an Irish priest. I'm talking about the odds on getting across the street if you're damned fool enough to walk against the light."

Sharkey held up a hand, saying he understood, saying he wished Big Mamoo peace, saying that they were friends if not brothers.

"Go easy on Orville, will you, Sharkey?" Big Mamoo said. "He told me you just pushed at him and pushed at him and treated him like a nigger. You scared him and that made him feel small."

"We were just working the game."

"I understand. Now I want you to understand. Him and me is lovers."

Sharkey and Dubrowski didn't comment.

"He don't know his she's a he," Big Mamoo went on, suddenly smiling.

"How the hell you work that?" Sharkey asked.

"A man with as many folds and creases as me, who knows how to pike his pecker, he got a dozen ways. And, Sharkey? You'll keep my secret, won't you?"

Sharkey held up his hand again.

Christ, you know a man for twenty-five years you don't need to speak.

24

"WHY'D YOU TALK TO ME LIKE THAT IN FRONT OF THE NIGGER?" Dubrowski asked, anger still mottling his cheeks.

"You were going to shut him up. You were pissing him off," Sharkey said.

"The day comes I got to worry about pissing off some faggot monster'll be the day I turn in my fucking badge."

"There was no profit in it. You want to hurt a man because there's profit in it, okay. But you were doing it just to tear the wings off that poor motherfucking fly."

"That asshole sees a man, doubled over, handkerchief to his mouth, going up on the elevator with another he takes for a bone-breaker, lugging a hank of clothesline, and he don't even call the police?"

"Virgil's relationship with the police ain't been exactly cordial."

"Sometimes I think you're two parts nigger," Dubrowski said.

"How's that?" Sharkey replied.

"The way you talk their lingo."

"Well, yes, it's a talent."

"I don't understand it."

"Exactly what don't you understand?"

"Where you learned their lingo."

"Out on the streets. When I walked a beat. Minifee and me. He never could learn the trick either. You've got to listen. You've got to have an ear. It's the inclination of the syllable, the intonation of the emphasis, the accent on the positive note," Sharkey said.

"Cut the shit."

"You think I'm kidding you? I ain't kidding you. It ain't what you say, it's the way that you say it. Like you say 'mothafucka' like that. That tells the man you're confronting that you are about to say bad things about him, do bad things to him, if he don't stop doing whatever's he's doing which is getting you on edge.

"You say 'motherfucker' real fast, clipped at the end like that," Sharkey went on. "You hear what I say? You hear how I say it? 'Motherfucker.' That means you are casting him an insult of the third degree. This is not yet a knifing offense but it's escalating the tension.

"Now you say 'mother-fucker,' two separate words like that, accent on the first syllable, and you are now at a second-degree incitement," Sharkey said. "When you get to 'moth-a-fuck-a' you have overstepped. You have got an angry opponent on your hands. It is time to flee or fight."

Dubrowski was frowning, taking it all in.

"On another occasion you might say 'mmmmmmmotha-fucker,' giving it lots of *m*. That shows appreciation for something this other dude's said or done.

" 'Moth*er*-fuck*er*,' heavy on the *ers*," Sharkey said, "and you've got an expression of doubt or incredulity. String it out another second and you got dismay. Another second more and you got a situation where you're calling the other man a liar and you are dangerously close to 'moth-a-fuck-a.'

"Also you have the high-pitched 'motherfucker' expressing joy," Sharkey said, "and the growling 'motherfucker' which is like puppies playing. A playful threat, you understand?"

"I think you're pulling my leg," Dubrowski said.

"Not I, motherfucker," Sharkey said.

"I say you're a silver-tongued Irish sonofabitch and I say you're pulling my leg," Dubrowski said, all his anger and irritation drained away, the insult to his pride forgiven if not forgotten.

"See, there you go," Sharkey said, "you call me a sonofabitch and I smile. Because you said it a certain way. You say it another way and I'd have to punch you in the mouth."

"You still ain't told me where you learned all this crap."

"I used to box them in the ring. I'm the one who busted Leroy Scarlet's jaw over to the Legion Hall one Friday night."

"That's right," Dubrowski said. "I remember that fight."

Everybody remembered that fight, a local legend, nearly forty years old.

"So, you had a good lunch?" Sharkey asked.

"Not bad," Dubrowski replied.

"What did you have?"

"Some antipasto. A plate of lasagna. A little linguini with mussles. A couple glasses of wine."

"Fachrissake, do you hear yourself? What's the matter with you, eating like that? No wonder everybody calls you Moby Dick. You know what's this Moby Dick?"

"Sure, I know. He's a fucking whale, right? Whale's got a ding-dong on him like a telephone pole, right? The whores ask me how come the other cops call me Moby Dick, I tell 'em because I got a ding-dong like a fucking whale. It gives me a reputation."

"What happens when they find out you can't measure up to the advertisement?"

"Well, it's too late by then, ain't it? Fachrissakes, Sharkey, use your head."

They were slapping it back and forth like partners, like friends, and Dubrowski was feeling very good about it.

"Hey, if I didn't tell you when you told me, I'm very sorry about the Vicks VapoRub and your camel hair."

"You told me."

"I'll pay for the cleaning."

"You told me that, too. Forget it."

Sharkey was also feeling pretty good.

"You want to have some lunch?" Dubrowski asked.

"After what you just told me you ate, you want to eat again? It's a no. I got a date for lunch. Hey, I really mean I got a date. Tomorrow we'll have lunch. I'll meet you back here in an hour and a half, two hours. You take the car."

"I know, I know. You'll grab a cab."

"I'll grab a bus back to the station and get my car. Who the hell can afford a cab? Hey. Maybe tomorrow we'll have lunch."

25

ELVIRA LEEDS WAS LYING IN BED, NAKED. ENGLISH ACCENT, milkmaid's skin, plump titties like two pouter pigeons, fine blond hair like baby down between her lemon-curd thighs. The last of the courtesans, she called herself, no whore she.

She was making phone calls, lining up the women for a private stag in honor of Bobby Hennessy, a party stalwart, sixty-seven years of age, who was getting ready to tie the knot for the fifth time.

It was scheduled for Friday night.

Sharkey sat on his tailbone, slouched down in a pink satin slipper chair, his fedora tipped forward, shading his eyes, his stained tweed topcoat thrown open, legs spread, feeling the hint of a hard-on. Wondering if he should partake of Elvira's ice-cream pussy for old times' sake. Wondering if she was offended or merely relieved that he'd stopped making demands on her for a freebie ever since he'd taken up with what Elvira called his chocolate drop. He'd never told her about Roma, but you could be sure that there were no secrets among pimps and whores.

He'd been using Elvira for the City Hall smokers and stags since as far back as he could remember. She never seemed to age, so he could pretend he hadn't aged when he sat with her in her candy box bedroom.

He listened to the conversations as Elvira sold her subcontractors on the benefits of partying with a bunch of city and county top cops, some of the City Hall crowd, a couple of the big cigars from the Cook County Central Committee of the Regular Democratic Organization.

"They're looking for pretty," Elvira said. "They're looking for an evening's companionship. They're looking for intelligence and good conversation. Ladies who know how to listen.

Yes, it's a bachelor party but that doesn't mean they expect you to strip down the minute you walk through the door. They got a tippy-tap dancer with a trick crotch to do the public entertaining. It's practically a political do, for heaven's sake. After the cocktails? After's what comes after the cocktails. Yes, it might well be that one of these gentlemen asks for a little private consultation. Maybe a quiet hotel room. No foursomes, fivesomes. No high-wire acts. No vaudeville turns. They're not into music hall. No lesbian acts, no."

She looked at Sharkey and raised an eyebrow. He shrugged. She shook her head, pretending annoyance, yet smiling. "Well, you never can tell about men, even cops and sheriffs, now can you? Kinky sex? That all depends. Some six-and-a-half-foot chief of detectives wants to put on a girl's panties, put on her bra, and dance around, how serious can that be? No, no, no. No third degree. No punching and kicking or burning with cigarettes or cigars. I think I can guarantee that."

She glanced at Sharkey and he made a face of outrage and astonishment.

"I can guarantee that," Elvira went on. "Well, if a six-and-a-half-foot chief of detectives rips the back off a bra, the crotch out of a pair of panties, of course there will be a clothing allowance. My God, I'm not a bookkeeper. Perhaps you'll have to voucher for it. What difference does that make?"

Sharkey shook his head and held up his hand with a little space between thumb and finger.

"Petty cash. Any damage will be paid for out of petty cash. These are executives, Darnell, after all. They know all about contingency funds. So, can I count on you? Friday night. This Friday night coming. Well, if you have a regular on Friday nights he should be more understanding and make allowances for a special event like this. My client pays top rates. You know that. Bonuses? Well, bonuses if it turns out there are reasons for bonuses but you can't expect me to make extra presents part of the guarantee. The usual favor, however, is part of the offer. Two free busts, you get picked up soliciting. Well, I know you don't make a habit getting picked up soliciting. Don't I know that? You got how many saved up? Eight. My God, you've been working for this client a lot, haven't you." She laughed. "So maybe you could murder somebody you don't like and cash them in all at once."

She hung up and, making a small funnel of her lower lip, blew the soft blond hair out of her eyes.

"I don't know if your business is worth the trouble, Ray," she said.

"What the hell you talking about? You were on the streets twenty years ago. I made your reputation."

"I'm not saying that's not true but, on the other hand, you might say that I made yours as well."

She squirmed a little, getting settled against the pillows, and veiled her eyes.

"You want a little refreshment, Ray?"

He pushed himself off the back of his neck and straightened up in the chair.

"I was up to see my wife," he said, as though that was an answer to her question.

She didn't have to be told what restrictions that imposed upon him. Catholic sins and prohibitions had to be sliced with a razor. But it wasn't only that. With everything available to him you'd think Ray Sharkey would be, would've always been, a greedy taster, the prince of one-night stands, but he'd never been like that. The oddly comforting thing about being with Ray—when she'd been with Ray—was that a woman knew she was the only one he was having anything to do with while they were doing it together. And now, with the brown lady in his life, he was as true to her as he'd once been to Elvira.

The wife, sick or well, always there in the background, of course.

She studied his Irish Catholic face, always scrubbed and shiny. It bore the curious innocence of the emotionally uncommitted, men who lived in the service of a peculiar honor, mysteriously defined.

"Are you going to be at the party, Ray?" she asked.

"Well, I'll stay long enough to see that things are going smooth like I usually do."

"Why don't you stick around for after, save me from the attention of strangers?"

"I think Mike Tierney took a shine to you last year."

"Is that the man who runs the patronage list for the mayor?"

"That's the man."

"Well, isn't that nice to know."

He stood up and walked to the bedroom door.

"Don't bother getting up," he said.

"I won't."

"By the way. In case there's any commotion at the party, don't worry about it. It'll be under control."

"What kind of commotion?"

"The party could get itself raided."

"You mean like a joke on the bridegroom?"

"Yeah, like that."

"It won't count as one arrest?"

He shook his head.

"Then, that's okay. What's a little commotion? It might even save the girls a little wear and tear."

26

SHARKEY SAT DOWN ON THE EDGE OF THE BED IN THE FLAT HE'D shared with Flo for so many years but scarcely ever dropped into anymore, except to check his answering machine, keeping up the pretense that he still lived there full time.

The pink satin spread and pillow shams, her favorites, cheaply reproduced the look of a courtesan's bedroom, the influence of a thousand motion pictures, misleading advertisements of carnal pleasures denied by the reality. Everything a stage set, nothing quite what it seemed.

Sometimes all you had to go on was instinct, if you meant to escape the seduction of appearances.

And Sharkey's instincts, backed by an accumulation of small evidence, warned him that his life was rushing headlong toward a crisis.

It wasn't just that The Candidate had sicced his little fucking lapdog, Kitty Brennan, on him at a public affair. It was something more, something he couldn't quite put his finger on. He'd have to have a talk with Cavan and find out what his Chinaman could do for him but he had the feeling the answer was going be nothing much. It was always the vague threat of disaster that came true, that blew your heart away.

He had no doubt that Leddy was a tethered goat, staked out for Sharkey to gorge upon. The Candidate and his cronies hoping to catch him with bloody bites of graft dripping from his jaws.

He didn't yet know how Dubrowski fit in. He didn't know if they'd gotten to him. It was hard to tell. Especially when the two of them were working a case together, because when two cops worked a case together other things got shoved aside.

Professionalism, the desire to do the job, was stronger than practically anything he could think of, except love and lust. Even then he felt better working alone than sharing information with another cop.

He reached for the phone and dialed the number he'd looked up on Leddy. A woman answered.

"I want to speak to Frank Leddy," he said.

"To who?"

"To Frankie Blue Shoes."

That seemed to reassure her that a friend was calling.

She told him to hang on. A minute later Leddy was on the phone.

"Who's this?" he asked.

"Sharkey."

"Oh. So you got a time and a place for me?"

"I want you to come to a party."

"You kidding me?"

"No, I ain't kidding you. A friend of mine, Bobby Hennessy . . . you know Bobby Hennessy?"

"Should I know him?"

"Well, he's the man what's getting married and some of his friends are throwing a little stag for him and that's how come I'm inviting you to his party."

"I suppose it'd only be polite if I brought a little gift," Leddy said.

"I was about to say. A gift of money is the custom."

"When, where, and what time?"

"Friday night. Come around midnight. At Schaller's Pump. You know Schaller's Pump?"

"Isn't that the tavern in the Eleventh Ward right across the street from Democratic Headquarters?"

"That's the place. So you can come?"

"I'll make it a point."

"You don't have to stay long, you don't want to. I know what a busy man you are."

"You mean I don't have to stay for the entertainment? All I've got to do is stop by and pay my respects to Bobby Hennessy, drop off my gift, and be on my way?"

"That's up to you. You want to stay for the entertainment, stay for the entertainment. I'm only saying you don't have to. You understand what I mean?"

"Can I bring a friend? I don't like traveling around by myself."

"I can understand that," Sharkey said. "You're afraid of walking around alone on these streets, all the criminal element around. So bring a friend but don't bring an army. If you and this friend got any brains you won't spoil the line of your jackets with anything large and heavy. There's going to be a lot of police officials and police officers at this party and I'm sure you'll agree it wouldn't be smart for you or your friend to be carrying."

"Whatever you say. I'll just walk in, pay my respects, drop off the gift, and walk out."

"That sounds all right to me," Sharkey said. "By the way, would you put your gift in a blue envelope?"

"A blue envelope?"

"It's the custom. You know, blue for the bridegroom?"

"I never heard of that."

"Sure you did. I just told you."

After he hung up, he picked up the receiver again and called around until he got a hold of Connell, the commander of the Cowboys.

27

It was one of those stores that crouch in decaying neighborhoods, in which things seem to grow and multiply until every shelf and counter is choked with merchandise. The kind of enterprise run by immigrant families or some old couple who live in the back rooms, selling a little something of everything as other stores close up from lack of trade or insurance rates that soar after each holdup or broken window.

They start out selling candy, newspapers, and smokes. The next thing you know they're selling milk and dairy products out of a chiller and then some beer. Then they put in a couple of gondolas with packaged goods. Then it's dogfood and a few staples. Then condoms and simple pharmaceuticals.

The business license inspectors cite them for violations. Sanitation comes in and does the same. Building Codes also. They fail to pay the fines. Pretty soon they owe more money than the inventory's worth. If they're closed down a whole neighborhood has to go without the convenience of a place to buy a quart of milk, a pack of rubbers, a pint of hooch, or a snort folded up in an aluminum foil packet.

They're allowed to stay open for humanitarian reasons. The inspectors get together and set a figure. The storekeeper pays the levy every month and the inspectors divide it up. It's a Chicago arrangement.

The owners of the Ace High Groceries and Dairy Store worked eighteen-, twenty-hour days, afraid to close in case some thirsty drunk needed a pint at two o'clock in the morning or some welfare mother needed a bottle of milk for a crying baby at five in the morning or some hoodlum decided to drive by and toss a concrete block through the window. (They could catch the license plate.)

The residents of the area thought the oriental couple were

Korean or Chinese or Thai. They were Vietnamese, and he'd been a captain when they drove out the French and a colonel when he fought beside the Americans and was himself driven out.

He had skin like polished ivory and small black eyes like black beads of glass.

He sat on a stool behind the counter, behind the cash register, a small clearing in a wilderness of goods, a newspaper always in front of his face, his right hand never far from a nine-shot automatic with which he was very skilled.

If he died and his old woman died, they'd have to seal the doors and board up the windows, leaving them to dry out and mummify right where they fell, because there wasn't a soul on earth who'd be able to sort out the confusion of the shop. Either that or put a torch to it.

It only took half a glance to tell him that the bulky man who walked though the narrow corridors between the merchandise from door to register was a cop and he took his hand away from the gun.

Sharkey was foot weary from slogging the streets around the Hotel Westley, marching into this tavern, that tavern, looking for a week-old memory of one or two men who might've walked in and picked up a third. Three men who might've done something, said something, that might be construed as funny, strange, off the wall, out of the ordinary in a neighborhood where strange was commonplace.

"This neighborhood, somebody toting around a toilet paper carton and a sack of Kitty Litter could be looking for a spot to build their house," Dubrowski had said, making fun of their chances before they split to work twice the shops in half the time.

So, now, they'd run out of saloons and taverns and even liquor stores. They were working the leavings. The places somebody passing by *might* have stopped into but probably hadn't.

"You got a pack of Wrigley's?" Sharkey asked.

The storekeeper pointed a finger at a display of chewing gum and Life Savers right under Sharkey's nose.

"I don't see any cinnamon," Sharkey said.

"Spearmint's better," the storekeeper grunted.

"So, that's a quarter?" Sharkey asked, choosing a pack.

"That's fifty cents."

"I didn't know this was a high-rent district," Sharkey said, tossing down two quarters.

"It's a high-crime district."

"You get a lot of it?"

"I get enough."

"It bother you?"

The storekeeper's right hand moved six inches. He came up with the gun.

What the hell's going on nowadays, Sharkey thought, old men packing guns like a bunch of vigilantes.

"Yes, I got a permit," the storekeeper said, before Sharkey even formed the question.

"A permit's one thing. You know how to use that goddamn cannon?"

The storekeeper grinned, showing a beautiful set of gleaming white false teeth.

Sharkey unwrapped all five sticks of gum, one after the other, folding each stick twice and popping it into his mouth. The old man watched him with a look on his face that might have passed for admiration.

"You got good teeth," he said. "I had good teeth before the Cong kicked them out."

"And you're here to talk about it?"

"I know how to use this goddamn thing and these goddamn things," the old man said, setting down the newspaper and holding up his hands. "That gum all you wanted?"

"You open Sundays?"

"I'm opened every day, including Christmas. Including Tet."

"A week ago Sunday, three men stop in here?" Sharkey asked.

"You mean together?"

"That's what I mean."

"You mean three men, two of which looked to be holding on to the third one?"

"I'd say so."

"Two of which bought a length of clothesline and maybe a sack of Kitty Litter?"

Sharkey felt that litttle bounce he always got when foot-soldiering paid off, when you hit the jackpot and information you thought was buried so deep you'd never find it came tumbling out.

"That's right. And maybe asked if you had an empty cardboard box?"

"I sold them the line and Kitty Litter. I gave them the box."

"They didn't happen to tell you why they wanted the Kitty Litter and the box?"

"They didn't mean to tell me but they told me. They were the type who like to make jokes and break wind. One of them said to the other one that it'd come in handy when they beat the shit out of the third man. A joke, see? He was making an elaborate joke. Softening up their victim. Scaring him half to death before they even had to lift a finger. The other man said maybe they wouldn't have any use for it and it'd be a waste of money. The first man said that would be all right, he needed it at home for his cat anyway."

"Oh, no," Sharkey said, "they actually used the box and the cat litter before they went home."

The old man nodded his head, closed his eyes, and looked inscrutable, there not being much by way of violence and cruelty that he hadn't seen.

"Can you give me descriptions?" Sharkey asked.

"One man was six feet one or two, a hundred and fifty, sixty pounds. He had colorless hair puffed out all around his head. Not blond, not white, but colorless. Perhaps he was an albino Negro, though his eyes were not pale gray. They were dark brown. He wore a pair of red and yellow running shoes, with a padded tongue and green laces.

"The other man, the one who bought the cat litter and made the joke, was your size and weight, heavier in the shoulders and upper arms. Brown hair, cut short. He had a scar, two or three inches long, on the side of his cheek, almost at the jawline. He wore thin leather gloves. The gloves were meant to save his hands."

"I understand," Sharkey said.

"He took one glove off," the old man said. "He was having trouble getting change out of his pocket. He had scratches on his hand. So he really had a cat at home."

"You've got an eye," Sharkey said, praising the old man's powers of observation. "You don't miss much."

"That's how I got away after the Cong kicked in my face."

Sharkey was two steps toward the door when the thought struck. He tapped his breast pocket and there it was, the rap sheet on Albert. He unfolded it and showed the photo to the storekeeper.

"That's one of them," the old man said.

Sharkey said, "Thanks," and walked out feeling very satisfied with Lady Luck. The facts were, you didn't have a considerable amount of dumb-ass luck, you never got anywhere. The downside of the downside was you had to do the donkey work even if Lady Luck never gave you the kiss on the schnozz.

Well, he had his smacker. Now what was he going to do with it? He'd pull the plug on that Albert and Leddy and whoever else might've hired him to break C. Pike's bones, but there was a matter of timing here, of using Albert to catch the bigger fish, to keep Albert safe until he was ready to drop the hammer because lifting him now could queer the money pass at Bobby Hennessy's bachelor party. You couldn't go off half-cocked in these situations.

28

WHEN SHARKEY GOT BACK TO THE WESTLEY WHERE HE AND DUbrowski had agreed to meet, Dubrowski was leaning on the fender of the department car, which he'd moved into the passenger unloading zone, nonchalantly cleaning his fingernails with a small silver penknife, even though he would have been a lot more comfortable in the lobby out of the cold. You didn't have to be a brain to figure out that he was making the point that he had no intention of doing anything extra until Sharkey got there.

Sharkey hesitated with one foot in the gutter. There was something about the picture on the street that wasn't sitting quite right with him but he couldn't get a handle on it, so he walked on across the street and said, "While you been loafing around giving yourself a manicure I found the store where the bone-breakers bought the clothesline and the Kitty Litter and got the cardboard box. And I got them linked to Pike."

"You got an identification?

"I got a description. Let's go in and see if we can do ourselves any good. It still bothers me," Sharkey said.

"What bothers you?" Dubrowski asked.

"No bag."

"No what? Look, Ray, if we're going to have conversations we got to facilitate the situation. You got to speak to me in whole sentences. You got to tell me what's on your mind."

Sharkey kept forgetting that he wasn't talking to himself like he'd been doing most of the time for years. He wasn't even talking to a partner who understood half-sentences, solitary words, and even grunts because they'd been together so long. Like a wife and a husband sitting on the other side of the breakfast table reading each other's minds.

"No suitcase in the room."

"So whoever beat the crap out of Pike could've taken it with them," Dubrowski said.

"What for?"

"Search it when they got the time."

"Whoever had the time to do what they did to Pike," Sharkey replied, "had the time to tear a piece of luggage apart."

They went into the lobby of the Westley.

"They left two hundred thirty-eight bucks in the man's pocket," Sharkey said. "Every shark I know tells his bone-breakers to grab every nickel, every dime, even after they bust somebody's arms and legs."

"So, maybe it was a good-looking suitcase and whoever done him was going on a trip."

"Maybe," Sharkey said.

Inside, both Kendicott and Big Mamoo were behind the counter.

Big Mamoo raised his plucked eyebrows and cut his eyes toward his little lover as Sharkey and Dubrowski approached.

Sharkey gave him a little nod and, out of the side of his mouth, told Dubrowski to remember to keep the fat boy's secret.

"You back?" Kendicott asked, showing a little aggressiveness in front of his paramour. Big Mamoo gave him a nudge with his elbow and said, "Be good," then smiled brightly at Sharkey and went on to ask him what they could do for the police.

"Two things," Sharkey said. "Number one, I got what I think is a description of the two men who did it to the man in room 224. One was about my size and weight. Brown hair, cut short. Scar on the side of his cheek and jaw. He wore thin leather gloves."

"Like I said," Kendicott said.

"You didn't say the brown hair," Dubrowski said. "You didn't say the scar."

"Hey, brown hair," Big Mamoo said, "that ain't much of a clue."

"I want your opinion, I'll ask for it. I'm talking to your friend."

"I'm just saying," Big Mamoo said, casting a glance at Sharkey, who raised his eyebrows in sympathy and agreement, saying that he didn't know who'd stuck the wild hair up Dubrowski's ass and made him so pushy, either.

"Listen here . . ." Dubrowski said. "Hey, what's your name? I can't go around calling you Big Mamoo. That sounds foolish."

Big Mamoo looked concerned and frightened for a moment, wondering if the white cop was going to give him away.

"I'll call you Shirley," Dubrowski said, grinning like a shark. "How about that? Shirley okay with you?"

"Virginia," Big Mamoo said softly. My name's Virginia."

"The other man could've been six feet one or two and skinny," Sharkey said. "Could've been an albino. Had this hair without any color, you understand what I'm saying?"

Kendicott and Big Mamoo nodded like a couple of crows.

"Had on a pair of red and yellow felony flyers with green laces," Sharkey went on.

"I didn't actually see that man but it could've been whoever I saw out of the corner of my eye going up the stairs," Big Mamoo said.

"So you didn't see anybody fits that description around here?" Dubrowski said. He was still looking at Kendicott, still trying to intimidate the man a little.

"Doesn't have to be only the days in question. Anytime," Sharkey said.

"If I saw any six-foot Watusi with white hair, I would've mentioned it," Kendicott said.

"Okay. So, number two," Sharkey said. "You any ideas what could've happened to the dead man's luggage?"

Kendicott shrugged.

"What'd he come in with? Could you describe it to me again?"

"Garment bag. Dark green garment bag folded over. The kind with pockets on the side."

"You didn't see anybody come down with a bag like that? You didn't see any other guest come down with an extra bag like that?"

"No, I didn't."

"You got any ideas, Virginia?" Dubrowski asked.

"About the bag you're talking about?"

"That's correct."

"Somebody could've dumped it down the chute."

"The chute?"

"The garbage chute."

"Those garbage chutes still in use?" Sharkey asked.

"Oh, no. We got padlocks on every one of them chutes," Kendicott said.

"But people are always busting them off and tossing their garbage down the chutes anyhow," Big Mamoo said. "They ain't supposed to cook in their rooms but they get these little Sterno stoves and they heat up soup, make coffee," he went on to explain. "They don't want the maid to find the cans in the wastepaper baskets. You know? They don't want to try to sneak the cans past us." She smiled proudly at Kendicott. "Orville, here, gives them hell, he catches them."

"Where do the chutes end up?" Dubrowski asked.

"Down in the basement."

"Let's go down and have a look."

"You mind I don't go along?" Big Mamoo said.

"That's okay," Sharkey said. "Mr. Kendicott's all we need."

"Fachrissake, we going to go poking around in a bunch of garbage?" Dubrowski said.

"There isn't any garbage in the basement," Kendicott said.

Making a face of disgust and long-suffering patience, Dubrowski followed Sharkey and Kendicott down to the first basement. The asbestos pipes were shedding and there was a smell of niter in the dusty air.

They approached a big wire-mesh cage with three wide-mouthed, square galvanized metal conduits yawning on the wall above its open top. There was half a foot of garbage, empty cans and food packages, newspapers and a busted bag from which pads of Kotex spilled laying around. Sharkey opened the inward-slanting door and kicked at the pile of refuse. A rat exploded from the center of it and as quickly burrowed in and disappeared again.

Kendicott looked distressed.

"You got to do something about this," Dubrowski said. "You got to start coming down here more often."

"Things pile up," Kendicott said, not realizing he was making a joke until Dubrowski hooted.

"Okay, okay," Sharkey said. "You got a rake, something like that?"

Kendicott went over to the corner and brought back a long stick with a hoe blade on the end. Sharkey scraped through the mess for half an hour, then Dubrowski moved it around for another.

Dubrowski tried to look up into the mouths of the chutes.

"You see anything?" Sharkey asked.

"Black as a bunch of nigger assholes up there," Dubrowski said. Then he looked at Kendicott, who'd turned his face away, and said, "I can't see a fucking thing, Sharkey."

"So we try it from the other end."

They tramped back up the stairs to the lobby and then on up the once-grand staircase to the second floor.

Dubrowski walked over to the chute in the corridor that faced room 224 and heaved on the lock. The shank was loose. He took off the lock and opened the door. A rush of stinking air hit him in the face and he backed off a step or two.

He took a flashlight from his pocket and stuck his arm and head into the opening and then withdrew.

"Not a goddamn thing."

Sharkey took the flashlight from Dubrowski. "Let me have a look." When he came back out he said, "I see a strap. I see something. Somebody go downstairs and get that hoe. Maybe we can poke around down there and break it loose."

"If it's there, maybe you just push it around the bend where it gets stuck even worse. Then we can't get to it from either end without a major operation," Dubrowski said. "We don't want to be fucking around here all day. Somebody's got to reach down there."

"Can't do it. Can't get our shoulders through the goddamn opening," Sharkey said.

"Maybe you and me can't but Mr. Kendicott here's pretty small. He could do it."

"Oh, no," Kendicott said.

"I could hold you by the feet and you could reach down and help us out," Dubrowski said. "I think you could reach it."

Kendicott scurried away a few feet. "No!"

"Fachrissake, give us a little cooperation here, Orville," Dubrowski said. "I wouldn't drop you."

"Didn't you ever get lowered upside down into a manhole to get a ball when you was a kid, Mr. Kendicott?" Sharkey said. "I think you could have a better chance at dragging up whatever's down there than us trying to poke it down around the bend with that hoe."

He was looking at Kendicott in this calculating way, a little smile on his face, as though he was testing Kendicott's courage.

"I'll get myself all dirty," Kendicott said.

Sharkey took off his topcoat. "Well I got this old coat I'm wearing. You can slide on it." He started to arrange it in the chute. "Remind me, Wally, I got to take my camel hair to the cleaners. I been forgetting," he said, as though he didn't expect Kendicott to make any more protests.

Kendicott's face closed down as he carefully removed his spectacles and placed them on the carpet close to the wall. He loosened his tie and unbuttoned his cuffs, rolling his sleeves up past his elbows.

Dubrowski stood there puffing out his cheeks but not saying anything until Kendicott presented himself to be helped into the chute.

Dubrowski held his ankles as Kendicott extended his body and reached down until his fingertips touched the strap Sharkey'd spotted. He sneaked it up into his fist and told Dubrowski to haul him back up.

When he was on his feet, the remains of a dark green garment bag with pockets dangled from his hand. It was covered with all sorts of travel tags to London, Cairo, Amsterdam, Tel

Aviv and had been ripped to shreds, every seam and layer pulled apart, even the handle sliced open.

Later on, out in the car out of the cold with this new piece of evidence, Sharkey slouched in the runner's seat, his hat tipped forward, his filthy coat folded up in his lap, thinking it out.

"Nothing of any special interest about the garment bag," he said. "Except . . ."

"Except what? Except they took the time to rip it up," Dubrowski said.

"Except that and his last trip was to Tel Aviv."

"So what?"

"So, I'm wondering what he was doing going to Tel Aviv."

"Maybe he was of the Hebrew persuasion."

"The other day you thought he was a guido connected to the mob."

"So I changed my mind based on new evidence."

"He wasn't Jewish," Sharkey said.

"Now, how the hell would you know that? They practically took away his face."

"The poor sonofabitch's pecker was hanging out of his shorts and I noticed he wasn't clipped. You're one hell of a detective, didn't even notice a thing like that."

"So, well, fachrissake, you don't have to be a hebe to visit Israel. They got all kinds of Christian holy places there, too."

"I don't think our Mr. Pike was a tourist and I don't think he was on a pilgrimage."

"So, what do you think?"

"I think he was a mule."

"Oh, fachrissake," Dubrowski said, "how much dope is anybody going to bring through in the seams or the handle of a goddamn suitcase?"

"Then there's the shit. They were poking around in the man's shit.

"What're we talking about here?"

"Swallowing balloons or condoms full of dope. How the fuck do I know? I'm just thinking out loud," Sharkey said.

Dubrowski started reaching for the ignition key, turning his head to the side to give him the extra reach, and saw Sharkey staring past his ear out the window.

"What're you staring at?"

"Look at that."

Dubrowski leaned back and turned his head. "Somebody's getting his ass towed for too much overtime parking."

"So, we better find out how long that vehicle's been standing there abandoned," Sharkey said, getting out of the car and strolling across the street.

"Yo, what've we got here, McIlhenny?" he called out as he approached the tow truck operator.

29

"SO, YOU'RE FRANKIE BLUE SHOES," THE CANDIDATE SAID, smiling at Frank Leddy with a kind of possessive pride.

"Yes, sir," Leddy said, immediately warmed by the quality of the greeting given him by the skillful politician, purveyor extraordinaire of Irish honey cake.

"Your name caught my ear the first time it was mentioned," The Candidate went on. "I've been wondering about it ever since."

"What's that, sir?"

"Why do they call you Frankie Blue Shoes? I don't see you wearing blue shoes."

"No, sir, I never wear blue shoes."

"So, how come, you don't mind my asking."

"The hair. The sideburns."

"I think you'll have to run that train by me one more time."

"The resemblance," Leddy said, lifting his head slightly and turning his head a trifle.

"I'm still waiting at the station," The Candidate said, a little mournfully.

"Elvis."

"Who?"

"Elvis Presley. 'Blue Suede Shoes.' "

The Candidate's face was a study in neutrality and confusion.

"Mr. Leddy bears a resemblance to the singer, Elvis Presley," Finnegan said. "You know Elvis Presley."

"I thought he was dead," The Candidate said.

"Well, he is," Finnegan said, "but Mr. Leddy—"

"Call me Frankie," Leddy said.

"—looks like Elvis Presley looked when he was alive."

"I looked more like him when I was a kid," Leddy said.

"So, *then* you wore blue suede shoes and that's how come the name?" The Candidate said.

"No, sir. But I had a pair of blue and white sneakers. They was mostly white with this blue lightning bolt on the side."

The Candidate nodded but anybody could see that he was still in the dark.

"So, what's the situation with Sergeant Sharkey?" The Candidate asked, shaking himself like a dog shedding water, turning to things he could better understand.

"He wants the money handed over to him at Bobby Hennessy's bachelor party over to Schaller's Pump."

The Candidate looked up at Finnegan. "You telling me that Bobby Hennessy's getting married again?"

"Fifth time."

"The man must be seventy years old."

"Sixty-seven to be exact."

"Well, God bless him. We get an invitation? Get the phone, Finnegan, and ask my secretary is there an invitation in the pile for Bobby Hennessy's bachelor party. If there isn't, then arrange to get a couple. For you, me, Quinn, and Kenna. This cop thinks he's going to catch a money pass without a crowd to witness it, he's got another think coming."

Finnegan hurried off to make the call, but there was a troubled expression on his face. The Candidate might think that Sharkey was going to be trapped that easily, but he knew better. He knew that Sharkey was slyer than a fox and slipperier than an eel and Finnegan was ready to bet his future that there was going to be something up Sharkey's sleeve besides his arm come Friday night.

"So, Mr. Leddy," The Candidate said. "Would you mind telling me again how you got the name Frankie Blue Shoes?"

30

SHARKEY AND DUBROWSKI FOLLOWED THE TOWED VEHICLE BACK to the police garage.

By the time they got there, Motor Vehicles had already run the plates on the maroon and gray 1976 Mercury sedan. It was registered to one Carmine D'Angelo, residing at 1121 Thirty-seventh Street near Wentworth over by Comiskey Park.

They popped out the lock on the door and looked around inside. The man kept a clean car. There was nothing on the floor or on the back shelf or on the seats, except for the wrapper from a package of mints tucked into the crack in the cushion.

The glove compartment contained a pair of fleece-lined gloves, a half-empty package of Kleenex, charts that could be filled out in case of accident, a couple of road maps, and a thin billfold which contained a driver's license and an automobile registration face to face.

The license was issued to Carmine D'Angelo, 1121 Thirty-seventh Chicago, Illinois, male, hair gray, eyes brown, height five feet eight inches, weight one hundred eighty pounds, date of birth, June 9, 1926. The photo bore a resemblance to the battered face of the Westley Hotel victim. At least it was a much better than even bet.

The address proved to be a three-flat in good repair and of fine appearance.

Sharkey and Dubrowski climbed the short flight of stairs to the porch and went through the outer door into the vestibule. A check of the nameplates on the mailboxes failed to turn up a Carmine D'Angelo.

Sharkey pushed the button for the first-floor flat. After pushing it a second time and waiting another minute, he tried the second-floor flat.

The third floor produced a squawk from the speaker. It was

one of the old-fashioned speaker tubes you blew into to tell the person in the vestibule that you were ready to listen to what he or she had to say.

Sharkey identified himself as a police officer and gave his badge number in case the person in the flat was cautious enough to want to check with the station. He said he wanted to ask a few questions about a certain Carmine D'Angelo who resided at that address or had done so within the last year. The tenant of the third-floor flat buzzed them through.

"Fachrissake," Dubrowski complained, "the only one at home would have to be on the top floor."

"You want to wait down here?" Sharkey asked.

"No, I don't want to wait down here. Go ahead, go ahead," Dubrowski said, waving Sharkey on.

He was panting like a beached whale by the time they got to the top floor. An old Italian woman with a dark mustache and white hair was waiting for them at the open door to her flat. She grinned when she saw Dubrowski's condition.

"You need more exercise," she said.

"I just had my exercise," Dubrowski grumbled.

"That's what I'm saying. You could use all the exercise you can get. My husband was an elephant like you. I told him and told him he had to lose some weight, get more exercise. Come in, come in. You want a little glass of red wine?" She turned her back and walked down the hall toward the kitchen, expecting them to follow, which they did. She never stopped talking. "You think he'd listen? He wouldn't listen. He dropped dead one night. Fell over dead into a dish of fettuccini. Sit down. I'll get you a glass of wine. Don't tell me that business about how you're on duty. A glass of wine won't make you drunk."

The kitchen was painted yellow and white. Yellow and white checked oilcloth was on the table. They sat down while she poured three glasses of wine.

"You want to know about Carmine?" she asked.

"His car was impounded, Mrs. . . . ?

"Tartaglia. Rose Tartaglia."

She placed two glasses of red wine on the table.

"Where's the car now?" she asked, bringing her own glass to the table and sitting down.

"It was towed to the police garage," Sharkey said.

"It's not damaged?"

"Well, we had to pop the lock."

"Carmine's not going to like that. He loved that car."

"It won't matter to him anymore, Mrs. Tartaglia."

Tears filled her eyes but didn't spill. She sighed and raised her glass to her lips.

"Are you a relative, Mrs. Tartaglia?"

"No. I'm no relation. Just a friend. Just a landlady."

"You own this house? You rented him a flat?"

"I don't own this house. I rent this flat. My husband and me lived here for eighteen years until he got so fat and fell over into the fettuccini. I put an ad in the neighborhood shopper. I needed the money renting out the spare room would bring in and I was lonely. Nobody around the house."

"How long ago did you rent Mr. D'Angelo the room?"

She thought about it, wanting to be precise, before she said, "Nine months."

"How come he's got no name on the mailbox?"

"I think he got all his mail at a post office box."

"Did he go to work every morning?" Sharkey asked.

"He went out on business, he said, but not exactly to work."

"How's that?"

"He'd just gone into business on his own."

"What was that?"

"He bought and sold diamonds, rubies, emeralds, all kinds of jewels. He used to work for another company but he thought he could do better by hisself."

"He ever tell you where he worked before he decided to go out on his own?" Sharkey asked.

"Three Seas Import-Export. I thought that was funny."

"What was funny?"

"Three Seas. I always heard there was seven seas."

"How come you didn't call the police when Mr. D'Angelo was missing for over a week?" Dubrowski suddenly asked.

"He told me he was going on a buying trip to Tel Aviv. He didn't know exactly how long he'd be gone. So I didn't have any reason to worry, did I? I mean I guess I had reason but I didn't know I had reason. What happened to him?"

"Somebody killed him, Mrs. Tartaglia."

"Killed him? How killed him?" she asked as though the generic answer wasn't of much use to her understanding.

"Beat him to death."

The tears finally spilled out of Mrs. Tartaglia's eyes.

Downstairs again, Sharkey said, "How do you want to work it?"

"How do I want to work what?" Dubrowski replied.

"Somebody should go down the customs, ask around, see if Pike—D'Angelo—declared anything coming in. Also somebody should go have a talk to the company he used to work for."

"So, we can do that."

"No sense both of us chewing the same cabbage. I mean there's no sense both of us doing what one of us can do."

"So, what do you want to do?"

"I don't give a rat's ass. One or the other."

Dubrowski stood there thinking about it.

"So?" Sharkey said.

"So, it makes no never mind to me either."

Sharkey sighed as though annoyed that the decisions had to be left up to him but if he went off and did something on his own without consultation Dubrowski got his bowels in an uproar.

"I'll go over to Three Seas," he said.

"Well . . ."

"You want to go over to Three Seas?" Sharkey asked, letting his irritation show.

"No, that's okay. You go talk to the people at Three Seas."

"All right then." He looked at his wristwatch. "Tomorrow, first thing, you go down and talk to customs and I'll have a look around Three Seas."

31

The offices of the Three Seas Import-Export were located on West Washington in a crummy brick building next to a railroad spur and a vast empty lot with which it shared a chain-link fence rusting away in big sections.

The first floor was occupied by a factory making condoms. Looking through the glass inset in the door, on his way up the stairs, Sharkey could see long lines of black and Hispanic women blowing up the little suckers on these pipes that delivered jets of air, testing for pinholes.

The second floor had offices, fruit and spice brokers, a small-job printer, this and that.

Three Seas was on the third floor. It occupied two rooms. Sharkey had an idea the owners could've operated out of their hat.

The first room—the outer reception—was about as big as a double closet.

There was a woman wearing big glasses that seemed to cover half her face sitting behind a desk sorting through a file drawer which she could reach without getting up out of her chair. She looked up, startled, when he walked in, as though visitors were so rare that anybody walking in must be there for no good purpose.

He flashed her the gold.

She stood up and took off her glasses, transforming herself from an owl to a bunny rabbit in one amazing trick.

"You have a Carmine D'Angelo working for you?" Sharkey asked.

"We had. He's not with us anymore," she said, after wetting her lips.

"He quit?"

She stood there like a rabbit caught in the glare of a car's headlamps, unable to move.

"He get fired?" Sharkey went on, trying to help her along.

"I don't know if I'm the one you should be asking these questions," she murmured.

He gave her his best smile, the one he polished up and displayed maybe once or twice a year, no more than that. She half turned away from the dazzle and colored up. She had the kind of complexion his sister Wilda had. Very fair, the kind that colored up at a glance, except Wilda didn't blush very often.

"May I please sit down?" he asked.

Her chair was the only chair in the tiny room. She looked around, confused, embarrassed, and concerned.

"Oh, I'm sorry," he said. "I didn't notice you only got one chair until right this minute."

She was extending her arm toward her chair and stepping back a pace.

"No, no. I mean if I took your chair, where would you sit? Unless you sat on my lap."

She smiled wildly. "I could get a chair from Mr. Dickman's office."

"Won't Mr. Dickman mind?"

"He's not in."

"Has Mr. Dickman maybe got two chairs in his office?"

"Yes."

"So, Miss . . . I didn't catch your name."

"Nancy. Nancy Ames."

"Pretty name. My name is Sharkey. Ray Sharkey. So would that be all right, we sit in Mr. Dickman's office?"

She was beside herself with doubt but this big, white-haired cop with the clean, polished face was smiling at her in a kindly way—in a very *friendly* way—and what would be the harm? Just to sit and talk in Marvin's office. You never could tell when good fortune might pass your way, that man on the white horse.

She opened the door to the inner office for him, but Sharkey placed a hand on her back and insisted she go in before him.

He had the kind of manners . . . she thought.

He also insisted she take Marvin's chair behind the desk while he took the other. While they were shuffling the deck, he noticed a studio portrait on the desk of a man with thinning hair, a pretty woman, and two small children, a girl and a boy.

"You want some coffee or tea?" she asked.

"I don't think I'll impose on Mr. Dickman's hospitality when he ain't here," he said. "Unless you'd like a cup of something? I'd be happy to make it."

"Oh, no," she said, and colored up again.

"So, where were we?"

"You wanted to know if Mr. D'Angelo quit or was fired."

"Did you tell me?"

Suddenly she looked like she was about to cry.

"What's the matter?"

"I think Mr. D'Angelo could be in some kind of trouble, even dead."

"Why do you think that?"

"I saw in the paper that a man by the name of Pike was murdered in a hotel called the Westley. Pike was a name Mr. D'Angelo used sometimes when he traveled for the company."

"So, there are probably a lot of Pikes around."

"I know. I thought of that. But it was just that it'd be such a coincidence."

"What's that?"

"Mr. Dickman had an appointment at the Westley about five or six days before I read about Mr. Pike in the papers. That's why you're here, isn't it, about Mr. D'Angelo?"

"I'm one of the detectives on the case, yes. So, we're going to have to have some dates here. You got Mr. Dickman's appointment book?"

She put her hand on the drawer and then, thinking better of it, put her hand back on the desk blotter.

"I don't know if I should let you look at that. I mean would I be doing the wrong thing, you coming in here and looking at his personal papers without showing me a warrant?"

"I wish I had a secretary like you," Sharkey said. "That is, if flatfeet like myself had secretaries." He took out his notebook. "I got to do it all for myself."

She smiled, still looking doubtful.

Sharkey wondered, sitting there, if she was playing him all the time he thought he was playing her.

"I'm just trying to make it easy on everybody. I could get a warrant. Come back and tear the place apart. But I've got no reason to do that. I mean all I'm doing is trying to get some simple answers to some simple questions about the relationship, if any, between Mr. D'Angelo and his employer. You understand what I'm saying?"

She nodded, but he could see that she was setting herself up to be stubborn.

He stood up. "Okay, I can leave and come back."

She jumped up, her face flaming again, and reached out as though ready to stop him, just as the door to the outer office opened. She stumbled coming around the desk and Sharkey caught her. He turned his head and saw the thickset man standing in the doorway with a white kid, about nineteen, twenty, with a blond Afro hair-do, right behind him.

"What the hell's going on here?" the thickset man said.

"I'm the police," Sharkey said.

Sharkey thought he saw a flash of fight-or-flight in the kid's eyes, but he kept a hold on himself and just stood there smiling a little vague smile meant to appear casual.

"I told him he'd have to have a warrant, Mr. Dickman," Nancy said, pushing away from Sharkey. He had a pleasant impression of her soft resilience pressing just a little harder against him as she pushed off.

"So, for a minute there I thought you were assaulting my secretary," Dickman said.

"Well, no, I wouldn't do that," Sharkey said, very seriously, not cracking a smile to match Dickman's own.

"You want to see me?" Dickman asked.

"Now that you're here, it'll make things easier for Miss Ames, I think." Sharkey turned to her and gave her the million-dollar smile again. She left the office in some confusion.

The fuzzy-wuzzy kid said, "So, you change your mind, Mr. Dickman, give me a call," and went bouncing out behind her in a pair of red, yellow, and green felony flyers.

"So, I'll sit down," Dickman said. "Won't you do the same?"

"Why were you meeting with Carmine D'Angelo at the Westley Hotel where he'd checked in under the name C. Pike?" Sharkey asked, taking the chair, hitting Dickman with it right away, letting him know that fucking around and playing games wouldn't be allowed. "Was he working for you at the time or wasn't he working for you at the time? Miss Ames was a little confused on that point."

Dickman started to stand up.

"No," Sharkey said.

"Miss Ames has my calendar," Dickman explained, wondering what Sharkey was saying no about.

"Maybe she has, but I got a feeling there's another one in your desk drawer. So, take a look. I don't want one of these situations where you ask her for the calendar or the appointment book and she says she ain't got it, she thought you had it, and you say, no, she's got it, and et cetera, et cetera. You understand what I'm saying here?"

Dickman settled back into his chair.

"So, take a look," Sharkey said.

Dickman opened the drawer and took out an appointment book.

"Look at that, will you," Sharkey said.

"Just a minute here," Dickman said, "You're trying to make it look like I'm not willing to cooperate. I'm perfectly willing to cooperate as soon as I know what it is you want."

"Thank you very much. That's what we're getting to here. I want to know when you had the meeting with Carmine D'Angelo."

"I didn't keep the appointment," Dickman said, after a flicker of hesitation.

The first lie, right there? Sharkey wondered.

"What's the name of the kid with the fright wig?" Sharkey asked, catching Dickman off balance. There he was getting his brain all geared up for a series of questions about the meeting with D'Angelo, ready to do the old juggling act, when Sharkey hit him with another question altogether.

"What? What?"

"The kid in the Times Square sneakers. He got a name?"

"Waddel. Zulu Waddel," Dickman went on.

"Zulu?"

"That's what they call him. You know, the hair?"

"The hair," Sharkey said, right on the beat, so they sounded like a vaudeville team. "His mother didn't name him Zulu?"

"Fletcher Waddel, I think."

"He work for you?" Sharkey asked.

"No. He was looking for a job."

"What day did you say you had the meeting with D'Angelo?"

Dickman tickled the pages of the calendar.

"The seventh, this month."

"That'd be a Friday," Sharkey said.

"That's right."

"He was murdered around that time. You know that?"

"What do you mean murdered?"

"I mean somebody beat him to death. Well, actually they gagged him with a sock, then they beat him and left him to choke on his own vomit."

"My God."

"You're sure you didn't go over to the Westley, make the meeting, find your ex-employee dead, and cop a sneak?" Sharkey said.

"No. I never made the meeting."

"Who'd blame you, taking a walk, finding something like that? Nobody would blame you, so telling me the truth wouldn't necessarily be a bad move."

"I'm telling you the truth. I never went."

"Why didn't you?"

"Because I decided he was working a game on me."

"How's that?"

"He was going to try to sell me goods he got from contacts he made while he was working for me."

"Explain it to me."

"I'm import-export."

"I saw that on your door."

"Import-export looks like an easy business, right? You go buy things in other countries, you get a customs broker to handle the paperwork, you take delivery and job it out."

"That sounds good."

"Good and simple. But there's a couple things you got to understand. A considerable amount of trust is necessary for parties to do business thousands of miles away. Not only do I have to know I can trust the man I'm buying from but he's got to know I know how to job out the goods so I can come back and do business again. Nobody wants to get involved in onetime deals. It's not worth the cost, credit checks of the other party, references, all like that."

"You're giving me an education here," Sharkey said.

"Carmine learned all he had to know about the business from me, so he quits and—"

"When did he quit?" Sharkey asked.

"—decides to go into business for hisself. What? Let me think. Let me think. He quit sometime last September."

"And you don't see him since?"

"I don't see him, I don't hear from him, until he calls me and tells me he's going to be at this Hotel Westley with a bundle of goods."

"What kind of goods?"

Dickman popped his eyebrows as though he was surprised Sharkey didn't already know.

"Gemstones for the jewelry trade. Mostly diamonds. You bring them in about this time of year because the jewelry stores are replenishing their stock after Christmas and the manufacturers have merchandise to make."

"Could you turn a profit if you made a deal with D'Angelo?"

"If he got the goods in Tel Aviv from the contact he made while he was working for me, and the price was right, I could've made a nice profit."

"But you decided not to do business with him?"

"Why should I do business with a goniff who steals my contact? Why should I make it easy for him? Let him shop the stuff around to other wholesalers. They figure out he's on his own with a load of goods he's got to unload before he can do business again, and they'd squeeze his nuts. He'd find out you can't make a living on stones nobody wants to buy except they set a price what cuts your throat."

"You act like you're a little pissed off at this D'Angelo."

"A lot pissed off," Dickman said. "I mean I was. Now, you tell me the poor sonofabitch got hisself killed, I ain't so mad at him anymore."

"I can understand that," Sharkey said. "What I can't understand is why a man with a high temper like yourself wouldn't at least take the opportunity to go over there and tell this goniff what you just told me. Read him the fucking riot act."

"I didn't even want to be in the same room with the sonofabitch. I never wanted to see the fucker again."

"Well, you don't have to worry about that anymore."

Sharkey stood up, pushed back the skirts of his coat, put his hands in the pockets of his suit coat with the thumbs exposed, and assumed the friendly, confidential air he'd seen Spencer Tracy assume in many films.

"Tell me, will you, Mr. Dickman, who do I talk to down at

customs to check on what D'Angelo brought into the country?"

Dickman didn't know where to look.

"Have we got a little problem here, Mr. Dickman?"

"Well, I'm not sure that D'Angelo brought the goods in the usual way."

"You mean he smuggled them? Who would've guessed?"

He surprised Dickman by the breezy way he took the news.

"You could do me a favor, Mr. Dickman," Sharkey said.

"What's that?"

"You could let me borrow that photograph of you and your family on your desk."

"What?" Dickman's mouth twitched as though he was starting to smile, then he scratched that and frowned instead. "Maybe I should call my lawyer," he said.

"That's your right," Sharkey said. "You can call your lawyer and I'll go get a writ and by the time it's over you'll've spent a bundle, I'll've wasted half a day, a day, I'll've walked away with the picture anyway, but you'll've made your lawyer happy. You can do that."

"Why do you want the picture?"

"I'm going to be right up front with you, Mr. Dickman. I'm going to show it to a couple of people over at the Westley Hotel and see if they can make you."

Dickman reached into his hip picket and took out his wallet. "Those prints cost me thirty-nine ninety-five each. I've got a wallet size in here." He found it and plucked it out of the plastic sleeve. "How about that?" he said, handing it to Sharkey.

Sharkey took a look. "This'll do just fine, Mr. Dickman, and I thank you for your cooperation."

32

SHARKEY AND DUBROWSKI PICKED UP ANOTHER HOMICIDE ON Tuesday. A slasher had ripped up a hooker from belly to throat.

They stood there watching the mobile lab techs going through the motions.

"Nothing to find," Dubrowski said.

"And nobody to care. What the hell are we even doing here? We're not going to find the crazy what did this little job of work. Not unless he walks into the stationhouse and signs a confession."

"Even then . . ." Dubrowski said.

"Yeah, even then some lawyer would get him off on a diminished capacity defense," Sharkey agreed.

"Besides . . ." Dubrowski said.

"Who gives a fuck. She's better out of it," Sharkey said, realizing with some surprise that here he was understanding incomplete sentences. They were starting to speak in shorthand. He was getting married to Dubrowski, the fucking whale, whether he liked it or not. "So, we got everything there is to get?"

A uniform who'd just arrived to help move the crowd along walked up and asked "Was she robbed?"

"No."

"Just somebody dissatisfied with the service, huh?"

"Hey, Wally, you want to stop over to the Westley, have another talk with Kendicott and Big Mamoo?" Sharkey asked.

"We ain't doing nobody any good here," Dubrowski said.

Sharkey took out the picture of Dickman and his family and handed it to Kendicott.

"You ever see this man?" he asked.

"No, I never," Kendicott said, handing it back.

Sharkey handed it to Big Mamoo, who shook his head.

Dubrowski snatched it from Big Mamoo's fingers, gave it a hard look, then passed it back to Sharkey as though it were a playing card.

"Who's the man with the wife and kiddies?" Big Mamoo asked.

"Used to be C. Pike's boss. C. Pike was a man by the name of Carmine D'Angelo," Sharkey said. "Ring a bell?"

Big Mamoo shook his head again and Kendicott looked worried, as though he feared they were going to start up with him again.

"Never heard the name?"

"No, never."

Sharkey smiled. "We've got to keep asking. You know what I mean?"

"Oh, sure."

Back in the car Dubrowski pouted for a couple of minutes and then said, "How are we going to work it here? You going to do interviews and keep the information to yourself?"

"What are you talking about?"

"The photograph. You never showed me the photograph."

"I just showed you the goddamn photograph."

"You didn't show me the photograph before you showed Kendicott and that fat he-she the photograph."

"How about you?"

"How about me what?"

"You find out anything down at customs?"

"D'Angelo made no declarations."

"So, there you go. I showed you the photograph but you didn't tell me what you found out down at customs."

"You showed me the photograph when you got around to it. After you showed it to Kendicott and that fat broad."

"Here's the goddamn photograph," Sharkey said. "Have a good look."

"How am I going to study a photograph while I'm driving?"

"I'm just saying, what the hell you think I'm doing, trying to keep something from you?"

"Well, I don't really know about that, do I?"

"It slipped my mind," Sharkey said. And it really had slipped his mind, he thought. Well, actually it wasn't so much that it had slipped his mind but that he wasn't in the habit of talking things over with anybody. There was something about that that made him uncomfortable all of a sudden. No wife, no daughter, no partner, no real friends to talk things over with. Something not so good about that. "What's your excuse, not telling me what customs had to say?"

"You never ask. It's like you don't give a fuck, the work we do together."

Sharkey gestured with the photograph.

"That's a picture of Marvin Dickman. D'Angelo worked for him. But he quit and went out on his own, tapping the contacts he'd made while he was working for Dickman."

"What contacts?"

"Diamond merchants. Dealers in precious stones."

"So you think this Dickman has D'Angelo punished because he stole his trade connections?"

"Fachrissake, use your brain. Suppose this D'Angelo brings a bag of stones through customs without a declaration?"

"Smuggling? You know the man was smuggling?"

"No, I don't know that. What I know is that there's a strong possibility. But look it over. He travels under an alias. He checks into a marginal hotel. Somebody beats the crap out of him looking for something."

"So, what do you think we got here?"

"You know what happens? What happens is we forget. We get so tied up in the new wrinkles the crooks are dreaming up, we forget the old dodges. We forget the old goods. We forget gold and counterfeit and gemstones, we're so busy with dope.

"What I think we got here is a man brings some stones through customs in his stomach, maybe in balloons he swallowed like they used to try to run drugs. Maybe not, but it's a bet. What do I know? Maybe cut stones can just be swallowed as is or maybe you wrap them up in a piece of bread. Whatever."

"Jesus," Dubrowski said, swallowing and wincing as though he could feel a fifteen-carat stone going down.

"Dickman says D'Angelo called him and made an appointment for the Sunday night when he checked into the Westley."

"He's trying to do business with the man he gave a fast shuffle?"

"Why not? He probably figures what's wrong with going out

on his own. Free enterprise, it's the American way. Dickman's not the only prospective buyer but why shouldn't he be entitled to a look, D'Angelo's old employer. So, Dickman's got this appointment to look at some stones at the Westley. He claims he never made the appointment. So, maybe he don't show his face but he could've hired them bone-breakers, the one with the cat scratches and the one with the shoe on the stairs. And maybe they beat the shit out of D'Angelo when he won't give up the stones and then go poking around in it looking for them afterwards."

"Wait a minute, wait a minute. D'Angelo's got an appointment with Dickman on Sunday, that means he's got the stones in his hand not his belly unless the poor sonofabitch had a bad case of constipation."

"He knows there's always the possibility of a hijack. If not from Dickman then from one of the other prospective buyers. He's no fool. He's dealing smuggled goods. He's got nobody to complain to if they try to screw him. So he wants them hidden but he wants them available."

"Jesus," Dubrowski said, "what are you telling me here?"

"He's going to keep on shitting the stones and swallowing the stones until he's got a deal."

"Ah, Jesus, I don't want to hear about it," Dubrowski said as though he were a fastidious man deeply offended by such strategies.

They drove along in silence, Sharkey thinking about what he was holding back from Dubrowski, the identification of Albert—Leddy's bone-breaker—by the Vietnamese storekeeper and his description of the tall, skinny freak with him. Him bumping into Zulu at the Three Seas. It was something he wanted to keep to himself, at least until the day after tomorrow when Leddy came to make the payoff at Bobby Hennessy's party.

"We better go see if we can find a true name on that hooker," Sharkey said.

33

A COUPLE OF HUNDRED THOUSAND YEARS AGO THERE'S NO doubt a bunch of the boys gathered in a cave to celebrate the last night of some yabbo's freedom before being tied to some female for the rest of his life. The details of how they worked it are naturally obscured in the mists of time, but five'll get you twenty that they started off with a little food, a little strong drink, a little entertainment from some local kooch dancer, and maybe a couple of willing round-heeled ladies from down the road to give the yabbo a last taste of what he was going to be missing before settling down with Harriet or whoever.

A million years from now, if anything that looks vaguely like people are still around, there's bound to be something very similar going on.

Bobby Hennessy's bachelor party and stag, held at Schaller's Pump, the tavern on South Halstead, promised to be a grand affair right off the bat.

Hennessy's friends had arranged for a bunch of X-rated films to be run continuously on the forty-inch projection screen in the back room where the latest broadcast sporting events were usually shown.

In the barroom, there were two twenty-six-inch sets hung up overhead, one at each end of the mahogany, the smaller screens provided for the drinkers who were afraid to stray too far from the taps, it being intended that the act of lifting their heads from time to time, to see who'd hit the homer or scored the touchdown, would keep them from falling asleep in the puddles of stale beer and—maybe—drowning. None of the regular customers were at the bar, however, Hennessy's friends having engaged not only the combination banquet and family room for the entire night but the barroom, too. So, the TV sets were also showing X-rated, friends of Hennessy's having lugged down VCRs for the occasion.

Two private rooms upstairs had been enagaged for the night in case Hennessy or any of the guests wanted to partake of the ladies supplied by Elvira Leeds (who was also present to make certain that nothing violent or unseemly took place). She went around reassuring her girls that she and her can of Mace were only a scream away.

The trestle tables were covered with white paper cloths and loaded with sliced hams, turkeys, pork and beef roasts, sausages, potato salad, macaroni salad, five-bean salad, coleslaw, six kinds of bread, eight varieties of cheese, bowls of red, green, and white dips, potato chips and Fritos, washtubs full of beer and bottles of champagne.

Mixed drinks and straight shots were available at the bar.

Forty-eight men, several in tuxedos, were already well into the party before the guest of honor arrived in the company of his very old and good friend Dan Sharkey. John Keir, the president of the Cook County Board of Commissioners, and Con Quirty, chairman of the Democratic Central Committee of Cook County, were also in Hennessy's company.

Finny Cavan, the deputy police superintendent, and Alderman Patrick McMullen from the Forty-second, Bobby Hennessy's ward, were right behind them.

Ray Sharkey had stationed himself at the door next to Harry Finney, whose job it was to present a top hat into which new arrivals might drop the envelopes filled with gifts of money meant to allay the costs of the honeymoon or furnish the parlor or whatever might be preferred.

"Ah, Jesus, ain't it good to see you, Harry,"—or something like it—each arriving guest would say as he came into the room, plucking the envelope from this pocket or that. "So, you're the man in the top hat tonight."

He said hello to everyone he knew, which was practically everyone, and shook the hands of the few he didn't, introducing himself as one of the evening's hosts. Some had a word of greeting for Sharkey and some didn't. "Anything you want, you don't see, all you got to do is give me the word and I'll see what I can do," he said, standing there beaming, showing his white crockery smile, playing his role of greeter, the City Hall Pimp, arranger of the feast of tit and ass assembled discreetly at the tables, all that powdered flesh scattered around, making a show. As he shook this hand and that, wondering about the cracks that were appearing in the structure of his life, the sound of beams cracking and masonry crumbling in his ears, threatening to bury him in the wreckage of little things become big things, of good intentions and response to necessity gone wrong, he looked into their eyes, trying to work it out by their responses who'd heard the word that his neck was on the block and who hadn't heard or didn't believe a cop with his connections could be in any danger.

At eleven o'clock The Candidate arrived with Finnegan, Quinn, and Kenna, all of them grinning, as sly as cats invited to a feast of sparrows.

"Surprised to see me, are you, Sharkey?" The Candidate said, shaking Sharkey's hand.

"Why would I be surprised to see a man who's a friend to presidents, popes, and kings and who must surely be a friend of Bobby Hennessy's? Aren't you known to everyone in the city, high and low, and are they not known to you?"

"My God, you've got the tongue of an Irish poet, Sharkey. And is your dear dad here tonight?"

"You'll find him by the keg," Sharkey said, matching The Candidate phony brogue for phony brogue, Irish honey cake for Irish honey cake.

He shook Kenna's hand and, holding Quinn's hand a moment longer, drawing the old pol in close, whispered in his ear, "You've signed up on a losing team this time."

Laughing about it, the little jokes and gibes, passed around like souvenir daggers tipped with little drops of poison.

When it came Finnegan's turn, the lawyer smiled and said, "I understand from a mutual friend that I wasn't welcome here."

"Why would you not? Do you know Bobby Hennessy well?"

"I know him."

"Then drop your good wishes into Finney's hat and go on in and enjoy yourself. Look around and take what pleases you. You're safe here, all the boys together playing in the sandbox."

"I'll do that, Sharkey. Yes, I will," Finnegan said. He held his arms out from his sides. "You want to pat me down for a wire?"

"What would be the use of that?" Sharkey said, widening his eyes and lifting his brows. "We're all friends here tonight. This is a celebration of a happy event. It's not the time or place to be conducting any business."

The mayor, with his entourage, made an appearance fifteen minutes later, handed Finney an envelope, went over to give congratulations to Bobby Hennessy, paused to shake The Candidate's hand, and was gone again, he being smart enough to know a stag party was no place for a mayor to be when the clothes started coming off the ladies.

By twelve o'clock Mike Villano, committeeman from the Tenth, was drunk and Jack Halloran, the alderman from the Thirty-third, was sitting on the laps of two of Elvira's ladies, both of whom had lowered their bodices and removed their skimpy bras.

At least one and perhaps several of the celebrants had made use of Elvira's ladies and the rooms upstairs, the extra service fees being charged to the individual partakers and not to the general cost of the shindig, such extras properly deemed to be an expense due the piper that called the tune.

Mike Tierney, the mayor's right-hand man, chief of protocol, keeper of the patronage lists, probably the most powerful man in the room at the moment, was looking down Elvira's dress, which seemed to amuse her.

Shirley Bitty, tricked out in shorts and halter, white collar and cuffs, black tie, gloves, and a top hat similar to the one Finney minded, had already tip-tapped through a half a dozen numbers during which one piece and another of her already scanty attire had been tossed into the faces of the crowd and her snappy-snap crotch had been unsnapped.

At one o'clock she was sitting on Bobby Hennessy's face—him laying on his back on the floor, a cushion beneath his old gray head—and the party was in general disarray.

Sharkey was sitting near the door by himself, Finney having left, it being doubtful that any more guests bearing gifts for the hat would arrive. But on the off chance that there might be such a latecomer Sharkey had volunteered to keep the vigil and hold the hat.

Looking around, he spotted The Candidate, Finnegan, Kenna, and Quinn, sitting in a group. The Candidate, at least, appeared to have grown weary. The other three glanced at their watches and the clock on the wall, starting to fidget as the time for Leddy to show up grew near, ready to stick it out until hell froze over so they could bear witness to the payoff which would give them the hammer with which to beat in Sharkey's head.

As he watched, two of Elvira's girls, spotting four lonely men, went over and squirmed onto the laps of Quinn and Finnegan.

Now, Sharkey thought, timing is everything, as he glanced out the window and saw a car pull up out of which Leddy and his bone-breaker emerged. They strolled toward the entrance of Schaller's Pump, Albert, the bone-breaker, looking right and left as he'd no doubt seen gangster bodyguards do in a hundred televison films.

Across the street, out of the shadow of the alleys, came half-a-dozen men, in dark clothes and armored vests, automatic weapons held at port.

It was just as Leddy and Albert pushed through the door that Sharkey saw the driver get out from behind the wheel of Leddy's car. It was Zulu. For Christ's sake, Sharkey thought, they were like a bunch of snakes all squirming around in the same nest together. Zulu's hair was shining like a halo around his head, his footgear a splash of bright color under the street-lamps. Although he didn't know exactly what was going on, but knowing that the cops crossing the street were not just going to a bachelor party armed and armored, Zulu started yelling to Leddy to watch his rear.

Albert started turning to meet the threat but Leddy, having a smarter, quicker head, grabbed him by the arm and rushed him into the tavern.

As the Cowboys came busting through, Leddy turned his head and smiled at their leader, Connell, and made a point of dropping the blue envelope into the top hat which Sharkey held.

Then all hell broke loose, as hookers screamed, Shirley Bitty tried to snap up the panel of her crotch, Bobby Hennessy, who'd been let in on the gag by Sharkey, started laughing so hard it looked like he was having a heart attack, rolling around on the tavern floor, The Candidate standing up in a hurry and dumping a half-naked woman from his lap, Finnegan pinned there with his hand up the party girl's skirt as seven porno stars cavorted on the forty-inch screen and the jukebox blared a hard metal version of "When Irish Eyes Are Smiling."

Mike Villano came stumbling down the stairs with his trousers down around his knees and The Candidate turned around to face the wall so that he wouldn't be seen as Kenna and Quinn fought their way through the milling crowd trying to make it across the room, having spotted the blue envelope drop into the hat.

Finny Cavan, the ranking cop in the place, was up on the table of honor demanding to know what the hell was going on at the top of his lungs as the Cowboys pushed and prodded everybody against the back wall with riot guns held at port.

Sharkey got up on his chair to get the bigger picture and saw Elvira Leeds up on another chair, staying out of the crush. They looked across the swarm of frightened, startled, angry faces and grinned at each other.

Kenna was flailing out at somebody who'd stepped on his shoes and a couple of the Cowboys were moving in on him, ready to push the big sonofabitch back. The Candidate had found a chair against the wall just to let everyone know he was complying with the shouted orders and was not a combatant.

For a second there Sharkey prayed to God that Connell's men wouldn't get fired up by the general commotion, the curses and accidental blows given and received, the sight of all the powdered tit and long stockinged legs pumping up the adrenaline, and start dealing in real violence.

And then he saw Connell looking his way, grinning and nodding, reassuring him that he and the boys knew that it was all a joke, a gag played on Bobby Hennessy and all the high-powered guests attending.

Sharkey saw Finnegan smothered by the hooker, desperately trying to see through the crook of her elbow or over her shoulder, trying to keep an eye on Sharkey and the top hat with the blue envelope on top.

And in a long moment when the hat and he were lost to Finnegan's view, Sharkey stepped down, plucked the blue envelope from the top of the pile of envelopes in the hat, and plunged it down underneath the floating ice in one of the tubs half-filled with chilling cans of beer.

34

Outside the Pussy Cat there was party trash from the week before, broken ornaments and crepe paper ribbons in the gutters, fag ends of filter-tipped cigarettes like the tracks of small urban animals wandering the concrete. Red neon bleeding all over it. Two-fifteen on a Saturday morning at the beginning of winter.

It had turned bitter cold overnight. The wind Chicagoans called the Hawk flew over the empty lots, the eyeless windows, flying low, talons scraping the big painted plate-glass window, prying into doorways where derelicts sought shelter, chattering in rage down the alleys.

It was warm inside the club, the heat of so many bodies still filling up the corners.

It had been a good night for Charlie Lincoln and his friend Billy Smith, who was, not incidentally, Jasper Tourette's cousin, though neither man made much of the fact. There hadn't been much by way of tips, but the music had been tasty and the audience appreciative. For a few hours there they'd all been back in Kansas City, back in New Orleans, birthing the blues, a little piece of ancient history.

Charlie had his cornet in its red velvet string-mouthed bag tucked under his arm, his hand holding it by the stem, like a drillmaster holds his baton. He held a briefcase with sheet music in his other hand.

Billy was taking his clarinet to pieces and putting it away in the foam nests of the scuffed leather case.

Charlie was licorice and Billy was coffee. Charlie was forty and Billy was almost twenty years younger.

"Chicago days, Chicago nights, Vi'lent lovin', gentle fights . . ." Billy crooned, looking up from under his brows at the white woman sitting in the chair waiting for Charlie to escort her back to her hotel, trying it on with his friend's old friend who'd appeared unexpected and unannounced at a ringside table, her red hair shining purple in the blue spot, sipping a highball and showing her legs and teeth.

"No, no, no, brother," Charlie whispered in his ear, warming it with his breath, coming in close, sideways, slideways, chucking him with a confidential shoulder alongside his bent head, "no, no. This is an old friend. She ain't just another head of hair. She ain't a box of candy going to be passed around."

Wilda smiled and turned her head away, knowing exactly the drift of what was being said, understanding young Billy's eyes on her legs, trying to look up her skirt, understanding Charlie's pride that Billy thought he'd been there more than once, more than twice, and might be willing to let Billy have a taste. Brotherly love. A musician's sharing piece.

Friendship's not enough for men, she thought, they want every other man to think that they've been there with every woman who gives them a smile and says hello. Men don't really want to be friends with women. They don't even really want to be lovers. They want to be possessors of women, users of women, never friends.

They didn't need women for friends. They had friends. They had other men. They talked about being friends with women because they believed that was a way to a woman's treasure.

Her brother Ray had once, within her hearing, given her brother Michael a piece of conventional male wisdom about seducing reluctant women. All you had to do, he said, was hang around long enough, the patient and understanding pal, until one day something made her mad enough or sad enough to welcome you in for a taste.

She and Charlie had been friends, no more than friends, ever since she'd walked into a club in Kansas City and admired the way he played the horn. He wanted more than that, no doubt. She wouldn't trust him in a dark alley, a dark flat, a dark bedroom, especially not if he'd consumed a pint or smoked a pair of muggles or snorted a line. Not if he was made bold or crazy by some invitation she might or might not know she'd extended.

Every time a woman was with a man she had to weigh the dangers. Even Grandpa Sullivan used to get red in the face, his hand on her thigh, when she was nine or ten, sitting on his lap, wiggling her bottom, giving him looks from beneath her lashes like the looks she saw her mother and her aunts give the men. Understanding a little of the power, learning more about the power women had over men, as long as you were smart enough and strong enough to keep them on a leash. A woman had to be very careful about arousing the beast.

Women wanted to be friends with some men, a lot of men, and lovers to only a few . . . belonging to one, maybe two, maybe three at most in a lifetime. Men didn't think about belonging to a woman. That was just not their desire. It was no part of their vocabulary.

Women wanted to be friends to a lot of men in hopes that they might then be able to understand the few they might want to spend a lifetime with.

Not understanding their ways with sex. That was easy. But understanding their other hungers, touching their fears, pitying their feelings of despair, were things as hard to do as a human being was ever asked to do.

The men she knew said the same thing about women, complaining about how impossible it was to track their moods, get beneath the skin, understand their need for long discussions and the silences that so often followed.

They would never understand one another, men and women, their heads worked differently. They spoke a different language. She'd learned that over the years and accepted it as a fact of life but the knowledge didn't make her happy.

"She is toothsome," Billy said, pitching his voice with a musician's skill so that, soft and low as it might be, it traveled twenty feet, meaning her to overhear.

The aging cleanup man hit the bank of switches, bringing up all the lights and suddenly the room wasn't a softly lit neon cavern anymore but just a big barn of a room, the walls splashed with cheap water paint, the stage hung with velvet at three dollars a yard, the tables strewn with half-filled ashtrays, used napkins, and dirty glasses.

The harsh white lights made everybody blink, even the cleanup man who'd been ready for the glare and wore a pair of blue-colored sunshades. But the bright lights didn't wash out their skins, didn't make them white. It made the woman whiter. The skin that had almost glowed in the dim lights was suddenly startlingly, harshly white. Milk-white almost.

She threw up a hand as though hiding from the raw brutality of the lights, as though all too aware of how cruel they would be on a woman on the hard side of forty. Then she lowered her hand and turned her face a little, making the most of the illumination, like an actress instinctively finding her key light, equally aware that though the dew was off the rose she looked a great deal better than most women her age.

The men stared at her, all thinking almost the same thought. That they'd never seen skin so white—like milk—or hair so red—as bright as a flash of blood.

She had practically no eyebrows, didn't draw pencil lines on her face, allowed pale arches to suggest the shape of her eye wells. Nothing pushy about her presentation. Lipstick on her lips no rosier than a little nibbling might make them. Cheeks pale, unblushed and unblushing. Cool, cool eyes, like gutter slush, a degree or two above freezing. Men had spent a lot in hopes that those eyes would warm.

"I'd eat through a yard of garbage to get to her crotch," the cleanup man said, as he passed the two musicians, his back to the woman, pushing the broom, pretending he only did it for a hobby.

Somewhere in the back of their heads they all cringed with the old, old fear. Lynchings of colored men for daring to touch a white woman told by eyewitnesses were not so old as to be forgotten.

But, oh Lord, how her flesh would shine, naked in their beds. How their bodies would look together. Colored and white. Brown and white.

And didn't she know it?

Didn't she sometimes take such combinations under consideration? Hadn't she lain with colored men and brown men and yellow men? Charlie knew she had, though she'd never lain with him. They were merely friends. She'd made a friend of him years ago and he'd allowed it because he thought it might be the way to her treasure.

So he knew it and she knew it, that he'd do much to have her, but would stop well short of forcing himself on her.

He put on a pair of wire-rimmed eyeglasses. They made him look like a preacher or a colored executive down at the commodities market. Uncle Tom or one of his many nephews.

No way out of that. Every step toward the white world was a step away from the black.

"Time to walk you home, Wilda," he said.

They walked out in a row, Charlie leading the way, Billy bringing up the rear, and Wilda in between.

For a moment she felt hemmed in, vulnerable, news stories of rape in nightclubs, pool halls, afterhours joints, flashing in her mind like little firecrackers going off. Date rape. Assault at the hands of friends.

Women are never far from fear, night or day. Never far from unexpected, unintended consequences following the most innocent excursions, everyday excursions to the store for a pack of smokes, to a movie, to a place where people meet to say hello for old times' sake or the sake of new beginnings.

At the exit Charlie paused and Wilda started until she realized that he was standing aside to let her precede him through the door, holding it open for her. She went out into the refrigerator of the night. Her shoes felt as though they were made of paper. How silly not to have worn boots.

They backed off from the cold wind, chattering around them and hitting the door and wall like blades thrown by a knife thrower, outlining them against the building, pinning them there.

"You don't have to walk me, Charlie. We could call and I could wait here for a cab," Wilda said.

"Not likely. Not here. Not this hour," he said.

"But you live the other way, you say, up Orleans Street. Cabrini-Green?"

He nodded. "Right by Seward Park."

"My hotel's the other direction. Jefferson and Arcade Place. How many blocks? This hour of the morning. This weather. I can't ask you to walk all the way down there, all the way back here, and then you'd have to walk yourselves home."

The neon in the windows blinked out. The pavement turned blue.

"We could freeze standing here discussing," he said. "We at least walk you down to the Merchandise Mart. Then we'll see. Maybe we spot a nighthawk cruising. Then we decide."

"Give me your arm then," she said, making up for her start, that little flash of fear in the doorway, putting her hand in the crook of his arm, the hard metal of the cornet inside the velvet bag against her knuckles, reaching out with the other hand to draw Billy closer, allowing him the pressure of his arm against her breast.

They all started out with a long step on the same foot like high-stepping chorus dancers starting a routine.

All of a sudden Wilda felt as though she were celebrating. She was back in Chicago. Home again.

She stumbled.

"Oops," Billy said, and she laughed and tucked her hand back into the crook of his elbow.

They strode along, Dorothy, the Tin Man, and the Scarecrow on the yellow brick road, laughing into one another's faces.

35

WHAT'S THE MEANING BEHIND THE SPECTACLE I JUST witnessed downstairs?" Finny Cavan demanded.

They were upstairs in one of the bedrooms, the bed rumpled from the action that had gone on upon it not minutes before, the room filled with the odor of sex, perfume, cigar smoke, and whiskey.

Cavan was sitting on the bed. Sharkey was sitting on the stool to the dressing table. And Tim Connell, looking like a Ninja warrior, was standing in front of Cavan, a look of hurt surprise on his face.

"Meaning?" Connell said. "There wasn't no meaning. Sharkey calls me up and tells me you want to play a little joke on a certain Bobby Hennessy, who, I understand, is about to get hisself married for the sixth or seventh time."

"Fifth," Sharkey said, as though anxious to keep the record straight.

"Let me get this straight," Cavan said. "Sharkey, here, asks you to raid a party attended by half the important men in city government?"

Connell grinned. "That was the idea."

"He asked you to use public funds and official personnel to pull a practical joke?"

"We come in our own cars and used our own gas," Connel said. "All the guys what was in the raid was off duty."

"Did you tell them to help themselves to food and drinks after?" Sharkey asked in a quick aside.

"Yes, thank you, Ray."

Cavan looked at Sharkey. "Is what Sergeant Connell says the truth?"

"I can explain."

Cavan arranged the pillows against the headboard and lay back as though prepared for a long story.

"I'm ready to listen."

"Don't you think maybe it'd be a good idea to have Sergeant Connell go downstairs first and make sure everybody's got the message that it was just a gag?"

"I think that would be a very good idea. Make sure nobody's had a heart attack. Make sure everybody understands it was a practical joke in honor of Bobby Hennessy's approaching nuptials and that any complaints of injury or embarrassment should be carefully considered in view of the circumstances."

"You mean the hookers," Connell said.

Cavan winced at the bluntness of the man.

"Use a little discretion, for God's sake, Connell. You'll be speaking for me."

"Yes, sir," Connell said, and went down to complete his mission.

Cavan turned his heavily lidded eyes—eyes like those of a wise old tortoise—to Sharkey and said, "Now, give it to me, Ray. Give me the details of how you dreamed up a stupid stunt like this."

"You know how it is, Finny. I'm asked to put together these parties, these smokers, year after year, several times a year. My reputation's on the line each and every time."

"Your reputation as what?"

"As the man who knows how to throw a party, do the guest of honor proud, please the visiting firemen, keep one and all feeling sweet."

"So you lay on the beef, beer, and broads. You lay on plenty of them three things and you got it made."

Sharkey laughed like a long-suffering expert—a seasoned veteran of the catering wars—listening to the casual opinion of someone who merely partook but did not have to agonize over the temperature of the keg beer and texture of the bean dip, let alone the attractiveness of the party girls and the freshness of the novelty acts.

"It's not so easy, Finny. You take the star attraction. I mean you got fads and passing fancies there. For a long time all you can get is belly dancers willing to strip down to their G's. Then you got acts what do it with animals. Then you got tap dancers wearing collars and ties but no shirts like Shirley Bitty and her snap crotch."

"I like Shirley Bitty," Cavan said.

"I know that. She's a crowd pleaser. A sure thing. So tonight I give the boys something familiar. I give them Shirley Bitty for old times' sake. You know, like they say for the bride. 'Something old, something new, something borrowed, something blue.' So I get the idea I'll do the same for the bridegroom. I'll do the same for Bobby Hennessy."

There was a little bit of a commotion outside the bedroom door, somebody demanding to be let in. Cavan had his driver, Jimmy Clay, out there watching the landing and they could hear Clay saying to whoever it was, "Please, sir, wait until the superintendent ain't occupied."

Cavan ignored the fuss.

"So Shirley Bitty was the something old?"

"The top hat for the gift envelopes was borrowed," Sharkey said, being very serious about it all.

There was a banging at the door.

"And it was your smart idea that Connell and his Cowboys should bust in here and stage a raid?" Cavan asked.

"Just for the hell of it, you understand what I'm saying?" Sharkey said. "Just for a joke. Just for something *new*."

"Those ugly fuckers busting in here like that you could have had incidents. Bobby Hennessy, hisself, could've keeled over in a faint."

"Give me a little credit, Finny, fachrissake," Sharkey said. "I already called up Bobby and told him what I planned to do. He thought it was a hell of a gag."

The doorknob rattled. Cavan got off the bed. "Hold on, goddammit," he shouted. "So, okay, maybe no harm done."

"Believe me, they'll be talking about the gag for a month down at City Hall."

"Okay. One more thing—"

The door opened up. Jimmy Clay was trying to hold back an irate J. J. Finnegan, warning him that he'd be under arrest in a minute if he wasn't careful, and Finnegan warning the cop right back that he'd have him up on charges if he didn't take his hands off the suit.

"—what was the something blue?"

"The envelope," Finnegan screamed.

Cavan turned around to look at Finnegan as though wondering what in the hell he was doing there practically foaming at the mouth. He waved his driver back and Jimmy Clay nodded and closed the door after leaving the room.

"Envelope?" Cavan said.

"The fucking blue envelope Frankie Blue Shoes—"

"Is this part of the gag, Sharkey?" Cavan asked. "All this goddamn—"

"—dropped into the gift hat," Finnegan shouted.

"—talk about blue envelopes and blue shoes?"

"Frank Leddy dropped a blue envelope filled with five thousand dollars in small bills into the gift hat for Bobby Hennessy's coming wedding."

"That was very generous of this Frank Leddy," Cavan said.

"It wasn't really for Bobby Hennessy. Frank Leddy—"

"Frankie Blue Shoes," Sharkey explained for Cavan's information.

"—doesn't even know Bobby Hennessy, for God's sake," Finnegan said, beside himself with anger and frustration.

"So why was he being so generous?"

"It was a drop. It was a pass. It was a payoff to Ray Sharkey here. This City Hall Pimp you got yourself, here, is a shrewd sonofabitch. He wouldn't take the payoff where somebody could see. He took the payoff where *everybody* could see."

"You're confusing me, Mr. Finnegan," Cavan said. "Payoff for what?"

"For doing a favor for Leddy. For getting a case of hijacking against him dismissed. For conspiring with his brother Judge Sharkey to set free a persistent felon."

"And how do you know all this, Mr. Finnegan?" Cavan said,

the skin on his face hardening up as though somebody had sprayed him with a coat of instant-drying clear varnish.

"Because Mr. Leddy is my client," Finnegan said, realizing the position he'd thrown himself into, trying to find an easy way to wiggle back out.

"And you advised him to bribe a police officer and a municipal judge?" Cavan asked, the warning very clear that Finnegan had damned well better watch what he said.

After a stuttering pause, Finnegan said, "That's privileged information."

"What isn't privileged information?" Sharkey said. "Does the fact that you came here with The Candidate and his political advisers mean he's your client, too?"

"I have several clients, Sergeant," Finnegan said, a little twist to his lip indicating his disdain.

"Does it maybe mean that one of your clients put up the money for another client with promises that if anything went wrong the charges would disappear off the court records before Leddy ever had to face the Judge?"

"I didn't come up here to answer questions."

"What exactly did you come up here for, Mr. Finnegan?" Cavan asked in his softest voice.

"To report the possibility—the probability—that a criminal act was committed here tonight."

"Of which you and others were aware before the fact. If you intended to bear witness to the fact that a police officer accepted a bribe from a criminal who later avoided the consequences of a criminal act just so you could beat the drums about police corruption, you didn't think it through," Sharkey said. "First of all, if you bear witness to a criminal act and don't report it at the time, it could make you an accessory after the fact. And second of all, questions would be asked about how come you knew about the possibility of a bribe changing hands if you weren't in on it. You and maybe The Candidate, the man you work for. You'd have to give your reasons and name your sources, which means Leddy would have to put his foot into the boiling soup. Which means he'd give you up or give The Candidate up or give up anybody else because he'd know you used him and didn't really care to protect him. Unless you win the election, Finnegan. Unless The Candidate gets to sit in the big chair on the fifth floor. Then he could wave the magic wand. But, see, you were so eager to get me, to use me as the horrible example of police corruption and bad government, that you didn't think it through."

"So, all right, you made your case, Sharkey," Cavan said. "Go tell Jimmy to go downstairs and bring up the hat."

Sharkey did that and then they waited, the three of them, standing around like three commuters waiting for the El until Clay came back with the top hat filled with gift envelopes.

Cavan dumped it on the bed.

There were mostly white envelopes, but there were a few buff and gray and blue ones.

Cavan opened every blue one, finding checks and cash but nothing like five thousand dollars.

"So, there it is Mr. Finnegan," Cavan said.

"He's got it on him. He lifted it out of the hat in the confusion," Finnegan said.

"Unless your client, this Mr. Blue Shoes, is ready to file a charge against Sergeant Sharkey here. Unless he's prepared to bear witness against him in a court of law, swearing that he did, indeed, deliver such a bribe in such a manner as you describe, I think you'd better sew up your mouth and get your ass out of here."

"Wait a second, Superintendent Cavan," Sharkey said, turning formal and official at this point in what had started out as farce and sunk to low burlesque comedy, "I'd like to be searched." He held his arms out from his sides.

"Are you demanding a search of Sergeant Sharkey's person?" Cavan asked the lawyer.

"I'm not asking Mr. Finnegan to put hisself in jeopardy of a suit for slander," Sharkey said, "I'm just asking to be searched so there's no doubt in anybody's mind."

"You understand you don't have to submit to this?" Cavan said, acting very solemn.

"I understand, sir," Sharkey said, still standing there like a well-dressed scarecrow.

Cavan patted him down carefully, taking Sharkey's belongings from his pockets and placing them on the bed.

"No blue envelope here, Mr. Finnegan," Cavan said. "No five thousand in small bills. Are you satisfied that my search was diligent and thorough?"

"You want to pat me down?" Sharkey asked the lawyer.

"No, no," Finnegan said, knowing they were gaming him but knowing he'd been outclassed, outmatched, and outnumbered. How would it look if word got out that The Candidate had been present at a stag party, complete with hookers and naked dancers, that got raided by the vice division's special squad? There were a lot of ways to tell a story.

"So, why don't you go back downstairs and join the fun?" Cavan said. "I'm sure the party's not over yet. The last time I looked, it seemed you had an interest in a little redhead wearing a blue dress."

36

WILDA, CHARLIE, AND BILLY HADN'T EVEN NOTICED THE POLICE car pass them going the other way, they'd been so busy laughing and having fun. Now they didn't even hear the car slipping up behind them close to the gutter. They were still being giddy until they saw their shadows spring up and grow long from the headlights and then the spot behind them. Then they tensed up and faltered in their stride. Wilda almost stumbled.

"Hey, you, come here," the cop in the runner's seat said.

They all turned in unison, arms still locked together, laughter stilled.

Seeing what it was, who it was, Charlie rearranged his face. Made it respectful. Made it nonthreatening, nonjudgmental.

"Get over here," the cop said.

"Yes?" Charlie said, taking his arm away from Wilda's small gloved hand, walking over, leaning over, putting his hand on the window frame as he bent down.

He felt Billy walk up and stand right behind him and wished he hadn't. Wished he'd kept his young, aggressive black face back in the shadows while he dealt with these white cops who were on the prod, looking for strokes, apologies, the nigger shuffle.

"Where you going?" the cop asked.

"Home. We were working here at the—"

"Where's home?"

"Seward Park."

"You live in the park?" An edge of snotty sarcasm there.

"Sedgewick and Locust."

"You're walking the wrong way."

"We're seeing the lady back to her hotel."

"Where do you live?" the cop asked Billy.

"He lives with me," Charlie said.

"Did I ask you where he lived? I already asked you where *you* lived. But I didn't ask you where *he* lived, did I? I asked him. Didn't I ask him where he lives, Bumper?"

The other cop, the driver, looking embarrassed about being used for a ricochet board the way his partner was doing, said, "That's right, Dennis," just to go along with it. Cop solidarity.

Charlie stamped his feet a little and ducked his head aside, away from a bite of wind, hoping the cop would let him out of the loop. Off the hook. Would stop pushing it, mining him for answers to questions without real consequence, asking for the display. Asking him to bend over in submission. Hinting for it.

Charlie couldn't give it to him. All at once he knew that he wouldn't give it to him. Not with Billy standing there at his shoulder. Not after trying to teach his young protégé the right way, the manly way. Keeping him away from hard drugs, loose women and all that. Knocking it into his head that his way, Charlie's way, might look a little harder but that the payoff was sweeter, being a man who could lift his head up anywhere, stand upon his dignity with anyone. Showing Billy that his way was a better way than the way of Jasper Tourette, Billy's cousin.

"When I'm talking to you I expect you to answer me, boy. When I'm talking to your brother, you shut up," Dennis said, less aggressively, almost sweetly, meaning to disconnect but making the insult greater.

Charlie made a quarter-turn to the rhythm of his lightly stamping feet, peering over his shoulder, catching a glimpse of Wilda standing there on the sidewalk, witness to his humiliation. Even from a distance he could see her pale eyes as flat as two dimes. There was a little smile on her mouth as though she were about to tell a joke but was waiting for someone to listen.

"I asked you where you live," Charlie heard the cop, Dennis, say to Billy.

"With my friend. Like he say. Sedgewick and Locust. Seward Park. Cabrini-Green."

Charlie turned his head the other way and saw Billy with the same tight little smile on his mouth, answering the cop's questions. Speaking in syncopation. Emphasizing every word like a drum beat. Spacing them out. Saying more than he had to say, as though he were talking to somebody who was mentally retarded.

"What do you do?" Dennis asked.

"I play the clarinet."

"What do you do for a living?"

Billy's tight smile broke. He was too good-natured to keep the insolence alive. "I work over to the Fire Academy."

"You a fireman?" Dennis asked, letting his eyebrows pop up, making a joke about Billy possibly being a fireman.

"I got my application in. I'm in the building maintenance crew. Hey, I work for the city, just like you guys do, pal."

"I'm not your 'pal.' You want to call me something, you call me 'officer.' You call me 'sir.' Maybe we both get our checks from City Hall but you don't work for the city the same way we work for the city. It's more like you sweep up the shit behind the men who do the real work of the city."

Billy lost his good nature. He turned away. "Oh, fuck you, ossifer."

"Listen, officer, you want us to respect you," Charlie said softly but quickly, hoping to distract him, "call you 'officer,' call you 'sir', you got to show us the same respect. Shouldn't call us 'boys'. Should call us 'mister.' "

But it wasn't doing any good. Dennis was out of the blue and white one side and the one called Bumper out the other, coming around, his hand resting on the butt of his gun, shouting at Billy, "Don't you walk away from us, we're talking to you. Don't you use your mouth on an officer of the law."

Billy turned around to face Dennis's rush and put his hands up, holding the clarinet case in front of his face to take the blow he thought was coming.

"Sonofabitch," Dennis said, slipping his club out of its harness, bringing it up to knock the clarinet case aside, backing Billy across the sidewalk and against the wall, the stick held in both hands across Billy's throat.

Charlie gave a yell and started to move.

"Don't you move, you nigger sonofabitch," Bumper yelled, his voice up a register, sounding like a frightened woman, adrenaline pumping, drawing his voice thin.

Rage leaped in them, the white men and the black men, like dogs off the leash, rushing from the dark alleys.

Wilda screamed. It stopped them dead in their tracks, all four, the cops and the black men under attack. They all looked at her as though they thought she was crazy, as though she were interfering in something that wasn't any of her business. As though none of them wanted anything to stop what they were getting into until it played itself out.

"Spread yourself against the wall, goddammit," Dennis said.

"Ease off, Dennis," Bumper said. "Ease off a little." Tossing glances at Wilda, wondering what she might do next, scream again, even take off her shoe and come at them. Knowing that they had to lower the intensity of this confrontation, get it under control, work it according to the numbers, according to the book. Easy on the language. Easy on the temper. Keep the adrenaline in the belly. All the time moving Charlie around to the wall where Billy now stood with his hands over his head, clarinet case hooked in one hand by his thumb, palms flat again the bricks, body at an angle, legs spread, taking the search without a murmur.

Charlie took the position without being told and let the cop pat him down.

"Okay, now get in the back of the car. Don't lip me. Don't drag your feet. Just get in the back of the car," Dennis told Billy.

"What for?"

"I told you not to lip me, you—"

"Hey, Dennis," Bumper warned.

"I'm on top of it, Bumper. I got it under control. Don't you worry."

He walked Billy over to the blue and white, ready with the club, but not laying another finger on him.

Ah, shit, Bumper thought, now I got to follow his lead. I got to put this one in the back of the car, too.

As Charlie followed Billy into the blue and white, Dennis snatched his briefcase out of his hand.

"What for you grabbing my briefcase?" Charlie protested.

Dennis put the briefcase flat on the seat in front and sat beside it. He snapped the latches.

"That's private property," Charlie said.

"I'm doing a lawful search."

"What the hell you talking about? You got no cause. Unless you planning to arrest us, you got no cause. You planning to arrest us?" Billy demanded.

"You a lawyer? You a musician *and* a fireman *and* a lawyer?"

"I knows my rights."

"You're busted. Okay, that's the way you want it, you're busted."

Bumper slammed the door on Charlie and Billy and walked around the car. He got in behind the wheel. He was shaking his head a little, wondering how he'd let it happen, letting Dennis go so far.

Charlie realized they were on their way to the stationhouse.

"What about Mrs. Carrigan?" he asked.

"What about her?" Dennis said.

"Well, just look at her. She's out there all alone—what time is it?—past two in the morning? You can't leave her standing there in a neighborhood like this."

"You should've thought about that before you messed up."

"Nobody messed up. This is all a misunderstanding that just got out of hand. The least you could do is give her a ride up to Wacker and see we can find her a cab."

"We ain't a limousine service," Dennis said.

"You're supposed to serve the public," Billy said. "You're supposed to do what's right, what's decent."

Bumper touched the accelerator and revved the engine as though the blue and white were impatient, as though he had no control of the vehicle.

But he didn't say anything and Dennis didn't say anything. Dennis tapped his partner's arm and Bumper released the brake.

"Officer," Wilda called, staying where she was, taking not one step closer. "Where are you taking my friends? What station?"

"Eighteenth. One-thirteen West Chicago."

"Don't worry, Charlie. I'll be down to get you out as soon as I get my money from the hotel," she called.

Bumper goosed the engine with his toe.

"Do what's right. Leaving a woman alone on the street this

time of the morning," Billy said in a pitying voice meant to make the white men feel small.

"Any woman hanging around a place like the Pussy Cat must know how to take care of herself," Bumper said, convincing himself she'd be all right.

They drove off and left Wilda standing there in her thin cloth coat with the fake fur collar.

37

THERE WERE JUST THE TWO OF THEM IN THE ROOM. SERGEANT Ray Sharkey, Merry Prankster, City Hall Pimp, and Phineas Aloysius Xavier Bosco Terrence Cavan, deputy superintendent of the Bureau of Investigative Services *and* the administrative assistant to the superintendent of police, Sharkey's Chinaman, mentor, and protector (but rarely confidant), sitting across from each other on a bed used for whoring.

"So you outfoxed the sonofabitch," Cavan said, waiting for Sharkey to laugh and agree.

But Sharkey knew that would be the wrong thing to do. He shouldn't act cocky. The proper demeanor was contrite until he got a clue from Cavan's expression that he could act otherwise.

"What I don't understand is why you went through all the trouble," Cavan said.

"I wanted to give the boys a—"

"No, no. Don't try that crap on me a second time. You could've hired two actors in Keystone Kop outfits and walrus mustaches. It would've made a better gag. You wanted it heavy. So tell me why."

When Sharkey didn't answer right away, Cavan went on. "All right, I'll tell you. Because you wanted to scare the shit out of Finnegan and The Candidate. You wanted to give them a bad couple of minutes. That's always been your trouble, Ray. You always go a little too fucking far."

"Why would I want to give them a bad couple of minutes, Finny?" Sharkey asked. "You know a reason why I'd want to do that?"

Cavan's eyes went dull for a second, his shoulders slumped, the sharp, dapper, fighting-cock energy he exuded failing him. He looked around vaguely, an old man suddenly irritated by all the petty annoyances surrounding him.

"We should've brought up a bottle," he said. "A little something to wet our whistle." He tried a little laugh. Falling back on the old saws, the stale maxims, trying to create a feeling of lasting fellowship.

"You could've done better by me, Finny," Ray said. "You could've let me know they were going after me."

"Better? How better?"

"You didn't have to leave me in the dark."

"What could they do to you? What could they shout about? A police sergeant taking a little graft, squeezing a little blood out of the goniffs. Fachrissake, the voters would laugh at that."

"But they wouldn't laugh so hard if it was some of the top brass involved, would they? They wouldn't laugh if it was a deputy superintendent on the take, maybe even the superintendent, maybe even higher. So you had to cut me loose? You couldn't afford to be tied to a crooked cop with the opposition running a sting on me? You couldn't stand up for me, couldn't walk beside an old friend?"

"I never said I'd walk beside you in a situation like this, Ray. Never. That's not the way it works and you know it. I've always walked *behind* you, Ray. I've always done that. Or in front of you when you needed somebody to run interference. But beside you. No, Ray. I never done that, because that way, if somebody takes a shot at you they could hit me and if there's one thing I ain't, it's a damn fool."

Sharkey was just looking at him. Cavan thought about how it was. You started off giving a guy a favor, giving a kid a hand, knowing how proud he'd be to have the sponsorship of an older man, a man with experience and clout.

Then the years went by and you were still twelve, fifteen years older than this kid, but twelve, fifteen years wasn't as big a difference when you were in your sixties and seventies as it had been when you were in your thirties.

Kids grew up.

Now they were both a couple of old dogs trying to sort out what was promised and what had not been promised twenty-five years before. The terms of an agreement never written down in the first place, a Chicago understanding—like spitting on your palms and shaking when you were kids—had been lost to memory and the contract never redefined.

Ray was looking at him unblinkingly and there was no ritual drink to ease the situation, to give him something to do with his hands.

"If you're talking friendship, that's a different story," Cavan said. "We been friends a long time now. And, that way, I'm sorry I had to let you down. But we're talking about saving asses, here, and you know the rules. You save your own ass first and then you see what you can do for friends."

"All you had to do was give me the word. It wouldn't've made much difference. I'm going to have to save my ass all by myself anyway. I know that," Sharkey said.

"We're talking survival here. I ain't saved a dime. I can't afford to go out without a pension."

"Hey, I know that song. It's the same one every cop on the take I ever knew sings. It's the one I'm singing, so I know all the words. So, okay, Finny, no hard feelings," Sharkey said, and raising a hand in farewell, he walked out the door, down the hall, down the stairs, and, when nobody was looking, retrieved the blue envelope with the five grand in it from the tub of icewater and bottled beer.

38

AFTER A WHILE WILDA COULD FEEL THE FREEZING CEMENT SENDing warnings through the thin soles of her shoes, into her feet, clutching at her ankles. Standing there wasn't going to accomplish a thing. She started walking south toward Wacker Drive. She could hear the thin streams of traffic on the double-decker roadway, Wacker Drive off to her right, people coming and going even at this hour when threads of false dawn lay like a hushed promise on the Lake off to her left.

She crossed Ohio, hurried to Grand. Stood there for a minute hoping for a cab.

She could hear the traffic in the quiet and sense the light over the lake in the dark but she felt as though she were walking in a wasteland with safety too far away to reach.

She was no good at streets, no good at distances, no good at directions, and it'd been six years away from Chicago.

New Orleans, Kansas City, Miami, Atlanta, Los Angeles, New York. Six years in strange cities, faraway places, among streets and alleys even less familiar than these. Always lost. Never knowing how far she was from the places where she slept.

On across Illinois, her heels beating out paradiddles, stumbling rhythms on the pavement. She'd never sold her body. That she'd never done. Not really. Not from a house and not on the streets. What made her think of that? she wondered, walking on a lonely street past 3:00 A.M.

She crossed Hubbard, reached the corner of the Mart on Kinzie, listening to the traffic on Wacker, sensing the light. All alone in the middle of a ravaged city. The Hawk scraped at her cheeks, tried to get its beak up her skirts, between her legs, chilling her bladder, causing an urgency.

Walking faster did some good, but it forced her to breathe harder, faster, sucking in the cold air until it cut her chest, sticking knives inside.

She turned off Orleans at Wacker and crossed the river at Lake. Somehow she thought she'd be safer if she crossed the river.

A black low-rider swung off the ramp at her back. She turned right on Canal, walking south, then turned west on Washington. The low-rider tracked her, shifting down until its engine merely idled, turning over with a throaty rumble.

"Hey, white pussy cat, pussy cat, pussy, pussy, pussy," a silky, insinuating voice crooned from the window of the car that paced her.

She brought her head up, straightened her back, the terror instantaneous (don't show it) cutting like a razor blade from groin to breast. Her heart rattled around in her chest like a tin toy out of control. She put her hand up to stop it, grabbed the collar of her coat, held it tight, wanting to shout at them to leave her alone but knowing there was mortal danger in admitting they were even there. How many? How old? To what purpose out on the streets this hour of the morning?

"You lookin' for a daddy, pussy cat? You lost in the wild streets? You searching for some warm and comfort?"

She should have gone straight down Canal to the Chicago and North Western Station, she thought, never mind the jog off the main road, never mind thinking there might be safety in the less traveled side streets.

She felt a terrible weakness in her knees, her legs, her loins. She was going to wet herself. Mustn't run, mustn't even hurry. In control. Haughty but not snippy. Unafraid but not arrogant. Don't look at them. Don't anger them. Don't invite them by the slightest sidelong glance to stop the car, get out of the car. Just keep walking. Tip-tap. Tip-tap.

She was walking faster. Without knowing it, but knowing it, she was walking faster. She was trotting. She was running. There was laughter chasing her down the hollow tunnel of the street.

"Gonna get a piece of poon. Gonna get a piece of tang."

The low-rider stopped. A teenage black got out of the back seat, scrambling over the shoulder of his friend in front.

"Look at the pussy run. Just look at her run."

The low-rider swept ahead of her, jumped the curb, blocked her way, sent her cowering against the wall.

It sat there rumbling and growling softly—urban tiger—as the driver and another one got out and approached her. Grinning whitely. Their arms stretched out, corralling her against the wall.

She felt a scream crowding up, clawing past her constricted throat, pounding painfully at her teeth. She opened her mouth but nothing came.

Her bladder let go.

She could hear her urine splattering on the sidewalk, soiling her shoes.

She could feel it wetting her legs and stockings.

She could smell it, sharp with the smell of fear, as sharp as splintered bones in the nose.

"Oh, fachrissakes, will you looka that?" one of the boys said in passionate disgust. "Will you fuckin'-A looka that?"

"Peeee-youuu."

A part of her mind examined what was happening as though she were an observer of an experiment in anthropology. Was urinating a survival technique among certain mammals? Would it be a lifesaver for Wilda Carrigan? She closed her eyes, she was afraid she was going to faint.

She heard the slam of the car doors, hooting laughter, the engine rumble rising to a roar. The tires screamed on the pavement.

She opened her eyes. They'd left their mark on the roadway.

She hurried toward her hotel.

Why had they gone away and left her alone?

How would she have lived the rest of her life if they'd stayed?

39

WILDA HOPED THE DESK CLERK AT THE RALSTON WOULD BE DOZing, wouldn't notice her wet stockings, her poor appearance.

But the desk clerk was a young man studying to be somebody someday and was alert to every possibility. You could never tell when opportunity might come your way in the most unlikely disguise. He looked up from his book and stared the woman up and down, the creamy skin, the flaming hair, the soft mouth like a promise, shaping itself into a kiss, trembling with some subtle invitation. He took inventory, his round glasses giving him the bewildered but sinister look of an owl. He saw the stained stockings. When she opened the coat he saw the thin dress clinging to her crotch, a slick of perspiration along the swell of her breasts in spite of the cold outside.

She went up to the desk and gave him a smile, pushing her hips against the counter as though pressing herself against his knees right through the wood.

"Do me a favor and call a taxi, will you? I'm going up to my room. Two-twenty."

"You going back out?" he asked, as though he really wanted to know, really wondered what a woman her age, with her looks, was doing coming back to a hotel at three-thirty in the A.M. and ordering a taxi to go right out again.

It was really none of his business and ordinarily Wilda would have told him to mind his P's and Q's and just do what he'd been told, but somehow just the fact that he wasn't leering at her, threatening her with rape and violence, made her feel kindly, even affectionate, toward him.

"I have to go out again—isn't it awful, this time of the morning, this cold out—and help a couple of friends who got themselves into a little bit of trouble because of me. So give me my key and call me a taxi so I can go do it. Okay?"

"Oh, sure, okay. I didn't mean to act nosy."

"That's all right. I wasn't scolding. No need to apologize."

They laughed, with surprise on their faces, as though laughter at such a time and in such a place was something more wonderful than they could say.

Wilda took her key and hurried to the elevator.

Up in her room she went right into the bathroom and voided her bladder again.

"Didn't think there'd be any left," she said aloud. "Felt like I peed a river." Making a joke of it now that the danger and terror were past. Taking comfort from the sound of her own voice.

She stripped off her stockings while she sat on the toilet and kicked out of her underpants when she was finished. Washed and dried her crotch and legs. Got fresh step-ins from her lingerie case folded on the dresser top and put them on. Looked for stockings or a pair of pantyhose but couldn't find a pair that weren't full of runs. So she'd go out with bare legs. So what?

Then she went over to the corner of the rug where she'd tucked her thin wad of money. What she didn't want to carry with her on the street. Not trusting hotel clerks and hotel safes, having had reason to doubt them in the past. She squatted there and counted out what she had. A hundred twenty dollars. Twenty more in her purse. Twenty in bills and a couple of dollars in change.

She put all the money she had into her change purse and closed it with a satisfying snap. She began to feel on top of things. Wilda Sharkey Carrigan could take care of herself. Could take care of her friends, too. Why not? She'd been on her own a long, long time.

She started to cry and had to sit down on the edge of the bed, it shook her so hard and came on so suddenly. She sat there crying for Billy and Charlie. Crying for trouble that traveled with her wherever she went, like a ghost that wouldn't let go of her arm. Crying for herself.

40

SHE STEPPED OUT OF THE TAXICAB LIKE A WOMAN GOING OUT ON a date, face washed and carefully made up (time taken for the sake of appearances while her friends despaired, she thought, ashamed of herself and her vanity), bare legs almost blue with cold, a scarf around her flaming hair.

There was four dollars showing on the meter. It would probably be that much more before she was out of the station with Charlie and Billy, but they couldn't very well step out into the cold dawn with the long walk back to New Orleans Street facing them without transportation waiting, and she didn't want to have to ask the cop at the desk the favor of calling for another cab. So, "Wait," she said, and tip-tapped into the funky heat and animal smells of the reception hall. Tip-tapped over to where Jim Titus, the desk sergeant, sat, green plastic shade protecting his eyes from the glare, scratching in a ledger.

He glanced up and she made a moment of taking off her scarf, shaking her hair loose, unbuttoning the buttons of her coat, throwing it open as though the heat already oppressed her. Giving him a look at the elegant woman she was, the kind of woman she was, coming out in the dark before dawn to help out two friends. That kind of woman. Pretty woman with flame-red hair and milk-white skin. A gently puzzled look, confused by the harshness of the world but unafraid of it. Loyal and true-blue to her friends. Showing how she could be loyal and true-blue to you if you'd only give her reason to be grateful.

There were cops and detectives, men and women, in uniform and in plainclothes, coming in and going out. All of them pausing to look at the wonder of her hair, the soft brilliance of her milk-white skin.

"You had two gentlemen, two gentlemen of color, brought into your station earlier this evening?" Wilda said, lifting the end of the sentence.

Her voice was soft, full of rough whispery growls like the feel of velvet stroked against the grain, little shadows of the South, little promises of laughter.

Titus had to shake himself and make himself remember this beauty standing in front of his desk was the whore, the nigger lover, the streetwalker that Dennis Machoose had raved on about while Bumper Slattery stood there looking uncomfortable. Christ, the look of her, the white skin and strawberry hair—milk and jelly bread—the body underneath the dress stretched across full breasts, swelling up from the V where she'd tucked a little frothy handkerchief. The soft material clinging to her hips, dipping into the valley at the bottom of her belly.

The things she promised just standing there had his heart going so fast and hard he could feel the shaking in his chest. For a minute there he was afraid to even talk for fear she'd hear a tremble in his voice.

"Names?" he said.

"Charlie Lincoln and Billy . . . I can't remember Billy's last name."

"Good friends, are they?" Titus said, making his judgment about the casual way she apparently took up with men. Making that little comment in the sly way of jealous housewives and hungry men.

"Charlie Lincoln is an old, old friend," Wilda said, trying hard to keep the edge out of her voice. "His friend is a new acquaintance of mine. But they were brought in together and I suppose they were booked together if they were booked, and—"

"I got the idea," Titus said, making a small production of running his finger down the pages of the daybook.

"No Charlie or Billy. Sorry, miss," he said, very polite, wanting to keep her there just so he could look at her.

This pretty little frown, like the frown of a cat, appeared

between her eyes, on the milk-white, flawless forehead. "You think maybe the officers never brought my friends in after all?"

"Well, there's a Lincoln down here, but no Charlie or Billy. Got a Harold Lincoln and a William Smith."

A little flash of annoyance (anger?) in the cool eyes.

"You've got to help me on this, Sergeant," Wilda said. "You're going to have to lead me by the hand through this unfamiliar territory. You get many people—two people, two men, two colored men, one with the last name of Lincoln—coming in here every night? You get much of that?"

So now she was showing her claws. Now she was giving him a little of the cutting edge of her temper.

That made Titus feel better. It was very hard dealing with a beautiful whore. Ugly whores were easy, but it was very difficult knowing just what tack to take with a gorgeous tramp. Very hard when what you wanted to do was ask her out and beg her to tell you why she was throwing herself away in the life. Why she wasn't ready to run away with you, anywhere she wanted to run, and live happily ever after. When all you wanted to do was kiss her face and wash her feet with your tongue and eat her crotch with a silver spoon, for God's sake.

"You're just staring at me, Sergeant. You're not answering me. Why is that?" Wilda said.

"Well, Smith, that's a name we get a lot of. It's very easy to forget a name like Smith. I've got to tell you frankly, miss . . ."

"Mrs. Mrs. Carrigan. What have you got to tell me frankly?"

"It comes as something of a surprise to see a lady like yourself coming into my station this hour of the morning asking after a couple of . . ." he stopped, stuttered, skipped, and went her way, "men of color brought in on drunk and disorderly."

"They weren't drunk and disorderly so far as I could tell. I know *I* wasn't drunk or disorderly."

"You were singing, walking arm in arm along the public thoroughfare at three in the morning. Disturbing the peace. You was at least disturbing the peace."

"I don't think there were any citizens asleep, that part of town. But I'm not here to debate with you, Sergeant. I'm here to see about getting my friend Mr. Lincoln and his friend Mr. Smith out of here."

"Do you know what I think, miss?" Titus said, leaning over his hands. "I think—"

"I think I know what you think, Sergeant," Wilda said, almost snappishly, annoyed at the attention, the background comments, of the cops and detectives milling around the reception area, coming and going. Not at all pleased by their attentions, the way they were acting like a bunch of construction workers who whistled and scratched and panted like a pack of dogs whenever a woman under eighty walked by. Like a pack of high school kids, nudging one another, saying how bold they could be given half a chance. Not at all pleased, listening to all that in the background, feeling their eyes all over her body, she a woman among them because of charitable necessity, on serious business.

The way she said it shut him up, decided him against giving her any good fatherly advice, a mature, beautiful white woman like herself running around with a bunch of niggers.

"Bench bail's been set at one hundred dollars," Titus said.

Wilda smiled and went into her purse. Counted out the hundred dollars. Looked at him as though very pleased with herself, for having done it right.

"Apiece," Titus said.

She looked bewildered, casting her eyes around as though looking for someone to come help interpret the strange language he was speaking.

"Each," Titus said. "One hundred dollars each."

She counted what was left. Even the change. Forty-two dollars and thirty-eight cents. The taxi waiting outside, twelve, maybe fifteen dollars before they all got home.

"You can only bail out one of them," Titus said, cool as a cucumber, official in manner. "Take your pick."

Wilda didn't hesitate. Charlie would know better what to do. "Mr. Lincoln," she said. "I'd like to bail out Mr. Harold Lincoln."

"Just wait over there, miss. It'll take a few minutes."

"I've got a taxi waiting on the meter," she said.

"Well, that's up to you."

The goddamn callousness of it, the plain and utter disregard of simple courtesy, brought tears she thought had been all cried out rising, pinching her nose, constricting her throat, misting her eyes.

She hurried out to the waiting cab and paid him off, having an idea of how long the process of release was going to take.

When Charlie was brought out of the holding cage in back,

his cornet bag and belongings already returned to him at the checkout cage, he looked rumpled and whey-faced, washed out, not at all like the proud African he'd appeared to be when first they'd met at that club in Kansas City ten years before.

He looked like a city nigger, a little seedy around the edges, sly-eyed, crafty, looking for a way out of the trap he found himself in, glad to be kicked loose, ready with the yessirs and nosirs. He didn't look capable of helping anybody, least of all himself.

He hesitated there in the middle of the filthy linoleum, his horn bag clutched in his arms like a bum's bindle, casting uncertain glances around, his eyes red where they weren't yellow, his teeth yellow too when he skinned them, smiling at the cops walking by—who didn't smile back, not even the black ones. Then he saw Wilda just standing up to walk toward him, and for a second she saw the shame that flashed in his eyes and she could have cried all over again.

Charlie started walking toward her and she walked a little faster and some of the people watching stared because they looked like two people in one of those wartime movies, meeting at the train station, in the bombed-out city square, outside a prison camp, lovers reunited, and they were afraid, the white cops and the black cops, that the stunningly beautiful white whore was going to kiss the black man on the mouth. Right there in front of them. Kiss him on the mouth.

But all they did was shake hands, he politely, she as though conferring a gift.

"I want to thank you for coming for us, Wilda," Charlie said.

"Did you think I wouldn't?" she asked, immediately angry.

"Uh?" he said, surprised at her anger.

"You think I'd let you down?" she asked softly, the flash of anger abating, reading his eyes.

"Sitting in the cage you get to wondering if everybody you ever knew just that minute forgot all about you."

He turned his head, looking right and left, turned his body, clutching the cornet, his expression expectant.

"I didn't have enough to bail you both," Wilda said.

He stared at her as though he didn't quite understand what she'd said.

"I'm about sixty dollars short. More if you figure what the taxi home'll cost. You have any money on you?"

"Not enough or we'd already be out."

"You got anybody you could call?"

"This hour of the morning?"

"How about you call your employer? What's his name?"

"Jasper Tourette? Billy's cousin?"

"So there," she said.

"I can try and find him. But, this hour of the morning, no telling where he might be."

She looked at the toes of her shoes as though she expected a solution to their predicament to be written there on the imitation alligator caps.

"I've got a brother who's a policeman," she said.

"You never told me."

"Oh, yes. He's a detective sergeant."

"Well, then, maybe you—"

"Can give him a call?"

"You got any reason not to give him a call?"

"I don't like to ask him for favors—"

"I can understand that."

"—But I will. I certainly will," she said, understanding that Charlie couldn't ask—or for some reason didn't want to ask—Jasper Tourette for the favor. "Well," she continued, trying to lighten things up, "what's this—your name's Harold? How come they call you Charlie?"

"Because we got two front names, just like white folks," Charlie said, letting his bitterness show.

41

RAY HAD KNOWN FROM THE BEGINNING THAT HE'D HAVE TO PAY up sooner or later.

He'd always believed you paid for whatever you got out of life and nothing that'd ever happened to him had told him different. You got something or you took something and life would hand you the tab, one way or another.

Screwing Flo that night after the Sharkey fight had cost him a good part of his life. Avenging the murder of Minifee had given him a reputation for being undependable, had cost him. Muscling into Shelley Orchid's gambling operation was going to cost him. Roma Chounard was surely going to cost him.

Sometimes, alone with Roma in the little flat in which he spent more and more of his time when he wasn't on the job, he felt warm, safe, and at home. She'd be softly clattering around the kitchen, humming to herself (as his mother used to do long ago), and he'd be in the parlor in an easy chair (that was almost the twin of the chair his father still had), and he'd be almost overwhelmed by this feeling of contentment.

She was sleeping in the bedroom. He could hear her move every now and then, the bedsprings speaking in the dark.

It was funny how she slept differently than Flo had slept.

Roma moved boldly, seeking her comfort, claiming her space. Flo had always turned with small, stealthy movements as though she didn't belong and feared discovery.

He fell asleep and dreamed and in the dream he was a boy again, walking through the summer streets looking for a game of marbles with a kid by the name of Leroy Scarlet.

He awoke from the dream with tears on his face; you paid for such sweet memories with weeping, with a sense of loss so great it felt as though someone had dug into your heart and guts and scooped them out, leaving you hollow, like the discarded husk of some insect.

Roma was sitting on the footstool, her elbows on her knees, her head thrust forward as though studying his sadness, an expression on her face caught somewhere halfway between pity and curiosity.

"You must have the damnedest dreams," she murmured.

"They ain't so bad."

He held out his arms and she slipped forward onto her knees and leaned her body into him between his legs. And they stayed like that, like two people comforting each other against the terrors of the world, just the way husbands and wives are supposed to do.

"Did I wake you? Did I yell out in my sleep or something?"

"No, no. You didn't wake me up, your dream woke me up."

She was forever saying things he didn't understand, didn't know how to take, this alien woman.

"Are you coming to bed?" she asked after a while.

"I'm up. I might as well stay up. I think I picked up a lead last night on that killing down to the Westley Hotel."

"What one was that?"

"Didn't I tell you?"

"No, you didn't tell me."

"Well, maybe Dubrowski and me'll wrap it up today, tomorrow, and I'll tell you."

Sitting there having a cop's domestic conversation as the dawn started breaking.

She stirred, her face burrowing into his shirt.

"My God you stink. You stink of sweat and whiskey. You drunk?"

"No, I ain't drunk. I might've been drunk a couple of hours ago, but I ain't drunk now."

"So, that's just the way you smell. You white bodies got a funny smell."

"But at least we got rhythm," he said.

"You better not go back to work smelling like that. You better take the time for a shower, clean socks and underwear."

She started untying his tie, which was already loose. She helped him out of his shoes and stripped off his socks and unbuckled his belt.

When he was naked she said, "What the hell, you going to spend an hour getting sweet, you might as well take another minute."

"Hey, that an insult?" he asked, joining in her teasing.

"That's an ob-ser-va-tion," she said.

She felt like silk when he put his arms around her. She felt like velvet when she climbed into his lap, straddling him, fitting him into her.

42

RAY STEPPED OUT OF THE CAR IN THE STATION PARKING LOT—the hour with Roma, the smell and touch of her still clinging to his body like a second skin—wondering what his feeling of satisfaction, yet deprivation, was all about.

He'd gone at her like a kid with an ice cream cone, trying to take it slow, not wanting to gobble it up because it was so good, but eating it like you were starving and then it was gone and you wanted more of it. You wanted more of it and were afraid that even if you had more of it, it would never be enough. You loved the stuff so goddamn much.

He stumbled when he heard his mind say "loved" inside his brain. What the hell was love all about? How the hell could you use the same word for what you felt for an ice cream cone, a mother, a family, a job, a wife, a goddam black hooker he'd traded for the hooker concession at a crap game?

His sweat turned to ice and a tremor shook him so badly he almost dropped his keys. He was cold in the time it took to walk across the parking lot.

Then he was inside and hot as hell again.

"What have we got here, a steam bath?" Ray said, as he came flinging through the door. "You renting towels, Titus? You taking a little graft here running a bathhouse for queers?"

There was a woman in a fur-collared coat and thin high-heeled shoes standing at the public telephone on the wall, just hanging up the receiver.

He put on his sweet face, serious angel face, looking at the legs in the shoes and under the coat. Nice legs. Bare legs. Vanilla ice cream legs. What kind of a woman went out with bare legs in this kind of weather? Bare, white legs with the backs of the knees the kind that could make a man get down on all fours and howl. He was ready to bet the front of her knees were dimpled. If that proved to be true there were men who would pay a fortune to get down there between those legs while she held him with the vise of those dimpled knees.

A man could go to jail even *thinking* about such pleasures.

She turned toward him as though she heard his thoughts, her eyebrows (hardly there) lifting, red hair shifting in the draft from the closing door, holding up her hands, this marvelous smile on her face as though the look on his face pleased her beyond words.

"For Christ's sake! Wilda!" he nearly shouted.

"I was just trying to call you," Wilda said, as though astonished at the coincidence, as though fate had intervened to bring her brother to her. "I been trying to call you for an hour."

"Well, I wasn't home, was I?" he said, stooping a little, bending his knees a little, so he could step in and scoop her up off her feet.

"Where the hell were you, Ray, this hour of the morning?"

"I could ask you the same."

"I was waiting here so I could call you. I didn't want to wake you up in the middle of the night. Where were you? I called and called."

"I was out protecting the people of the city, wasn't I?"

"My brother, the cop. Gimme a hug," she said, holding her arms out to him and taking a step toward him.

They put their cheeks together. Wilda moved her head a bit and kissed the corner of his mouth.

His heart lurched and the adrenaline started pumping and he felt his scrotum cringe. He knew what he was feeling—what he felt each and every time Wilda came home and they touched the first time—was the wrong thing for a brother to feel for a sister.

But he knew in the bone—and kept the thought in a secret place—that he would give almost anything to lie with his sister, against her milk-white flesh, her red hair crowning on the pillow, glowing at the bottom of her belly.

He felt himself getting an erection and was overcome by shame.

Wilda must have felt it too because she backed him off, holding him by the shoulders. She gave him a knowing smile that had something of a precocious child about it and something of a stranger.

"What's a nice girl like you doing in a joint like this?" Ray asked.

"Trying to bail out a couple of friends of mine got themselves into a little misunderstanding because of me."

"How's that?"

"We were leaving a jazz club after closing. They were going to walk me back to my hotel. See that I was kept safe. These two cops stopped us."

"Why'd they do that? What were your friends doing?"

"They were walking me home like I said. We were just walking along arm in arm singing to keep warm."

"Your friends have a couple too many?" he asked, cocking his head to one side, giving her a knowing—an understanding—smile.

"Nothing like that."

"So what reason did the officers give for stopping you and your friends?"

"They didn't like their complexions."

"Oh, for Christ's sake, Wilda . . ."

Her eyes narrowed, glinting blades above cheeks suddenly tight as drums, her mouth wide and harsh, showing the skull beneath the skin.

"I don't want to hear it, Ray."

"Hear what?"

"My friends, Charlie Lincoln and Billy Smith, are perfectly respectable working men. Musicians when they find the work. Laborers otherwise. Perfectly decent men who—"

He took her by the arm just above the elbow and moved her back until she had to sit on the bench. He sat beside her.

"I've got no doubt, Wilda. I'm not saying they ain't good people. I'm not saying I maybe wouldn't like to have them for friends. I got plenty of colored friends."

"Cops," she said, harshly, as though they were a special breed of wolf that only ran together in a pack no matter what the color of their pelts might be.

"I'm saying I got plenty of friends in a lot of different jobs, a lot of different places. What I'm talking about here is suitability."

"White people go to jazz clubs all the time."

"Not white women on their own. You were on your own. Weren't you on your own?"

"I just got back into town so, yes, I was on my own."

"So a white woman on her own walks into a colored jazz club, sits down, has a drink, takes up with a couple of colored men—"

"One of whom I've known for nine or ten—"

"I don't care you grew up with him," Ray said, his voice barely held under control, he wanted to shout at her so badly. "I'm saying you took up with a couple of colored men and left the club at what? Two in the morning. Two-thirty in the morning? After they closed up. Where's this club?"

"Orleans Court."

"Right there a hop away from Cabrini-Green. Walking through a colored neighborhood with two—"

"Why don't you say it?" she said, challenging him, her voice growing louder.

"Say what?"

"Niggers. Two niggers. Isn't that what you almost keep saying?"

"Keep your voice down, goddammit," he whispered fiercely. "Don't tell me what I almost say. Sometimes I say nigger, you want to know. Sometimes I say that. It's like I say Jesus Christ. I'm not going to argue nonsense with you, Wilda. I'm trying to tell you something about the way you act. The dangerous way you sometimes act."

"I can take care of myself," she said, defiantly, just like she used to do when she was a little kid and was told not to do this or that.

"I'm not going to comment on that," Ray said. "So you don't mind putting yourself in danger. What I'm saying is that you were putting your colored friends in danger. You understand that?"

"Things shouldn't be that way."

"They shouldn't be that way, Wilda. You're right. But that's the way they are and I'm telling you to start operating in the real world before you get yourself killed or you get somebody who likes you killed. So now I'll go see what I can do. What'd you say their names were?"

"I already bailed out one of them. I had enough for one but not for two," she said. "The one still in jail's called Billy Smith."

"All right, so let me go see," he said and got up and walked over to the desk.

"I got to ask you, Sharkey," Titus said.

"What do you got to ask?"

"That beautiful hooker over there. You seem to be old friends. But I don't remember seeing her around."

Ray almost said it right out, that the pretty woman Titus was calling a hooker was his sister, but it wouldn't form in his mouth, wouldn't work its way past his teeth and tongue. What the hell was she getting him into here? If he asked a favor for Wilda and said it was because she was his sister, the word would go out, Sharkey's sister slept with coons. For God's sake.

"We're acquainted from way back," he said.

"But how come I don't see her around?"

"She comes and goes."

"They all come and go."

"What's going on here, Titus, you surprised I know a woman you don't know?"

"She's no kitten. She's been around any length of time, she should've passed under my eye once or twice."

"She ain't what you think. Take my word."

"So, what's your interest? Is she a prospect?"

"Prospective what?"

"Prospective entertainer. Prospective snitch. Prospective connection."

"Connection to what?"

"The dinges. Whatever the dinges are into."

Ray looked at Wilda over his shoulder, a rush of anger filling up his belly and rushing into his chest, turning his face red, giving his feelings away.

"This one she couldn't bail, how you got him booked?" Sharkey asked.

"Nothing. They were picked up on a chickenshit gripe. The patrolmen and the coons had a shouting match and it got personal."

"So you're just letting this one cool off a little?"

"That's all. He didn't have such a big lippy mouth, he could've walked out of here with his buddy. So now he could be looking at a drunk and disorderly."

Ray made a face.

"I told you it was nothing."

"That's it?"

"They was singing at the top of their lungs."

"Anything else?"

"Resisting."

"Somebody work them over? They marked up?"

"No. It's just down for resisting."

"I understand resisting."

"It's not a cover for any damage done to them."

"So one's already out the door?"

"You want me to do you the favor and kick the other one out the door?"

Ray thought about it. He thought about Wilda. He thought about colored men dumb enough to be walking the streets of that neighborhood, especially with a white woman, particularly that hour of the night. He thought about how fools like that deserved a little inconvenience.

"So you want me to give him a pass?" Titus asked.

"What? No. No, that's all right. Keep the asshole. He needs a lesson."

He turned his head, looking back at Wilda, frowning to show his dismay with what he was being told. When he turned back to face Titus, he was grinning.

Titus was savvy enough not to answer the smile with one of his own, they were doing an act for the redhead.

"In fact why don't you just make that sucker do the stations of the cross?"

Then he walked back and told Wilda that there'd been an administrative mix-up and her friend Billy Smith had somehow been sent to another stationhouse.

43

WILDA ASKED SHARKEY TO STOP BY A DRUGSTORE SO SHE COULD buy some pantyhose before he dropped her off back at her hotel.

"I'm going to go back to the station and ask around," he lied, trying to keep his eyes off her legs as she put the pantyhose on under her skirt. "See what I can do to expedite this matter. I'll locate your friend, don't you worry."

There was a bar just down the street from the hotel. She turned her head to look at it as they drove by.

"You want to buy me a drink?" she asked.

"First thing in the morning?"

"I'm a little shaky. A little tired. I haven't had any sleep. I could use a drink."

"All right."

He parked the car at the curb and they walked back to the bar.

All the drinkers at the bar on the morning shift seemed to catch a breath as they walked in. Wilda didn't know if it was at the sight of a pretty, red-haired woman or because they spotted Ray for a cop. He was looking into the eyes of everyone who dared looked back, as they walked down the bar, staring with his cop's eyes, looking for guilt, judging their capacity for crime.

They settled themselves on stools and the bartender strolled over.

"You're going to give my friend a little of your time?" Wilda asked.

"I'll give it every minute I can give it, Wilda. You've got to understand, I got other duties, other obligations."

He looked up sharply at the bartender. Looked at him hard

as though he wanted to know just what the hell he thought he was doing standing there.

"Anything?" the barkeep asked.

"Wilda?" Sharkey said.

"Gin and tonic, squeeze of lime."

"Short beer and a whiskey," Sharkey said.

Sharkey waited until the beer was drawn, the shot glass filled. The barkeep placed them on the wood in front of Sharkey and glanced at Wilda.

"That's all we're going to want until we call you," Sharkey said.

The barkeep nodded and walked away.

"The way you do that," Wilda said.

"Do what?" Sharkey asked.

"Intimidate people with a look and a couple of words."

"What'd I say? Just what the hell did I say?"

"You're doing it now. You're doing it to me."

Sharkey held the shot glass to his mouth, the rim resting on his lower lip, the pinkie finger of his right hand slightly extended like some old Irish woman taking tea, pretending to elegance and fine manners, pausing there, regarding Wilda with his cop's eyes. He threw his head back and splashed the whiskey behind his teeth, the motion of a soldier taking poison, self-destructing, taking courage from the fatal act.

Still looking at her, he drank a third of the beer in the small glass, then took out a clean folded handkerchief from his back pocket and patted his lips. Then he finally broke the eye contact (she wouldn't blink first), and rolled his shoulder closer to her, looking over the other as though making sure nobody was listening in, the conspiratorial posture of ten generations of Old World Irish engaged in insurrection and intrigue.

"I've got to tell you something, Wilda. I don't know why I've got to tell you, but apparently I do. You're my sister. You're my blood. You think I'm—"

"You judge me, Ray. You—"

"—always thinking the worst of you."

"—always act like you're judging me."

"I'm not judging you. I'm concerned about your welfare. I'm not telling you that you shouldn't live your life. You live your life the way you want to. You don't ask me how you should live it. I don't expect that. You live your life in other cities far away from home. You live your life with people I don't even know their names. What do you think? I'm supposed to just sit with my hands folded and a smile on my kisser—I don't see or hear from you, how many years?—when you come back and ask me to do you this favor which—"

"I don't see it's very much of a favor."

"—I'm perfectly willing to do you. Perfectly willing to do for you," he said again, a little irritation, a little anger, pushing the words out. Just a little bit of the old clenched teeth, primate threat display. "I didn't say it was much but it's something you asked me to do and I'm doing it. You understand I can't walk into the system, tell everybody, 'Drop what you're doing. Never mind the rapists, the child abusers, the murderers. To hell with all that. My sister asks me this favor. She wants this drunk colored boy kicked loose—' "

"He wasn't drunk."

" '—so let's get our *fucking* priorities straight,' " he finished, his voice growing thin, rising above a whisper.

"You always go overboard, don't you, Ray? You always make everything ridiculous by exaggerating things. By using the most excessive, outrageous language."

She brushed out her hair with her fingers. She straightened up and made herself tall, stretching up like a preening swan, reaching out for the bartender's attention without having to speak. When he took a step toward her she said, "Do me again," deliberately giving the words a little spin, a little suggestiveness, tricking Sharkey into silence until the drink was mixed and served.

"It's not what you think," she said. "Me and my friends."

"Hey, your life, babe."

"You don't mean that. You don't *fucking* mean that," she said, turning her head so that she looked as though she were talking into her shoulder, joining him in the Irish conspiracy of whispers, plotting, quarreling, or making love-talk in confidence, as though every ear were listening, every stranger a counterspy, every conversation a plot.

Her eyes were filled with unshed tears. He reached out and touched the corner of her eye with his thumb, his fingers caressing her neck behind her ear, releasing a drop that ran down her cheek. "Hey, Wilda, you don't have to do that."

"You've got your ways and means and I've got mine," she

said, sniffing like a child, laughing a little at the same time. "I just want you to know that Charlie Lincoln is just an old friend of mine. I like the music. That's how we met. I hardly know his friend, Billy Smith. He's just a boy. I'm not fucking either one of them—"

"For Christ's sake—"

"—and don't intend to."

"—why are you doing talking to me this way?"

"You think I never heard the word?"

"I know you heard the word. It's me that doesn't want to hear you say the word. It ain't necessary, that kind of language, when you're talking to your brother."

"I just wanted you to know in case it might have something to do with what kind of effort you're putting out on Billy Smith's behalf, on my friend Charlie Lincoln's behalf."

"While we're on the subject. You see this Charlie Lincoln? He come back to the station with the money to bail his friend?"

She sat there silently.

"Don't strain yourself, Wilda. Don't strain yourself thinking up excuses for the man."

"It's not so easy raising money early in the morning," she said.

"Don't play around the edges, Wilda. You heard what I just said. These people are not dependable. They don't make good friends. For God's sake, Wilda, why can't you stick to your own kind?"

"Some good Irish Catholic like Bill Carrigan, liked to see if he could break my jaw?"

"I don't know about some goddamn slum mick from Brooklyn you decided to marry, your family never even got a look at him ahead of time. But like that, Wilda. I saw the man once and that's all it took for me to see he was a wrong number, but I kept my peace because you acted like everything was hunky-dory. All you had to do was tell me that the bastard was beating on you and I would've hopped a plane into New York and knee-capped the sonofabitch. But that's then and now's now." He covered her hand with his hand. "For Christ's sake, Wilda, trust me. I got people working on Smith's little difficulty."

She nodded her head slowly. What else could she do?

"It's good to see you, kid," he said. "Now, why don't you go up to your room and get a little shut-eye?"

She slid off the stool, catching her skirt with her hand before it slid too far up along her thigh. She kissed him on the cheek. She was three steps away before he called her, knowing she'd stop and even come back a step to hear what more he had to say, exercising his power over her. He took out his money clip and peeled off two fifty-dollar bills and five twenties. She wouldn't come any closer when he held them toward her, caught between the first two fingers of his hand.

"Here," he said, getting off the stool, practically lunging forward to capture one of her wrists, stuffing the two hundred into her hand.

"No!" she said, knowing she already had the attention of the men in the bar, struggling just a little trying to get her hand free.

"You shorted yourself bailing out your friend. Go on, take it. Do me the favor."

She took the money then, a little impish smile curling up the corners of her pink mouth, recalling the child she'd been. "You know what these dumbos are thinking, don't you, Ray?" she asked very softly. "They're thinking you're paying me off for services rendered."

44

BILLY SMITH SAT ON A ROLLED-UP MATTRESS, A NEARLY EMPTY pack of cigarettes in the pocket of his denim shirt, hiding behind his glasses, sitting there but feeling a powerful need to walk. To run. To start running, get up the speed, and just smash on through the barred door at the far end of the cage. Run through the streets of the city, back to Cabrini-Green, back to the Pussy Cat, back to his friend Charlie (wherever he might be, just as long as it was outside), and warn him about messing with white-skinned women. Back to his cousin, Jasper Tourette, who let him go his way and didn't offer much advice or help but was still family. Which had to count for something in this shitty world.

He'd heard the stories about Cook County Jail. Not as bad as State, it being only a facility to hold for trial or upon conviction for Class C felonies, incarceration for up to two years.

Bad enough all the same, the things that went on behind the walls. Worse, some said, than in the more orderly prisons because of the confusion of all the comings and goings. Plenty of opportunity for acts of violence and coercion. The victim soon to be out of sight and therefore out of mind.

"Grab a hole!" the trustee sang out. Everybody immediately stepped into the cells and Billy followed suit.

A white boy about eighteen or nineteen rolled out of the top bunk and stood beside Billy. A smile passed between them, the first crack in the grim facade Billy had assumed behind his dark glasses.

Billy wanted to ask why they were being locked up at the supper hour, since this was the first time he hadn't been on the move from jail to jail at mealtime, but he was afraid he'd give away the fact that he was so innocent and vulnerable.

But the white boy seemed to understand that fact without being told. "They're bringing in supper, is why we're locked down. It'll only take five, ten minutes," he said.

"Any good?" Billy asked.

"Sunday," he said. "Sundays they serve the best meal of the week. Creamed turkey on bread. Green beans and stewed peaches or apricots. They got tea but they also got containers of milk. My name's Jack Nellis," he went on as though he were part of the menu.

"Billy Smith."

"So, Billy Smith," Nellis went on, "trustees help with the serving. When the creamed turkey comes in the garbage cans, they go digging around in there for the biggest pieces. They keep out a couple loaves of bread. Got them a little jar of mayonnaise in there. After dinner, an hour, two hours, anybody still hungry, anybody wants a nice turkey sandwich with mayonnaise can buy one from the trustee, cell number one, three dollars."

"Racket," Billy said, eager for conversation and the comfort he knew it would bring, but still hiding behind his glasses and his silence.

"Guards make shit," said Moonlight, a tall, skinny black man, another cell mate. "They got to supplement their wages. A nickel here, a nickel there. Asshole's way of gettin' by."

"At least it keeps them out of jail," Billy said, inviting them into the joke, showing off how funny he could be.

Nellis stared at him blankly, trying to work it out, not getting it. "They *are* in jail, though. They're in jail just like we're in jail . . . except at least they got an angle," he said, as though an angle, a scam, an edge, was the most important thing in the world.

After the dinner of small bits of turkey buried in a starchy white sauce, boiled string beans, some stewed fruit, and a square of pink Jell-O, some took to their cots and mattresses and some walked along the length of the cage, stopping here and visiting there.

Billy sat down on his mattress again, taking small comfort in a full belly since the quality of the food was already giving him cramps, a churning of the gut that warned him he might soon have to use the toilet in the cell, dropping his denims, baring his ass, exposing himself to any eyes that wished to watch.

A figure, as squat and round as one of the galvanized metal garbage cans, planted itself in front of him. He looked up through his dark glasses, scarcely raising his head, pretending to be nearly unaware of the blocking of the fading light that pierced the dirty windows beyond the bars and perimeter corridor as the sun went down. A black man with a shaved head like an inverted bowl of bronze, a scar, shining pink, slashing him from eyebrow to chin, dipping in at the corner of the mouth (knife deflected on its way to the throat?), giving his face a smile of perpetual amusement or threat.

"Gimmie cigarette," he rumbled harshly, like a phlegm-masked cough rising from his belly.

A shaft of terror, as bright and sharp as a solid blade, pierced Billy's heart and bowels, bringing forth a sudden flatulence so surprising and powerful that it escaped his clenched buttocks before he could prevent it. He farted loudly and outrageously even as he heard himself say (contrary to any intention of prudence or self-preservation), "I ain't got any."

The squat monster was at first dismayed and then astonished at the boldness of the refusal, the goddamn insult implied in matching fart to words. He turned his head and glared when a catcall (uttered behind closed lips) chided him and somebody else remarked, "That fish farted right in your face, Deever."

As the laughter of the other inmates rattled through the cells, along the corridor, the marvel of Billy's retort already being told and retold, clattering from tongue to tongue and ear to ear, Deever's face twisted up in a grimace as though he were in some terrible pain or about to deliver some terrible punishment and he turned on his heel and walked away, his swinging shoulders and broad back saying, It ain't over, motherfucker, as clearly as though the words were written there.

Nellis reached over and poked Billy on the shoulder, making him turn around to receive the grins and stares (of admiration?) of Nellis, Moonlight, a Mexican with an air of patient waiting about him who wasn't called by any name, and Mackle, the man without legs, who was treated with some deference by those who seemed to be familiar with it all.

It was as though they'd claimed him as their own because his mattress roll was on the floor of their cell, the way men without true allegiances were apt to do.

Moonlight glanced over his shoulder and made a gesture with his head, smiling softly, and for no reason that he could understand (was he learning to read minds as well; was that a convict's skill?), Billy knew that Moonlight was telling him that there was more to be done. Having met a challenge, he must offer a challenge, and put the matter to rest somehow.

So, afraid that he might lose the contents of his bowels in the simple act of standing up, he did stand up and went walking the length of the aisle, his eyes (behind the shades) watching Deever standing against the steel shelf at the end of the cage opposite the trustees' cell.

He walked the length of the cage twice and each time he approached Deever he faced the scowling hoodlum as he passed, not making a direct challenge of it, but simply scanning Deever's face as though it were just one among many and not to be feared.

On the way he also passed a tattooed man who made a kissing motion with his lips and when Billy failed to respond the first time said, "Sheeee-it," when he passed him the second.

Then he went back to his cell, dropped his pants and relieved himself, unable to hold it anymore. He lit a cigarette, offering one to Nellis, who accepted it gratefully, apparently having none of his own or the means to buy any. Offering his pack all around, making friends. The old con taking a dump and holding sociable conversation.

As dusk fell, the blue light outside fading, the yellow lights of the electric fixtures growing brighter in contrast, softening the faces of the caged men, conversations sprang up and they could have been, from appearances alone, a bunch of laboring men at the end of a long, hard day, sharing one another's company.

Men wandered here and there, stopping in at this cell and that, as though strolling the streets of a neighborhood, visiting friends sitting out on the stoops and porches.

Even when the tattooed man and Deever wandered in, they made no gesture toward Billy and appeared to hold no grudges or harbor any evil purpose. They simply sat down where there was room and in the atmosphere of such friendliness Billy even handed around his pack of cigarettes. Deever said, "Thank you, kindly."

They all seemed to know one another.

"So, Moonlight, what did you say they got you for?" the tattooed man asked.

"Armed robbery, Beckett," Moonlight said.

"What you think they going to give you?"

"Three to five, out in eighteen months."

"That ain' so bad," Deever said.

"What you going to do when you get out?" Beckett asked, wiping away a year and a half as though it were no more than a weekend.

"Well, you know, they got these classes. You can take automobile mechanics, air conditioning, installing insulation. Like that. I'm thinking maybe I'll learn how to fix automobiles, you know? So when I get out I'll get me a job, good pay, and I'll get me a nice flat someplace nice. Some nice neighborhood. Then maybe I'll find me a nice woman, you know?"

Deever was grinning as though he was wondering what kind of fool Moonlight was trying to be. "What you *really* going to do when you get out, Moonlight?"

Moonlight, as soft-spoken as a professor, a man who looked

like he had potential, said, "Well, when I get out, first thing I'm going to do is get me a bottle and get drunk, then get me a woman and get laid, then get me a gun and rob a gas station."

They all laughed, twisting their heads from side to side, delighted with Moonlight's recitation of the true scheme of things.

Suddenly Beckett said, "You like gibs, Nellis?"

"When I can't get nothing else," Nellis said.

"Well, that's good," Beckett said, and Deever laughed, and all of a sudden Billy realized that during all of this comfortable conversation no one had ever looked at him or addressed a remark to him. It was as though he weren't even there. Now they'd all grown so still, like wary animals, listening for the rustle of their prey, that he was suddenly chilly with fear.

Just before they were locked down for the night Deever and Beckett casually got Moonlight out into the corridor for a private conversation. Nellis and Mackle stayed inside the cell with Billy, chatting about nothing, Nellis finally looking at Billy every once in a while with his soft smile, drawing him into the conversation, as though trying to capture his attention.

Billy had one ear out the door, but he couldn't make out what they were saying, only that Moonlight was refusing Deever and Beckett something they were asking him for.

"Ah, fachrissakes," Deever said loudly, giving up any further attempts at persuasion. Moonlight came back into the cell and got into his bunk.

"Grab a hole," the trustee hollered and when everybody was put away except for the ones that would have to sleep in the corridor, the cell doors clanged shut.

Then the trustee yelled, "Lights out," and the overheads went off.

Billy lay there on the thin mattress. Jails were like hospitals he thought. They never went to sleep. The night guards spoke in normal voices and walked around without trying to be quiet. Sounds of laughter came drifting down from number one cell where the trustees had light and special privileges. A hell of a note.

Then it was quiet all of a sudden and Billy fell into a fitful sleep as the first snowfall of winter began to drop out of the night sky.

45

WHEN SHARKEY WALKED THROUGH THE DOOR OF ORCHID'S HE saw Zulu, the kid with the fuzzy-wuzzy haircut, on the door. It came as no great surprise. Some handy kid was looking for a little work, the wise guys passed him around to see what he could do—would do—until they found a regular spot for him. So he'd done a little something for Dickman. It looked like he was in on the beating of D'Angelo, giving Albert a hand. It could be that Albert had been doing a little moonlighting, a little freelance roughhousing for Dickman. Unless it was Leddy who'd ordered the working-over.

Anyway, there was Zulu running with Albert and there was Leddy sitting in on the Chinese dinners with Orchid over to the Canton so it was not some amazing coincidence that the fuzzy-headed kid was working for Orchid now.

"Long time no see," Sharkey said.

The kid didn't try to pretend they'd never met before, over at Dickman's Three Seas Import-Export, but it was more than possible that he was unaware that Sharkey had spotted him driving Leddy's car and shouting out a warning. With a haircut like the one he sported he knew that people who saw him once would never forget him if they saw him again. That was the whole idea, standing out in a crowd, being somebody.

"You get around, officer," Zulu said.

"Zulu, ain't it?"

"Yes, sir."

"I wonder why."

Zulu grinned good-naturedly, but there was something swimming behind the eyes Sharkey had seen before in the eyes of madmen. This kid was death waiting to happen.

Sharkey looked him over, the tuxedo, the starched shirt front, the bow tie, the pair of brand-new multicolored sneakers.

"Will you look at yourself," Ray said.

"What's the complaint?" Zulu replied, holding his arms out wide, looking down at his shirt front, looking himself over.

"The feet. Don't you ever look down at your feet?"

"I got these arches," Zulu said, holding up one of his feet in its high-top. "I got these weak ankles. When I was a kid I couldn't even ice skate in the park, my ankles bent like noodles."

"What are we talking about ice skating, here? Are you planning on ice skating out here at the front of the house or what?"

"I was just saying these shoes keep my feet comfortable. They ain't cheap, you know. A hundred and forty bucks."

"For a pair of sneaks, for God's sake?" Ray said, appalled at the extravagance of it all. "So, at least get a pair of black. When were you hired?"

"Last week."

"I got to stop by more often," Sharkey said. "The place's falling apart."

He went over to the bar, looking around at the action. The cloakroom girl, maybe eighteen years old, followed him over, asking him if he wanted to check his hat and coat. He said he wasn't staying long enough for her to bother.

"That a new topcoat, Mr. Sharkey?" she asked.

He looked at the sleeve and the cuff that was showing wear. "Are you teasing me, Harriet?"

"No, sir. You're usually wearing that nice camel hair."

"Oh, for God's sake."

"What's the matter, I say something wrong?"

He handed her a five-dollar bill.

"No, no. You reminded me. I've got to get that coat to the cleaners and I always forget."

"Tie a string around your finger," she said, having gotten what she'd come for.

"Which one?" he asked.

"Well, you know, the big one in the middle," she said, giving him a little giggle, a little double entendre there, flipping the old lecher a wink over the shoulder. What the hell, it didn't hurt. Maybe she'd need a favor one day. She'd long since learned that aging men were easy and that a slightly dirty joke went a long way.

When Orchid spotted Sharkey and walked over to say hello, Sharkey said, "What's with the freak at the door?"

"Colorful, ain't he?" Orchid said.

"A riot."

"I thought he could be like a trademark, a conversation piece. You know what I mean?"

"You're starting to talk like me, Shelley, you better watch yourself."

"That's okay, I don't mind."

"Well, no, I don't suppose you would. Who gave you a reference on the fluff-head?"

"Frank Leddy. You know Frank Leddy? Frankie Blue Shoes? Sure you know Frank. I understand you done a favor for him."

"You people gossip a lot, don't you?" Sharkey said. "You see Leddy around?"

"He's right in the back, at the corner table, having himself a meal."

"Is that right? Well, it looks like I've saved myself a trip or a phone call."

He walked through the doorway into the small restaurant. Leddy was sitting at the corner table with a redheaded hostess and Albert. The kid who ran messages for him, the one who'd been sitting in back at the Kilarney Tavern, wasn't around.

"Excuse us," Sharkey said without any other preliminary.

The redhead got up at once, without comment. Albert started to open his mouth but Sharkey said, "Take off those gloves, you asshole. Everybody knows what you do, what a hard prick you think you are."

"Take a walk, Albert," Leddy said.

Sharkey sat down and smiled.

"How's the food?" he asked.

"Not bad."

"We try to keep a nice kitchen. You know I have an interest in this place?"

"I've been told."

"Sure you have. Shelley's got a big mouth. That kid at the door, you recommend him to Shelley?"

"He came in from Philadelphia a couple of weeks ago and—"

"Imported?"

"What do you mean imported?"

"I mean was he brought here for a particular purpose?"

"He's just a kid looking for a little travel. Wanted to see Chicago."

"Did you give him something to do?"

"I didn't have anything for him."

"Didn't have him give Albert a helping hand?"

"Doing what?"

"Negotiating for some gemstones?"

Leddy laughed. "What I know about gemstones you could stick in your eye."

"Maybe Albert does a little something on his own and on the side now and then?"

Leddy shrugged. "I don't own him."

"What does the kid do?"

"I don't know. Runs errands. Drives a car."

"I saw him driving your car the other night."

"That's right. He was around so I let him drive me over to your party. Everything come out all right?"

"That's all he does is run errands and drive?"

"Well, like that. He's only a kid."

"With bigger and better things in store for him?"

"I wouldn't know. He ain't working for me. He's working for Shelley right this minute."

"That's right, he is, ain't he?"

46

THREE OR FOUR TIMES A WEEK SHARKEY HAD TO STOP BY THE OLD flat in Bridgeport. Sometimes he caught himself calling it that and for a minute he'd stop in his tracks and think about it. Why he called the home he'd shared with Flo for so many years the old flat as though it were a place he'd already moved out of permanently, never intending to live there again.

The old flat, the old house, the old neighborhood.

In that minute he felt a hollow feeling in his gut, as though a piece of him were missing and he was only now and then aware of it.

If he wasn't going to live there, where was he going to live? He couldn't go on playing house with a colored hooker forever.

He stopped by around lunchtime if he could manage it and in the evening after work, just before he went over to the flat he shared with Roma.

He'd stop in and just sit in his old easy chair and sometimes read the paper. Usually he just sat, not even bothering to take off his hat and coat. Just sitting there, not even remembering. Waiting for the phone to ring. Not expecting any calls but waiting for the phone to ring in case Della called, or Michael called, or somebody called. Occasional evidence that he still lived in the old flat in Bridgeport.

Sometimes he went over around nine o'clock, ten o'clock, while Roma sat and watched television. He never told her where he was going and she never asked.

He went to the old flat and made calls from there. He called Flo up in Fond du Lac and occasionally was able to talk to her because she wasn't sleeping or lying up there in a drugged-out stupor.

It was better calling his wife from the old flat. He couldn't talk as freely with Roma in the next room at the other place.

Besides, he believed that Flo would be able to tell that he was calling from the old flat (not knowing a thing about the new one, of course), that she'd be able to tell the difference if he called from anywhere else. Something about the shape of the rooms and the position of the furniture. Some strangeness in his voice.

There were occasions when he slept in the old flat.

The next day Roma never asked him where he'd been as Flo would've done if he'd been even an hour late. Maybe that was one of the big advantages of just living with a woman like Roma. Maybe that was one of the disadvantages, too.

He was sitting in the dark when the phone rang. Even before he picked it up he knew what he'd be told.

"Mr. Sharkey?" a female voice that wasn't bothering to hide an edge of irritation.

"Yes, this is Ray Sharkey," he said.

"This is the Oxford Pavilion at Fond du Lac. We've been trying to locate you for the last three hours."

"I work."

"Yes, of course. We called the work number and were told you were not available."

"I'm a police officer. I'm very rarely at my desk."

"Oh, well that's all right, then."

She seemed relieved to find out that he was doing his job and not just goofing off while they cared for his dying wife.

He could just see the woman making a notation in some file, keeping the record neat.

"I'm afraid I have the unhappy duty to inform you that your wife, Florence Aurelia Sharkey, passed away suddenly at seven o'clock this evening," she said, her voice walking a fine line between efficiency and condolence.

"Suddenly?"

"She had a heart attack."

A startled laugh bubbled up out of his chest. He had to catch it and turn it into a cough. All that suffering from cancer and then she dies because of her heart.

"Are you all right, Mr. Sharkey?" she asked, her voice coming down the line like that of a disembodied ghost.

"Was it quick?" he asked.

"It would have been very quick."

"A blessing."

"Yes, I'd say it was a blessing. Shall we make the arrangements?"

"The arrangements?" he asked, wondering what she meant, his mind running back there somewhere, five minutes, ten minutes, before the phone rang. Holding on to that moment before the phone rang, his mind pretending he wasn't having this conversation.

"Where would you like us to send the body?"

He cleared his throat and realized that it was filled with unshed tears.

"Isn't it in the file?" he asked. "I thought we'd made arrangements for the mortuary. I thought we gave you a number."

"I'm sorry. I see it now. Tierney's. Is that right?"

"Yes, that's right."

"We'll take care of it, then. And, once again, please accept our condolences—"

Why did she say "once again"? he wondered. Had she already given him their condolences once and he hadn't heard?

"—Mr. Sharkey. It should give you a great deal of comfort to know that you did everything that was humanly possible."

"Yes."

"That was Tierney's, wasn't it?"

"Yes, Tierney's."

"I like to double check, triple check, details like that so that there are no embarrassing mistakes."

"Tierney's is right. We've been burying from Tierney's for years."

"That's all right then," she said, and, a moment after, said, "Goodbye," and hung up.

He sat there, a verse the funeral home had once had printed on their courtesy matchbook covers years ago running through his mind.

As we near this sad time, there's no cause for worry,
Your loved one will tell you as the time comes to bury.
Bring out the lace curtains and call Robert Tierney,
I'm nearing the end of life's pleasant journey.

Giving himself a reason to laugh because he wanted to cry.

47

CHARLIE LINCOLN FOUND HER AT HER HOTEL. HE CAME TO TELL her he'd been unlucky, that he'd been unable to raise the money to bail Billy Smith out of jail.

Wilda told him all about her brother Ray Sharkey trying to do her the favor but how there'd been some administrative mix-up and it would take a little time.

Lincoln didn't even bother asking how much time. It was as though all the manhood had been stolen from him. He'd lost all his hope for dignity. He'd been beaten by the casual power the cops had exerted over him and anybody could see he felt like a dog.

He'd brought along a bottle in a brown paper bag.

He held it up by the neck and said, "I thought we'd have this for a celebration. You want a drink, anyhow? It'll help pass the time." As though he intended to keep her company until Billy Smith was released, as though Billy Smith would come looking for them in Wilda's hotel without even knowing its name.

She could tell he'd already had a drink, probably a lot more than one.

She wanted to tell him that she didn't really like the idea of them spending the time together in her hotel room, but she didn't know how to make the point without offending him. She couldn't suggest thay they go over to the Pussy Cat because it was Sunday and she'd been told the club was dark on Sundays.

"You think to get any mix?" she asked.

"It's bourbon. It does good with tap water."

"It'll be warm. I've got no ice and I doubt they have room service here."

He frowned. "So, all right, warm is all right. Bourbon and water from the tap is all right."

"If you don't mind," she said, taking the bottle from him. "Just one, and then I'm afraid you'll have to go."

"What?"

"I mean I'll have to go."

"Why's that?" he asked with an edge to his voice as though waiting for the racial insult.

"I'm going over to my sister's house," she lied.

"Oh, then," he said, but didn't go on to say then what.

She went into the bathroom and there was only one glass. But there was a collapsing plastic cup in the cheap fitted case where she kept her toothbrush, toothpaste, and other toilet things. She mixed two drinks, taking the collapsible cup—the smallest one—for herself, making it only half as strong.

She meant it as a kindness, having a drink with him, to let him know she considered him a friend who needed what help a friend could give in time of need. She hoped he wouldn't think otherwise.

It was merely a kindness, but she should have known, having learned long since, that it was very dangerous to show men any kindness. They always mistook it for something else. So when she was close enough to hand him his drink, it came as an odd sort of surprise which was also expected when he kissed her before she'd even had a chance to take a sip.

It wasn't unpleasant, the feeling of his lips so thick and full upon her mouth. He tasted of cloves and she wondered idly if he'd popped a breath pastille on the way up the stairs. He embraced her and she had a little start of fear because she could feel how powerful he was, understood that he could force himself on her if he wanted to and she'd have no chance to fight him off. Even if she managed to scream before he stifled her breath with his big hand, she doubted if anyone would come to rescue her. She expected such screams were heard frequently coming from this room or that, spilling down the dimly lit, musty-smelling hallways.

She wanted to break away when he tried to insert his tongue into her mouth, past her teeth, but somehow she was afraid he might take that as an insult, so she just resisted passively. They were so sensitive about being black, letting you know in a hundred ways that they realized how repulsive you probably found them, no matter how often you let them know that the color of their skin didn't matter. No matter how often you told them—in all seriousness—how you sympathized with all the cruelty and horror they had been subjected to in America. No matter how much you raved over the contributions they'd made to American culture. Jazz and all.

They were no different than white men in taking advantage of something about themselves that they thought might buy them a little sympathy.

When he grasped her buttock in one hand and tried to touch her breast with the other, the glass still in it, she figured it was time to straighten out any funny ideas he might've gotten, her having a drink with him alone in a hotel room.

She broke free, turning her hip, doing a little swivel, taking a couple of steps and tripping, nearly falling.

Her spilling most of her drink, him spilling most of his.

"Oooops! Well, thank you," she said, laughing a little harder than the occasion demanded when he grabbed her arm. "No, no that's all right. You can let go my arm. Just a little fold in the rug there. See? That's where I keep my cash money when

I'm going out someplace where I don't know what could happen. You understand, I don't really trust hotel clerks?"

"I understand that," he said.

"So that's where I put my money, and when I came to get it *so I could bail you out* I guess I didn't straighten the rug out. I was in such a hurry, you understand. I didn't want you—I didn't want my *friend*—to have to stay in jail one minute longer than he had to."

"I understand that," Charlie said, losing a little of his intentness, a little of his focus.

"So, all right, I guess we need a little drink," Wilda said. "Don't you think we need a little drink? I'll make us a couple of drinks," she said, and went back into the bathroom to pour them a couple of short whiskeys with water.

When she came out he was sitting on the bed sideways, his upper body propped against the pillows but his legs half-dangling over the side, one foot on the floor. He was looking at her with slitted eyes. It was a speculative look, a dangerous look, and he didn't speak, not even to say thank you when she handed him his glass.

Wilda went over to the Danish modern armchair and sat down, making damn certain that her short skirt didn't ride up more than it had to, her knees angled away so that, lying as he was, he still wouldn't get a glimpse of anything much.

He lay there silently, sipping from his drink every now and then.

She was sorry she'd ever invited him into the room. She should have said the hotel didn't allow guests in the room and they really should go down and talk in the lobby.

If she'd been Charlie, what would she think was supposed to happen with this white woman who walked around town on her own, going into colored joints to listen to the music, inviting a black man into her hotel room?

"Charlie, I want to say that I always valued your friendship. You understand that?"

"That's nice, Wilda. That's nice to know. Because what it is, you understand, it's I don't see you from one goddamn year to the next and when I try to do right by you, treat you respectable, I get nothing but trouble for my pains. So, that's what it is, Wilda."

He shifted his weight on the bed and her stomach jumped because she thought he was going for her. She got up quickly, saying, "This needs a little more water," and hurried into the bathroom, closing the door and locking it. "Be right out," she called, so that him hearing her lock the door wouldn't make him mad.

As long as she was in there, playing for time, trying to get her thoughts together, figuring out how to get him out of there, she decided she might as well empty her bladder. What was it her brother Ray always said that some big fat cop instructor at the Police Academy had always told the trainees? "Two things a cop's got to know going in. Always wear high-tops when you're walking a beat, otherwise your ankles'll give out, and always take a leak every chance you get because you never know when you'll have to go without for three or four hours." She giggled, remembering that.

She quickly put her hand over her mouth so that Charlie wouldn't think she was laughing at him. Black men were so goddamn sensitive.

She sat there on the commode with her panties down around her ankles thinking about how she'd been in worse spots than this, because, after all, what was the worse that could happen? She'd let him do it. One thing she knew was that if you let them do it, ninety-nine times out of a hundred you could shovel them into a wastebasket afterward and roll them down the stairs for all they cared. They were like goddamn babies that way. Give them the sugar tit and they turned into kittens. Any whore knew that.

Jesus, Mary, and Joseph, was that what Ray was looking for in her face? Ray and those goddamn cops and that buffalo behind the desk at the Eighteenth? Did they peg her for a tramp? Worse, a nigger-loving, nigger-fucking whore. If Ray really thought that he'd murder her and say it was for her sake he'd done it.

So maybe what she'd do, she thought, wiping herself and pulling up her panties, rearranging her skirt, washing her hands, and pouring herself another little drink (never mind the water), maybe what she'd do would be to walk out there and tell Charlie that it was very nice of him to stop by, but she was very tired and had to take a nap before going over to her sister's. Had she told him she was going over to her sister's?

And if that didn't work, she decided, tired as she was, drunk as she was, she'd just get into bed and fuck him so at least, after it was over, she could get a little sleep.

She went back into the bedroom all smiles. Charlie was still lying on the bed, the empty paper cup fallen from his hand to the floor. He was fast asleep.

So Wilda took a last swallow of her whiskey, got her coat to put over herself, took off her shoes, and curled up in the battered Danish modern armchair. She'd slept in worse.

48

AT FIRST BILLY SMITH THOUGHT HE'D BEEN SLEEPING AND THE snick of the cell door opening up had awakened him. Then he realized that he hadn't been sleeping at all, that he'd been lying there half-awake for hours.

He lay on his side, back turned to the bunks where the Hispanic (what was the guy's name?) and Mackle, the legless man, slept, facing Moonlight's lower bunk and Nellis's upper bunk, his feet toward the toilet, his head toward the cell door. Which swung back now.

He had no way of knowing if this was the way the turnkeys made their rounds in the middle of night, stepping into the cells for this and that. His heart was hammering his heart and belly. It was all he could do to keep his breath running smooth and even. He wanted to gasp, breathe faster. He felt as though he couldn't get enough air.

He tried to grow eyes in the top of his head, afraid to open his regular eyes, afraid to roll over on his back, look behind him, see what danger might be coming.

They put their hands on him. His eyes flew open. He caught a glimpse of Deever's scarred face and Beckett's tattooed arm grabbing, the hand tearing at his wrist which was tucked under him, his hand protecting the sunglasses which had been his shield.

They were rolling him over onto his face and that's when he started to buck and fight, because now he knew what "gibs" meant. Now he knew their intention.

He reared up on his hands and knees, trying to throw off their weight, and felt another body fall on him from above.

"Get the fucker's ass out of them trousers, Nellis," Beckett hissed.

Billy opened his mouth, ready to give out a yell, and somebody stuffed a sock in it, gagging him. For a second he feared he was going to vomit and drown there, thrashing around like a landed fish, but terror washed the nausea away.

His right hand was wet and sticky. He realized he'd broken his glasses and a shard had cut his hand.

He twisted and turned, and bucked and heaved.

"How this sweet ass do rock and roll," somebody said, crooning softly, chuckling softly, as though commenting on the passionate contortions of a woman caught up in the act of love.

He managed to turn himself around and free his right arm. He lashed out and felt his wrist caught and held as though it had been clamped by a vise, a hand without pity. He opened his fingers against the pain cracking his wrist bones. Then there was a blade of slashing fire along his cheek and he knew the broken lens he meant to use as a weapon had been turned against him.

He was on his belly again, his trousers shucked off, his shorts ripped away, exposing his naked ass. Somebody sat on his head.

"Don't you lay no farts and gas my sweetheart to death before I give her some of my joystick."

Billy started to make grunting noises as loudly as he could and a fist came slamming down between his shoulder blades.

And then he felt his legs being spread apart and a thrusting, prodding pressure at his anus, his sphincter resisting, then giving way and a terrible tearing, burning in his rectum.

It went on, the ugly penetration, the pain, the shock, over and over again. Frantic signals urging his body to move, to fight or run, and the overpowering despair when his body would not move, could not move, and he knew how helpless he was against this unnatural assault.

Sometime during his ordeal, old Mackle, the legless man, was sitting on the floor beside his head, petting his face.

After a while, like a storm passing over, it became quiet. He heard the shuffle of feet hurrying away and the cell door closing.

And then the Mexican boy said something in Spanish and Mackle said, "Oh, yeah. Oh, yeah. Look at that. It's snowing."

As Billy Smith lay there bleeding on the prison mattress the snow fell and he heard Moonlight call out, calmly, almost softly, "Got a man sick in the cell block. Got a man not feeling good."

49

SHARKEY SLEPT IN THE OLD FLAT, IN THE OLD BEDROOM, IN THE old bed that night. He wanted to go back and tell Roma about his loss, ask her to comfort him. That was exactly why he didn't go. Not so much because it would tell her that he had nobody he needed at that moment of grief more than he needed her, but because he didn't want to let himself know it.

He undressed and went to bed in his underwear, lying there wondering how long he'd want to hold on to the pain before sharing it with anyone. Trying to decide who to share it with first. His father or his sister Della? His brother Michael or Jerry? Maybe he should call his brother Gabe. Priests were supposed to know the right words at times like this, but he was afraid all that Gabe would come up with was one of the old ones about Flo being in a better place—in the arms of Jesus—and he doubted that even his brother, the priest, believed that anymore.

In the morning, for half a minute in the gloom of the bedroom with the ecru shade pulled down to keep out the thin light of dawn, waking in the familiar room with the face of the suffering Jesus on the wall, the blood dripping into his eyes from the crown of thorns, Sharkey was twenty-five. He reached out a hand to touch Flo, his sleeping wife, and, feeling nothing there in the bed beside him, time flipped back. He began to cry, his face buried in the pillow as though afraid there might be someone in the house to hear.

Then he got up, shaved and showered, brushed his teeth, moved his bowels, found nothing in the refrigerator to ease his hunger, dressed carefully, decided not to wear the topcoat made filthy by Kendicott's slide down the garbage chute, and went out wearing nothing but his suit jacket, a scarf, and his fedora.

It was cold but there was no wind, the Hawk was nesting

somewhere down by the lake, waiting to fly when the sun rose higher, warming the land enough to rouse the biting wind. Every clear winter's day was a battle between the warming thermals stirred by the sun and the wind it aroused, with the people of Chicago caught in between.

His car's engine turned over on the third try and he said a little prayer of thanks because he didn't need small annoyances on what he knew was going to be a trying day.

He stopped at a diner on the way to the stationhouse, ordered a glass of orange juice, a cup of coffee, and a Danish, glancing at a newspaper left behind on the counter by another customer, trying to read the headlines, trying to make himself believe that this was just another day. Trying to get his head into that frame of mind because he knew he couldn't go back to the apartment and just sit there like a zombie waiting for life to start happening to him again.

Maybe he should call Fond du Lac and see if the arrangements for Flo were being made, if they were sending her on down to the funeral home by truck, plane, or train. Better she should be brought down in a hearse, even all that way. He didn't like the idea of her being crated up and shipped by commercial transport as though she were a commodity being rushed to market in the city along with a thousand other kinds of goods.

He changed a five-dollar bill into change at the register and went to the public phone in back, identified himself, asked what was being done about Florence Sharkey.

"Florence has been prepared. She'll begin the journey to Chicago via the railroad sometime this afternoon. She should be arriving in the city about five o'clock this evening."

He couldn't tell if it was the same woman who'd called to tell him about Flo's death the night before. He'd forgotten the sound of her voice in that brief length of time. It was even hard to focus on what she was saying, his mind having grabbed hold of the familiar way she called his wife by her first name, thinking that in the last four years this faceless, nameless clerk or secretary may have had more occasion to pass the time of day with Flo than he had. He had to ask her to repeat the information and when she was done he said, "Is it too late to make other arrangements?"

"Other arrangements?" she said, as though wondering what he could possibly have in mind. Was he going to tell her that there was a better way for shipping bodies? She who'd had a wealth of experience.

"I wonder could you drive my wife down to Chicago in a hearse."

"That would be a good deal more expensive. Not only the cost of the hearse, you understand, but the cost of a driver to and from the city."

"Yes, I understand that. It's just I'd rather . . ."

When he didn't go on, she quickly said, "We understand. We'll change the arrangement immediately." There was a curious mixture of pleasure and tenderness in her voice. The joy of profit and sympathy for such a caring husband all stirred together like lemon marmalade.

He was going to ask her when she thought the driver would arrive at Tierney's but was afraid the calculation would make her crisp again and he wanted to have the tenderness of her voice linger awhile.

So he thanked her and said he'd be waiting for his wife at Tierney's.

When he paid for his breakfast at the register, the counterman asked him wouldn't he be awfully cold without a topcoat.

Sharkey smiled his best smile, genuinely touched, and said he'd be in the car or in the office most of the time. He had a couple of topcoats but both of them were stained and needed cleaning.

"I don't seem to get around to some things," he said.

"I'm the same. Sometimes I spend my whole day off running errands, trying to clean up a list, but usually half the places I go to are closed, one reason or the other, I forgot their day off or somebody in the family died. You know what I mean?"

"I know exactly what you mean," Sharkey said, handing the guy a two-dollar tip for a two-dollar meal.

"Hey," the counterman said.

Sharkey strode out, waving away the man's thanks, feeling good about people.

The feeling stayed with him all the way to the station.

The first thing he saw coming through the doors was Pennyworth, in a silver wig this time, getting booked.

Titus was on the desk again, having probably flipped shifts.

"What the hell have we got here?" Sharkey asked. "We got an ambitious hooker?"

"He was out there flaunting hisself, teaching some youngster how to pike his pecker, turn him out on the game, and the sun not hardly up yet," the arresting uniformed officer said.

"What the hell is this, Pennyworth, you setting yourself up as a madam?"

"I was being charitable," Pennyworth said, very seriously. "This young man—"

"Boy," the uniform said.

"Well, you don't know that, do you?" Pennyworth said.

Sharkey raised his eyebrows, asking the cop, who shook his head and said, "Kid took off like a burnt bunny."

"So, we can't get Pennyworth on a contributing to the delinquency of a minor, here?" Titus said.

"I was merely giving a newcomer to the city a little on-the-job training," Pennyworth said.

"This hour of the morning, fachrissake, Pennyworth?" Sharkey said.

"I was starting him small-time doing the truckers on the way west."

"West? There a reason why you was on the road heading west?"

"Truckers going east got sunshine in their eyes. They don't like to stop even for comfort and entertainment," Pennyworth said.

"I'm afraid what we got here, Ray," Titus said, "is a persistent felon."

"Sheeeit," Pennyworth said, "I don't do no felonies."

"Well, we're getting mighty sick and tired of plucking your ass off the streets, Pennyworth," Titus said, "so we might just start booking you for greater crimes."

"You'd do that?" Pennyworth said. "You could do that? They could do that?" he rattled on, looking from Titus to the uniform to Sharkey.

"Of course he can do that. You're an outstanding public nuisance and if Sergeant Titus wants to upgrade you into the felony class, well, I think he can find a way."

"You mean legally?" Pennyworth asked, dumbfounded at the brazenness of it all.

"It's very difficult for us to stand here listening to you talking about legality, Pennyworth," Sharkey said. "You can understand that."

Pennyworth could clearly understand that and understood

that in a miserably unjust world one more injustice wouldn't even be cause for comment, let alone tears.

"Can I have a word with you, Detective Sharkey?" he said.

"Every time you call me detective and want a word with me, you're out trolling for a favor."

"Well, like they say, Sergeant, tit for tat. Tit for tat."

"Use the interrogation room?" Sharkey asked Titus.

"Interrogation room A," Titus said. "Go to it."

Once in the interrogation room, Pennyworth took off his wig and laid it on the scarred tabletop. He lifted his skirts and crossed his legs, resting his ankle on his knee the way a man would do. Sharkey didn't look up his dress, but if he had, he knew he'd see a mounded form like a woman's, Pennyworth's organ having been tied up in the crack of his ass. Pennyworth had once told him it was surprising how many men had intercourse with a hooker, never knowing that it was a man they prodded. He fished a pack of cigarettes out of his blouse and lit up.

"For God's sake, it ain't an easy life. You think my life's an easy life?" Pennyworth said.

"I don't. I know it's very hard. Everybody's life is very hard."

"Not Paul Newman's. Not Rita Moreno's."

"Well, maybe not them though I expect they got their share of troubles and sorrows. What did you want to have a word with me about, Pennyworth?"

"We have the usual agreement?"

"You can do me some good, I'll see if I can do you some good."

"This is some *personal* good I can do you."

"In that case, you know I'll do the very best I can."

"Somebody's talking about putting a hit out on you."

Somehow it came as no suprise.

"You trying to tell me there's somebody dumb enough to put a hit out on a cop? I'm no serious danger to anybody."

"Well, it looks like you're at least an aggravation."

"Rumors about people out to take my life ain't news. It's just a lot of donkey dust."

"The person talking about having your ticket punched is well known to you."

"Yes?"

"Shelley Orchid? You know why Shelley Orchid might have designs on your life and well-being?"

Sharkey laughed.

"You can laugh," Pennyworth said, more than slightly miffed by the reaction to his news, "but the man what told me about this inquiry about his services isn't known to make up stories."

"So why was this gunsel so runny-mouthed with you?"

"I was doing him and he had the idea him talking about doing you would arouse me to greater efforts, you know what I mean?"

"I don't need a play-by-play."

"What I mean is I was doing him in a very different way than he said Shelley Orchid was asking about doing you."

"I understood you the first time. What's this mechanic's name?"

"They call him Zulu Waddel. He's built like a stick with a rag mop on the end. Looks like a white nigger what with the hair and all. Wears felony flyers in three colors even when he's in a suit."

Pennyworth took Sharkey's silence to mean that he wanted more information.

"This Waddel's a new boy in town. He was bragging how he connected right off the bat. Was hired to do a little job."

"What kind of job?"

"Breaking bones."

"He say who and where?"

"He never said who but he dropped the name of the hotel without meaning to."

"Which was?"

"The Westley."

Sharkey was silent again and Pennyworth thought he was losing the interest he thought he'd had.

"The freak described what he done to this victim. How him and this other bone-breaker strung him up and beat him in the gut till his bowels let go."

"You live a very hard life, Pennyworth," Sharkey said.

Sharkey said nothing again for a long time.

"So is that worth a walk or what?" Pennyworth said.

"It's worth a walk. Fix your skirts for God's sake, Pennyworth. You're sitting there with them up around your ass like a goddamn whore."

They were standing at the counter arranging for Pennyworth's release when the call came in that a prisoner by the name of William Smith had been beaten and raped at Cook County and the warden wanted to know who was responsible for running a man around the stations of the cross who'd been picked up for nothing more serious than a drunk and disorderly.

50

SHARKEY HAD BEEN IN HOTEL LOBBIES LIKE THE ONE IN WHICH Wilda had come to roost a thousand times. They always smelled the same in the morning. He couldn't identify the separate elements of the odor but he recognized it as despair.

There was nobody behind the desk. In hotels like this the clerk did a little of everything. Half the time he wasn't there to greet the guests. There was a bell you rang if you wanted to see a human face.

Sharkey checked the box of registration cards and found Wilda's with the room notation on it. The key rack was on the wall at the end of the counter. He didn't even have to walk around to pick up the duplicate key.

Lousy security. A good cat burglar could wait for his chance, walk in here, lift as many keys as he wanted, and try the rooms one after the other until he found the ones where the people had forgotten to secure the night chain. People didn't realize that most hotel rooms were robbed with the guests asleep in their beds.

He went upstairs thinking about how fate had decided which one of the family he was going to tell first about Flo's death and how, sooner or later, Wilda would've been the one he'd have chosen to tell first anyway.

He walked along the corridor until he came to the right room. He knocked on the door. He heard Wilda's voice through the thickness of the door, muffled and faraway, half-asleep, but he couldn't make out the words. He heard footsteps, heavier than a woman's, approaching the other side of the door, and he backed off a step.

When the door opened, Charlie Lincoln was standing there in rumpled trousers and stockinged feet, clip bow tie hanging from one wing of his open shirt collar.

He read the look on Sharkey's face, shouted, "What the hell?" and started to close the door, but Sharkey had his shoulder against it, knocking Charlie back and aside, and was into the room just as Wilda opened the door to the bathroom and stood there in her slip, drying her hands on a towel, hair all disarrayed.

Charlie scooted backward to the side table and picked up the lamp sitting on it. He tore off the shade and, holding the stem, smashed the base in half on the radiator, making a weapon for himself.

Sharkey threw back his jacket and stuck his hand up and under the skirt, going for the gun holstered at his belt.

Wilda grabbed for a robe hanging on the hook as though trying to hide the damning evidence of her underwear.

When the gun was out, Charlie drew back his arm and said, "What's going on here?"

"Ray, for God's sake," Wilda said.

"Don't you try to use that, you black sonofabitch," Sharkey said.

Adrenaline pumping, fear and danger flooding the seedy room, everything exaggerated, time and space and the loudness of their voices.

"This is my friend, Charlie Lincoln," Wilda said, as though expecting that to explain everything.

The men held their positions, acting with what they knew to be prudence, the black man aware that the white man would shoot at the slightest provocation, the white man knowing that the black man might strike out if he so much as took away his attention for an instant, both of them able to recall experiences when men died just as the conflict seemed to be cooling down or was even all but over.

"Charlie, this is my brother. This is Sergeant Sharkey. He's the one I asked to help us out."

Slowly, slowly, the lamp came down.

"That don't change the scene, you motherfucker," Sharkey said. "I came to talk to my sister."

Charlie opened his fingers and the lamp fell to the floor.

"Talk about what, Ray? You find out where Billy Smith landed?" Wilda asked. "You get him out?"

"He's out. They're taking him home. He's probably already home right now."

Charlie's eyes widened. "What you mean 'they're taking him home'?" Knowing that cops didn't escort prisoners, especially black men, home when they let them out of jail. "What's wrong with Billy?"

Sharkey remembered the gun in his hand. He put it away. "There was a little trouble. A little accident. Your friend's all right. You go see."

"What do you mean a little—"

"You go see," Sharkey said, interrupting him in a flat voice. A flat voice that had a rusty edge to it, warning Charlie that there was a lot of anger in him and Charlie would be smart to get the hell out of there before it erupted and scalded him.

Charlie saw that the red-faced Irish cop, Irish brother, was holding himself back. The hell with delivering a message of mercy. The hell with decency. He'd come to make excuses to his sister for not being able to help her out when she'd come to him for help and he'd found her in her underwear, consorting with a nigger.

He kept his eyes on Sharkey as he slipped his feet into his shoes, picked up his jacket and overcoat.

"What do you mean a little accident?" he said again, as he circled his way around Sharkey to the door.

"I told you what to do. Why the hell don't you go do it?" Sharkey asked, almost plaintively. "Get out of here. Don't you know when somebody's handing you a pass?"

"Charlie!" Wilda said, as he stood there ready to walk out the door.

The men looked at her as though startled by her interference. She walked over and stood up on her toes, making a very tender gesture of it, her hand flat on Charlie's chest, and kissed him on the cheek. "You tell Billy Smith we did all we could and that I'm terribly sorry for whatever happened."

Charlie's eyes were frightened again. This goddamned white woman seemed determined to get him shot, but he couldn't say so, couldn't scold her or warn her, because that would be groveling before the Irish cop bastard. It was so goddamn hard to stand up straight and do the shuffle at the same goddamn time.

After he was gone, Wilda closed the door, turned around, and gave Sharkey a look. It was a look meant to burn him and chill him at the same time.

"So you can tell me. What happened to Billy Smith?"

"Some of the other men in his cell beat him up."

"That's not all, Ray. I know that's not all."

"It looks like they might've raped him."

"A bunch of goddamn animals, you men are," Wilda said contemptuously. "Screw anything with a hole. Screw a sheep. Screw a cat. Screw your fist."

"So, Wilda, what do I catch you screwing?"

"You think that's what happened, you go ahead and think that's what happened," she said, and started to walk past him to the bathroom.

He grabbed her and spun her around. "Goddammit, Wilda, I got eyes."

Instead of pulling away, she moved against him, positioning herself so that her belly pressed against his groin. She smiled a hateful smile up into his face and wet her lips with the tip of her tongue.

"So what is it, Ray? You jealous I might've let that black man—that black nigger—do me the way you want to do me?"

"Shut up, Wilda."

"You think I didn't feel your hard-on when you gave me that hug over at the station? I got a fucking seismograph down there between my legs, Ray, it can detect the slightest tremor."

"Wilda," he said, warning her.

"You jealous that some *dinge* is getting into my pants—"

"I told you to shut the fuck up, Wilda!"

"—where you been wanting to get just one time all your life?"

Just like that, there it was. A sudden flash of rage and despair and shame making her go and say it. Bringing it out into the open, taunting him with it, insulting him with it. Just spitting it out that way, not thinking, all the sweet longing and melancholy of his many waking dreams tossed at their feet in the seedy, smelly hotel room.

"I never laid a finger on you, Wilda. I never—"

"Tell me you never had the thought," she went on, not able

to stop herself, ready to bite her tongue even as the words lashed out like the little flicks of a whip, meant to draw blood, meant to wound.

"Hey, Wilda," he said, softly, like a man with no fight left in him, "I didn't come here to tell you about Billy Smith. I would've called you for that."

"What?" she said, reading the look on his face.

"I came to tell you Flo's dead."

"Ohhhh." She moved in close to him, put her arms around him. Drew his head down on her shoulder. "It's a blessing, Ray. She was in such torment. It's a blessing."

51

BILLY SMITH WAS OUT OF JAIL. HE WAS HOME WITH FAMILIAR black faces and caring black hands. He didn't even have to call for anyone. The minute he stepped out of the blue and white at the corner of his block (they wouldn't drop him in front of his house, that would've looked too much like a courtesy), the word went out and by the time he made the stoop the people were gathering, crooning softly at him, patting him gently with their hands.

He was holding a Kotex supplied by a female guard at Cook County Jail to his face and another had been packed into his crotch to stanch his torn and bleeding rectum. He walked with a waddle that made one of the neighbor children laugh and earned him a quick slap across the mouth.

His Aunt Hattie was there inside of fifteen minutes, her arms loaded with bags of groceries. She came into the disorderly flat he shared with Charlie Lincoln, took off her coat, and started making soup.

Then she drew a bath and helped him get his clothes off. When he protested, she tut-tutted and reminded him that she'd raised him from a child and had bathed him many times. He was grateful that she treated him like a child because a child could take absolutely no responsibility for what happened to it.

"They let you see a doctor?"

"They asked me did I want to see a doctor for the injuries somebody done me before they picked me up out of the gutter when I slipped on a wet patch getting into the van that was taking me to the place of release. I wasn't in no gutter. That's just what they said in front of witnesses. Getting the story right. Letting me know what the story was going to be. Everybody ready to lie that I was picked up out of the gutter." He noticed that he was crying.

She tut-tutted again, being wise, knowing that she couldn't do a thing about the system that had injured the boy so grievously. All she could do was help heal him as best she could.

When he was washed and dried, wearing fresh underwear, a doctor on the way, a folded handkerchief on his cheek instead of the Kotex, in bed between clean sheets, a bowl of his Aunt Hattie's soup in his belly, Charlie Lincoln came home and told Billy how he'd tried to get Billy out. How Wilda had revealed that her brother was a cop, Ray Sharkey, a sergeant, and how he'd failed them. How Charlie had confronted this Ray Sharkey in the hotel room where he'd spent the night with the white woman, making plans to get him out.

While Charlie was going on about it, Jasper Tourette walked in with Waylon Carteret, both of them standing there in their sinister black outfits, taking it all in.

Billy just lay back against the pillows, reading Charlie, reading all the little lies and half-truths Charlie was telling him, understanding that when all was said and done you couldn't even trust a friend. The only people you could trust were family and them only sometimes.

"So, Charlie, how come you don't come to me the minute that white pussy bail you out?" Tourette asked.

"I look all over, that hour, how do I know where anybody's hanging?"

"All right, I got the picture," Tourette said. "Now you give us a minute with my cousin."

"Hey," Charlie said.

"This is just between family, you understand?" Tourette said, putting his long-fingered hand on Charlie's shoulder.

"This between the men in the family. Why don't you just take my Aunt Hattie out to the kitchen and make her a cup of coffee, a cup of tea?"

"I made soup," Aunt Hattie said.

"So she gives you a bowl of her good soup."

Charlie and Aunt Hattie did as they'd been told.

Waylon stayed behind because he was an extension of Tourette.

"They stuck it up your ass, did they?" Tourette said. He saw the expression on his cousin Billy's face and took his hand. "You listen to me. You didn't give them nothing—I can see your face—they stole it. That's that."

"I ain't going to forget it," Billy said.

"Oh, no," Tourette said, "you ain't going to forget it but you going to *pretend* to forget it. You going to live with it. We going to take our time and wait until we got a chance at every one of them did you dirty. We going to stick it up their asses, each and every one, and twist it. We going to get our payback."

52

DOWN DEEP SHARKEY BELIEVED IN THE REALITY OF SIN, LIFE EVERlasting if you played the game according to the rules laid down by Mother Church, eternal suffering in the flames of hell if you didn't, and the comfort and protection to be found in your mother's arm. He had the Irish sentimentality about mother in full measure and, were he willing to reveal his deepest feelings—which he was not—he would've said that he saw nothing strange about it since everybody's first love—man or woman—was mother. And for a while, until life, circumstances and fate, caused her to disappoint you, it was the purest, sweetest love you'd ever know.

But Cora, his mother, was long dead. And by her own hand, so there was pain there even in her memory, and, for all the tenderness she'd just shown him, Wilda's rage against him burned through the hugs and kisses.

He'd never turned to Della for the kind of comfort he needed now when he was not only hurt and grieving but suffering great fear and loneliness.

So, even though he'd fought against it, merely nibbling at the edges of the relationship he really wanted with Roma, showing it only sometimes when drunk or in great heat, now he suddenly knew in the bone that he had nowhere else to turn. No one he would rather turn to, man or woman.

He rushed to the flat on Artesian, hurried up the stairs, fumbling with the key at the lock in his haste, finally bursting in and practically running through the flat from room to room calling for her, scarcely noticing, at first, the signs of struggle in the living room and the mess someone had made in the bedroom when her bag, missing from the closet, had been packed. Underwear and blouses he'd given her lying on the bed and floor. Shoes and stockings thrown around. Dresses dropped from their hangers in a pile. Roma gone.

53

THE PUSSY CAT WAS DARK ON MONDAYS, ONLY THE JANITOR there to give the place a general cleaning.

So, when Sharkey arrived at the door, he didn't really expect to find Tourette or Waylon Carteret or anybody else who might tell him where Roma might be found. The fact was he had no idea where Tourette lived. Though they spoke of each other as friends they were actually less than acquaintances, neither one of them having set foot across the threshold of the other's dwelling. What he was hoping for was that the janitor would have the information he needed to find Tourette.

As it turned out, after the janitor had opened the door and let him in, Tourette was there, sitting in the pool of a single spot over his favorite table, the table where Sharkey had threatened to shove fruit salad up his ass.

It looked very dramatic, him and Waylon sitting there under the light, purple shirts, black leather pants, brocaded vest, leather vest, eight-hundred-dollar leather jackets carelessly draped on the chairs beside them. Dark glasses turned to him as Sharkey walked across the floor. Giant insects waiting for their prey. And Roma sitting there, leaning back out of the light, hiding in the shadows.

As he came closer, never taking his eyes off her, she turned her head aside. She was wearing a plain blouse with a sweater thrown around her shoulders. Not a bit of flash and dash, plain black woman in a plain blouse and sweater hugging herself as the white man neared.

"Ho, Sharkey," Waylon said.

Sharkey reached the table and leaned his thighs against the edge, reached over and took Roma's wrist, drew her out into the spotlight, and saw the bruises and scrapes on her eyes and mouth. Someone had slit her nose with a knife where the nostril met her upper lip. It was an awkward place to bandage and no attempt had been made.

He reached over and laid his hand alongside her cheek so gently and tenderly that her eyes filled up with tears and then spilled over.

"When you wasn't at home, my heart squeezed up like a fist in my chest. I was going to start looking for you at the bus stations, the train stations, but I thought I'd ask Jasper first where you might be."

"Never dreaming she'd be with me?" Tourette asked with a strange wry twist to the words as bitter as bile.

Sharkey didn't even glance at him. He just kept on looking at Roma, holding on to her wrist with one hand, touching her with the other, leaning across the table awkwardly.

"You hear what I say?" Tourette said.

"What are you doing here, Roma?" Sharkey asked.

"You tell him, lover," Tourette said. "You tell him I told you it was time to come home so you come."

Sharkey released her and straightened up. She didn't try to move back out of the light but sat there looking up at him. Just before his hand had left her cheek, he'd felt the slight movement, left and right, that called Tourette a liar.

Now, he finally looked at the two men, first at Waylon, then at Tourette.

"What's going on here, Jasper?"

"I'm taking back my property. What business is it of yours?"

"It's my business, you fucking pimp."

"I'm a pimp and she's a whore."

"Not anymore. Not since she came to live with me."

"Not live with you. Wait for you at your pleasure in your little fuck pad."

"You don't know anything about it."

"I know more about it than you know about doing right by your friends.

"I hurt you in some way?"

"You wouldn't raise a finger to help my cousin."

"Who?"

"My cousin. Billy Smith. The young man you listened to playing the clarinet many times, right here."

"I had no idea."

"That's what I say. Everything between us has been about business. Nothing else. So I take back what's mine."

"I didn't do anything to hurt Billy Smith."

"You did. I got eyes and ears the same places you got eyes and ears. You told them to run poor Billy around the fucking stations of the cross, you did. Just for the fun of seeing the nigger run."

"It's no way to get back at me for the insult—you think it was a deliberate insult—taking it out on Roma. If you told her to come back why did you have to punish her?"

"Because I wasn't going with him," Roma said.

Waylon's hand started to come up. It was a thoughtless thing to do, like slapping a cat that'd hissed and scratched. Before the backhand ever landed he was on the floor, the chair kicked out from under him, Sharkey's foot on his throat.

"I ought to step down, crush your windpipe, teach you a fucking lesson, you fucking freak."

He eased the pressure and let Waylon breathe. Then he took his foot off altogether.

"Get your ass up and out of here," Sharkey said, "and don't be a fool. You fuckers kill me and there'll be black asses hanging from the lamppost."

"There you go, Sharkey," Tourette said softly, as Waylon

scrambled to his feet and moved away at a nod, "there you go." He looked at Roma. "What more do you need, girl? This man is a slave owner at heart. He don't care about you. You're nothing but a black piece of nookie. Wouldn't mess with a white woman because his wife ain't dead yet, but a nigger woman don't count."

"It don't matter," Roma said. "I want to be quits with both of you. I don't belong to anybody."

"Come on out of here," Sharkey said. "You bring a coat?"

"I don't need a coat," she said.

"All right."

She got up and walked over to her suitcase standing on the floor. She picked it up and took a few steps while Sharkey watched Tourette with one eye and Waylon with the other to see what they'd do.

"You can drive me to the bus stop," Roma said. "I'm going home to New Orleans."

"Go out to the car," Sharkey said. "Go ahead."

He stepped along sideways after her.

"I got to tell you, Tourette, all you had to do was ask the favor and I would've had your cousin on the street in five minutes."

"Why should I have to ask you a favor, white man? Why couldn't I just expect you to do what was right?"

Roma was in the car when Sharkey slipped in behind the wheel.

"I'm not going back to the flat on Artesian," Roma said.

"All right, I can understand that. I'll take you over to my place in Bridgeport. Tourette ain't got the address."

"Not there, either. You heard what I said? I meant what I said."

"I need to talk to you, Roma."

"About what? About fucking what? You going to tell me you're going to take care of me after what they done to me?"

"No, I'm going to ask you to take care of me. Flo's dead and I've got nobody to take care of me."

"Oh, oh, oh," she moaned, reaching out to put her hand on his sleeve, turning her head away, putting her other hand over her ruined face.

54

ANYBODY ASKED RAY SHARKEY, HE'D ADMIT IT WAS CRAZY. Maybe he even had a mental sickness. But whenever he walked into a funeral home, into the hush and the thick carpets and the heavy smell of flowers, he felt strangely calmed, insulated from the frenzy and rage outside in the real world.

Maybe Tierney's Funeral Home and all the funeral homes were not really part of the real world. Maybe they didn't even exist in real time. Maybe they were way stations, halfway houses on the way to somewhere else.

People sat around resting their feet, having an hour off from work, their business, their house repairs—whatever—from their personal worries, which tended to shrink to nearly nothing in the face of that final silence, that last great trial which ends all trials, talking in whispers, telling the old stories, laughing soft laughter, looking at the faces of the dear departed and remembering.

For a second he imagined Roma Chounard coming with him to a funeral. If you could put aside the fact that she was black, the scandal something like that would cause. But if they could walk into a funeral among people who were color-blind, in that kind of world. He expected he knew how the sympathy would flow from her. How she'd take the hands of the bereaved and warm them. How she'd croon to the widow and cry with the daughter. How she'd spread her warmth over them like a dark cloak. The way she did with him, blanketing his body with her body in their bed, making him forget his pains and sorrows, making him forget she was a black whore for hire.

He looked around to see who was already there this evening. He didn't see Flo's brother Harry or sister Gwen. Then, with a shock that momentarily frightened him, he remembered that Harry was already dead and Gwen living in California somewhere. She'd sent a night letter saying that she didn't think she could make it back to Chicago for the funeral.

So maybe Jerry was right when he asked what sense there was in coming to these death houses, going through the useless ceremonies, when so much time had passed and so many had already died that a person couldn't even keep it straight in his head who was alive and who was already gone.

Then he saw his sister Della in the first seat of the first row. Saw this solid little person sitting there attending the dead, patient and forgiving.

As though she could hear his thoughts whispering in her ear, Della turned around and smiled at him.

He walked down the aisle between the folding chairs and kneeled on the prayer stool, crossed himself, and did a quick Hail Mary. Not thinking about it, but just saying it in his head, old habits not easily put aside. Not even believing in the reasons for prayer, just saying it because Flo, the wife of many years, had believed in prayer. So it wasn't really a prayer, but just a tribute to Flo.

When he got up off his knees and turned around, intending to sit beside Della in the front row for a minute, he saw Kitty Brennan standing out in the reception room as though doubtful about where she was going.

So what the hell was this going to be all about?

He touched Della's hand as he started back the way he'd just come, her looking at him with the same smile, expecting him to sit down, him pointing up the aisle to the back of the room as he paused. She looked back at the woman, a stranger to her, and then gave Ray an inquiring look.

He bent over and murmured, "Somebody wants to talk to me, I think. I'll be back. You wait."

"I'll be here," she said. "Pa's going to be along tomorrow. He had trouble getting out of bed this morning."

Kitty Brennan took a step toward him as he came out of the slumber room, her eyes casting around like a trapped animal looking for a way out.

She was wearing a gray winter tweed suit and had a jet brooch pinned to the lapel as a badge of respect for the dead. A politician's thoughtfulness, walking in on the funeral of somebody she'd hardly seen in thirty years. She was alone, which was a surprise. The Candidate was very big on attending funerals, having been taught that there was no better place to earn credit with the voters.

Sharkey stopped in front of her, standing very close, invading her space, cop's trick of taking the advantage. She started as though she expected him to strike her or ask her to leave.

A skittish little woman, she was, Ray thought. Then he saw her little knob of a chin come up and her lips straighten, the small gloved hand flung out at him, and he realized that she was also a fighter, fighting an important fight against her own fear and natural shyness. Plenty of guts there. He felt oddly proud because this woman had come knowing he'd be there and because she was Irish.

"I'm sorry for your loss, Ray," she said, in a husky soft voice. Very appealing, that.

"Did you know my wife very well when we were kids?" Ray asked.

She looked startled. "For God's sake, Ray, we were all born and raised within six, seven blocks of one another. Of course I knew her."

"Did you come to the wedding?"

"Well, I didn't know her that well. I mean it was more my family knew her family. I was more Wilda's age. We used to play together when we were kids. We hung out together until she left home."

"That's right," he said, frowning a little. Something tugging at his memory, there.

"If anybody was to ask me to the wedding it would've been the groom," Kitty said. "I was more a friend of the groom's family. Of the groom."

She didn't want to come right out and goddamn say it. Couldn't demand that he remember he'd fucked her once in an empty lot and promptly forgot all about it. Went on to get married and live a life and never even acknowledged by word or gesture that he'd done that with her.

She was watching his eyes like a hawk. When he remembered, when it came back to him like the frames of a motion picture, brightly lit, clicking over in his head like a film in slow motion, she saw it.

"Do you remember we knew each other pretty good once upon a time, Ray?" she asked.

The memory was in his eyes. He looked away for a second

and when he returned his gaze to her face, he'd thrown up the veils, those Irish veils of secrecy and forgetfulness.

"I didn't have nothing to do with the invitations," he said, apologizing for that old oversight, as if an invitation to the wedding of the first man she'd given herself to was the thing that mattered.

He laughed. It was a harsh sound. "That why The Candidate's going after me, Kitty? Was it you sicced him on to me?"

"It wasn't my intention to single anybody out."

"The hell it wasn't. It was exactly your intention to strip me naked if you could before shooting me full of holes. Are you so hard up for an issue that you got to fall back on the old joke about sex, sin, and police corruption?

She stood there stiff-backed, a cat backed up against a wall by a bulldog.

"Am I supposed to be the cornerstone you're going to knock out of the wall that'll bring down City Hall?" he went on.

She shook herself and frowned, scratches appearing between her eyes and alongside her nose.

"It's all a goddamn game, Kitty, don't you know that? There's nothing else. Just a lot of thieves sitting around dealing out the cards."

"Like you say. It's just a game. There's nothing personal in it."

"That's what the mafia says—'Nothing personal. It's only business'—before they shoot a man."

For a moment it looked as though she was about to cry. Then she turned away, walked over to the guest book, signed her name, took a prayer card from the box, put it in her purse, and walked out without giving him another glance.

55

WHEN SHARKEY SAW WILDA COME THROUGH THE DOOR, HE caught his breath and he realized he'd been afraid she'd decided in the night to pack up and leave town because he'd failed her, because he'd interfered with her life again.

When he went to welcome and embrace her, he saw that she was in a cold rage, her milk-white complexion even whiter, drained of blood, so that a layer of the palest freckles appeared beneath the skin, as though another person he'd never known was coming to the surface after being so long hidden.

"I'm so glad you came," he said. "I was afraid . . ."

"Afraid of what, Ray?" she whispered fiercely. "Afraid you'd driven me away with all your rotten suspicions?"

"Wait a minute—"

"Never mind the minute. I've been waiting for years for you to learn to be a human being. You're all smiles and sweetness when you want to get your way but you've really got no heart, Ray. You've got no love for anybody."

"What are you talking about?" he said, trying to keep his voice down, their whispers like knives cutting across the room. "Nobody's got cause to say that. I always broke my ass taking care of this family, this whole goddamn family."

"It ain't a job to be proud of," she said, losing her refinement of speech, a Chicago kid again.

He grabbed her by the elbow. "You come with me."

She jerked her arm away.

"You come with me," he said again. "We don't want the whole world to know we're having words."

He walked along the corridor to one of the parlors and opened the door. He held it open so she could go in before him. There was no one sitting on any of the folding chairs but there was a small white coffin on the platform in front, with white beribboned candles at the head and foot. They could see the dead one was a child, a girl of eleven or twelve in a white knee-length dress, white ankle socks, and white patent-leather Mary Janes.

"This room's in use," Wilda said, calming herself somewhat.

"She won't mind if we keep it low. If we keep it civilized. I told you I was sorry for the way I acted in the hotel room. What do you want from me? I can't help the way I am. I saw you standing there in your slip with that black looking like he'd just got hisself dressed, the bed all mussed, what am I supposed to think?"

"Who cares what you thought? What right did you have to intrude that way even I was humping the liver out of Charlie Lincoln?"

"Watch your mouth, for God's sake, Wilda."

"It bother you your sister knows how to talk dirty, Ray? Where do you think I've been since I was thirteen? What do you think I've been doing? You think I went away to a convent? I know all about fucking, Ray. It's one of the things grown up people do."

"Well, if you're going to do it, all I'm saying is you should do it with your own kind."

"What a miserable hypocrite you are, Ray."

"Oh?"

"I went over to your flat. If you hadn't already left I was going to help you get ready and come over here with you. You weren't home, Ray."

He could feel the color flooding his face and neck, could feel the prickles along the backs of his hands. He cleared his throat, which was suddenly thick with phlegm.

"What are you trying to say?" Wilda said. "You trying to say that what you're doing with Roma is different than what you were afraid I was doing with Charlie?"

"I been alone for a long time, Wilda."

"I've been alone all my life," she said. "You men give me a laugh. You go around screwing this woman, that woman, with no thought at all for her feelings. It's what you want. The old cock without a conscience you like to laugh about. It doesn't matter to most of you, what the woman is. She can be blind, crippled, eight or eighty, black, white, yellow, or brown. Just so long as she's got the necessary plumbing.

"White men are the worst of all. All of you talking the good liberal fight, always ready to kiss a minority child. Fuck a black, brown, or yellow mother and toss her a tenner, a double sawbuck, but never marry her. Never love her or any child they might make. Condemn any female relative to hell who took a black man into her bed. The double standard gone wild. The double standard in spades."

"Who fucking wound you up?" he asked, finally finding anger to match her anger.

"A little joke there, Ray. In spades. A little racial slur there."

"I'm not going to let you crucify me for trying to take care of my sister. You give me nothing but goddamn trouble."

Wilda looked at the coffin. The subdued light was like the light at the bottom of a pond.

"Sure, Ray. It would've been better for you if I'd died when I was about as old as that child in the coffin there. It would've been easier for you and—swear to God—it would've been easier for me."

56

HE FOUND ROMA SITTING IN THE CHAIR NEAR THE WINDOW where Flo used to sit when they'd first moved into the flat—the second and last home they'd ever had—all those years ago.

She was dressed in none of the clothes he'd ever seen her in before. She was wearing a flowered housedress with a sweater thrown around her shoulders and her hair was combed back and caught with two barrettes at the sides and a small comb at the back. She had no makeup on her face. Her lips were dark, almost the color of red plums, almost purple.

"I borrowed one of your wife's dresses and a sweater," she said. "I hope you don't mind. There was bloodstains on my clothes. I got them soaking in the sink."

"If they fit you, you can take what you want."

"I couldn't do that," she said.

"I'm going to hurt Tourette badly for what he did to you."

She shook her head and even laughed a little bit, a rushing sound full of bitter amusement.

"Don't bother yourself. You should know, Jasper was only playing by the rules."

"Not by my rules."

"Well, there you go. Everybody goes around pretending there's one set of rules. One size fits all. That's not the way. There's one set for crooks and one for cops. Another set for niggers and another for honkies and another for slants. Break it down you even got one set for brights and—"

"Brights?"

"—another for bloods." She looked at her hands before she answered the question. "Light-skinned niggers. I'm a blood. You can see. So never mind, Jasper done what he thought he had a right to do. What I give him the right to do when he convinced me down in New Orleans that I'd do better in Chicago." She laughed the brutal laugh again. "Not so. Not so."

"You hungry? You want something to eat?"

She glanced up at him, from beneath her brows. It was coquettish.

"You asking me out?"

"I got to get back to the funeral home. I wouldn't have the time. I just thought there might be something in the house."

"There's nothing worth eating. I looked."

"Maybe a can of soup. Something. Until I get back. Then we can go out someplace if you want."

"That'd be a first," she said.

"I suppose it would be."

"Maybe we could all go out together."

"Who's we all?"

"Me and you and your sister and one of her friends. Maybe that musician, Charlie Lincoln."

"She told you about that?"

"We talked. So, maybe we could do that. See, that way, all four of us go sashaying into some restaurant, everybody'd think, look at those two nice liberal couples. My, my, a black couple and a white couple sitting down to dinner."

"I'm not ready for another argument about this," Sharkey said.

"I was just saying."

"So why don't you put on a coat and I'll drive you back to your place."

"You afraid some more of your friends and relatives might be stopping by?"

"No. No, I don't mean that. I just mean there's food there. If there ain't, we could pick up something on the way over. I'll come home after I do what's expected of me over to the funeral parlor.

"You mean you'll come back here?"

"I might stop back to take care of a couple of things but I mean I'll come *home*. Will you be there?"

"We'll just have to see," she said. "I'm a woman what owns herself. You understand?"

He nodded his head, no arguments. He reached out a hand and helped her to her feet. She stood up but he didn't let go. She moved closer to him and let him embrace her and then she hugged him back.

"So, all right," she said. "Let me go get a coat."

57

SOMETIMES MICHAEL WENT FOR DAYS WITHOUT STRAPPING ON his leg, just staying inside reading or sitting in the window watching the world go by. He'd have milk, bread, and cold cuts delivered from the mom and pop on the corner. The library had a wagon that went around giving shut-ins the chance to borrow some books and he'd long ago applied for the service. The most he might do, if it was a sunny day, would be to drag the wooden chair out on the front stoop, hopping along on his one leg, and sit himself down there. He'd noticed that people waved more often when he was outside in full view than when he was inside behind the windowpane.

So, when he finally put his leg back on, it was a chore and

didn't always sit well. First he powdered the stump, then he put on the elastic stocking. When he got the stump settled in the plastic cup, he threaded the end of the stocking through a hole and then started hauling on it, drawing the stocking off and out, sucking the stump into the cup, creating the suction that would keep it securely there.

Strong as he was, it was an awkward, difficult thing to manage and he cursed the necessity of it to himself, though he never otherwise complained aloud to anyone.

If he had his way, on this crisp cold day, he'd just as soon stay inside with a good book but he figured he had a mission. He had to try to get Ray to make up the quarrel he'd had with Wilda over at the funeral home and see if there was any way to persuade her to stay.

He'd wondered, but never asked, why Wilda had run away from home when she was just a kid. Thirteen years old, and small for her age even. It wasn't as though she'd looked like some grown-up woman with well-developed breasts and that way of looking at men that suggested she knew a lot more than she really knew, like some he'd met since. He remembered her as being a skinny little kid with hardly anything in front, legs all banged up from roughhousing, practically always wearing dirty Keds. Very white skin except where her face, neck, and arms were sunburned in summer. Freckles that appeared when she was in distress. A cloud of red hair. Plain blue eyes that didn't flinch from anything.

He remembered her looking at a dog lying in the street, crushed by a passing truck, its bowels crushed out of its body. She'd cried later on but she never flinched from the cruel sight of it at the time.

He'd thought about it over the years, why a girl that young would want to leave her family. They might not have had all that much, with six kids and the hard Depression years early on, from which it had been so difficult to recover. But by the time Wilda got up and left they were enjoying the prosperity of war along with everybody else. She might not have had everything a kid might've wanted in her childhood, but she certainly had everything Dan and Cora could give.

So, what about it? Why had she left? Why did any young girl leave?

Sometimes they left because they were messed with by a

father, a brother, or some other male relative. Michael knew—would've sworn on a stack of Bibles—that there'd been none of that, though more and more it seemed those things were kept so secret nobody could ever know for sure, stacks of Bibles or no stacks of Bibles.

Or a girl could feel badgered, psychologically tortured, or diminished beyond bearing by an overpowering family. Though they'd quarreled and fought with the best of the households in Bridgeport, no one had ever picked on Wilda that way and, in fact, you might have even said it'd been the other way around, Wilda being the teaser and instigator of trouble, almost as busy that way as Ray.

Too much love that smothered, not enough love and chilled, maturing too soon, remaining childish too long. Because they're trying to distance themselves from some guilt unknown to anyone else. Because they are compelled to fulfill the prophecies of the doomsayers in the family—and every family's got a few of those—predicting that this child or that child will follow in the footsteps of some older relative. In Wilda's case that she was so much like Aunt Josephine, Dan's younger sister, a runaway at fifteen and a wanderer ever since, that it was inevitable that she become a national tramp as well.

Because she, like generations of boys and young men in which it was deemed more acceptable, was infected with that most mysterious of diseases, wanderlust. That longing that plucks the heart out of your body at the sound of a distant train whistle in the night, the sight of airplanes blinking their way across the sky. Feelings he'd had himself and might have answered had things been otherwise, had he not lost the leg and a certain sense of self that was lost with it.

Just because.

Well, whatever the reason she'd left thirty years before, she'd turned the corner on forty now and it was time for her to settle down somewhere. And Michael could see no reason why that somewhere shouldn't be Chicago, where she'd have the support of her family.

Just because she and Ray didn't get along, were like a couple of goddamn cats, purring at each other, licking each other's faces when they met, and then unsheathing their claws, spitting in anger, sooner or later, was no reason why they couldn't find a way to settle whatever it was between them, hide it, bury it, whatever, so they could live in the same kind of cautious harmony in which most brothers and sisters lived.

It was because there was a special love between them, as powerful as that of lovers and just as apt to generate jealousy and anger. Well, they'd just have to struggle with that and sort that out as well, because he wanted Wilda to stay home. He wanted them to find a flat in which they could live in harmony and brotherly-sisterly intimacy together. He wanted someone with whom he could share his deepest secrets and receive the gift of hers.

He stood up and stomped on the artificial foot with the sock tacked to the plastic shin and the shoe already in place. He got into his trousers and put on a sock that didn't match because he'd lost the other in the laundromat. At least the shoe was the other of a pair. Found a white shirt, fresh from the hand laundry a week ago, and unfolded it, taking pleasure in the crisp hiss of the cloth, heavy with starch, separating. Then a sweater and then his heavy shearling coat, a gift from Ray one Christmas. He treasured and cared for the coat. It looked scarcely worn, a beautiful coat of leather the color of toffee.

He found his crushed tweed hat on a hook behind the closet door and went out into the cold.

Three blocks from his flat he caught the El which dropped him at a station seven blocks from Ray's flat in Bridgeport.

He had no plan. He didn't even know if Ray would be at home—there'd been no answer when he called and another call to the stationhouse informed him that Sergeant Sharkey was on compassionate leave—but he expected that Ray would turn up sooner or later. There'd be a lot of sorting out of Flo's clothes and other things to do.

Michael knew where the spare key was kept in the loose plate where a radiator had once stood to heat the landing. He'd just let himself in and sit in the living room and wait. He was very good at waiting.

Ray's car wasn't parked out front. Neither was one of those unmarked detective vehicles—junkers with heavy-duty antennas and a dashboard stripped of all automotive amenities, standing out like sore thumbs—parked at the curb.

He clumped up the stairs, making as little noise as possible, still and always embarrassed by the sound of it, like the tinkling of a leper's bell, marking the approach of a crippled man. He didn't even bother knocking on the door but found the key behind the plate and opened up the flat.

He walked down the hallway, bathroom to the left, spare bedroom to the right, then the kitchen on one side and the dining room on the other, calling out, "Ho? Anybody home?" just in case Ray was home after all.

He peeked into the kitchen and the open door to the bedroom beyond it, then turned into the dining room, clumped across the floor to the parlor, and stepped across the threshold into the gloom of the shade-drawn room just as he saw a motion off to his right near the television set which made him shy away and catch his foot on the edge of the rug.

He felt himself going down, throwing out a hand to catch himself, felt something punch him in the side and heard the shot.

Twisted and landed partway on his back, his leg wrenching loose, as the gunman rushed past him.

"What the hell . . ." Michael said aloud before relaxing to the floor, succumbing to the pain and finally passing out, never finishing the exclamation, asking the question of the empty room.

What was a fuzzy-wuzzy doing in Chicago?

58

WHEN RAY FOUND HIM, A FEW HOURS LATER, MICHAEL WAS JUST coming to, struggling to right himself, holding on to his side, thinking, My God I been cut, Owney Farrel or Buddy Doll has cut me, they cut off my leg.

"Easy, easy, easy," Ray said, pushing him back against the floor, standing up and taking off his jacket, rolling it up to make a pillow.

"Ray?" Michael said. "Jesus Christ, Ray, can't we have a

little light in here? Why do you keep the shades pulled down all the time?"

"Flo's worried the sun'll fade the rug while she's gone," Ray said, then caught himself and exchanged looks with his brother before going on with it, opening Michael's coat, pulling up the sweater, seeing where the bullet had grazed him, probing gently with his fingers until Michael hollered.

"I can feel the bullet just under the skin. It could've busted a couple of ribs, but that's okay."

"It is, is it, fachrissake? You ain't the one hurting."

"Shit, I've taken hits like that and then had lunch and a nooner."

"Ruined my coat," Michael said.

"A little blood on the inside. That'll clean up and you can get a girlfriend to sew up the hole. Embroider a little shamrock on it. You'll be a fashion note."

He got up and left, coming back in a minute with a clean towel which he folded into a thick pad and placed against the wound, though the bleeding had stopped, only some serum seepage still oozing.

"Somebody was out to kill you, Ray."

"My God, what do you know? You're a fucking detective," Ray said, making a sarcastic joke out of it.

"You know any coloreds don't like you?"

Ray held up ten fingers spread into fans. "Pick one."

"I mean enough to want to kill you."

"Was it a nigger shot you?"

"It was so dark in here, especially coming in from that bright sun outside, that I wouldn't've been able to tell, except for the guy's hair."

"How's that?"

"It was all fluffed out around his head. You know, what they call an Afro."

"You didn't happen to see his feet?" Ray said.

"Why the hell would I be looking at his feet?"

"I just thought you might've got a glimpse on the way down. It don't matter. I got an idea I know who the shooter was, one'll get you ten."

Sure I know, Ray thought, after he'd insisted on an ambulance to take Michael over to Passavant Pavilion and was sitting there in the living room, the green shades still drawn against the sun, though it was already fading into late afternoon. I know Zulu Waddel—that white-faced, crazy sonofabitch, eager to make his name as a hard type—was sent to do me. And it looks like that crazy Shelley Orchid ordered it. But can I put money on the word of a pimp who's turned on me and a transvestite who'd lie his mother into slavery for a twenty-dollar bill?

I'm sitting in the middle of a snake pit, all the snakes curling around each other in a cozy mess. Dickman claiming he hired Zulu for small errands now and then. J. J. Finnegan, if not The Candidate directly, trying to set him up with a sting and, failing that, so pissed off that maybe he decided to get even a simpler, quicker way. Leddy known to Finnegan—used by Finnegan—and Albert working for Leddy, maybe doing a little moonlighting on the side, helping out Zulu when they went to break D'Angelo's bones.

Orchid hiring Zulu as a bouncer to work the door and throw out nasty drunks, and maybe to guard his body now that he thought he was such a big criminal type, another ear into which he could pour the tale of how that sonofabitch Ray Sharkey'd abused him and taken advantage, until one night drunk or sober, but surely goaded into a rage, giving the order to the baby gun. "Go get fucking Sharkey. Kill the sonofabitch."

But there was Jasper Tourette, his enemy now because he'd failed to help that musician—not even knowing Smith was Tourette's goddamn cousin—and surely capable of putting out a contract in his sensitive nigger pride. Tourette had set up the appointment for Leddy and may have known about the sting even then, taking pleasure in seeing the white men tear at one another. So he knew Leddy and Leddy employed Albert and there you were back to Zulu again.

So, forget about making a case. He wasn't a prosecutor who'd have to prove something in a court of law. He had to take that Zulu out. But Zulu was only a hired hand, a mechanic. He had to take down a boss and it really didn't matter which one. The death of one would be warning to the other. So it might as well be Orchid, whose mouth would only add to his troubles sooner or later anyway.

He got up from the chair, peeked around a shade to see if there was anybody lurking in the doorways, alleys, and shadows, then went to get his jacket off the floor. It was a crumpled mess. He went into the bedroom closet and took the only jacket, a summer-weight cord, off the hanger. He knew how cold it was outside; he could use a topcoat. So for lack of any other he put on the camel hair, pocket stain and all, scarcely noticing the weight of Dan's gun still in the pocket.

59

IT WAS AS COLD AS A REFRIGERATOR INSIDE THE CAR. SHARKEY and Dubrowski were muffled up to the ears and were wearing gloves. They couldn't use the heater because they'd have to run the engine and the exhaust steaming out the tail pipe would be a dead giveaway that cops were on a stakeout.

The Friday night crowd kept on going in and out of the glass doors of the restaurant. You could see them getting rid of their coats just beyond the vestibule going in and putting them back on before going out.

"I see you're wearing your camel hair," Dubrowski said. "How much do I owe you?"

"You don't owe me."

"The stain come out okay?"

"I ain't had it in the cleaners yet."

"Well, you should take care of that."

Sharkey shifted a little and pulled the skirt of the coat over his knee. He could feel the bump of Dan's service revolver, unwrapped and loaded now, against his leg. A cold piece, its registry lost in a mountain of old records somewhere if they existed at all.

"What's this all about?" Dubrowski asked. "Why the hell we staking out the Canton? This got anything to do with D'Angelo? This got anything to do with that?"

Sharkey shifted in the runner's seat so he could face Dubrowski in a sincere way.

"I don't know how to approach this," he finally said.

"Approach what?"

"This situation. It's got something to do with D'Angelo, yes. It's also got to do with something personal."

Dubrowski was clearly out in the wilderness, wondering what the hell Sharkey was getting at. For once he kept his mouth shut and waited.

"I want to be straight with you."

Still Dubrowski waited, beginning to feel slightly embarrassed as though afraid that Sharkey was going to make some intimate confession he didn't really want to hear, also feeling wary as though Sharkey was about to stuff him full of some of his famous Irish honey cake.

"I don't have to tell you that there's people out to bite me on the ass do I?" Sharkey asked.

Dubrowski felt the guilty color rising past his collar. He immediately went on the defensive. "How the fuck would I know that? Would you mind telling me? It ain't as though you and me swap secrets."

"The gossip in the fucking chicken yard is how. The bullshit that runs down the gutters. Fachrissake, you got to brush rumors off the chairs over to Schaller's or 'Hara's or Flannery's before you can even sit down. You understand what I'm saying?"

"I never heard anything about anybody trying to bite your ass. Who's trying to bite your ass?"

"Shelley Orchid for one. Maybe a pimp by the name of Jasper Tourette for—"

"I heard of this Tourette."

"—another. And a bunch of schemers by the name of Finnegan and Leddy and this Kitty Brennan—"

"I heard of Kitty Brennan, she's—"

"Fachrissake, I ain't asking you who you know, who you don't know. I'm telling you all these assholes could be in a conspiracy to chop me off at the knees, slit my throat, gut me, and hang me up as a campaign issue. They could all be in The Candidate's employ."

"So, what's that got to do with us being here staking out a fucking Chinese restaurant?"

"Because I got reason to believe that there's going to be a meeting, all these people, and they're meeting so they can compare notes about me and drag me under."

He heard himself making up all this complicated crap and it hit him like some sort of revelation, a goddamn religious epiphany. He was like practically every cop he ever knew, so used to laying down the con with the cons, trading lies with the liars, stealing the truth just like the thieves stole the truth, that you kept on shoveling the bullshit even with your own. You forgot how to be straight with anybody anymore. Your veins and arteries were clogged with hidden motives and secret agendas.

"That's what they could be doing, so I want to see who shows up, who sits in on the meeting. Also . . ."

"Hey, you told me never to do that," Dubrowski said, starting to grin.

"Do what?"

"Say 'also' and then stop like you just did. Now I got to say also what."

Sharkey grinned back at Dubrowski. He felt a warm spot under his ribs for the big walrus.

"So, okay," Dubrowski said. "Also what?"

"I got some information on the D'Angelo murder I ain't shared with you."

The grin immediately left Dubrowski's face.

"You got to understand, all these years, ever since Minifee, I never felt comfortable working with a partner. Remember we—"

"I know that."

"—only worked together a few months and I couldn't handle it. I don't want you thinking it was just you, Wally. It wasn't just you. I just couldn't work with anybody."

"Because you lost your partner?"

"I never told anybody what I'm going to tell you right this minute. I ain't sure I ever even admitted it to myself. It was my fault Minifee died with a broken bottle up his ass in that alley. I called in sick—"

"He shouldn't have been walking that beat alone," Dubrowski said. "The captain and the duty sergeant shouldn't've let him."

Sharkey gave him a little smile of thanks but waved his hand as though brushing away the attempt to shift the blame, if that was what it was.

"I called in sick, but I wasn't sick. I had a hot date at a dance hall over to Pilsen. So that's what happened."

They were quiet for a minute. What more was there to say about it, that old failure and betrayal?

"So, I got in the habit of working alone even when they teamed me up with somebody. I was useful other ways and I had Finny Cavan in my corner, otherwise they would have shown me the door years and years ago. I ain't stupid. I worked my way."

He reached into his pocket and took out the file photo of Albert, Alberto Carbonne aka Albert Bug-Eye aka A. Chooch. He handed it to Dubrowski.

"This is a bone-breaker works for Frankie 'Blue Shoes' Leddy by the name of Albert. On the back I got written down the address of a mom and pop grocery store run by a tough old Vietnamese who'll put Carmine D'Angelo—C. Pike—with him and another mauler on Sunday night. He'll give you an identification and swear to the fact that he gave Albert a cardboard carton and sold him a hank of clothesline and a sack of Kitty Litter. Also . . ." He smiled. "Also he'll give you a description of a tall, skinny freak, a white boy with a blond Afro hairdo.

"You're a good cop, Wally. It's all you're going to need to close the case."

"Where the hell are you going to be?"

"Well, I'll tell you, Wally, I don't really know."

They were silent for a while, both of them thinking their own thoughts, one or the other looking out the car windows toward the Canton.

"We're going to sit here much longer, I'm going to have to go wring out my sock," Dubrowski said.

"We can arrange that."

"I could go piss against the telephone pole."

"Some cop passing by'd collar you for waving your whale's dick at the passing motorists."

"Jesus Christ, don't make me laugh. I'll piss my pants right here."

They were quiet again, both of them sitting there feeling very friendly, like partners, a couple of cop wives.

"Ray?" Dubrowski said.

"Yeah?"

"I got to tell you something."

"What's that?"

"I got approached."

"About what?"

"You."

"By who?"

"Jack Quinn."

"What the fuck do I have to do here, Wally? Do I have to jump on your chest and pull your teeth out of your head? What, what, what?"

"He wanted me to spy on you. You're right, they're after your ass."

"There you go."

"Why are they after you, Ray?"

Sharkey shrugged. "I guess I've made a million enemies, Wally. I didn't know I was doing it, but I think that's what I did. A million enemies and no friends."

After another long silence, Dubrowski said, "Well, I don't know about that."

"So, what's the rest?" Sharkey asked.

"They come to me, The Candidate's people, this Jack Quinn. They made me an offer. I'm supposed to keep an eye on you and do a fink if you step in any shit."

"They pay you anything?"

"I didn't say yes."

"Christ, Wally, when are you going to learn?" Sharkey said, grinning at his partner. "You tell them sure you'll keep an eye out, sure you'll do a fink. You take their money and you give them nothing."

He glanced past Dubrowski's shoulder at movement across the street.

"Here we go," Sharkey said.

"Here we go where?"

"You stay here, but keep an eye out. I'm going to have a talk—"

"You mean a face-off?"

"—with somebody. I don't expect any trouble but you never know."

"Wait a fucking second here," Dubrowski protested.

But Sharkey was already out of the car and crossing the street.

60

SHARKEY COULD SEE THROUGH THE PLATE-GLASS FRONT DOORS Orchid and Zulu and that bunch piled up in the little lobby, getting their coats, and he didn't want them outside the restaurant on the sidewalk where they could scatter out. He wanted them inside, all packed together.

As he stepped up onto the sidewalk, he could see that other patrons were bunched up just behind Orchid's crowd, everybody shooting the shit, getting into their coats, laughing and scratching, their bellies filled with all that good Chinese crap.

It felt right. This was the minute. He'd never get a better chance and he had everything in place.

He pushed through the door, working his way in. Somebody—he didn't know from which crowd—said, "What the fuck, take it easy, asshole."

Sharkey could see yet another party on their feet, everybody chipping in a ten, a twenty, paying the bill. More people who could be expected to bear witness and add to the confusion of testimony when the police started asking questions.

Sharkey was in the middle of the crowd, their arms stretched out everywhere, hats and coats going on. Orchid was by the counter to the wardrobe waiting for his coat.

Sharkey stepped up next to him and nudged him with the gun, finding the spot under the ribs where the bullet would enter, exploding upward at an angle, taking out his heart.

Orchid turned his head to see who was poking him and a look of surprise started working its way across his mouth, in his eyes. There was a muffled pop like somebody had dropped an umbrella or an overshoe, only louder, and the expression on Orchid's face changed. He fell down and crumpled backward against Zulu's legs just as he turned, ready to help Orchid with his coat.

One of the hookers in the group screamed. It sounded like a mild protest over somebody nudging her.

Zulu looked at Sharkey and, seeing the expression on Sharkey's face, knew what could happen to him any second. He panicked and started pushing his way past everybody clogging the door, elbowing and shouldering them aside as Too-Too, Leddy, and Chicklet crowded around, stooping down to see what had happened to Orchid.

Zulu broke out and was through the door, Sharkey moving after him, hampered by the crush of bodies.

A couple of women in the restaurant finally got the message that something serious had occurred—maybe a crime of violence—and they started to scream. Men were on their feet, craning their necks, trying to see what the trouble was.

Zulu was running for his life, having figured it out in one snap of the fingers, that if Sharkey put Orchid down, he'd be next. Sharkey burst through the doors.

Zulu turned left and went footing it down the alley toward the parking lot in back.

Dubrowski was out of the stakeout vehicle. He saw Sharkey pulling out his service revolver and plucked his own from the holster riding his hip.

Dubrowski had a shorter way to go crossing the street and beat Sharkey to the mouth of the alley. "Stop or I'll shoot," he sang out, in a picture perfect challenge. Zulu didn't stop. Dubrowski fired twice. Zulu flipped over three times before he lay still, crumpled up against the dumpster standing there, the toes of his multicolored high-tops pointing to the night sky.

Sharkey pushed past Dubrowski and was the first to reach Zulu. With his body shielding the action, he slipped Dan's revolver into Zulu's pocket.

He glanced down at his pocket and saw the bullet hole and the scorched material. He spotted a projection on the dumpster and rubbed against it so that the pocket caught and tore, the filthy metal side of the box completing the damage to the camel hair topcoat. Then he squatted down to check on the body again as Dubrowski finally lumbered up.

61

AFTER THEY CALLED IN THE SHOOTING, THEY WAITED, DUBROWSKI giving Sharkey little sidelong glances, trying to figure out whether he'd been set up and how he'd been had.

When Finny Cavan arrived in person, it wasn't altogether unexpected, because Sharkey's name had been connected to the killing. It was further proof that just about everybody had been out to get him, one way or another. At least there was nobody ready and willing to lift a finger to help him.

Getting Sharkey off to one side, beyond anybody's earshot, Cavan said, "Did you know that man in there, Shelley Orchid?"

"Sure, I knew him. I know practically every two-bit grifter and goniff in the city."

"But rumor has it that you and him were more than acquaintances, Ray."

"Like friends?"

"Like business partners." He waited, but when Sharkey failed to say anything Cavan said, "You want to tell me?"

"No, I don't want to tell you, Finny."

"Did you hear about Orchid coming in to have a little talk with me?"

"How would I hear that? You don't tell me much of anything anymore. What did you talk about?"

"He was going to talk about a certain cop that was covering his ass and taking a slice of that gambling operation Orchid's running in that restaurant. He was out looking for the best deal he could make for hisself," Cavan said.

"You mean he was talking to this one and that one?"

"That's what I mean."

"Well, I did hear rumors about that. I heard he had words with The Candidate."

"That's a possibility."

"So what did you say to him, Finny?"

"I told him to go peddle his papers."

"That was nice of you."

Cavan turned his head and half-turned his body as though looking through walls back to where the ambulance crew was getting Orchid's body into the wagon. "Well, now he's got nothing to talk about, has he? There's at least one lucky cop in town tonight if anything that goniff, Orchid, tried to tell me was true."

"That's right, I guess."

"So, you don't want to tell me?" Cavan asked again.

"Tell you what, Finny?"

Cavan turned away and started walking back to his car.

"Finny?" Sharkey called.

Cavan stopped and turned around.

"I want to thank you for the flowers you sent for Flo."

Cavan nodded and went on his way. His radio started squawking and the radios in other cars started squawking. It was all a garble to Sharkey from where he was standing.

He went back and joined Dubrowski.

"You finished here?" he asked.

"I've got to wait for Internal Affairs. It was my gun that did the fuzzy-wuzzy kid."

"You got the other gun? The one he was carrying?"

"I put it back in his pocket. Let the mobile lab boys do what they got to do. They won't find anything on it, cold weather like this, everybody wearing gloves."

"That's right."

"Except the kid wasn't wearing gloves. Just the left one. I guess he didn't have time to put the other one on when he started running."

"Shot the other gonzo and started running," Sharkey agreed, nodding his head.

"The gun in his pocket?"

"Yeah?"

"It's an old sheriff's department piece."

"You could tell?"

"Yes, I could."

"Well," Sharkey said, "there's a lot of them floating around. They used to auction off their old pieces, you know."

"I understand what you're saying," Dubrowski said.

"I wasn't saying anything special, Wally. I was just making conversation. So, you mind if I take the car and get the hell out of here? We'll work on the report together tomorrow morning."

"I'll be around for a while. Somebody'll give me a ride back to the station," Dubrowski said.

Sharkey took off his glove and stuck out his right hand. It caught Dubrowski off guard. He started to stick out his own hand, hesitated, drew it back, took off his own glove before sticking out his hand out again. They shook, looking into each other's eyes.

"So, I'm sorry I got you into this," Sharkey said.

"That's okay," Dubrowski said.

"I'll do the same for you if you ever find yourself in a similar situation."

Dubrowski nodded and Sharkey walked away.

62

DRIVING BACK TO THE FLAT ON ARTESIAN, HE JUST KNEW IN HIS blood and bones that Roma would be there waiting for him.

It was over. So much was over.

Flo finally dead and buried, out of her pain and suffering. Not only the pain and suffering of the cancer that took her but the tortures of her whole life, nothing turning out anything like the way she would have liked it. Not a bit like she thought it was going to be when she captured him that night in her father's car after his fight with Leroy Scarlet.

Keeping two establishments, the expense of that, was over. He'd only need one place now. Just a place somewhere, maybe not even in the city, maybe out in some small town by a lake, just big enough for him and Roma. Where they could keep themselves to themselves and try to build a life completely different than the one she'd led and he'd led.

Quit the force. Quit the games and the schemes. No more City Hall Pimp. No more of that.

Maybe take Helen out of the mental facility. She wasn't mental. She just had these fits, and maybe in another environment (up at this magical lake) they could take care of her themselves, him and Roma. Let people think whatever they goddamn wanted to think about a white man, a black woman, and another who had spells and was oddly like a child.

He parked the car at the curb and stepped out into the cold. He huffed and puffed, blowing his breath in clouds toward the lighted windows. All the working-class people, black and white, inside their homes. Some watching the late news. Most of them asleep, the men done with work, the kids in off the streets, the dishes washed up, the women resting their feet, waiting for another day.

The way it'd been in the flat in Bridgeport for those three or four good years early in the marriage before little Helen started getting sick with one thing after the other and then the seizures. Before everything started falling apart.

Now he could start putting some of the pieces back together.

He walked up the steps to the porch, went into the vestibule, climbed the stairs to the third floor, and put his key into the lock.

There was a light on in the living room.

"Roma," he called. "Roma, I'm home."

He stepped into the living room.

Cavan was sitting in Sharkey's easy chair. He was wearing his hat and coat. There was a uniformed cop standing in the bay window.

"I didn't see any cars downstairs," Sharkey said, his throat husky with a certain knowledge.

"I didn't want you running, Ray. There'd've been no sense in that," Cavan said. "I got the call when I got back in my car."

"What are you after me for, Finny?"

"You want to go into the bedroom, have another look at what you done?"

Sharkey started to say that he hadn't done anything, but thought better of it. Because he had done things. He'd done plenty.

Charlie Press, the coroner's assistant, was standing there, a pair of rubber gloves on his hands.

Roma was on the bed, her legs sprawled out in a lewd manner. She'd been struck repeatedly in the face. Wounds on top of wounds she'd already carried.

Sharkey touched her ankle and looked at Press.

Press shook his head from side to side. "She wasn't violated, Sharkey," he said.

"Can I?"

"The body's not supposed to be moved until photographed," Press said, and then thought better of it. "Go ahead."

He turned his back as Sharkey rearranged her legs so that she looked modest lying there.

"It's the damnedest thing," Sharkey said.

"What's that?"

Sharkey shook his head, not knowing how to tell this white man how it could be that Ray Sharkey had fallen in love with a black New Orleans hooker.

He walked out of the bedroom and went into the kitchen. There was another uniform standing at the back door.

Sharkey poured himself a glass of water from the faucet and said, "Riley, ain't it?"

"That's right, Sergeant."

Sharkey took a bottle of rye out of the kitchen cabinet over the sink. "You want to ask Superintendent Cavan to come out here a minute."

When the officer left the room, Sharkey walked out the door and hurried down the back stairs, on his way to kill Jasper Tourette.

63

SHARKEY WAS OUT ON MINIMUM BAIL, A FACT THE CANDIDATE and others might've made much of, except the primaries were over by the time he was arraigned for the unlawful deaths of one Jasper Tourette and one Waylon Carteret. He was out and living in the Bridgeport flat in which he'd lived with Flo for over twenty years.

The rooms echoed when he walked through them getting ready to appear in court, to stand and hear the verdict, all his dirty laundry washed and hung out to dry for all to see.

He always shaved right after he stepped out of a hot shower, standing there in front of the mirror naked, letting the water drops dry untoweled, cooling him off, focusing his mind like a splash of aftershave, taking inventory of face and body. The jowls blurring the jaw line. The neck starting to thin out. The scars of old bullet wounds, knife wounds, lead pipe wounds, sometimes pink, sometimes white, sometimes almost purple, shining on his fair, freckled Irish skin.

As he shaved he felt the scars of street wars and surgery with the fingertips of his left hand, tracing out the appendectomy, the removal of his gallbladder, the mining for bits of lead and steel. His fingers remembered the touch of his chest and belly when he'd been sixteen and unmarred, when he'd lost his cherry (in a very half-assed way) to an older woman.

He took the last swipe up the length of his throat, his head thrown back, then stood there for a long minute with his eyes closed, the safety razor in the faucet flow, imagining himself taking a blade in the heart.

When he lowered his head and opened his eyes he felt a rush of vertigo. Silvery wiggles the shape of sperm swam on the fringes of his vision. For a second he thought about stroking out, becoming as helpless as a baby, lying in bed, shitting in it, above it all, the struggle over, the need for power, money, fame, honor, and the love of beautiful women past.

A pink bottle of Flo's hand lotion was on the sink. He unscrewed the cap, poured a trifle into the cup of his hand, brought it up to his nose, and smelled it. The sweetness of flowers, violets, and roses.

He rubbed the lotion between his palms and oiled his forearms with it, then smelled his wrists. Funerals and corpses lying in their caskets.

He washed his hands and arms under the hot water faucet with the cake of Lifebuoy soap to get rid of the stink.

He picked a towel off the rack and scrubbed himself until his skin became electric.

Then he went into his bedroom and started dressing.

The white underwear shorts he wore buttoned in front, the kind of underwear called union suits. He bought them by the dozen and changed two, sometimes three, times a day, discarding them when they showed the slightest persistent stain at seat or crotch. He always wore an undershirt.

When dressed in a suit or uniform he still wore garters and dark-colored calf-length silk socks with clocks up the sides.

He hated to feel a sag at his ankles or a pleat at his crotch or a label on a shirt collar biting his neck. He liked everything snug, not constricting, but snug, tight, and trim.

Shirts, suits, jackets and vests, slacks and topcoats were tailored to an old-fashioned cut, tucked in at the waist, with no fullness through the chest. He wanted the cloth to just barely restrict his movements so he could feel every breath straining slightly against the buttons, every arm swing and upper body turn pressing against the cloth, constantly reminding him of body attitude, strength, and posture. Leaving enough room for a shoulder holster, which he always wore when in uniform instead of the belt holster clipped to the hip.

He strapped on his wristwatch. Tightened it until he could feel the pulse of his blood against the leather, then backed off a single notch. He'd once read about ancient fighting Celts and the Moros of the Philippines who had bound their arms and legs with leather thongs before going into battle so the bleeding of sword and knife wounds would be contained, tourniquets applied before the need.

Buttoned up, his shirt felt like he imagined the tunic knights wore underneath their chain mail shirts must have felt. When he kicked his legs to set the cuffs of his trousers he could feel his thighs filling them out, his calves touching the cloth lightly, his ankles, as slender as a dancing girl's, not touching.

Jerry, having had long experience on the bench, had advised Ray to wear a conservative suit.

"All my suits are conservative," Ray'd said.

"Wear the same one every day of the trial. If you have to change, if you spill something in your lap or on your sleeve and you have to change, wear another as much like the first as you can manage. Nothing new. Black shoes well polished. Shirt fresh every morning."

"I always wear a fresh shirt. Most of the time I change in the middle of the day and then again before I go out at night."

"You're a fashion plate. Nobody disputes that. Don't change your shirt during the day when you're in court. Some woman sitting on the jury's going to notice that, is going to think either you got your wife doing three washes a week or you got a Mex maid doing them for you. Maybe starching them. Hand ironing them."

"I send my shirts out."

"Even worse. That costs what? A buck and a quarter a shirt nowadays? They've got you charged with unlawful homicide. The murder of a couple of black pimps. Can you understand that, strange as it may seem, that's probably the least of your worries. You're actually up for extortion, usury, graft, consorting with thieves, running businesses on the side, and pimping for the politicians, not one of whom will admit they knew what was going on in the back rooms at the little parties you catered. You're the bone the powers that be are throwing to the dogs. So, you don't want to look rich, you don't want to look poor. You want to look hardworking and respectable. A man struggling to support a handicapped daughter and a dying wife all these years. You should be wearing wash and wear, not one hundred percent Egyptian cotton which you've got to iron."

"Who the hell's going to know I wear one hundred percent cotton?"

"This housewife sitting on the jury. She's got an eye for things like that. It validates her life."

"So who am I supposed to think I'm kidding? Every twisted sodomist, filthy twangy boy and wife beater, every pimp, killer, and bum living like a pig under a bridge, comes into court all dressed up in a blue serge suit, white shirt, and maroon tie. Looking respectable. Looking like a pillar of the community. *Trying* to look."

"Listen to me. It's like flattery. You flatter somebody outrageously. Even though they know you're doing it, the person getting the strokes is gratified. You flattered them. You took the trouble. You bent the knee. You made the display."

"What display? What the hell you talking about a display?"

"You bent over and showed your ass like the monkeys do. You were properly submissive."

"Fuck that. I ain't showing any submission. I ain't showing my ass."

"You'd better do it. You'd better show your ass and bend the knee and lick shit off their shoes if that's what it takes to make you look sweet to that jury. Wear a nice old suit and never wear your uniform. Don't remind them you're a cop they're saying went bad."

He'd wear his uniform. At least at this last appearance. What did Jerry know about pride?

He zipped up his fly and looped his arms, one after the other, through the suspenders buttoned to his trousers.

He sat down on the mattress to put on his shoes. Not slip-ons or even narrow lace-ups but black high-top brogans, the kind of shoes the old beat cops used to wear walking the neighborhood streets, keeping Chicago safe. He hardly ever wore them, hadn't put them on for years in fact. But they were polished every week. He polished them himself, sitting in the easy chair in the living room, stroking the old leather with the brush, smelling the smell of yesterdays.

The leather creaked when he stood up, standing in front of the wardrobe mirror to put on his black tie, carefully knotting it, his face looking back at him. His eyes staring like blue lasers back at him. He drew the knot tight until it was the size of a walnut, no fancy, wide, soft, stylish knot for him.

His uniform jacket was on its hanger, hooked over the top of the facing wardrobe door, looking like another presence in the room. Another Ray Sharkey.

Reaching for it, he hesitated. His shoulder harness and gun—not the service issue gun he'd turned in but the magnum he'd bought for himself with his own money—were hanging on the hook inside the door. How crazy it'd be to go in to face the grand jury wearing the gun.

The gun was the thing. It made a man different. Gave him the right to enforce his will on others. Not the right, the means. If you were an officer of the law, the right as well, when not abused. Whoever failed to abuse it? It was in a cop's way of speaking to square citizens, polite "sirs" and "madams," smarmy smile—a threat display—waiting for them to bend the knee, show their asses, lick spit, and beg mercy.

He reached out for the harness, removed the gun, and placed it on the top shelf underneath one of his hats. Then he got into the leather rig and tightened the straps. Even empty the harness was part of the warrior's battle dress, the strap across his chest giving him an acute awareness of the beating of his heart, the pump of action.

He put his hand to his crotch, settling his balls—the heavy stones of courage—along his left thigh.

"Well, fuck 'em, Jerry," he said aloud, "they can shoot me but they can't eat me."

He brushed the jacket of his uniform, with its discreet hash marks of service running up one sleeve, the sergeant's stripes on the other, the ribbons of commendation and valor set in a row above his pocket, with his hand. He slid his arms into the silk-lined sleeves and settled it on his shoulders, pulling down the skirt in back so the collar would hang across his back and shoulders just right. It fit him as neatly as it had when he'd bought it twenty years before.

The visored cap with the swag of gold braid and the insignia of rank finished off the making of Sergeant Ray Sharkey.

What he saw in the mirror pleased him. He even smiled.

He took off the cap and put it into a paper bag.

He took the soiled and torn camel hair topcoat off the hanger and put it on. When this was over he'd take it to the cleaners, or have somebody take it to the cleaners, and get the stain out, sew up the tear.

He was almost ready to go down and face the music. He took down his old fedora and put it on, taking his time, arranging it at just the proper conservative angle. Nothing flashy. Nothing unruly.

Epilogue

WILDA DROVE THE RENTED CAR OUT TO THE CEMETERY, HURrying along at first until she caught the tail end of the funeral cortege then slowing down to its pace.

She'd offered the keys to Ray, holding them out in her gloved hand (the woman giving deference to the man), but he'd refused with a shake of the head and no explanation.

She knew he was afraid he'd feel awkward behind the wheel after being so long away from the city streets, city traffic, so she didn't offer twice.

They were silent for a long while, Wilda paying attention to the road and the last car in the procession, afraid of losing them, uncertain of her way in the city that was her home, scarcely known, hardly remembered, relearned each and every time she returned, all its streets and neighborhoods appearing as sudden revelations, surprising, frightening, or wonderful.

From the look in his faded eyes Wilda knew that Ray was marking changes along the way, filling in, altering, updating the map stored in his memory.

"It'd be a helluvalot faster, they took The Dan Ryan down to Stevenson Expressway," he suddenly said, as though the idea had been bottled up in him for miles instead of blocks.

"I bet they'll catch the Stevenson at Ashland. It'll go quickly from there."

"Showing off the grief," he said. "The thing I always hated most about funerals. Showing the neighborhood your grief. Sackcloth and ashes. Weeping and wailing."

"Leaping into open graves."

"Aunt Josephine," he said, mentioning Dan's sister, the wayward aunt, Wilda's prototype, and laughed. "She always was the one for the grand gesture. I wonder how she died. You ever find out how she died?"

"She died in Bellevue," she said. "That's what Michael said. She died in the wards. She died fighting off the six-eyed spiders and the giant cockroaches, the death's-head moths as big as her head and mice with silver knives for teeth, he said. Her heart gave out. It was a race with her liver, what would take her, anyway. He went back to see her buried, did you know?"

She could tell when he turned his head away that he considered seeing off the dead and taking care of the family his job, but he hadn't been around to perform it.

"What did Mr. Cromarty have to say to you?" she asked, changing the subject.

He didn't answer. She glanced at him. He was staring straight ahead, looking out the window, looking ahead at the end of the funeral cortege but really looking backward. To what? To Roma's funeral? To their mother's death by suicide? To Aunt Josephine? To what and when?

"What, what?" he said, feeling her eyes on him, even though he'd not heard the words.

"Mr. Cromarty said you were tried and convicted for killing Roma, didn't he?"

"Everybody gets it wrong, don't they?"

"You were tried for shooting those bastards who beat her to death, weren't you?"

"Well, in a manner of speaking."

"What does that mean?"

"It means it don't matter for what crimes or misdemeanors I was tried, convicted, and sentenced. I was put away for living with a nigger, for breaking cop rules, Irish rules, you understand what I'm saying?"

"No, I don't."

"Well, you should've hung around and sat in on the trial instead of leaving town the way you did."

She jerked the wheel a little bit as though he'd slapped her in the face and made a sound halfway between a choking protest and a sob.

He reached out without looking at her and placed his hand over her hand.

"Listen to me. Listen to me. I'm always so goddamned hard on everybody."

"Yourself, too, Ray. On yourself, too. So, you still haven't told me why you didn't set Mr. Cromarty straight."

"Because it don't matter, Wilda. Because I had it coming, one way or another, so what difference does it make? I might just as well have been the one who done it to Roma."

They were at the cemetery.

Wilda parked at the curb some distance from the last car in the cortege.

They got out and followed the other mourners up the gentle slope of the hill to the place where the raw earth marked Della's last resting place.

People took a good look at him now. He took Wilda's elbow in his hand and steered her around the gravesite and canvas marquee, skirting the gathering of mourners, climbing the hill until they could look down the slope when they turned.

Every once in a while somebody, Jerry or Michael or somebody else would glance around expectantly as though willing Ray and Wilda to join them.

The murmur of the priest's prayers and the responses scarcely reached them standing upslope the way they were.

After everyone had broken off a flower and laid it on the casket, after the machine started cranking it down into the earth, after the gathering broke up and started down the hill to the cars, still glancing back at them but leaving them alone, Ray and Wilda finally walked down to stand beside the grave.

A couple of grave diggers were standing well back. Wilda noticed that one of them was discreetly cupping a cigarette in the curved palm of his hand, respect for the dead and the grieving.

"You want to go have a drink, have a talk?" Ray asked.

"You still don't want to go to Jerry's house for the wake?" she replied.

"We'll think about it."

They drove back to the city in silence until they found a likely looking tavern.

It was an old-fashioned neighborhood saloon. The coolness inside was of a different order than the coolness of the funeral home. It still had a family room off to the side that hadn't been invaded by pool tables. They took a table near the window and Sharkey went to the barroom to order from a bartender in a white butcher's apron tied around his waist who smiled benignly and set up a whiskey sour, a shot of rye, and a small beer on a tray.

Back at the table Wilda watched as Sharkey downed the shot with the short snappy motions of a much younger man, then took a swallow of the beer like an old one, leaning forward, careful not to dribble on his tie, looking up like an aged dog, fearful and melancholy.

"I've committed all the sins," he said.

"Ray," she said, warning him to leave off, give over.

"All the sins but one," he went on. Insistent, meaning to have his confession.

"You're not as bad as you make out," she said, desperate for him to stop, fearing that he was going to say something she didn't want to hear.

"All the sins but one," he repeated. "I never committed incest. Though I wanted to. God knows I wanted to."

She threw her head from side to side sharply, as though tossing a stray curl out of her eyes or denying what he was saying, not wanting to listen.

"Did you hear me, Wilda?"

"I don't want to hear you. I don't want you to put any of the blame on me. I've got enough blame of my own."

"I'm not putting anything on you, Wilda. I'm just saying I wanted to sleep with you, sleep with my own sister, but I didn't. I make that something to be proud of. I mean, I'm not proud of the wanting to sleep with you—"

"It's nothing to talk about."

"—but maybe I can be proud of not trying to do anything about it."

"Please, Ray."

"It's the reason I got so mad when I saw you in the police station worrying about that colored man. It was why I was ready to kill when I found you in that hotel room with that Charlie Lincoln. It wasn't only that they were black, it was that I was so jealous. I just wanted you to know."

"I knew, Ray. Don't you think I knew?"

"I remember you told me."

"So, that's all ancient history."

"The snows of yesteryear," he said.

"That's right. We've got to keep on looking toward tomorrow."

"You've got plans?"

"I was thinking. I had this idea."

She hesitated, afraid that he would disbelieve her and laugh at her.

"Tell me," he said.

"I was thinking of finally staying put in Chicago. It's the only place I can call home. You, too?"

"I ain't going anywhere."

"So, I was thinking that maybe we could get ourselves a flat together. Two bedrooms, maybe three."

"Didn't you hear what I just told you?"

"I heard you. If we didn't do anything about it when we were kids why should we be afraid that we'd do anything about it now that we're old? You're past seventy for God's sake and—"

"That don't mean I'm past it," he protested, automatically boasting about his virility, his appetite for women, his ability to satisfy that appetite if the occasion arose.

"I wasn't suggesting you were past it. I'm just saying I don't want you to spoil my dream, this idea I've got, bringing up things that never happened; would never happen . . ."

She'd said they hadn't done anything and wouldn't do anything, he thought, catching up with her. So maybe, once upon a time, she'd thought about what it would be like just like he'd thought about it.

". . . so we can forget you even said it," she finished. Then she went on as though nothing else had been said, repeating herself like a child getting back into the fairy tale. "So maybe we could get ourselves a flat together; two bedrooms, maybe three, so you could have a den."

"In Bridgeport?" he said, knowing it would never happen.

"Sure, in the old neighborhood," she said. "I could keep the house. Or I could even get a part-time job if you think we couldn't make it on your pension."

"We could make it on my pension," he said, going along as he'd gone along with her grand ideas and schemes before.

"So, what do you think about my idea?"

"I think it's a grand idea," he said.

"We could get your furniture out of storage where it's been sitting these fourteen years and we could . . ." She was laughing the funny, throaty laugh of her girlhood, young womanhood, as though she had secrets she would share and stories she would tell only after long and proper coaxing. The two of them living together, the brother and sister, in the Irish way.

He felt cold inside his overcoat with the black arm band on the sleeve all of a sudden, knowing how lonely he was going to be when she left town again.

"Hey, maybe we should go over to Jerry's, say hello to the family, say hello to Pa," he said.